"*Angie's War* is a powerful story that is a timeless reflection of the emotions associated with three generations of combat. As a combat veteran of both the Iraq and Afghanistan campaigns, I can fully relate to the American heroes and their families — both past and present."

—**Lieutenant Colonel Chris Morris,** Special Forces Officer, United States Army

"At last ... A novel about war that also starkly portrays the anguish and pain of those who wait at home while their loved ones are far away in the fight. A must-read for every American."

—**Susan Warden,** Marriage and Family Therapist, Prairie Village, KS

"Congratulations on *Angie's War*, Gary. Well done! I usually don't read war novels, but when we were together in the jungles of Vietnam, sharing foxholes in life-or-death firefights, we developed a bond, a connection that cannot be severed. *Angie's War* brings back both sad and joyful memories that we can continue to share in our remaining earthly years."

—**Specialist-4 John Baca,** D Co., 1st Bn, 12th Cav, 1st Cavalry Division, July, 1969 — February, 1970 — Medal of Honor for Extreme Heroism on February 10, 1970

"I loved *Angie's War*. It's a heartbreakingly beautiful story of love, and war, and loss, and redemption. You won't be able to put it down."

—**Ruth Walsh,** Mind-Body Healer, Overland Park, KS

"As in *One Young Soldier,* Gary DeRigne has brilliantly poured his combat experiences, his homecoming struggles, and his very soul into *Angie's War.* You can feel it on every page."

—**Steve Koppenhoefer,** 1st Lieutenant, Infantry, 1st Cavalry Division, 1969

"A masterpiece. DeRigne is a gifted storyteller, and *Angie's War* is destined to become an American classic."

—**Bob Babcock,** Vietnam Infantry Platoon Leader and Military Author of eight books

"Having fought alongside Gary DeRigne in the First Air Cavalry Division, I found myself sometimes remembering and weeping, and always reflecting, as I followed the characters in *Angie's War* from the jungles of Vietnam to the streets of Mogadishu, the mountains of Afghanistan, and the sands of Iraq, and always, always, at home. This is a necessary read for everyone wanting to better understand American warriors, their families, and their lives."

—**Basil B. Clark,** Retired Professor, University of Pikeville, KY

"Intriguing and riveting account of the emotional traumatic impact on soldiers in combat. As an infantry combat veteran of Vietnam, I was impressed that every word rings true. DeRigne captures the pure essence of combat experiences and their impact upon us."

—**Jonathan B. Dodson,** Infantry Platoon Leader and Company Commander—Vietnam, 1969-70

"Gripping. *Angie's War* is an excellent read. It is rare that a story reaches the reader on such an emotional level, yet is so enlightening. DeRigne's novel delivers on both."

—**Dr. Michael Steiert,** Prairie Village, KS

Angie's War

[signature] 4/9/22

Angie's War

A NOVEL

GARY M. DERIGNE

Deeds Publishing | Athens

Published by Deeds Publishing in Athens, GA
www.deedspublishing.com

Printed in The United States of America

Cover design by Mark Babcock. Text layout by Matt King.
Cover photo by Dana Clarke, cover model: Susan Warren
Author photo by Betsy Hudgens

ISBN 978-1-947309-78-4

Books are available in quantity for promotional or premium use. For information, email info@deedspublishing.com.

The terminology used to describe the enemy in *Angie's War* is that which was pervasive during the time of the Vietnam War. It is used by the author to realistically portray the language used by the American soldiers in this novel.

First Edition, 2019

10 9 8 7 6 5 4 3 2 1

To my grandsons, Graham and Wyatt.
May you live full, happy lives in a secure and prosperous America.

To my friend John Baca, who received the Medal of Honor for his incredible heroism in Vietnam, and who has since led such an exemplary life, caring for others. John, may you always know peace.

To the men and women of the Armed Forces of the United States, who endure so much, risk so much, and sacrifice so much to keep America free. May you never be forgotten.

1

17 August 1969
Tay Ninh Province, Republic of Vietnam
Tony Giles

Angie...Sweet, beautiful Angie.

Except for the simple gold wedding band on her left hand, she was completely naked, sitting astride him, her perfect, supple legs squeezing his hips, her deep green eyes staring directly into his. Long, thick, raven hair tumbled carelessly over her shoulders, reaching the tops of her full breasts, which bounced slowly, rhythmically, as she moved on him. Angie was smiling, that sensual way she smiled when they made love, as though their bodies, their minds, and their spirits were all connected. It was almost as if they were one person, the closeness he felt to her was so intense.

He heard her beautiful, soft whisper: "Tony! Oh Tony! You feel so good inside me!" Then she broke the rhythm of her movement to squeeze him harder between her legs as she gasped with her orgasm, "Oh! Oh! Tony! Oh, God! I love you so much!" A passionate whisper, just loud enough that only he could hear.

He was hard with the wanting of her. The image of her in his mind was so vivid, he could even perfectly visualize the little bumps at the edges of her nipples that he loved to tease with his tongue. She was so real. She was there…

But she wasn't.

And as he realized that, he was overcome by an intense sorrow, a pain in his chest so real he felt his heart would literally break.

From behind him came another whisper, this time a distinctly male voice: "Tony! Can't you hear me? Hal says take a break, man!"

With great reluctance, Tony broke out of his daydream and came back to grim reality. The dense Vietnamese jungle materialized around him, so thick he could see only a few feet. He observed, rather than commanded, his right hand wielding an Army-issue machete, mechanically chopping through thick jungle foliage; bamboo and palmetto, and wait-a-minute vines, with their little barbs that tore at his arms and hands. In his left hand, his off hand, was the grip of a battered, war-weary M-16 rifle, pointed carelessly forward, suspended by an improvised sling that hung from his shoulder.

His entire body was soaked in sweat, the worst of it dripping from his face onto a filthy, past-saturated, olive-drab hand towel that hung around his neck. The rucksack that agonized his shoulders weighed nearly eighty pounds, full as it was from the morning's re-supply with rifle ammunition, plastic explosives, Claymore mines, smoke grenades, C-rations, a few packs of cigarettes, a few quarts of precious water, and a jungle camouflage nylon poncho liner, his only defense against the rains that soaked him nearly every night as he tried to catch just a little sleep on the steaming jungle floor.

Tony was the point man for an American infantry company, breaking trail for the eighty or so men who followed him through the jungle as they moved slowly, carefully, single file, through the few hundred meters they covered each day in their ongoing mission of "long-range reconnaissance in force," or as it was once called, "Search and Destroy."

They were operating in Tay Ninh Province in an area northwest of Saigon known for its curved shape on the map as "The Fishhook." Most days they were less than a kilometer, a "click," from the Cambodian border, trying to "find, engage, and destroy" units of the North Vietnamese Army who infiltrated constantly from the Ho Chi Minh Trail just inside Cambodia. The North Vietnamese Army. The "NVA." The "gooks."

Only that wasn't the mission Tony and the other men truly believed in. Each, in his own way, knew that America had given up on trying to win this particular war. President Nixon, inaugurated earlier that year, had announced that it was simply a matter of time before America withdrew its forces from South Vietnam and left the Vietnamese to their own defense. "Peace with Honor" Nixon had called it.

On the day they had heard that announcement, Tony and the other GIs in this company, and all across Vietnam, feeling betrayed by their own government and their own people for sending them to risk life and limb in a war they were no longer even trying to win, had immediately adopted a different mission, a more personal one: simply to survive this horrible war, and make it home alive and in one piece. No one wanted to be the "last poor dumb bastard to die in Vietnam."

The word to take a break had come up the line to Danny Nakamura, Tony's backup man, from Hal Wilson, the squad leader, after Hal heard it from the company commander's radio operator. The company commander, Army Captain David Larkin, known by his radio call sign as "Patriot 6" and by his men simply as "6," had ordered the company to take a ten-minute break only after more than two hours of ass-kicking, single file hump through the dark, hellish jungle.

With a few more slashes of his machete Tony finished chopping through the next wall of bamboo that stood in his way, so he could see ahead a few more feet. Then he stood for a moment, bent forward under the load of the heavy rucksack and all his ammo and gear, looking carefully at the jungle ahead for any sign of the enemy. Still panting from his exertion, he sheathed the big knife and walked closer to a nearby tree, where he turned around and half-sat, half-fell backwards, so the weight of the rucksack was propped lightly against the tree just as his butt hit the ground.

There was some talent to that, getting just far enough away from the tree that the rucksack only leaned on it. Too far away, he would have missed the tree entirely and wound up on his back on the ground, like an upside-down turtle. Ugly. He could almost hear the quiet laughter that would have floated up from the grunts behind him if he'd done that. Too close, the rucksack might have hit the tree too hard, might have ruptured one of the soft plastic canteens inside, costing him part of his precious water. But Tony had practiced this move hundreds of times before, and made it perfectly. Just as his rump touched the ground he felt the rucksack stop against the tree.

Three-point landing.

He made sure to keep his body facing forward so he could keep an eye out for gooks to his front, though it was unlikely any would approach through the thick bamboo that lay directly ahead. He'd have to chop through more of it or find a way around it after the break, so the company could continue the march.

Tony lifted the heavy steel helmet from his head and dropped it upside down on the ground, the leather band and canvas webbing inside the helmet liner drenched with sweat. He carefully laid his rifle on the ground next to the helmet, facing forward, the pistol grip to the right, the selector switch on "Auto." Normally he would have left the rifle on "Safe," but Tony was the point man, first man in the line of march, and if the gooks did come at him suddenly from the front, if he had to pick the rifle up and fire quickly, he didn't want to be fumbling with the selector switch, which some genius on the M-16 design team had put on the left side of the receiver, where it was hard to reach in some positions by a right-handed rifleman.

The selector switch on the communist AK-47s they fought against was on the right, where Tony felt it ought to be, so the shooter could move it with either the thumb or the trigger finger. But Tony was sure some gook soldiers bitched about the position of the AK's selector switch too. That's what soldiers did, he knew, besides killing each other. They bitched.

At any rate, as an experienced point man, Tony had managed to stay alive more than once because he'd been quick with his M-16, had out-gunned an enemy soldier before the other guy could kill him. Especially when he was on point, Tony never forgot to keep his rifle at the ready.

The company worked off a battalion fire base, which in the vernacular of the Air Cavalry was called a "Landing Zone," in this case "LZ" Sherman. They had been off the LZ, working in the jungle for over a month this trip out; thirty-six days by Tony's count. He hadn't had a bath or a haircut for that long. He'd shaved about a week before when Patriot 6, the company commander, had ordered everyone to do it, using filthy water from a bomb crater, with no soap or shaving cream. Drinking water was too precious to use for shaving, and soap and shaving cream were luxuries, too heavy to carry, too easy to do without.

There had been one change of jungle fatigues since leaving the LZ, but that had been over two weeks before, and his were now rank with sweat, mud, and jungle muck. Mercifully he'd long ago stopped being able to smell the stench of his own sweat. But he could still smell the jungle rot that spotted his hands, arms, and legs. Jungle rot; the oozing, pus-filled sores that wouldn't heal until the next time the men came out of the field and got a couple of showers; sores that grew a little bigger every day, and always left scars, and always stunk like something that had died.

Tony pulled a half-crushed pack of cigarettes out of the webbing inside his helmet, shook the pack to free one, then pulled it out with his lips. He fished his Zippo lighter out of his shirt pocket, lit the cigarette, sucked smoke deep into his lungs, and blew it out again. Then he un-did the parachute cord from around his calves, loosened his drenched, filthy fatigue pant legs, rolled up the right one, and set about using the cigarette to burn off the leeches that had attached themselves to his legs during the morning's walk, and were sucking his blood. There were twelve on his right leg alone, the biggest of them the size of his little finger, all full of his blood. "Sorry, guys. Ride's over," he said absently. Leeches were an everyday thing that he'd long ago gotten used to, and the animosity he'd once felt for the little blood-suckers had long since disappeared, re-directed toward the enemy, and the government that had sent him here.

Normally a very calm man, even in moments of great danger, this morning Tony was agitated, unable to concentrate on much of any-thing beyond the thoughts of his wife, Angie. The cigarette smoke in his lungs settled him down a little, but not much. He finished burning off the leeches, rolled his pants back down, lapped them over the tops of his moldy jungle boots, and laced the parachute cord back around his lower legs, up to a point just below his knees. It kept some of the leeches out, and helped keep his pants from snagging and tearing on the jungle brush.

Before putting the cigarette lighter back into his pocket, he looked wistfully for a moment at the engraving on the side; two hearts, one overlapping the other, with the words "Tony & Angie, Forever" in-scribed underneath. She'd given it to him the morning he'd boarded the plane in Newark, headed for Vietnam.

Tony looked down into his upended helmet at Angie's picture there in the webbing, and even the plastic bag that protected it didn't keep her beautiful dark eyes from seeming to look right back into his. He stared at it for a moment, and the tears began again. He blinked them back, then reached into the upper pocket of his fatigue shirt and took out her latest letter, the cigarette dangling from his lips, smoke curling into his eyes.

The letter had come that morning with the resupply chopper. Mick Delaney, his platoon sergeant and close friend, had handed it to him at the same time he gave him the word that that they would move out in fifteen minutes.

Tony had known instantly from the familiar handwriting that the letter was from Angie. So with a big smile on his face he'd sliced the envelope open cleanly with his belt knife, being careful to save it to keep the letter in as he carried it with him to read and re-read later, as he always did. Letters from home were the only mercy, the only tenderness that could be clung to in this merciless place.

He had taken the letter out and unfolded it, the smile leaving his face as he began to read. The words had hit him like a fist in the heart.

Tony,

I'm sorry to have to tell you this, but it has to be over between us. I want a divorce. I can't stand this waiting anymore. Not knowing every night while I lie awake in our bed whether you're alive, or dead, or hurt somewhere in the jungle. I know I'm a coward, but I have to stop caring about you. I just can't live like this anymore.

Angela

She had signed it simply, "Angela." Not "You are my love and my life, forever, Angie," as she sometimes did, or even, "Love, Angie" as she usually did. Just "Angela."

A Dear John letter.

He'd known other soldiers to get them over the months he'd been in Vietnam, and had always felt enormously sorry for them, seeing the heartbreak so clearly on their tough young faces. But he could never really imagine what they were going through, couldn't imagine what it would be like to get one of those letters himself, because he had been so absolutely certain that it could never happen to him. If there was only one thing he believed he could be sure of in this very uncertain world, it was the love that he shared with Angie. Before today, if anyone had even suggested the possibility that she would send him a Dear John letter, he would have laughed in their face.

But now it *had* happened.

He'd read the letter repeatedly, first in disbelief, then in mortal sadness. He'd read it over and over again to make sure there was no way he could've misunderstood, until the words of his own personal Dear John letter were burned indelibly into his mind, and his heart. He'd sat, stupefied, for a while, unable to grasp it, unable to think what to do.

Then the word had come up the line for the grunts to saddle up and get ready to move out. Third platoon had the point today, and his squad would lead the platoon. That meant that Tony would walk point, and Danny would be behind him, his backup, the guy who would do his best to cover Tony's ass while he chopped his way through the morass of jungle.

He had to talk to her, find out why this was happening. He had to go home!

But he knew, because it had been tried many times before by other grunts, that the Army would never send him home for what they termed "marital strife." If they did, he knew, every soldier in Vietnam would suddenly develop marital problems.

He'd folded the letter back up, put it into its envelope, tucked it into the breast pocket of his filthy jungle fatigue shirt, and carefully buttoned both buttons of the flap, to make absolutely sure the letter was secure. Then, in silence, he had put on all his gear and made ready to move out.

Mick had made his way up to Tony, a folded map of their sector of the jungle in his hand.

"Morning again, Tony. How you doin' today? Another great day in the 'Nam, eh?"

Tony didn't smile at Mick's little irony as he usually would have, and said only, "I guess." He stared off into the jungle behind Mick.

"You OK, buddy?" Mick asked. "Bad night?"

"I'm OK." Tony hadn't decided yet what to do about Angie's letter, and he wasn't going to share the news with anyone, even his closest friend, until he'd made up his mind. Tony was wise well beyond his years, and mature enough to keep his mouth shut until he could calm down a little and think his way through this.

But Mick kept looking at him in silence, looking straight into his eyes, and could see that something was wrong.

"Vivid dream about home…about Angie," Tony said finally, his eyes darting to Mick's face, then away again. He had to give Mick something to get him to leave him alone, so he could think.

"Ah. I'm sorry, man. Those are tough. I thought I'd quit having them after being here for two or three months, but then one night there it all was again. Just about broke my heart. But you got a letter from her today, didn't you? Get a chance to read it?"

Tony nodded, didn't say more.

"Everything OK at home?"

"Yeah," he lied.

"Well …." Mick paused, unable to think what else to say. It didn't occur to him that Tony had gotten a Dear John letter. Not when Tony had told him so many times how close he and Angie were, how much they loved each other. And he knew he had to get the column moving before "6" went into another of his raging fits. "Here's where we're going today, Tony. About 305 degrees on your compass ought to get us there. It's just over a click, and as thick as this jungle is, it'll probably take most of the day to get there. Terrain's dead flat so no landmarks to guide you, as usual. Just shoot the azimuth, and when you think we're about there, call it back and we'll call in Redleg for a marking round to spot us. Same-old same-old. OK?"

"Yeah. Any new intel on the gooks?"

"No. Just the usual. They're thick as ticks on a dog. Be careful, man."

"OK. I need to talk to you and the LT tonight, Mick."

"Sure, Tony. What about?"

"I need to get an R & R to Hawaii. And I need it soon." An idea had formed in Tony's mind while they'd been talking. If he could get an R & R to Hawaii, maybe he could get Angie to meet him there so they could talk through this, so she could see he was OK and only had a few more months to go. If she wouldn't come, then at least he could try to sneak back home from there and see her. It was illegal to do that, he knew, and if the Army caught him they'd put him in the stockade for a while and then send him back to Vietnam. But it was the best he could come up with.

Tony also knew that if he told Mick and the LT about the Dear John letter, his chances of getting an R & R would disappear. There were standing orders that no one with known marital problems would get an R & R to Hawaii. It would be too easy for them to go AWOL, Absent Without Leave, from there and fly back to the States. And once on the mainland, they could just disappear, desert, and maybe never be found.

Mick thought he understood. After the dream, Tony was really missing his wife, really needed to see her. "I'll let the LT know, and we can talk about it tonight then."

"Thanks, Mick."

"You sure you're OK?"

"Yeah, I'm all right. Soon as we get movin' I'll be fine." Tony wasn't a man to shirk his responsibility onto anyone else, no matter the situation.

"See you later then. Go ahead and move out when you're ready. I'm going to walk in the LT's spot for a while, right behind your squad. He's back with 6, probably getting his ass chewed again."

Tony gave a weak smile. Their platoon leader, a 1st Lieutenant named Ed Thorsen, "the LT," was a super-bright West Point officer who cared greatly about his men, and only minimally about what he often referred to as "this fucking, goddamned, fucked-up war." His ass-chewings by the company commander, who was regarded by the men as a very poor officer and a terrible leader, were frequent, and often loud. The LT had become a hero among the men in the company because he so frequently challenged 6's poor decisions, and just as frequently got his ass chewed out. But the berating seemed to have little effect. The LT didn't stop standing up for what he believed in, and always stood up to 6 for the men. And so the endless stream of reprimands continued.

Mick headed back to his fighting hole to get his equipment on, and Tony walked over to Danny Nakamura, who was standing a few feet away with all his gear on, finishing up a can of C-Ration Ham and Lima Beans, eating them cold.

"Ugh. How do you eat that shit cold, Danny? I can't even eat ham and limas heated up."

Danny just shrugged, smiled, and kept eating.

"Anyway, you heard most of that. Time to go. We're headed out on 305 degrees, about a click, no landmarks between here and there. Lots of gooks around. Pretty much like every other day."

"Got it. Any friendlies around?" Danny, who was an activated Hawaii National Guardsman, was Okinawan by ancestry, and with his short muscular body, black hair, and oriental features, was certain that to other American soldiers, he looked like a gook, even though he per-

sonally saw little resemblance between Okinawan and Vietnamese facial features. So when he walked point and Tony backed him up, he was
almost as afraid of running into another American unit as he was of
running into the North Vietnamese or Viet Cong.

"Mick didn't mention it, so I'm sure there aren't. We're out here all
alone, as usual."

"Yeah. As usual. OK, Tony. Ready when you are."

"And keep your Okinawan ESP cranked up. OK?"

"Always do. Right now, it's telling me you had a dream about your
wife last night."

Tony was forced to smile a little despite his anguish. "Fuck you,
Danny. That was your little Okinawan ears that told you that, not your
ESP."

Danny flashed a big grin. "Oh, yeah. Sometimes I get those confused."

"My ass."

"You have a nice ass, Tony. I can hardly keep my eyes off it while
we're humpin' through this beautiful jungle."

Tony just shook his head. Danny's crazy sense of humor was part of
what kept Tony going in this hell hole. He'd been known to crack jokes
in the middle of firefights.

After checking his compass to get his bearings, Tony made his way
past the fighting holes his squad had dug the evening before, now lit-
tered with C-ration trash and other junk. He moved through the fields
of fire they'd chopped to give them a clear killing field, should the
gooks attack in the night. In doing so he had to step around the piles
of shit the grunts were supposed to bury, but seldom did, in their total
disdain for this despised country they found themselves in.

And with his machete, which he always kept razor sharp, he began
to hack his way into the jungle. Danny was right behind him, his rifle
held in both hands across his chest, his eyes searching the jungle for
any threat to Tony, or to himself.

2

Tony was twenty years old, just two years out of high school. He'd been a star football player while there, quarterback of the varsity team since he'd been a sophomore. He was that good. He was an even six feet tall, and normally weighed about a hundred and eighty pounds. He figured he was down by five or ten since coming to Vietnam, because of the heat, the strenuous all-day humps through the jungle, the awful C-Rations they ate when they had anything to eat at all, the bad water, and the frequent bouts with diarrhea and other crud, from just being in this nasty place. He had dark curly hair, almost black, naturally olive skin from his Italian heritage, and a handsome, chiseled face. He was lean and muscular, with broad shoulders and narrow hips. In another, kinder universe he would have been a movie actor, or at least a model for an Army recruiting poster. Instead he was in the most dangerous of jobs among the most dangerous of jobs, point man for an American infantry company, working the jungles right along the Cambodian border in South Vietnam.

The thing that usually made Tony an outstanding point man was his ability to clear his mind of everything except his job, and focus entirely on the jungle ahead of him. He paid close attention to every tree branch, every clump of bamboo, every cluster of jungle grass. He listened intently to the sounds around him, the insects and lizards and the occasional monkey. It wasn't so much what he was looking at or listening to, as it was the out-of-the-way thing he was looking *for*, the unusual sound he was listening *for*. He was looking for things that didn't belong: a straight line in the overall disordered crookedness of the jungle might be a trip wire or the upright of a bunker. The odd dark spot on the jungle floor might be a scuff left by the rubber Ho Chi Minh sandal of a passing *gook*.

But this morning, from the get-go until this break had been called nearly two hours later, Tony had thought only of Angie.

He'd remembered the first time he'd ever seen her. It was on the first day of their junior year in high school, and he'd literally bumped into her as he'd entered a classroom talking to one of his friends, her there talking to the teacher. She'd turned to face him and he'd said, "Excuse me." But their eyes had met and locked, and that had been that. He'd fallen in love on the spot. Stepping away he'd looked down at her and realized that, even apart from her gorgeous eyes, she was the most beautiful girl he'd ever seen. An incredible figure for a girl of sixteen, thick black hair that fell in waves and curls around her face. And that face! High cheekbones, a beautiful full mouth, and those deep green eyes that smiled playfully at him.

"That's OK," she'd said, before turning back to her conversation.

He'd memorized her name from the teacher's roll call; Angela. "Angel." He'd waited for her after class, shyly introduced himself, asked her out for that very night, maybe a hamburger and a Coke? She'd said, "I'd like that!" right away, not playing games. Gave him her address, told him she had to be home early so why not pick her up at 6:00?

Apparently, she'd been smitten as quickly as he, because they became inseparable from that very day. Couldn't get enough of each other. He'd started to kiss her goodnight in the car at the end of the first date, lightly on the lips, and she'd put her hand behind his head, drawn him close, kissed him slowly and deeply before pulling away with a little sigh, smiling at him as she pulled the door latch, said, "See you tomorrow in class?" Then she'd stepped out of the car and run to the door, turned and waved to him as she opened it and slipped inside.

They'd made love for the first time only a few weeks later, skipped school one day when her parents were away and went to her house, and made love in her bedroom. Just couldn't wait any longer. It had been the first time for both of them, and it was by far the most beautiful, touching experience Tony had ever known.

Angela and Anthony. Angie and Tony. They became nothing short of a school legend. Everyone knew they would marry one day, and they had, right after high school. But then, only a year later, the notice from the draft board had come, inevitably leading him to Vietnam. And away from Angie, his soul-mate, the unquestioned love of his life.

But now there was that letter. Tony just didn't get it. He'd re-read her letter from a few days before, and it sounded OK. She seemed a little stressed, and worried about him, but she'd said all the loving things she usually said. Now this. He didn't get it.

Tony's whole life was tied to Angie. He'd heard other guys complaining about their wives, even joking about them, ridiculing them to the other soldiers. He'd never do that. Angie was everything to him. He'd had football scholarship offers to some interesting smaller colleges, but he hadn't even considered them seriously, because he just wanted to be with her, be married to her. He'd figured he'd do his tour in Vietnam, do the best he could, and then return home to her, start a family, work the refinery, go home to her every night. That's all he wanted.

Still leaning back against the tree, smoking a second cigarette, Tony was reading the letter again when LT Thorsen pushed quietly through

the tangle of brush behind him, and called softly, "Tony, it's the LT."
Thorsen came forward, watchful, then took a knee beside Tony.

"How you doin' Tony? Mick said you needed to talk to us tonight?"
Thorsen spoke very softly, aware that there might always be NVA nearby.

"Yeah, LT. I really need to get an R&R to Hawaii, and soon if I can.
I've been here over six months, and I should be up for one. I really need
to see my wife."

"OK, Tony. When we stop for the night I'll radio the XO back in
Tay Ninh, and see what we can do. You sure deserve one, and you're
right. You should be up for one soon. But it might take a while. But, are
you sure you're OK for now? You OK to be on point?"

"Yeah, I'm OK for now, LT. Thanks for looking in on me. Talk to
you tonight."

Once the LT had gone Tony folded the letter, put it back into its
envelope, and shoved the envelope back into his shirt pocket. Then he
picked up his rifle and put it back on "safe," shifted his legs to get his
knees under him, rocked forward, leaned on the rifle, and pushed himself up off the ground. Bending down carefully under the heavy pack
he picked up his helmet. Angie's picture was still there in the webbing,
her beautiful face smiling up at him. He stared at it a moment, tears
coming again to his eyes, and then he put the helmet on his head.

He dropped the cigarette and ground it into the forest mulch with
his boot. Then he pulled his machete from the sheath on the side of
his rucksack, checked the edge with his thumb, stepped forward up the
path he'd created, and began to chop at the bamboo cluster growing to
his front. Danny was on his feet behind him already, equipment and
helmet on, rifle at the ready, eyes searching the dense jungle ahead.

And so it was, just over a half hour later, that Tony was again daydreaming about making love with his wife, and failed to see the gook
sign in the jungle ahead of him. It wasn't much. Just a few blades of

grass bent the wrong way, at the edge of an area where the foliage was a bit less dense than what he'd been pushing and chopping his way through all morning. Normally he would have noticed it. Except that he was thinking so intensely about Angie, his heart in his throat with fear of losing her.

And then the world exploded around him as an NVA soldier in a spider hole opened fire on him with an AK-47, catching Tony with a burst across the top of his legs, knocking him backwards onto the jungle floor. Tony's rifle flew from his left hand into the thick brush, and his machete flipped end-over-end to the other side.

There was little pain at first, just the dull feeling of having been hit with something heavy, like a baseball bat, across the legs. He fell awkwardly onto his rucksack and rolled off to one side. Then as the bullets continued to snap around his head and the streaking green tracers cut paths through the air above him, he thought to pull the rucksack strap releases, and got fully out of it. He started to crawl around the pack to use it for cover, but his legs wouldn't respond to his head, and he looked down and saw blood pouring from the wounds.

His whole body went cold then, as he realized he would die quickly if he couldn't stop the bleeding. He looked back for Danny, saw him firing away from behind the fallen log Tony had just stepped over, his M-16 on full-automatic, putting out as much firepower as he could to try to suppress the gook fire.

Tony's eyes met Danny's through the pall of gun smoke, a naked plea for help.

Danny slipped out of his rucksack, threw off his helmet, laid his rifle aside, and slithered over the log and began a low crawl toward Tony. The gook fire intensified even more with a new target in the open, and tracers flew all around them. The noise was hellish, totally deafening, so outrageous Tony literally couldn't think.

There had been many times since he'd come to Vietnam when Tony had seriously feared for his life. But this time, with these wounds, he was truly afraid that he was going to die within the next few minutes. And even more than he feared his own death, he feared that he'd never see Angie again, would never know ... *Why?*

3

2018, Kansas City
Mick Delaney

I'm Mick Delaney, Tony's platoon sergeant the day he walked into that ambush. It's me telling his story, along with Angie's story and my own, almost fifty years later. It has taken me all this time to fully understand what happened that day, and all that has happened since, because of it. You will wonder, as you read some of this, how I know it. Just read on ...

***

I had been in Vietnam a little less than five months that day, having gone there as a volunteer at the ripe old age of twenty-two to help defend South Vietnam and America against the Communist threat. Or that's what I'd believed until I'd been there awhile, and learned first-hand how fucked up that war was.

My family and my childhood had been essentially destroyed by the death of my Uncle Tim, my mother's younger brother, in the Korean War in 1951. He died on a snow-covered ridge, killed by attacking Chinese soldiers while single-handedly trying to defend a gap in the

American lines, armed with only his rifle and a few hand grenades. His heroism earned him a posthumous Silver Star. But his death broke my mother's heart.

My childhood was overshadowed by her depression, bitterness, and anger over his loss in a war she didn't understand or support. Like most Americans back then, she couldn't point to the Korean peninsula on a map, and certainly couldn't understand why South Korea's defense was important to America or her people. She never understood why her beloved little brother had to give his life to defend the world against the obscure notion of Communist expansionism.

By the time I was fourteen, she and my father had divorced, and Dad had moved to the west coast to get as far away from her as possible. I had watched her make his life a living hell since my uncle's death, and couldn't really blame him for finally leaving. But I did miss him.

My older sister Sarah, who had looked after me throughout our childhood and early teens in the absence of our parents' interest or attention, had married and left home by then. So I was left pretty much on my own with my still grieving and emotionally absentee mother, a fatherless kid trying to grow up in one of the rougher parts of Kansas City.

It was no surprise then that only a couple of years later, at sixteen, I had become a rebellious, difficult teenager, a minor hell-raiser who hung around with the wrong crowd, smoked, drank, and committed numerous petty crimes, just for the hell of it. Mom was distraught by what she saw me turning into. But I was a big, lanky, almost-grown young man by then, a full head taller than my mom, and she wasn't about to intimidate me into changing my ways.

But then in my senior year in high school, I met and fell in love with a beautiful, sweet young woman named Katie, who for some unexplained reason also fell in love with me. Katie made me feel truly loved for the first time in my life by someone other than Sarah, and our relationship settled me down. I spent less and less time with my buddies from the wrong crowd, and more and more time with Katie. Because of her influence, I somehow squeaked through the rest of high school with grades just good enough to graduate.

With no money for college and bored with school anyway, I took a job as an entry-level draftsman with a company called Langton Manufacturing. By working all the overtime I could get and saving every penny I could, I soon had enough money to rent a small apartment. It was a third-floor walk-up, barely big enough to turn around in, hot in the summer and cold in the winter. But it was ours, Katie's and mine. It became our sanctuary, the place where we could go to be alone, away from the world, and simply love each other. We spent all our free time together there.

We were married a few months after graduation in a small ceremony in Katie's family church. Katie's parents were a little apprehensive that we were marrying so young, but Katie talked them into giving their approval. My mom eagerly approved, relieved that she would no longer, in any way, be responsible for me. Katie and I took up our lives as a young married couple, me working at Langton Manufacturing to support us, her going to junior college and working a part-time job to pay her tuition.

We were happy!

But by then it was 1965, and Lyndon Johnson was well into forsaking his 1964 campaign promises by deploying tens of thousands of American Marines and Army troops to fight the Communist Viet Cong and North Vietnamese on the ground in Vietnam. Since I wasn't in college and we had no children yet, I wasn't surprised when I got my draft notice later that year.

With memories of my father's and uncles' honored service during World War II, and my Uncle Tim's heroic death in Korea, I was inclined to follow family tradition and go do my part in Vietnam. But

Katie, my sister Sarah, and pretty much everyone in my extended family reminded me of how tough it would be for my mother, with all she had already suffered, if I went to war. Even though Mom and I had a pretty poor relationship, I still loved her. I got it.

So to avoid being drafted I enlisted in the Army National Guard, an infantry battalion near my home in Kansas City, Kansas. In those days, joining the Guard or Reserves was considered an almost certain way of avoiding the war. I took my six months' training with the regular Army, then settled in back at home for what I thought would be five-and-a-half years of boring monthly Guard meetings and annual summer camps, but an otherwise peaceful, happy life with Katie.

And no war.

Our plan didn't quite work out. President Johnson, before declining to run for re-election in 1968 (a cowardly bug-out, in my opinion, since he got us into the war in the first place) acceded to the wishes of his generals, and agreed to activate several National Guard and Army Reserve Brigades for the first time since the Korean War, to provide additional fodder for what had grown to be a massive ground war in Vietnam.

My battalion was activated and relocated to Fort Carson, Colorado, in May of 1968. There we underwent refresher training in the high desert, to prepare us somehow for a jungle war. After the first few weeks we began being reassigned, one-by-one, to combat duty in Vietnam. Our men were sent off to war as individual replacements for the more than five hundred casualties America was suffering there each week.

Somehow my name was continually overlooked in the reassignment levy, and the end of 1968 approached with no orders for me to go to Vietnam. By then Katie and I were living in another tiny apartment off-post in Colorado Springs, and I had been promoted to sergeant and had pretty easy duty at Fort Carson. It looked like I would remain there for the rest of the activation, which was scheduled to end late in 1969.

But somehow I felt like I was missing out. Men in my family had fought in all the wars, all the way back to the Civil War. And everyone in my family had been proud of their service. I couldn't forget my Uncle Tim and his death at the hands of Chinese Communists in Korea. Weren't these just more Communists we were fighting in Vietnam? If I went, maybe I'd have the chance to avenge his death. Besides, most of my buddies from the National Guard were already there, and I wasn't. I felt guilty about that.

With all that going on in my head, and without talking to Katie about it beforehand, I committed what she later described as an irrational act: I requested reassignment to the 1st Cavalry Division, my Uncle Tim's old unit from Korea, which was then in the forefront of the fighting in Vietnam. I volunteered for the war.

Katie was understandably pissed. Didn't I love her anymore? Why would I want to leave her to go fight in a war few Americans supported, or even understood? And maybe not come back? Didn't I know about the war protests? Hadn't I seen the news about college campuses on fire, people rioting in the streets, the marches on Washington to get the war stopped?

She cried…a lot. And I felt bad. But I still believed I should go.

A few weeks later I got my orders for Vietnam, and had the awful experience of calling my mother from Colorado to break the news to her.

She only said, "I knew it!" and began sobbing into the phone.

I felt terrible. But even still, I believed I was right in volunteering to go. Somehow, I felt like I owed it to someone. Although to this day, I've never been quite certain…to whom.

I didn't tell Mom I'd volunteered.

The thirty-day leave at home before I left for Vietnam was a miserable time. Everyone in my family treated me as though I had been sentenced to death. Katie was constantly sad, and I would often wake up at night to the sound of her crying.

I was almost relieved when the day finally came in mid-April for me to go. Leaving a tearful Katie and my sister, Sarah, in the terminal, I climbed on board a TWA airliner in Kansas City, gave Katie and Sarah a last wave goodbye, and left on the journey that would change my life forever.

4

A few days later I was in hot, muggy, smelly, dangerous Vietnam. Early one morning I found myself stepping off of a resupply helicopter into a jungle clearing to join my infantry company, officially designated Company D, 2nd Battalion, 9th Cavalry Regiment, 1st Cavalry Division (Airmobile), but known better by the company commander's radio call sign, "Patriot 6."

The soldiers I encountered there didn't look much like soldiers at all. Instead they resembled a gang of some sort, made up of ragged, filthy, smelly, unshaven, teen-age thugs, wearing all faded green and carrying all manner of automatic weapons, grenades, machetes, and other lethal stuff. They seemed somehow angry that I was there, and I was greeted by most, including my platoon sergeant and squad leader, with less than friendly enthusiasm.

"Welcome to your new world, grunt!"

This, I later learned, was understandable. I was replacing one of their friends who had been killed in a firefight a couple of days before. They were still grieving and angry over the loss. And I had not yet earned the right to be one of them. Hell, I was still relatively clean and had on almost-brand-new jungle fatigues. Theirs were generally faded and torn, and grungier than I'd ever seen clothing before.

I was assigned to the Third Platoon, First Squad, known as Patriot 3-1, or just "3-1." To my surprise a couple of the guys in the squad were actually friendly to me right off. They said hello, shook hands, and even smiled, and began trying to show me the ropes. One was a California surfer named Jonathan West, who I would later learn had a great singing voice and played terrific guitar. The other was a twenty-year-old Italian kid from New Jersey with olive skin, black hair, and serious eyes, named Tony Giles. The three of us got to know each other well over the next few days, and found we had a lot in common. For one thing, we had all married young, and we were all very much in love with our wives. We made a pact that we would help each other survive the war and go home to them.

The platoon sergeant made me a point man right off despite my National Guard sergeant's rank, explaining that I was just a cherry, I had never been shot at, and had yet to demonstrate any value to him even as a soldier, let alone any leadership ability in combat.

Fair enough, I thought. *He's right.*

There were few trails in the dense, triple canopy jungle we patrolled, and to walk one was an almost certain way to trip some sort of booby-trap or stumble into a full-scale ambush. So instead we made our way single file through the jungle, the point man picking and hacking the path through dense vegetation. The first day I walked point the fear and the physical stress of it in that unbearable heat and humidity nearly killed me. But over time I toughened up, physically as well as mentally. It was all part of the process.

The overwhelming sense of it after a few days in the bush was that we were simply bait, live meat, humping miserably, laden like pack mules, through the jungle every day, the Army hoping we would blunder into some of the enemy so we could "close with, engage, and destroy" them. We of course were hoping we wouldn't blunder into any of the enemy since, because they were dug in and waiting quietly for us while we were fully exposed and making a lot of noise approaching them, the chances were that they would surprise us, and kill or fuck-up more of us than we could kill or fuck-up of them.

That's what it was all about in that war, really, to the higher-ups. Who got the bigger body count? A firefight was considered a success if we killed twenty of them, but they only killed four or five of us. It seemed that nobody in command thought much about the families of the four or five of our guys we'd lost that day, or the wounded who might have gone home to spend the rest of their lives in wheelchairs.

It didn't take me long to figure out that it was a really terrible way to run a war, especially if you were a grunt, and most especially if you were the point man. And it didn't take me long to realize that I'd made a terrible mistake by volunteering to go there. After a few weeks there and my first few firefights, I calculated that I had about as much chance of making any real difference in the war against Communists as I had of making it home alive and in one piece. Not much. I had given up a beautiful, safe life with Katie to go to Vietnam and fight in a war we weren't even trying to win.

Three months later, one day in July, we got into a really bad firefight and lost our squad leader, a good Alabama boy named Carl Engle, and several other men from Third Platoon. An altogether sad day, and a story I'll save for later. But after we'd put Carl's mangled body onto a chopper to begin its journey to his grieving family back home, the company commander, Captain Larkin, called me over and told me I'd be taking over my platoon. Not the 3-1 Squad, the whole Third Platoon. Seemed our platoon sergeant had been one of the wounded that day, and had to be replaced. With my National Guard time (which was apparently recognized by then) I was the senior sergeant left in the platoon. And besides, none of the more Vietnam-experienced NCOs wanted the job. I didn't really want the job either, but I was given no choice. "It's an order, not a request," Larkin said.

So that's how I came to be Tony's platoon sergeant, and his friend, on the day he walked into that ambush.

5

Two hours into that morning 6 called the first break, and after passing the word forward to the point squad, I sat down like everyone else to get the weight off my feet and shoulders. LT Thorsen came up from his "meeting" with 6, pissed off as usual by the CO's bullshit.

"Hey, LT," I said with a big cheerful smile. "How's your morning going?" I kept my voice low since we weren't all that far from 6.

He just glared at me. "How's it going up here?"

"Same old, same old. Except that Tony didn't seem like himself this morning. Said he'd had a dream about his wife last night, fucked up his head."

"Yeah. Those are a bitch. He OK?"

"Said he would be, once we got moving. Seems like things are going all right, maybe a little slower than usual."

"I'll head up and see how he's doing." And the LT made his way forward, careful not to step on any of the grunts sitting on the path, alternately facing right and left as we always did.

When he came back a little later he said, "He seems OK. Told him I'd try to get him an R&R to Hawaii to see his wife."

"Great. I could use one too, you know. If you can get two. I'd love to see my wife's cute little freckled face. And her other parts."

"You haven't been here long enough, Mick. Besides, you're just too important to the welfare of this platoon. What would we do without you?" A mirthful smile adorned his dirty, bearded face.

"I'd love to let you try, LT. Besides, I'm pretty old for this shit. I'm almost as old as you are." Not much of a retort, but all I could think of at the time.

I saw Fragman, just ahead of me, getting up, ready to move out. So I dragged myself up onto my feet, put my helmet on, and got ready for the next couple of hours of boring, back-breaking hump. LT Thorsen headed back to rejoin 6 so they could continue their talk.

POP-POP-POP-POP-POP! It was only a little while later that I heard the first shots of the ambush.

Fuck! Tony's up there!

I went to my knees, shrugged out of my rucksack, got back to my feet, and began moving forward in a crouch.

POP-POP-POP-POP-POP! More rounds from the gook AK. As I got close to the front of the column I saw a couple of their green tracers zip by, and I hit the ground and began crawling forward. What only seconds before had been near-silence except for the metallic ringing of Tony's machete, was now the ear-shattering roar of automatic weapons firing in both directions.

I heard one of our guys scream "Hey, gook! Your mother sucks GI cocks!" Scared as I was for Tony, and for myself, I had to smile a bit at that. I doubted that any of the North Vietnamese could understand English. But whoever had screamed that wasn't going to miss any chances to add insult to the injuries he was so aggressively trying to inflict on the NVA.

It was easy to distinguish between the sounds of the enemy AK-47s and the American M-16s and a bit later, our M-60 machine gun starting up. It wasn't certain from the noise level who was putting out more fire. But I could see red American tracers streaking toward the NVA, and I could certainly see the green North Vietnamese tracers as they zipped our way. And there was a hell of a lot of smoke.

As always in the beginning of a gunfight I was absolutely terrified, my gut turning to water, and fear pounding in my chest. But I had learned from the twenty or so other firefights I'd been in by then to suppress the fear, at least enough to function. I knew that when fear took over and froze you up, you were dead. I also knew, had repeatedly accepted, that I probably wasn't going home alive anyway.

I crawled up alongside Hal Wilson, the 3-1 squad leader and another close friend. Hal was a slender blonde Tennessee boy, originally from Boston, a really physically and mentally tough guy with a super big brain who had a strange sort of combo-accent that always amused me a bit when I heard him speak. Only this day he wasn't speaking, he was screaming into my ear over the gunfire.

"Motherfuckers got Tony!"

FUCK!

Through the thickening gun-smoke I could barely see Tony on the ground to our front, ten yards or so beyond a good-sized log that was just in front of us, perpendicular to the line of fire. But I could tell he was still moving, looking back at us. And I could see Danny Nakamura crawling toward him, and Fragman, the big, strong black man on loan from our weapons squad, following closely behind. A little rise in the ground just in front of where Tony had fallen was keeping the gooks from getting fire low enough to hit them, and, for the moment, from hitting Tony again. I made my way up to the log and moved off to the left of them a little, to help put as much suppressing firepower onto the gooks as possible. I put magazine after magazine of fully automatic M-16 fire into the spots from which the green tracers were still coming at us.

Danny and Fragman got Tony the rest of the way out of his rucksack straps and began dragging him toward the cover of the log. I could see blood streaming from Tony's legs, and the terrified look on his face. Danny and Fragman were staying low, pulling with all their might, low-crawling as fast as they could drag him.

"Hal!" I screamed, though he was only four feet away. "Get the Doc up here, and have them call in a Medevac! Tony's hurt bad!"

"I'm right here!" I heard Doc Benedetto shout from my right. He had followed me up, knowing he would be needed.

"Medevac's on its way, Mick!" I heard Hal yell from just to my left. I just nodded at them. Should have known.

Danny and Fragman were rapidly making their way back to us, dragging Tony for all they were worth toward a low spot behind the log where we'd taken cover. I motioned Hal to slide over to one side of the low spot while I moved to the other, so we could help them get Tony over. Doc Benedetto was right beside us, and had already taken the tourniquet that he wore as a belt off his waist so he could get it onto one of Tony's legs as soon as he was over. He had a second tourniquet out of his medical bag, ready on the ground. The Doc, who was a conscientious objector and didn't carry a weapon, knew his stuff, and had already saved many lives before that day.

I felt a hand on my back. The LT. I turned to him. "Tony's hit bad, LT." He could see the rest for himself.

"I shoulda been up here with you guys. Fuckin' 6!"

I just nodded, nothing else to say. He was right.

The LT's radioman, Firedog, was right behind him, radio handset to his ear, talking away. "Redleg is on its way, LT! Cobras won't be far behind."

The LT just nodded to him.

Just then we heard the shriek-rumble of a 105-millimeter artillery shell streaking in overhead, and saw the white air-burst of the marking round about fifty meters out and fifty meters in the air, right behind where the gooks were dug in.

"Right on it!" the LT screamed above the noise. "Fire for effect!"

Firedog shouted into the handset. "Right on target! Fire for effect! I say again, Fire for Effect!" And round after round of cannon fire began screaming in overhead and detonating with huge explosions in the trees behind the gooks.

Exhausted and terrified, sweat running in their eyes, Danny and Fragman finally reached the far side of the log, dragging Tony along. He seemed barely conscious, skin pale from fear and loss of blood, but still alive, blood still streamed from his legs. The gook fire finally seemed to be slowing down a bit, with our suppressing fire still pouring out and the artillery exploding in the jungle right behind their position.

Hal and I had our helmets and gear off and were shifting our weight around, getting ready to pull Tony over the log. Danny and Fragman moved off to the side, still on the other side of the log, and dragged Tony right up to it, ready to push him up and over.

"You guys ready?" I tried to yell above the noise.

They shouted back, "Ready!"

"Go!" And both Danny and Fragman pushed Tony up onto the log as Hal and I rose on our knees to grab him and pull him over.

But something on his fatigue shirt caught on a stub on the log just as we got him on top of it, and he was suddenly, unexpectedly stuck there. His eyes opened, and he looked straight at me. I saw terror there, but also a strong spark of life. I knew he would make it if we could just get him free.

Danny and Fragman continued to push, and Hal and I, rising higher on our knees in the dwindling gunfire, pulled for all we were worth.

6

17 August 1969
Tay Ninh Province, Republic of Vietnam
Tony Giles

At that point, Tony felt himself break free, and he began to tumble toward the "safe" side of the log. But then came a blow, like being hit by a batted baseball, right in the center of his back. And there was a searing pain that cut right through him. He gasped at the violence of it, and his eyes went wide. He knew without looking that he'd been hit again, and that the bullets had come through his chest.

The beating of his heart slowed as his body ran out of blood, and darkness overcame him.

But then there was a light. At first it was just a tiny point of light, very far away. But then it came closer and closer, became brighter and brighter, until it seemed the entire universe was bathed in beautiful, soft light. Tony's spirit began to free itself from his shattered body, and as it did, he became very calm. There was no more fear, and no more pain.

He began to feel as though he was floating, safe, in pure love. It felt like God's love.

As the overwhelming sense of peace consumed him he again saw his beautiful, sensuous wife Angie, who he loved more than he had ever believed he could love anyone. She was again naked, her perfect, pure body sitting atop him in their bed. She was looking down at him as they made love.

And she was smiling.

With the last beat of his heart, Tony smiled back.

7

We were so close! If only Tony hadn't gotten caught on that log he would have made it over alive, and the Doc would have saved him. But instead, Tony came across the log spurting blood from the new wounds in his chest, and flopped limply into my arms.

Strangely, he was smiling.

We got him flat on the ground and Doc took his pulse, then pulled one of his eyes open wide to see if there was even a spark of life. But by then the bleeding from all his wounds had nearly stopped, and his normally olive Italian skin had gone pale.

Tony's dead! He's gone!

I reached over the log to help Danny up and over, while Hal helped Fragman. No one took a shot at any of us, and in fact the firing from the NVA had nearly stopped.

With Tony's body there on the ground among us, there on the "safe" side of the log, my sadness at his death transformed into rage, and the rage overcame me. I took my helmet off and smashed it into the ground. "FUCK!" I screamed, my palms pressed into my eyes. "This

FUCKING war! And the FUCKING gooks! And the MOTHER-FUCKERS who sent us here! GODDAMN IT!"

The men around me stared at me, perhaps thinking that their platoon sergeant had finally gone over the edge.

I had seen more death in the few months I'd been in Vietnam than I'd ever thought I would see in a lifetime. I thought I was hardened to it, the maiming and killing, both the giving and the receiving. But Tony's death simply overwhelmed me. Although there was a lot I should have been doing, I just sat there for a while. As I did so Tony's body gradually lost any resemblance to my friend, and turned into a pale, staring corpse. Gently, I reached over and closed his eyes, eyes that had already gone opaque.

I thought about his wife, Angie, who he talked about so often, and whose picture he'd shown me proudly so many times. She was a beautiful woman who had meant everything to Tony, and to whom he had meant everything as well.

How will she survive this? What will she do?

After a bit I got control of myself, and during a little lull in shooting, finally thought to say to Danny and Fragman, "Thank you, guys, for trying to save him. That was an incredible act of heroism, and I can never thank you enough."

Danny shook his head, shaking it off. "Couldn't just leave him out there, man. He would have done the same for me."

Fragman just kept looking at Tony, his face a mask. "Back in Watts I wouldn't have pissed on this honky to put him out if he'd been on fire. But that was Tony out there, man, and I didn't even think about it before goin' to help Danny bring him back. Fuck, man, I am so goddamn sad." And he wiped his eyes on his forearm, and turned away to find his weapons and his gear.

LT Thorsen was nearby, Firedog right next to him on the radio. I heard Firedog talking to the lead pilot of a Cobra gunship flight, and moments later one of Hal's men threw a yellow smoke grenade to mark our position. The Cobras began making passes over the enemy bunkers to our front, mini-guns and grenade launchers firing away with each pass.

Thorsen made his way over to where I was sitting, next to Tony's body.

"I'm really sorry about Tony, Mick!" he shouted, to be heard above the outrageous noise of the Cobra attack. "I know what good friends you were. Such a waste." I could see the LT was containing his own emotions. Sadness? Rage?

His sadness won the battle over his rage, and I could see it on his face. There were tears in his eyes, too. "I guess he won't be needing that R&R now."

"No, I guess not."

8

17 August 1969
Tay Ninh Province, Republic of Vietnam

The Cobra gunships had finished their passes and pulled away, and the jungle became eerily silent. The NVA weren't shooting, we weren't shooting, no artillery was landing. Nothing. Just a weird pall of silence, except for the loud ringing in my ears, and probably everyone else's. And all that smoke, and the acrid smell of a gunfight, and the smell of Tony's drying blood.

"You stay here and make sure his body gets on its way home, Mick. I'm going to take a patrol out to see what's out there."

"No, c'mon, LT. You know 6 doesn't want you taking squad-sized patrols out. You'll just get your ass chewed again."

"Fuck 6. I'm sure my fitness reports are already fucked, therefore my career. Nothing much else to lose. I'll do it my way."

Firedog's radio crackled to life. "3-6, this is Patriot 6 Alpha." It was the company commander's radio operator, calling for the LT. "6 wants you at the CP."

"Now what the fuck?"

"He probably just wants an update, LT. And he's too chickenshit to come up here to get it."

38

"Tell him I'm on my way, Firedog. Mick, you'd better go out with the patrol. But be careful! I don't want to lose anyone else today."

"OK, LT. Watch your temper with 6. You don't need him chewing you any more new assholes."

"OK, OK, I know. You be careful."

Thorsen picked up his rifle, stood up, bent over behind the partial cover of the log, and helped Firedog to his feet. In a crouch, the two of them headed to the company command post, where Captain Larkin waited.

"Hal," I called. "Get Loon on the radio and tell him to saddle up his squad. We're going to run a patrol to see what's out there. You're the platoon leader while the LT and I are both gone. Don't let anybody shoot us coming back in."

"OK, Mick."

While I waited for Loon to get his squad ready for the patrol, I sat with Tony's body. I heard a Huey landing in a small clearing behind us. Knowing he would be evacuated before I got back from the patrol, I realized I'd never see my good friend again. Not in this lifetime, anyway.

I checked for his dog tags, and seeing that one was on a chain around his neck, I took my belt knife and cut the other one out of the laces on his right boot. Working around all the drying blood as best I could, I snapped it onto the neck chain with the other one, with the crucifix that was also there. Then I started going through his pockets to make sure there were no grenades or live ammo there that might endanger anyone handling his body.

In one of his shirt pockets I came across the letter he'd received from Angie that morning. It was in an open envelope, a corner of it stained with his blood. I put it into my own pocket, knowing the Army would only destroy it if I left it on him, and thinking vaguely that the LT might want to send it back to his wife. The engraved cigarette lighter was there too, but I left it there, and I left his wedding ring on his finger. There was another letter in one of the cargo pockets in his pants, and I put it into my own pocket as well.

That grisly job done I got up on my knees and got my fighting gear in shape for the patrol. Just the pistol belt and harness, one canteen, frag and smoke grenades, and two bandoliers of rifle magazines.

As Loon and his squad came up to me I once again put my hand on Tony's face, to say a final goodbye. There were no eloquent words forming in my messed up mind, so I just said, "Goodbye, buddy. I hope you're in a really good place now, where no one or nothing can ever hurt you again." Again, the tears.

"What a shame," said Loon. "He was a good guy." Loon was a really good Canadian kid, white-blonde hair, stout build, who had enlisted in the American Army and volunteered for Vietnam because, as he had put it when I first met him, "Canada has decided to sit this one out. So I thought I'd come down to give you Yanks a hand. And you know, Canadians are better soldiers anyway."

"Sure is a shame," I said. "Let's go out about fifty meters, Loon. Your patrol. I'm along for the ride. I'll walk right behind Pete." Pete was his radio operator. "Take it nice and slow. Let's try really hard not to get anyone else hurt today. But we need to know what's out there."

"OK, Mick." Loon would be fifth man back, behind his point man, his backup man, his machine gunner, and the assistant gunner/loader/ammo bearer. Pete would be after Loon, and I'd be after Pete. Then would come the rest of the squad, in this case, just a rifleman and an M-79 grenade launcher man. We didn't have a scout dog with us, so we'd be using our own noses to find the NVA.

"Hal, would you see if you can find a poncho, and get Tony's body wrapped up and back to the chopper? Better hustle; it sounds like it's already on the ground."

"Just heard on the radio. They're sending up a body bag, Mick. But sure, we'll take care of it."

Loon's point man, a short, curly-haired Belgian kid we called Termite because his real name was unpronounceable, had stepped over the log and was making his way into the blasted-out jungle. The rest of the squad followed behind. When my turn came, I made my way over the log, and looked down to see a bloody piece of Tony's shirt still snagged on it.

A little ways later (it seemed a very short distance, now that no one was shooting at us) I reached Tony's rucksack and fighting gear. I stooped down and picked up the helmet, saw Angie's picture inside the webbing and pulled it out. There, staring at me, was that beautiful face, those gorgeous green eyes. I was so sad for her. I put the photo in my pocket with Tony's other effects. Then I dropped the helmet, moved forward and tapped Pete on the shoulder. "Call Hal and tell him to come get this stuff," I whispered. "Don't want the gooks to get it."

"OK, Mick," and he made the radio call.

A little farther on, word came back from Termite, whispered man-to-man to me. "Spider hole up here. Dead gook in it."

At least we got one of the fuckers.

When I reached the spot, I saw a dead Vietnamese kid, couldn't have been more than fifteen or sixteen, hanging part way outside his spider hole, part of his head blown away by some of our stuff. Not in a kind sort of mood I pushed his head back with my boot, spit in his grisly dead face, and then shoved him back into the hole. "That's all the buryin' you get, motherfucker."

We patrolled in a loop, finding three other NVA bodies and several blood trails, but making no further contact. There were several bunkers, all at least partially destroyed by artillery or the Cobra strike. We didn't bother to look inside the ruins. At each one we just stopped to listen for movement, which we never heard, then moved carefully through. If 6 or battalion wanted us to get into the bunkers we'd need to move the whole company forward.

I got on Pete's radio. "Patriot Niner-Niner, this is Patriot 3-5. We have a patrol coming in. Don't shoot us. Patriot 3-6, we have three NVA bodies and several blood trails. Several bunkers, all pretty well blown."

The LT was on his radio. "Roger that, 3-5. Come on in."

One by one we stepped back over Tony's log, and returned to our starting point. Tony's body was gone, and the helicopter had already taken off. His gear had been sent back with him. The guys who had brought in his pack and helmet never found his rifle.

The LT was there. "Let's get saddled up, Mick. Battalion has decided to request an Arclight on this spot tonight. We have to get a click away from here before the B-52s can drop their bombs. Third platoon will be company drag. Let's put 3-2 on platoon point, Hal's squad on drag. We're going back over the same path we cut getting here, so we can make tracks. So make sure everyone has their eyes peeled for an ambush."

"Got it, LT." I began sorting out the platoon for the forced march we would make. It was about noon, so we only had a few hours to get a thousand meters away and dig in for the night.

We made the march without incident, and 6 called a halt just an hour or so before dark. We hastily got our fighting holes dug, Claymores and trip flares out. The men ate their C-Rations, and we sent out our listening posts.

The LT, Firedog, Doc, and I sat on the ground behind our shared fighting hole in the last light of that horrible day. We were worn out, emotionally fucked up, very sad, and angry at Tony's death. I pulled Tony's letters and Angie's picture out of my pocket, held them in my hands for a while, looked at both envelopes. The one with the blood on it was postmarked only two days after the other. *She writes often,* I thought. *Just like Katie.*

Maybe just to feel closer to Tony, maybe to help me understand why he hadn't seemed himself that morning—I've never been sure exactly why. But I took the most recent letter out of its envelope and unfolded it in the fading light.

I was shocked to read the Dear John letter.

Tony,

I'm sorry to have to tell you this, but it has to be over between us. I want a divorce. I can't stand this waiting anymore. Not knowing every night while I lie awake in our bed whether you're alive, or dead, or hurt somewhere in the jungle. I know I'm a coward, but I have to stop caring about you. I just can't live like this anymore.

Angela

I read it once, then again, then again, before handing it to the LT. "That fucking bitch!" I almost shouted. I couldn't believe it. I pulled her picture out of my pocket, took it out of its plastic, and stared at it.

How could someone this sweet looking, with that look of love in her eyes, do something like that?

"Jesus Christ!" the LT said, as he handed the letter back. "So that's what had him so fucked up this morning. I should have read him better, Mick. I should have taken him off point."

"I know, LT. I should have read him better, too. Guess I was just in too much of a rush to get us moving so 6 wouldn't have another excuse to get pissed off at us. But after reading this, if anyone's to blame for Tony's death, besides the fucking gooks and our own fucking government, it's Angie, that bitch."

I read the other letter, only a few days older. It seemed the normal letter of a loving but worried wife. It was signed "All my love, always, Angie."

What?

I handed it to the LT too, and he read it quickly and handed it back, shaking his head. Neither of us could understand. We sat in silence, each lost in our own thoughts, as the sky fully darkened. A little while later we began to see rapid flashes in the distance, followed by a loud, deep rumbling, and we felt the ground shaking beneath us like an earthquake. The Arclight.

"Wouldn't want to be those poor motherfuckers," the LT said absently.

I remember sitting up most of the night, exhausted though I was, thinking about Tony. I thought about how he'd looked as he died, how the light had gone out of his eyes, and his body had turned into just that... a body. No longer a young man. No longer my friend.

Where has his spirit gone? Where is he now? Is he still nearby, as I've sometimes heard? Is his spirit still back where he was killed, where the Arclight just hit? I hope not there. Not in that devastation. If I listen hard enough, can I hear him talking to me or feel his presence?

I tried. I tried really hard. But I didn't feel anything. He simply seemed...gone.

What in the hell are we all doing here? Once it was decided that we're not even going to try to win this war, what exactly is the point of us even being here? Why do they keep sending us to endure this, for so many of us to die? What did Tony die for? What value is there to anyone in Tony's death? What value that could somehow offset the pain it's causing?

Why does God allow things like this stupid fucked-up war to happen? Why did God let Tony die like this?

I had no answers. Only questions. And Angie's letters. And that picture of her beautiful face. And my thirst, and my hunger, and my sickness of the war. And the darkness, and the mosquitoes buzzing around my neck and ears, and the Fuck-you lizards calling in the night.

The sound of distant artillery fire. And my homesickness for Katie, whose latest letter was still in one of my pockets, unopened.

9

"Angie. It's almost time for the news, honey. Come on down and eat something, and let's watch the news," Angie's mother pleaded from the kitchen below.

Angela Giles sat at the dressing table in her bedroom, staring into the mirror. It was the room her father had built for her himself, above the kitchen, when she was fourteen. It was the room where she and Tony had first made love one warm fall afternoon when she was still seventeen and he was barely eighteen, when they'd skipped out on high school, unable to wait any longer; the room where she and Tony had stayed through his thirty-day leave, before he'd left for Vietnam.

How could anyone have ever called me pretty? She asked herself absently. *I'm a wreck.*

Since she'd been about fourteen, everyone had told her how beautiful she was. Her breasts had developed earlier than some girls, and with her slim hips, her figure was striking. With her beautifully sculptured face, green eyes, and black hair, she was, as some had said, a knockout. She'd been homecoming queen, and Tony had been the king. She'd modeled some while still in high school, and had even been told she had a great future in modeling, maybe in acting. And she'd earned an academic scholarship to Rutgers, the State University of New Jersey. She was no dummy, either.

But Tony had been all she'd ever wanted, ever since they'd first met. And he'd felt exactly the same for her. There had been no one else for either of them since their first date. They'd been married right out of high school, unable to wait for that, either. And they'd had an amazing life together, just living and loving each other, him working the job at the refinery, her turning down the scholarship and going instead to junior college to be near him.

Until he'd been drafted.

That's when the horror had started. First, he'd gone to Basic Training at Fort Dix, New Jersey. But that wasn't too far away, and she'd been able to see him twice when he got overnight passes. Then he'd been sent to infantry AIT at Fort Polk, all the way down in Louisiana. She hadn't been able to see him the whole nine weeks, and that had been horrible. But then, when he'd come home, he'd confirmed her worst fear. He had thirty days' leave to spend at home with her. And then he was going to Vietnam.

The time had flown by so quickly she couldn't believe it when they woke up one morning after an almost-sleepless night, and it was the day Tony was to leave. She'd cried, unable to stop herself, all the way up to Newark to the airport. She'd wanted to be strong for him, but she simply couldn't. She'd hugged him fiercely one last time before he climbed the stairs to the plane, while tears ran down her face. He had turned to wave goodbye, tears in his own eyes, and then he'd disappeared into the plane. Moments later the door had closed, and a few minutes after that the plane, and Tony, were gone.

The emptiness he'd left behind had been palpable, as though there was an actual vacuum in the air where Tony and the plane had been.

But Angie had stood and looked and felt the emptiness until her mother and father had pulled her away, back to the car, back to this now empty room in this now empty home, where she would wait on pins and needles for 365 days, until Tony could return.

Now it was almost six months later, and Angie was indeed a wreck. The dark circles under her eyes almost matched the shadows under her cheekbones. She'd lost so much weight from her face, she thought her cheekbones looked like those huge knobs on the bumper of her dad's old Buick.

It had been over three weeks since Angie had mailed Tony the Dear John letter.

Before she had written it, she had always watched the war news with mixed emotions, hoping somehow to catch a glimpse of Tony, yet knowing that if she did, it would be because he was in the middle of a fight somewhere, or maybe one of the wounded. But now with the letter on its way, she watched the news with special anticipation. She hadn't told her mom about the letter. She had only hoped, somehow, that it would bring him home.

Angie was nineteen years old, and she and Tony had been married for just over a year when he'd left for Vietnam.

She was also pregnant, a little more than six months along.

They had conceived the baby during Tony's last few days at home, before he'd shipped over. She hadn't been sure she was pregnant until nearly two months later, thinking perhaps she'd missed one period because she was so nervous and upset all the time. By the time she was sure, she had learned from his letters that Tony had been assigned to the 1st Cavalry Division, and he'd been honest enough to tell her just a little of what it was like. So she hadn't told him about the baby, figuring he didn't need anything else to worry about.

The next four months had crawled by, and as her belly had grown bigger, her worry and fear of losing Tony had grown as well. And somewhere during those months, for reasons she never fully understood, Angie also developed a second, almost debilitating fear; although her mother reassured her that the danger was very low, Angie somehow became very afraid that she would not survive childbirth…that she would die bringing the baby into the world. If that happened, and if something did happen to Tony, that would leave their child an orphan, with neither a mother nor a father to care for it.

With those two fears nagging her constantly, Angie had withdrawn into herself more with every day that passed. She now concentrated on only one thing: *She had to get Tony home!* He had to be there when the baby was born. He just had to be! And once he was home she knew she'd find a way to keep him there.

She knew she wasn't being logical, or even rational; she understood all that. But she loved Tony so much, and was so afraid that she herself might die, that she became obsessed with finding a way to get him back home again. Surely the Army could spare one soldier from the hundreds of thousands in Vietnam. Surely it wouldn't make that much difference to them if Tony came home. And it meant everything to her. *Absolutely everything!*

Desperate, she had gone to the local Army recruiter, an older sergeant with many stripes on his sleeves and lots of ribbons and badges on his chest. She had told him her story and asked him to help her get Tony home. She figured that if there was a way to do it, he would know how.

"I'm sorry, ma'am," the recruiter had said respectfully, "but I've done two tours there, and I'm pretty sure I'd know. The Army won't bring him home because you're having a baby. I'm afraid you'll have to wait it out. Maybe he can get an R&R to Hawaii or somewhere you can get to, and you can go and see him there. But it looks like you'd have to do it pretty soon. How far along are you?"

But by then Angie wasn't listening anymore. She had begun to cry, silently, tears streaming from her eyes. The recruiter had comforted her as best a soldier could, but there was nothing he could do. She had left feeling that there was no burden in the world greater than hers. She was desperate.

Days later, as she'd been pouring her heart out to Ellen, her closest girlfriend from high-school, Ellen had given her a ray of hope. "Angie, I have a cousin down in Kentucky. Her husband was in Vietnam in the infantry like Tony, and she got so scared waiting for him to come home that she wrote him a letter telling him she couldn't stand it anymore, that she wanted a divorce. The Army sent him home on some kind of emergency hardship leave, so he could try to save his marriage."

"Really?" asked Angie, desperate for any hope.

"Yeah. I guess he got hold of the Red Cross or something, and they helped him get the leave. He was home in two weeks. He only got to stay for a few days, and they made him go back. But he came home for a little while, at least."

What she didn't tell Angie was that this had happened over three years before, when the war had first begun. And she didn't know that the trick had been tried so many times since then that the Army had been forced to pass tight rules about such emergency leaves.

But Angie, desperate for anything that would bring Tony home, had clung to this thread of hope. And one night a few days later, as she lay awake, worrying about Tony and the baby and herself, she had decided to try it. She was convinced there was no other way. So she'd gotten out of bed, snapped on the light, and taken out her box of writing paper.

And she had written the letter.

The next morning, convinced after another sleepless night that there was no other way to bring Tony home before the baby was born, she had mailed it. And every day since then had been absolute torture, worse than even before. She couldn't write more letters, couldn't give it away. She got one brief letter from Tony, but could tell by what it said that he hadn't received hers yet. She could only wait. Wait and hate herself for what she'd done.

Angie pushed back from the dressing table and rose to her feet, weak from her exhaustion and worry, the weight of her unborn baby an extra burden. She made her way slowly down the stairs, her mother waiting in the kitchen to put her arm around her and hug her lovingly as she walked her to the table. She only picked at the snack her mother had made her, taking a few sips of milk and then getting up to go into the living room and watch the news. It was stiflingly hot outside on that late August evening in 1969, and a window air conditioner chugged away in the dining room, struggling with the overwhelming task of keeping the ground floor of the house cool enough for its occupants to bear.

She turned on the television, made sure it was on Channel 5, and then sat down on their sagging old couch. As the set warmed up she first heard the voice of Walter Cronkite talking about a battle going on in the Michelin Rubber Plantation north of Saigon. Then as the picture grew brighter she saw film of American soldiers fighting an unseen enemy with rifles and machine guns. There was footage of two soldiers carrying another on a stretcher. The wounded soldier was shirtless, his head and face bandaged, his chest covered with blood. Angie stopped breathing until she was sure it wasn't Tony, then let out a breath and slumped further into the sofa.

This war was killing her!

10

20 August 1969
Watertown, New Jersey, USA

A few minutes later, still watching the news, Angie caught movement out of the corner of her eye from the street in front of the house. She turned to look and saw a plain olive drab Chevy sedan pull to the curb, a white star on the passenger door.

She stopped breathing again.

Two men got out, uniformed Army officers. They paused to carefully straighten their uniform jackets and put on their caps before walking to the front door.

Her front door.

Seeing them there, Angie's whole body went numb.

The knock came. Angie's mother, who had not seen the men approach, was startled by the soft tapping on the door. She got up from her chair, went slowly to the door, and pulled it open. "Yes?" she asked fearfully.

Angie heard muffled words from one of the men, the last one clearly "Giles." And then her mom stepped back without a word of her own, a stricken look on her face, and allowed the two inside.

Angie stood up from the couch, her stomach bulging on her thin frame.

Maybe, she thought, *Maybe it's a mistake. Maybe he's just been hurt.* But she could see the little cross on the lapel of one of the men, and knew they didn't send a chaplain to the home of the wounded.

"Mrs. Anthony Giles?" asked the other officer, his voice soft. Angie recognized the gold oak leaves on his shoulders as the rank insignia of a major, and the crossed rifles of the infantry on his lapel. The same crossed rifles Tony wore on his dress uniform.

"Is your husband Specialist Anthony Giles with the 1st Cavalry Division?"

Angie couldn't speak. She could only nod her head slowly, her face a mask.

"Mrs. Giles, I'm sorry to have to tell you this." He paused, not wanting to go on. "But Specialist Giles ... Anthony ... was killed in combat three days ago in Vietnam."

Angie sat down heavily on the couch. Her mother went to her and sat down beside her. Angie was very pale. She didn't cry. She didn't say anything. Her eyes could not focus.

Finally she looked up at the major and said, "Are you sure?"

"Yes, ma'am. His body's been positively identified."

Angie looked down and became silent. *His body? His body!?* That just wouldn't sink in.

"We're awfully sorry, ma'am."

Then the two officers stood there, waiting for Angie to absorb what she'd been told, to respond in some way that assured them she understood. Finally, she looked up again.

"We are so deeply sorry, ma'am," said the chaplain. "But perhaps you can take some comfort knowing that your husband was a very brave man, and that he died serving his country. He's in the arms of God now, ma'am."

She looked up. "What ...?"

"Serving his country, ma'am," the major said. "He was killed in the war against Communist aggression. He was fighting for the freedom of the South Vietnamese, and ultimately, for the freedom of Americans."

She couldn't seem to grasp the meaning of what he was saying for a while.

"Yes," she said finally, looking down, her hands on her big belly, and tears now beginning to stream down her cheeks. "I see what you mean." The bitterness was evident in her words. "His unborn child and I will take great comfort from his heroic death."

"He was a good soldier, ma'am, and a brave man. You can be very proud of him," the major said. Her irony appeared to be totally lost on both men. Again, the two officers stood silently, shifted uncomfortably on their feet, not knowing what else to say.

Angie seemed to drift off for a while, but then, remembering them, she looked up. "Thank you," she said darkly. "You've done your job now. You may go."

"You're sure you're OK, ma'am?" asked the chaplain. "May we pray with you before we go?"

"No," said Angie, her voice flat. She rose again heavily from the couch. "That won't be necessary. I've been doing a lot of praying, and it doesn't seem to have helped. Thank you for coming. You may go."

"Well then, goodbye, ma'am. We're awfully sorry." And with that the two officers left. Angie just stood there, staring at the closed door, frozen in place. Her mother stood next to her, not knowing what to do.

Angie's grief was so deep, so intensely painful, that she thought she would die. She wanted to die so the unimaginable horror of what she'd been told would go away. She was six months pregnant, and her baby's father, her beloved Tony, was dead. He had died not knowing that he was going to be a father. And maybe he had died believing that she was going to leave him, that she wanted a divorce. Maybe he had died with a broken heart.

The heaviness of her body dragged her back down to the couch, and she sat unmoving, her weight feeling like a thousand pounds on the sagging springs. She put her face in her hands and began to cry, deep wracking sobs that caused her whole body to heave. Her mother sat down next to her, put her arms around her shoulders, and held her, both of them sobbing.

They were still sitting there crying quietly together when Angie's dad came home from work nearly two hours later. When he came through the front door, and saw his wife and daughter there on the couch, he knew instantly what had happened.

Quietly, only to himself, he said, "I told him not to go to that goddamned war!"

11

Mick Delaney

A few days after Tony was killed our battalion chaplain rode the chopper into a jungle clearing where we were being resupplied, to perform worship services for those of us who cared to attend. I went, along with many of the others. The chaplain handed out crucifixes to the Christians, simple devices on beaded chains that we could wear around our necks. I got one and put it on. I noticed that most of the other men did, too.

I was able to have a private conversation with the chaplain after the service and told him the story of Tony's death and how saddened I was by it, and how confused I was about the whole war and what we were doing there. He let me talk for a while, sometimes with tears in my eyes, about Tony, and what a great friend he'd been, and about Carl Engle and Sugarbear, and how much I missed them all. I told him how bad I felt that I hadn't read Tony better that morning, hadn't kept him off the point. How I felt at least partially responsible for his death. I didn't tell him about the Dear John letter.

Once I'd finished my story he looked at me thoughtfully for a moment, then finally spoke. I don't remember his actual words after all these years, but I remember he was able to say something that made me feel a little better about it all, as though the sacrifices we were making really were for a good cause, and that God was on our side. He told me that Tony was undoubtedly in a better place, with God, and would never again suffer or come to any harm.

I remember coming away thinking that the chaplain was a good man, and that he truly believed in his God and the words he spoke to me about the value and the "rightness" of the work we were doing, and the sacrifices we were making.

I certainly hope so. A few days later we got word that the chaplain had been lying on his cot back at battalion headquarters in Tay Ninh one evening when a big 122mm rocket, fired from outside the base by the local Viet Cong, had dropped through the roof of his hooch, fallen between his legs, and buried itself in the ground under him before exploding. It tore off both legs almost to the hip, shattered his genitals, and nearly gutted him. By luck, the grace of God, or whatever, his hooch was next to the battalion medics' shack, and three of the medics rushed into the building and were able to put tourniquets on the stumps where his legs had been, quickly enough to save his life. He was going home a totally different man than had come to Vietnam.

We heard about it out in the field, of course, and I remember once again being very confused. *Why would God allow such a thing to happen to such a good man, someone who obviously believed in Him, and communicated His word so effectively to a group of young men who so badly needed to hear those reassurances?* I remember that this really disturbed me for a few days after the chaplain's maiming. And then I remember pushing it all away from me (actually internalizing it more deeply), and deciding once again that if I thought too much about the circumstances I was in, what I was doing, the friends I had lost, and the slim chance I felt I had of making it home in one piece, I'd go insane.

So I just quit thinking about it. That happened a lot in that war, as I'm sure it does in any war. The mind has a way of protecting itself. I didn't pray to God for an explanation, or even for guidance after that. I wore my little crucifix on the chain with my dog tag, and I just quit thinking about it.

12

16 September 1969
Watertown, New Jersey, USA
Angie Giles

Nearly a month passed before Angie finally got word from the Army that Tony's body would be arriving at Newark Airport the following day. She had counted every one of those days as they dragged by, but in her later memory that time was simply a blur, so buried was she in the incredible grief and sorrow she felt. She spent most of her time lying on her bed, crying, thinking about Tony, wondering if he'd received her letter before he died, and wondering if he'd died thinking she was planning to divorce him and that she didn't love him anymore. It was driving her crazy, not knowing. And making it even worse, she knew she would probably never know.

Only her mother's gentle but constant reminders of the baby she was carrying, Tony's baby, kept her going, kept her putting food into her body that she didn't want to eat, kept her going to the doctor so she could get some help sleeping. She couldn't lose Tony's baby! The baby was all she had of him.

A letter had arrived for her from a Lieutenant Thorsen, with the same APO address as Tony's letters, about two weeks after the two

Army officers came to the house. She tore it open thinking it would tell her something, at least give her a clue about whether or not Tony had received her letter before he was killed. But there was nothing about that. It just said that Lieutenant Thorsen had been Tony's platoon leader and talked about what a good soldier Tony had been, how brave he was, how he always looked out for the other men, and how much everyone liked and respected him. It told about him walking point for the company the day he was killed and said he had died instantly, and that they knew he didn't suffer. Then it said how sorry he was for Tony's death.

The last line was, "Tony talked about you often, and everyone here knew he loved you very much. I am deeply sorry for your loss." She couldn't tell anything from it, and reading about Tony made her miss him so much and hate herself all the more for having written that letter.

Against their objections, Angie's parents drove her to Newark to meet the plane carrying Tony's body. She insisted that she had to be there. They made a little convoy, her mom and dad in her dad's Buick, Angie alone in the back seat, following Tony's parents and his little brother in their car, who were in turn following the funeral home's Cadillac hearse. They drove through constant rain on a chilly, totally overcast September afternoon.

At the airport they watched through the terminal windows as the hearse driver was summoned to the plane by a uniformed Army sergeant, and a big aluminum box was moved by hand down the cargo conveyor from the plane's hold. The sergeant, two baggage handlers, and the hearse driver gently lifted the box from the conveyor and slid it into the back of the hearse. Then the sergeant made his way into the terminal and introduced himself as Sergeant First Class Jeffers. But Sergeant Jeffers hadn't known Tony in Vietnam. He was up from Fort Belvoir, Virginia, he said, come to escort Tony's body to the funeral home and help make the funeral arrangements with Tony's family. He took special time with Angie, and seemed genuinely sympathetic at Tony's loss.

They drove back to Watertown, still in the rain. Angie cried all the way back home. It had somehow become even worse, knowing that Tony's body was so close, in the box, in the hearse, only two cars in front of the one she rode in.

The next morning she got a call from Sergeant Jeffers to let her know that she could come to the funeral home and view Tony's body if she chose to. His wounds, Jeffers said, were in a place she wouldn't be able to see, so it wouldn't be necessary to keep the coffin closed, as they had to with so many military funerals. Jeffers would arrange a private viewing for her, her parents, and Tony's family, for later that afternoon.

Angie's father was working, so her mother drove her to the funeral home. Tony's parents and brother, it was explained, would come later that day, so Angie and her mom could view Tony's body alone. Sergeant Jeffers and the funeral director walked them into a room set aside for such viewings and then the funeral director left them alone to approach the open coffin. The lights were intentionally dimmed, Angie supposed, just bright enough that she could see.

Tony was lying on his back, his eyes closed, his deeply tanned face at peace under the funeral home makeup, his hands folded on his chest. He was wearing his Army dress uniform, a big yellow patch with a horse's head on his right shoulder, and several badges and ribbons that she hadn't seen before over his left breast pocket. Angie broke down completely as she saw him there, her knees collapsing under her, so that her mother and Sergeant Jeffers had to hold her upright. She sobbed, tears pouring from her eyes, for her Tony. The grief had become unbearable again.

The funeral was on a Saturday, three days later. They were three days that felt like forever...

It was still dismally overcast, but the rain had slowed from a constant downpour to intermittent showers. There were many people at the service. Tony had been very well liked in high school, and many of his classmates and their families came. There was all of Tony's family, of course, and Angie's mom and dad. Angie endured the visitation line as best she could, tears rolling from her eyes the entire time.

The service itself was a blur. Their pastor spoke his words of hopefulness, but they seemed hollow to Angie, and didn't really register with her. Then Sergeant Jeffers went to the podium and spoke of Tony's bravery in Vietnam, his excellent record as a soldier. And he told everyone, looking straight at Angie, how proud they should be of him for his service. Angie thought the unendurable funeral service would be over then.

But instead, Tony's father stood to speak.

"My name is Angelo Giles, and I'm Tony's father," he began. "I'm forty-seven this year. I served with General Patton in Europe during World War II, fighting against the Nazis. I made the forced march from France into Belgium during the Battle of the Bulge in December of '44, when we relieved the 101st Airborne Division at Bastogne. I was wounded twice during those months in Europe before we defeated Germany and liberated those enslaved nations. So I know about war, and I know about hardship, and I know about service to my country." He paused, looked around the room.

"This war in Vietnam," he began again, "well, I supported it when it started in 1965. Back then I believed, as most Americans did, that we were fighting there to save the rest of Southeast Asia, and ultimately ourselves, from communist aggression. To keep the communists from taking over the world. But that was before President Johnson, who got us into this mess, decided to bail out on us last year and declined to run for re-election. And that was before President Nixon was elected and came into office this January, declaring our new policy in Vietnam to be 'Peace with Honor.'

"I was a little confused by that at first because I thought, along with total victory, that our goal in any war is always 'Peace with Honor.' But I've been paying very close attention, as you might imagine, with my older son fighting there, and I've come to understand what 'Peace with Honor' really means." He paused.

"It means we're no longer trying to win the war against North Vietnam and the Viet Cong. It means we're simply buying time until we can train the South Vietnamese Army to defend their own country before we pack up and leave.

"Tony wrote to me often from Vietnam, separate letters that he sent to my office, where his mother wouldn't see them." He paused and looked at his wife, who was crying in the front row. "Because I'd been in a war myself, Tony knew I would understand what he was going through, so he told me about a lot of things that he didn't write his mother or Angie about."

That comment sent a shock up Angie's spine, and she wondered, just for an instant, whether Tony might have written his dad about the letter she'd sent him. But then she immediately realized that Angelo wouldn't have been able to keep from saying something to her about it if he had. And he wasn't even looking at her when he said it.

Angelo went on. "Tony told me that the American soldiers in Vietnam are very demoralized now that they know there is no intention to win the war, and that we're only buying time. They feel they've been betrayed by their own country, their own president, and most especially, by their own people, who they feel sent them there under false pretenses. He told me about all the drugs there are on the American fire bases and rear base camps. He told me about the racial problems between blacks and whites in the rear areas. He told me how it was sometimes difficult for the officers and NCOs to even motivate the men to do their jobs in the field, and about the frequent fraggings that happen in the rear areas where enlisted men kill, or try to kill, their own officers with hand grenades."

Tears filled his eyes and began to stream down his face. "What I want to know is, what happened to the America I fought for twenty-five short years ago? And how did I lose my son, who I loved more than my life, to a goddamned war that nobody supports, and nobody wants to try to win?"

He shouted. "Who had the right to take our Tony away and get him killed in some goddamned Asian country that nobody gives a damn about?! Who had the goddamned right to waste my boy's life?! WHO?!" He looked around the room, from face to face, looking for an answer. But no one except Sergeant Jeffers would look back at him. Even Angie's eyes were averted, looking at the floor.

He broke down completely then, and his wife, streaming tears, got up from her seat and went to him. She put her arm around his waist and walked him back to his seat, where he collapsed beside her, sobbing.

There was silence in the room, except for the sound of crying. And then the funeral director took charge of things again, and music began to play, and he walked to the front row of seats and helped Angie to her feet, to lead her and the other family members past the open coffin one last time. Angie stopped there and put her hand on Tony's hand there in the coffin. But it was cold and dead, and his face was a mask covered in makeup. And she knew that Tony wasn't in that body anymore.

After a few moments, with the other mourners lined up behind them, Angie's father gently pulled her away, and he and Angie's mother half-walked, half-carried the sobbing young woman out of the room. Solemnly, the rest of the mourners followed.

There was a smaller group at the graveside service. Sergeant Jeffers was there with an Army honor guard, and after a few final words from the pastor, he commanded them through the twenty-one-gun salute. Angie winced through each of the three volleys of fire, the shots ringing out and echoing across the little valley where Tony's body would lie. Then a bugler played *Taps*, and Angie's heart, already destroyed by Tony's loss, was broken again by the mournful sound. It left everyone there weeping in remorse.

Finally the honor guard folded the flag from Tony's coffin, and Sergeant Jeffers came forward and presented it to Angie, with the words, "On behalf of the President of the United States ...."

13

16 September 1969
Watertown, New Jersey, USA

The last thing Sergeant Jeffers did before leaving with his soldiers several hours after the funeral on that miserable day was to stop by Angie's parents' house and bring Angie a sealed cardboard box with the words "Giles, Anthony, Spec. 4, Co. D, 2nd Bn, 9th Cavalry, 1st Cavalry Division (Airmobile)" and Tony's Army serial number printed on top.

Angie invited Jeffers inside, and they sat down on the couch. "These are your husband's personal effects, Mrs. Giles. I kept them until after the funeral because I felt like you were having a really tough time of it, and I didn't want to burden you with any more than I had to all at once. But my detail and I have to leave now … they're waiting in the van outside … and it's my duty to make sure you have these things before I go."

Angie made a small gulp, and the tears began to flow more steadily again. "These are Tony's things?"

"Yes, ma'am. Would you like me to open the box for you?"

"Yes."

He took the box from her, took out a small pocketknife and slit the tape that sealed it, opened the flaps, and handed it back to her.

She looked inside, not knowing quite what to expect, but hoping that her letters to Tony would be there so she could know whether he had received her last one before he died. There was tissue around the few things that were inside, and she pulled it back.

There were no letters at all. None of the photos she had sent him. Only his cigarette lighter, the one she had given him with the two hearts that said, "Tony and Angie Forever" on it. His wedding ring was there, scratched up and dull. And a chain with a small crucifix and two stainless steel dog tags on it, one straight and new looking, the other bent and stained.

"Why is one of these dog tags like brand new, and the other one all bent up and old-looking?" she asked, not sure she wanted to know.

"Well, ma'am, out in the field combat soldiers like your husband usually wear one around their neck on a chain, and they usually tape it up with black tape so it doesn't shine in the dark and make noise. So it's protected from the rough environment. The other one is worn in the laces of one of the boots. I think the theory is that if a soldier is killed by an explosion or otherwise... you know... torn up... there's a better chance of the body being positively identified. The Army rule is that if the body isn't positively identified, the soldier is counted as missing, and then the family never really knows what happened."

Angie shook her head at the brutal logic of it, tears streaming from her eyes, and returned her attention to the box. The last thing in there was a black plastic wallet with a 1st Cavalry Division logo on the side. She took it out and opened it, but found only a slightly crumpled Army Immunization Record, and a few pieces of strange looking paper currency.

She looked up at Jeffers. "Where are all the letters I wrote him and the pictures I sent him?"

Jeffers looked down, seemed a little embarrassed. "Well, ma'am, the Army destroys all that stuff before sending the personal effects home. I'm sure it didn't happen with your husband, but there have been a couple of cases where a soldier had met someone on an R & R, or had another relationship besides his wife, and had letters or pictures from the other lady in his effects when they were sent home. You can imagine the pain on top of pain that would cause. So some time ago, they started destroying all photos and letters. I'm kind of surprised they left the cigarette lighter, since it was engraved with your name... a woman's name. They must have overlooked it."

"Not much here to remember him by." Her voice trailed off, and she seemed to become lost in thought. Now she would never know about the letter. She couldn't write that Lieutenant Thorsen, the officer who had written to her about Tony's death, and ask. It wasn't likely he would know about a letter Tony got, and if he didn't know, she certainly didn't want him to. Angie's despair rose in her again, and she began to cry harder.

"Again, ma'am. I am so sorry for your loss. I don't know what to say, except that I'm so sorry. He was a good soldier, ma'am. You can be very proud of him." He paused. "Is your baby due soon, ma'am?"

"About six more weeks."

"Well, here's my card, ma'am, if there's ever anything I can do." He gave Angie the card, then stood to leave. Angie set the box down and stood herself, extended her hand past her big belly.

"Thank you for bringing him home," she muttered, her face wet with tears.

As he held her hand, Sergeant Jeffers said, "I've been to Vietnam twice myself, ma'am, and it's a very, very hard life there. But bringing soldiers' bodies to their families... that's much tougher. I'll be glad when this war is over, and no one has to do that anymore." He paused, seeming unable to think of anything else to say.

Angie only nodded as she swiped at the tears that now stung her swollen cheeks.

"Well, good luck, ma'am." And with that he released her hand, turned, and left.

Angie stood looking after him as he walked to the van. He didn't bother to put his cap on. He opened the front passenger door, climbed into the seat, closed the door, and said something to the driver, who then started the motor and pulled away. He didn't look back.

14

30 October 1969
Tay Ninh Province, Vietnam
Mick Delaney

We had been on another typical day's ass-kicking hump through the densest part of the Vietnamese jungle. Dozer, the point man, was forced to hack his way forward with every step. At about three o'clock, Dozer made his way onto a trail that crossed our line of march and then angled off to our left, toward the Cambodian border. As he stepped out onto the trail to check it out he glimpsed two NVA soldiers, dressed in khaki uniforms and pith helmets, about twenty yards to his left. He made a couple of weird noises of fear in his throat, something like, "Uh, uh, UH!" and then quickly fired a burst at the gooks as he hit the ground. One of the enemy soldiers got off a burst of return fire that zipped above Dozer's head, and then the two NVA took off running, around a bend where they could no longer be seen.

I had been walking with the point squad, had heard the weird, "Uh, uh, UH!" from Dozer, then the gunshots, and had hunkered down quickly to avoid being hit. But when there was no more fire, I'd gotten up and walked forward with Tommy, the point squad leader, to see if anyone was hurt. Dozer sat behind a tree, his helmet off, a chagrined smile on his face.

Tommy said, "Jeez, Dozer, I thought you were having a baby up here, all that grunting you were doing." We all laughed.

"Scared the shit outa me, Tommy, you fuck. Walked right up on those fuckers, and I could see one of them turning to fire just as I was dropping my machete and trying to get my rifle into my gun hand. Guess I made some noise. Seemed like everything was happening in slow motion. Never been so scared."

Tommy laughed again. "Woulda scared the shit out of anybody, Dozer. I'm just fuckin' with ya. Did you hit anything?"

"I don't think so."

Just then LT Thorsen walked up to us, Firedog right behind him. "Having a little party, guys? Why isn't anyone shooting?"

"Nothing to shoot at, LT," I said. "Gooks took off."

"Well, get your heads down. I have some Redleg on the way." Just then the first artillery round, a white phosphorous shell, burst in the air about seventy-five meters to our front.

"Move it off to the left, LT," Tommy said. "The trail kind of angles over that way. But those fuckers are half a mile from here by now."

"Yeah, well, gotta keep the lifers happy." He called in the correction to the artillery battery, gave a "Fire for Effect," and several seconds later the first volley of high explosive rounds came screaming in and detonated out ahead of us in the jungle. After three or four minutes of continued fire, Thorsen called in a, "Cease Fire! Thanks, Redleg!" and the artillery stopped.

6 called Thorsen on the company network. "What do we have, 3-6?"

"Just spotted a couple of gooks on this trail we were getting ready to cross. They took off. We're getting a patrol ready to go check it out."

"Roger that. Keep me informed, 3-6."

"Roger that. 3-6 out."

"Mick, why don't we give these guys a break, and check this one out ourselves? We're just going up the trail a little ways to where Dozer saw the gooks before they took off."

"OK, LT. You want to walk point?" I was smiling.

"Fuck you, Mick," he laughed. "You're the enlisted man. You walk point. And try not to trip over your own big goddamned feet."

There was laughter from the point squad.

We walked the trail very carefully for the twenty yards or so to the spot where the NVA had been seen, but saw nothing except a couple of footprints in the fresh mud and a small bundle of folded papers lying beside the trail. I looked around carefully for wires or other indications that they might be booby-trapped, but saw none. They'd probably just dropped it in their haste to get away. But I knelt carefully, took my rifle by the stock, turned my head away, and pushed on the pile of papers with the muzzle. Nothing happened, so I reached over and picked them up, unfolded them, and showed them to the LT. There was a lot of Vietnamese writing and some photos of two NVA soldiers dropping a mortar round into a big mortar tube.

"Looks like a 107mm to me, LT. Big stuff."

"Yeah. Those guys must have been attached to a heavy mortar unit. That makes my asshole pucker. Let's get back to the company so we can saddle up and get the fuck out of here. I don't want to be here later if they start dropping that shit on us."

But back at the company, Captain Larkin had other ideas. He had already decided to set up the night defensive position (NDP) right where we were. Thorsen showed him the papers and said, "6, I strongly suggest we move away from this area before we set up. The gooks know right where we are."

"You over-dramatize, lieutenant. We're setting up here."

"But, 6 ...!"

"Shut up and get set up for the night, Lieutenant!"

Thorsen's face got red, angered by the stupidity of Larkin's decision. But he realized that no amount of argument would change Larkin's mind, so he spun on his heel, made his way back to the squad leaders, and began giving instructions for placement of the squads and the listening posts.

Seeing this, I said, "We're setting up here, LT? What, is Larkin insane? We're gonna get our ass kicked!"

"I know. I told the dumb sonofabitch. But these are his orders, and he's not going to change 'em," said Thorsen. "We get hit tonight, it's that motherfucker's fault for not moving us away from the contact point."

Thorsen sent Loon's squad out a hundred meters, directly across the trail, to run a loop pattern and look for gooks, bunkers, whatever. They came back without incident. "Sure feels spooky out there," Loon said when he returned.

Hal took part of the 3-1 squad out as a listening post, making sure they were well-concealed before making his way back to the perimeter. Men in the company were digging in, working diligently on their fighting holes before even eating. Everyone, apparently except 6, knew the danger of having the spotters from an NVA heavy mortar unit know exactly where we were.

LT Thorsen and I were down to our last C-Rations. We were standing side-by-side, arguing quietly and good naturedly over who was going to have to eat what out of the miserably bad, boring, canned rations. Finally I took out my P-38 can opener and opened a can of Beef and Potatoes, a greasy, salty, disgusting mess. As I pulled the lid out of the can I caught a whiff of the food.

"Uugh," I complained to the LT, still standing next to him. "Smells just like..."

BOOM! There was an explosion to our front, very close.

I found myself on the ground, bleeding from the shrapnel that had peppered my right side, my head, neck, arm, and hand. LT Thorsen was sitting on the ground next to me, blood pouring from wounds in his head, neck, and wrist.

Then the gooks opened fire with automatic weapons. My brain was fogged from a shrapnel hit in the head. I hugged the ground, dizzy and sick to my stomach, watching the familiar green tracers snapping by, what looked like only a couple of feet above me.

"Fuckin' gooks got us by the balls this time," I said as loud as I could to the LT, now lying on the ground a few feet away. I wondered, for perhaps the hundredth time in my tour, if I was about to die.

Then I heard American weapons starting to return fire, M-16s on full automatic, M-60 machine guns, and grenade launchers…quite a firefight. I searched around on the ground, saw my rifle, but when I reached for it, searing pain shot through my right shoulder, and the fingers on my right hand didn't seem to work right. I felt my shoulder with my left hand, and it came away bloody. There seemed to be a good-sized hole in my right forearm, but I couldn't see what was causing the hand to malfunction. It was sort of numb and hurting all at the same time. I couldn't find my helmet.

The mortar fire slowed and then stopped, suppressed by the American return fire. And the AK rounds stopped popping by, at least for the moment. I got to my knees, crawled over to the LT. Blood was running in my eyes from the head wound, and I wiped it off.

"Hey Doc," I yelled. "Give me a hand, will you? The LT's hit pretty bad." Thorsen was sitting up again by then, but his left hand was covering a wound in his neck, and blood was leaking out through his fingers. His right arm hung limply at his side.

It was getting dark quickly. I looked around, tried to collect my thoughts. It looked like the LT was out of it, so I knew I had to get the platoon organized. But I had to get the LT some help first. "Hey Doc, where are you?" I shouted. But there was no answer.

Just then the 1st platoon medic found us, and I pointed for him to take care of LT Thorsen. I was still dizzy, shaky from the wounds. I turned toward the perimeter, and in the darkness could barely make out the shapes of the other GIs. Hal came up to me from my right and said, "You better stay down, Mick. You look like shit. I'm going out to get the listening post in. The rest of the platoon perimeter is tight."

"OK," I said, relieved that I could just sit down for a while. I found Firedog a few feet away, lying on the ground next to a fighting hole, the radio carefully protected by his rucksack and the berm of the hole. "Hey, Firedog," I said, "put out a niner-niner. Hal's going out to bring in the listening post. They're the only ones out from 3-6. Make sure nobody fires on 'em."

"OK, Mick." He began his call. "Patriot Niner-Niner…this is 3-6 Alpha. We have a man going out to bring in our LP. Watch your fire."

I felt my head awkwardly with my left hand, could feel small holes and little lumps under the skin where the shrapnel had gone into my scalp above my right eye. It burned like fire to probe them, but they didn't seem too big, and the bleeding was slowing down. The numbness in my right hand was spreading up my arm, though, and my shoulder and head hurt like hell.

The first platoon medic finished with LT Thorsen and began working on me. He put bandages on my right forearm, my right shoulder at the neck, and my head. "How you feelin', Mick?" he asked.

"Like I was on the wrong end of batting practice. How's the LT?"

But before the medic could answer, the LT himself rasped, "I'm not that bad. But I can't talk. Throat's fucked up."

The medic turned back to me. "He'll be OK. Missed his jugular. But he won't be singing in the choir for a while."

"Fuckin' shame," I said. "I will so miss his rich baritone."

"Fuck you, Mick," rasped the LT with a weak smile. "Let's get the platoon organized."

"Sorry to disappoint you, LT, but they're way ahead of us," I said.

"Hal just came back in with the listening post, and the rest of the squads have finished putting out their trip flares and Claymores. I don't think they need us as much as we'd like to think they do."

"You'll be OK, too," said the medic as he finished with me. "Lots of blood, but everybody bleeds like hell here. I don't know about your hand being numb. Probably shock from the impact of the shrapnel. You got hit pretty good on that side."

But as the medic talked I noticed that some of the feeling was already coming back into my hand. And with it, a good deal of pain.

The mortar round had detonated only about fifteen feet from the LT and me. Thankfully, we were hit by 82mm NVA mortars, not the 107mm stuff pictured in the enemy papers we'd found. If a 107 had landed that close to us, we'd have been a fine, pink mist covering the nearby trees.

The LT and I were the only ones hit in third platoon, but several of the grunts from weapons platoon were down, being tended by Doc Benedetto and another medic.

LT Thorsen was on the radio. "6 this is 3-6," he rasped. "3-5 and I are both hit, but OK for now. Several other wounded around us. Will advise on any emergencies needing Medevac."

"This is 6 Alpha," came the response from Larkin's radioman, "Roger that."

"Hal went out to bring in the listening post alone?" asked the LT.

"Yeah. And he brought them all in with no one hurt. Now while we're lounging around, he's running the platoon."

"Jesus. Some balls. Sounds like gooks everywhere. I'm putting him in for something. A Silver Star I think."

"He deserves it."

Suddenly I heard a faint "POP" sound behind me, what sounded like twenty meters or so, then a dull "thud" just on the other side of the berm in front of the nearest fighting hole. "Down!" someone yelled, and the ChiCom grenade exploded. Almost immediately there were several more "POPs," and more grenades came flying in from directly in front of our fighting position.

15

Boom! Boom! Boom! The grenades detonated, all short of the American fighting holes.

GIs scrambled to return the assault with their own frags and threw several into the jungle in front of them. Boom! Boom! Boom! Boom! Boom! The frags went off, almost together.

AK-47 fire came back at us from the trees, rounds close to the ground, green tracers going everywhere. And another NVA mortar opened up, this time on our side of the perimeter. At about that same time, American artillery rounds began blasting the jungle, a hundred or so meters out, seemingly on all sides. The night lit up from every direction, gook mortars and automatic weapons fire coming into the perimeter, American artillery shrieking in overhead, loud as a freight train, then detonating in the jungle close by.

I felt a hand on my arm. It was the LT. "You work your way over to 3-1 and 3-2," he whispered, his voice nearly gone, "and stay with them. Let Hal know we're back on our feet. Get on 3-2's radio. I'll hang with 3-3 and the weapons squad. Hold off on rifle and machine gun fire unless you can see the gooks rushing us."

"OK, LT," I said. "Be careful. I'll see you in the morning."

"Yeah," said the LT. "In the morning."

I picked up my rifle in my left hand and began crawling toward one of the 3-2 fighting holes. Suddenly I heard a whistle, like a referee's whistle, from outside the perimeter, and the AK and mortar fire stopped almost instantly. Then I began to hear the gooks signaling to each other using their common signal, two pieces of bamboo tapped together to make a "tink-tink" sound, the imitation of a "Fuck-you" lizard. There would be a "tink-tink" in one direction and another "tink-tink" in another. Clearly lots of gooks out there, and clearly they weren't leaving.

The American artillery rounds continued to scream in overhead and explode in the jungle. But I knew from experience that the artillery wasn't doing any good because the gooks were between our perimeter and the points of detonation. Army rules wouldn't let us call the artillery in any closer unless we were being overrun, because the brass feared that a short round would land on us, kill our own people.

The enemy knew that. So they stayed in close.

I picked up my rifle with my left hand, made my way to the 3-2 hole, and crawled up behind it. I still had no helmet. My right hand was still partly numb. "It's Mick," I whispered, loud enough for them to hear. "I'm gonna hang out with you guys for a while."

"OK, Mick," I heard back. It was Hal. "Fuckin' ChiCom went off right on the other side of the berm here. Did you hear all those fuckin' gooks?"

"Yeah, I heard. Everyone OK?"

"Yeah. We're all OK."

Things quieted down. After a while the American artillery slowed, too.

I nodded off for a few minutes but was soon awakened by an artillery round impacting in the jungle nearby. I was groggy, hungry, and thirsty, mosquitoes buzzed around my face and ears, and I really wanted a cigarette, which was out of the question. And I hurt like hell. My right hand had gone numb again, and my head and shoulder were throbbing fiercely. "Just another night in paradise," I muttered to myself.

I got to my feet, still shaky, clutched my rifle in my left hand, and headed, bent low, toward the 3-1 fighting hole. I came upon Danny Nakamura first, sitting up on guard at the near end of it.

"Hey, Danny. How you doin,' buddy?" I whispered.

"OK, Mick. Thought those fuckers had us there for a while, though." Seeing my bandages in the near darkness he said, "You look like shit, Mick."

"Thanks. I'm OK. LT got hit pretty bad, but I think he's going to be OK, too. Voice is fucked up, though. Sounds like Carol Channing."

Danny laughed. "You're goin' back to the world, man. You got holes all over you."

"Naw. I don't think any of these are that bad. Hand still feels numb, though."

"You think these gooks are gone tonight?" Danny whispered.

"I doubt it. It doesn't feel right," I said.

"Sure doesn't. Creepy, man."

"You keep that little Okinawan head of yours down, buddy. Those gooks'll see you and think they're home, just walk on in here to say hello."

"Did I say, 'Fuck you,' Mick?" Danny laughed.

"I believe you did, buddy. I believe you did. See you later."

I made my way over to Jon West and Termite at the other end of the hole, facing out, in a whispered conversation. "Hear anything?"

"Yeah," said Termite. "Fuckers are movin' around out there. Every so often I hear one of 'em."

Just then we all heard the "tink-tink" signal, then another a-ways to our left. "They're gettin' ready to hit us again," I said. "You guys OK on frags and ammo?"

"We're OK, Mick," said Jon. Then, "You look fucked up, buddy. You OK?"

"Yeah. Bleedin's stopped. I'll be OK." I tried a smile there in the dark. "Might get me a few days of sack time in some aid station somewhere, though. Like you did when you got hit."

"Yeah, well, stay away from those boom-boom girls," whispered Jon. "I hear the clap is a terrible thing."

"Yeah, yeah," I said. "Your radio workin'?"

"No. You know about that piece of shit. It only works when we don't need it."

"OK. Well, I better get back up to 3-2 to call in this movement."

"Be careful, Mick."

"You guys, too."

I got to my feet, hunched low, and began making my way back toward 3-2. At that moment, I heard the "pop" of a ChiCom grenade primer being pulled, and I hit the ground. The frag landed near the 3-1 fighting hole I'd just left, and it detonated. I heard the "click" of the 3-1 grunts squeezing a Claymore detonator, and the Claymore went off with a bright flash and a huge explosion, blasting shrapnel into the jungle. Seconds later an artillery parachute flare ignited overhead, and I could make out the shapes of several NVA soldiers out in the trees, barely outside our perimeter.

The 3-1 and 3-2 squads began pouring rifle and machine-gun fire into them, and as the flare settled to the ground, the whole perimeter lit up. There was AK and machine gun fire coming in, frags flying in and out, Claymores going off, the grunts firing into the trees. There was the "Thunk," "Thunk," "Thunk" as the gooks began mortaring us again from two sides, and explosions as the rounds began detonating inside the perimeter.

I crawled up to the 3-2 fighting hole and grabbed the radio handset, but then realized I no longer had anything to say. Everybody knew we were being hit. I gave it back, shouted, "Control your fire, guys. Gonna be a long night." And then I began firing clumsily myself, left-handed, at the last shadowy shapes of the NVA soldiers as the flare drifted to the ground.

Realizing that the NVA meant to overrun the Delta company perimeter, Joe the FO, our artillery forward observer, began calling the 105-artillery fire in even closer. The big shells came screaming in directly overhead, only a few feet off the ground, before detonating on the far side of the Delta Company position. It sounded like a series of high speed locomotives going by, followed by deafening explosions. And everyone in the American perimeter knew that if one of our own artillery rounds fell even a little short, a lot our guys would end up in body bags.

But the NVA were in so close to the perimeter, Joe had no other choice. I began to wonder seriously whether or not we were going to survive this one. I wished I had my helmet, so I could maybe see Katie's picture the next time a flare popped. But I had no idea where it was.

The NVA mortars finally quit, and the AK fire tapered off. Soon, the artillery fire slowed down as well. I checked the 3-2 fighting holes for casualties, but everyone was OK. I made my way back to 3-1 and found Doc Benedetto already there, dressing a wound in Jon West's shoulder.

"You OK, Jon?" I whispered.

"Yeah. Just some shrapnel. Purple Heart number two for me. One more and I can get out of this shithole."

"Well, this one will get you a few days of down time. Buy you a beer in Tay Ninh."

"OK, man."

"Keep your fuckin' head down," I said, seriously.

"Right. Thanks for the motherly advice, Mick."

I smiled and moved away. I began to hear the engines of an Air Force C-130 overhead. That meant that "Spooky" the gunship was up there. We didn't see Spooky very often, and the fact that the big airplane was orbiting our position in the darkness was another indication of the precariousness of our situation. Spooky didn't come out for routine firefights.

The C-130 carried two 7.62 mm Gatling guns on its left side, facing outward and slightly downward, each capable of putting out 6,000 rounds per minute. Its technique was to fly passes over an enemy position with the plane banked low on the left side, and stream thousands of bullets into the target on the ground. Spooky had no lights on, of course, but I could make out the blue fire of the four turboprop engines as it passed overhead.

Someone put a strobe light on top of the bamboo thicket in the center of our perimeter, to mark our position for the big gunship. The strobe's flashes were incredibly bright in the semi-darkness of the battlefield.

Just then there was another bright flash and a huge "Krump!" to my right, and I was blown off my feet into the brush between the 3-1 and 3-2 fighting holes.

I woke up what must have been only seconds later to burning pain all down my right side from my neck to my leg. It was new pain on top of the old, but much more intense. I was dazed and sick to my stomach. I looked down in the light of the strobe to see blood pouring from wounds in my arm. My neck hurt like hell, and when I reached up to check it my fingers felt a good-sized hole, and my hand came away covered in blood. I tried to cry out "Doc!" but no sound came out.

I was suddenly very afraid.

I tried to get to my knees to crawl to the 3-2 fighting hole, but my right arm and leg collapsed under me, and I fell back to the ground. As

I did, I saw a pair of legs right in front of me, and I looked up, afraid they belonged to the NVA soldier who was about to kill me.

But it was only Fragman. He had his 90mm recoilless rifle, and was aiming it outside the perimeter toward the advancing NVA. I could see the enemy soldiers clearly in the light of a parachute flare. Fragman looked down at me and said, "Stay down, Mick. This motherfucker makes a hell of a blast."

My head fell back to the ground, and seconds later Fragman fired the 90mm. There was an unbelievable blast and shock wave as the big recoilless rifle fired thousands of the little steel darts into the jungle at the advancing gooks.

One of Spooky's Gatling guns opened up with a roar that sounded like a big RRRRRRRRRRRIIIIIIIIIIIIIIIIIIIIIPPPPPPPPPPPPPPPP PPPPP!

I watched as a big red waterfall, made by the thousands of red tracers, descended from the sky in a lazy arc that ended right outside the closest fighting hole, on top of the advancing North Vietnamese.

It's too close! my mind screamed. I tried to shout, "Get down!" to Fragman, but again, no sound came out. I watched, mesmerized, while the dazzling red waterfall approached, and listened to the gunfire and the rushing sound of thousands of bullets shredding the trees.

I thought about Katie, her sweet smile, the warmth of her arms around me.

And then I blacked out.

16

28 November 1969
Kansas City, Missouri

I remember waking up from a hard sleep on board a TWA 707 airliner as the big plane approached Kansas City's Municipal airport, trailing black smoke through the clear November sky. The loud noise of the flaps and landing gear being lowered had startled me awake, and at first I had no idea where I was or why I was there. I looked around me, saw the other passengers collecting their things, looked down to see myself in a dress green Army uniform with a Combat Infantryman's Badge and a bunch of new ribbons over the breast pocket. My right arm was out of the jacket sleeve, in a white sling that hung irritatingly from my neck.

The runway at KC Municipal was short for the big jet, so as soon as the main tires smoked at the end of the runway and the nose wheel was down, the pilot reversed thrust on all four engines, throwing all the passengers forward against our seatbelts as he slowed the plane to ground speed. We taxied over to one of the terminal gates where a ground controller was signaling us in.

As I realized where I was and came fully awake, I began to get really excited. *Home! I'm alive, I'm in one piece, and I'm home!*

Finally the stairway was pushed up and the plane's door opened. I was about eight rows back in the cabin, and it seemed like forever before the passengers ahead of me were up from their seats and out the door. But eventually my turn came.

I limped down the stairs, across the tarmac, and into the terminal, where I looked around and saw a smiling Katie there with her parents, my mother, and Sarah waiting for me. Katie flew into my arms, or rather my arm, and we kissed and hugged until we could hardly catch our breath. She clung to me, tears of joy on her face, as the rest of my family gathered around us, and there was round after round of hugs and kisses and "Welcome homes." There were many questions about my wounds, and I reassured everyone that none of them were serious. But I could see doubt in their eyes.

I tried not to notice the glares, the open looks of hostility, from many of the other travelers and the people who waited for them.

Katie's family began to drift away, and she left my side for a few minutes to see them off and thank them for coming. That left me alone with my mother and my sister, Sarah.

My mom had been through a lot in her life, coming from a poor sharecropper family with eleven kids, worrying through World War II with my dad and three of her brothers away in the war, and then losing her younger brother, my Uncle Tim, in Korea. She'd been very close to Tim, and his death had pretty much turned her sour on life.

Being close to her there in the airport terminal, I could see that the worry over my time in the war had aged her even more than the rest of her life already had. Even though she was only forty-five, she seemed old and tired to me. Even older and more tired than I felt. But she smiled at me and hugged me warmly, and said, "I'm glad you're home safe, Son. Are you sure you're all right? I've been so worried about you."

"I know, Mom. I'm sorry. You've had more than your share of worry in your life. But I'm home now and I'm OK. You don't need to worry about me anymore."

Sarah didn't say much. She just hugged me and said, "We're so glad you're home safe." Sarah and I didn't need words, really. She was four years older than me, but ever since we'd been kids, and she had taken care of me through my mother's bouts with anger and depression, we'd always seemed to be able to communicate without words. I hugged her back, held her for a while, and kissed her on the cheek.

It was really good to be home.

I walked Mom and Sarah to the parking lot and saw them off. Then Katie and I made our way to our car. It was a black Mustang fastback we'd bought new just before my National Guard unit had been activated in 1968, what seemed like a thousand years before. And Katie had it all polished up. It looked beautiful. I threw my bag into the tiny trunk, and Katie helped me into the passenger seat. Then she went around and climbed behind the wheel. There was something really sexy about a beautiful woman in a short dress sitting behind the wheel of a fast car. Especially given where I'd been, and for how long.

Katie took me for a leisurely ride across the river into Kansas City, Kansas, and ultimately to the modest house she had rented for us. I enjoyed the ride, especially the part where every time she used the clutch to shift gears, her dress rode up a little higher on her legs. But with some of my attention I also enjoyed the scenery of our city, which seemed to have changed little while I was gone. I was struck at how little anything seemed to have changed at home, when so much had changed for me.

"It's so good to have you back, Mick. To know you're out of danger. We all went nuts when we found out you'd been hurt, and we couldn't find out how bad it was. How are you feeling?"

"The wounds aren't that bad, Katie. Most of them are almost healed. Still a little stiff, but I think I'm going to get out of this sling as soon as we get home. And out of this uniform. I've only had these dress greens since yesterday. We flew home in jungle fatigues, and they fixed this uniform up for me in Oakland. But it doesn't feel comfortable. And…" I looked over at her, "I'm not used to wearing underwear, and I still have a touch of ringworm. These are kind of chafing me." I smiled wanly. "Mostly, I'm just tired."

She looked down at my uniform jacket. "What are those stains, Mick? I thought it was a new uniform?"

"Dried spit, courtesy of the friendly welcome-home committee at San Francisco International," I said sarcastically. "I saw one soldier not far from me get red paint thrown on him. And they kept chanting 'Baby-burner! Baby-burner!' at us as we got off the bus from Oakland. Wish they'd let us keep our rifles. Almost rather kill one of them than a fuckin' gook."

She just looked at me, her face sad, and shook her head. "Unbelievable," was all she said. She took her hand off the gear shift and put it on my thigh, and smiled at me. I put my hand on her thigh in return, and could feel the warmth of her body through the dress she wore. I didn't pay much attention to the outside scenery through the rest of the drive.

When we were finally at our new home, Katie got out, opened the garage door, and pulled the car inside. I was opening the passenger door when she came around and held it for me, and helped me out. We went in through the kitchen, and I saw a modest two-bedroom ranch, sparsely furnished with some of our old furniture and a few unfamiliar pieces. I went back into the garage, opened the trunk of the car, and pulled out my duffle bag, which was nearly empty. I lifted the lid off the big plastic trash can in the garage, dropped the bag inside, and closed the lid.

Katie just looked at me. Then she shrugged. "Do you want to take a shower?" she finally asked.

"I really do. I didn't get a real shower with hot water through the whole tour until I got hurt. I got a few at the hospital, but even then there was a shortage of hot water. They had hot showers in Oakland yesterday, but they would only let us stay in for a few minutes. I feel like I need to stand in there for hours to even try to get rid of all this filth that's soaked into my body."

She led me to our bedroom and helped me undress. I knew she could smell me, a putrid dead-flesh smell, but said nothing. As I took off my clothes she saw the still-healing jungle rot sores, and the fresh scars and stitch marks from the wounds on my neck, arms, chest, and side. And there was the shadow of ringworm on my upper thighs, although it had nearly faded.

"My God, Mick! I'm so, so sorry you had to go through that. Look at you!"

"My own fault. You know that. I had to go and volunteer. Wouldn't have had to go otherwise. Guess I learned that lesson!" I gave her another wan smile.

She started the shower and I stepped inside, running the water as hot as I could stand. She undressed and stepped in behind me, began to gently wash me with a washcloth and soap. The water ran dirty down the drain, with occasional blood where a sore opened under the washing. I was very aware of her nakedness, of her nipples brushing my back, of her hands on me. She turned me gently around, washed my chest and the front of my thighs, and then began gently to soap my genitals.

She kissed me then and stepped out of the shower, and pulled a towel around her. I stayed a few more minutes until the water began to run cold, then stepped out myself, dried off with a big, soft bath towel, and followed her into the bedroom. She was already under the covers, and I pulled them back, my heart pounding at the sheer beauty of her. She lay there on her back, unembarrassed by her nudity, her arms outstretched to me. I slipped under the clean, soft sheets, the sensation one of sheer luxury after my months in the mud and filth of Vietnam.

"I haven't been with anyone else, Katie. You don't need to worry about that. I only wanted you."

She smiled at me and said, "I haven't either, Mick. But you knew that. I'd never want to be with anyone else." We kissed, I rubbed my hands over her body, and unable to wait longer, slipped easily inside her. She stroked my hair and kissed my neck and we moved slowly together until I came, a deep, wracking orgasm that left me exhausted and drained. Then I fell asleep in her arms.

While I was asleep there in our bed, clean and dry and warm and safe for the first time in months, I had the first of what would become a constant series of dreams … nightmares, about the war.

17

2 May 1969
Near the Cambodian Border, Republic of Vietnam

It was my second day in the bush after first arriving in Vietnam. We had humped all that day, covering just over a click, and wound up very close to the Cambodian border. As we were moving into our night defensive position, the platoon sergeant, 3-5, approached Morales, my first squad leader. "Third squad has ambush tonight but they're short of men. You're going to have to send two of your squad out with them. Get 'em ready." Without looking very hard, Morales picked Jon West and me to go along.

The 3-3 squad had taken a position inside the company perimeter, behind the rest of third platoon, and the men were getting ready for the ambush patrol. The squad leader, another Californian named Mike Sands, who Jon seemed to know, was sitting with the other five in his squad, cleaning his rifle. When Jon and I approached, he told us to have a seat, introduced the men in the squad by their nicknames, and briefed us all on the ambush plan.

"We'll relax inside the perimeter for a while longer," said Sands. "So, get your gear ready, eat chow, camouflage your faces and hands, and rest a bit. We'll move out about an hour before dark. Rat will be on point. We'll head about four hundred meters northwest, to a spot where there's supposed to be an NVA supply trail coming out of Cambodia. If things go right we'll set up along the trail just before dark. We'll put Claymores out in a simple line setup, with maybe a twenty meter kill zone.

"Leave everything here except weapons, ammo, Claymores, water, and poncho liners. No smoking once we leave the perimeter. Tie everything down tight. I don't want any fuckin' noise." He went on to give us the watch schedule, two men on at a time, six men asleep. "Anyone snoring gets woke up as often as it takes to keep you quiet. On watch, you listen for gooks coming down the trail. If it seems like there's a large force, you sit tight and let them go by, maybe we'll call in artillery farther down the trail. If it's a small force that we can take out with our Claymores, you wait until all the gooks are in the kill zone and then blow all the Claymores at once. That'll wake everyone else, and if there's any return fire from the gooks we'll finish them off with frags and machine guns. We're taking two machine guns with us.

"Very important," said Sands, "the Claymore detonators will have the safeties off, so you can blow them fast if you need to. But don't step on one or roll onto one, because it'll go off, and we'll be fucked!"

Jon and I were assigned first watch. We would be on from about 20:00 until 21:30 and again from 02:00 until 03:30.

Jon helped me put on camouflage paint and silence my gear. We moved out about 18:30 with Rat on point, followed by Sands, two other 3-3 men, Jon and me, and two more 3-3 men bringing up the rear. The jungle was fairly thin there, and we had no trouble covering the four hundred meters. When Rat found the trail he motioned the squad to stop, and Sands moved everyone back until they were about ten meters from it, placing us in pairs about two meters apart. He, Rat, and a couple of the other 3-3 guys set up the Claymores along the trail, ran the wires back to the center of the ambush position, and attached them to the hand detonators. He moved Jon and me to the position where the detonators were laid out and had us watch as he moved the wire safeties to the "fire" position. He gave Jon a watch with a luminous dial and told us to wake him and Rat for the next watch, at 21:30.

We rubbed on bug juice, smearing it into the camouflage paint mess, and the rest of the grunts rolled up into their poncho liners. The bug juice had a sickly-sweet odor that I figured the gooks could smell for a mile.

Jon and I pulled our first watch uneventfully, although the time passed with miserable slowness. It seemed that every time I looked at the watch, only seconds had gone by.

Eventually our first watch was over, and Jon crawled over to wake Sands and Rat. Then we swapped positions with them, rolled into our poncho liners, and, surprisingly, I quickly fell asleep. Sometime later it began to rain, gently at first, but then hard for a while, and covered only by the thin nylon liners, we were quickly soaked. I lay there with the rain pounding on my face, soaked through, the mixture of bug juice and camouflage paint stinging unmercifully as it ran into my eyes. I looked over at Jon and found him still fast asleep. I tried not to think about how miserable I was and wondered how long it would be before I could sleep through a soaking rain like this.

The rain stopped after a while, but I was still awake at 02:00 when one of the 3-3 grunts came to wake Jon and me. We sat up, pulled off our poncho liners, and crawled over to the detonators for our second watch. With the rain stopped and most of the bug juice washed off, the mosquitoes were out in force. They buzzed my face and neck and bit mercilessly.

The second watch seemed to pass even more slowly than the first, and I found myself fighting to stay awake for the last half hour or so. Once I thought I heard movement along the trail and nudged Jon to listen while I began to feel around carefully for the Claymore detonators. But the noise soon stopped, and I eventually figured it must have been some small animal. Though the rain had stopped, the sky remained very black, and even with eyes well accustomed to the darkness, I couldn't see anything around me.

Finally, 03:30 came, and again Jon went to wake Sands and Rat. They crawled over a few minutes later and took the position, and Jon and I made our way quietly back to where we'd slept before to try to catch some more sleep.

I was just starting to doze off when I heard a dull metallic clanking sound coming from up the trail. I nudged Jon, who grabbed my arm to let me know that he heard it too, and we quietly unraveled ourselves from the poncho liners, and slowly pulled our rifles in close. We were only a few feet from Sands and Rat, and I thought about moving over to make sure they had heard too. But as I was about to move I heard the unmistakable low murmur of Vietnamese voices, and I figured everyone had heard that.

My hands trembling, I moved my weapon into firing position in front of me and quietly thumbed the selector switch from "Safe" to "Auto." We waited.

The gooks moved directly in front of us, and it was clear from the sounds of their equipment and the muffled scraping of their footsteps that there were only a few of them. They were moving at a moderate pace, not speed walking, but not stepping too carefully, either.

Suddenly I heard a Claymore detonator being squeezed, first once, then twice, with a "Click! Click!" sound. And then all the Claymores went off, one after another, with loud explosions and bright flashes of light. The noise was unbelievable, deafening. The night went from pitch black to strobe-like brightness as the Claymores flashed and blew, and sparks flew out into the kill zone.

With the first flash, I could see two of the North Vietnamese caught standing, turning toward the sound of the detonators. But with the second flash the two were falling, and with the later flashes and explosions I could see no one standing at all. It was a hellish scene, the intense flashes of light and incredible explosions, and the air filled suddenly with smoke and the stink of the explosives.

I lay there shaking, waiting for the return fire, or for the American machine guns to crank up, but there was none of that. After a few minutes my hearing started to come back, and I began to hear sickening moans and the sound of weeping from the kill zone, along with a few pained words I did not understand. That went on for a few minutes, then gradually died away. And then there was silence. Still no one in the squad fired a rifle or machine gun.

I heard Sands whispering into the radio, calling 6. "This is 3-3 actual," he whispered. "We took four or five gooks with Claymores. No return fire. They're all quiet now, over." A short while later: "Roger that. Out." Then he whispered: "Pass the word. We're pulling back another thirty meters or so until morning."

Quietly we pulled our gear together, and moved back away from the trail to a small clearing where we formed a circular perimeter and laid down, everyone facing outward, weapons in front of us. We stayed there for the rest of the night, some sleeping off and on, but everyone obviously psyched out by the ambush. I laid awake for the rest of the night, thinking about what had just happened, the horrible sounds of the dying Vietnamese, the incredible violence of what we had done.

Seeing violent death that close, even in the dark, had been a shattering, terrifying, and at the same time, disgusting experience. I couldn't believe what this squad had just done to the people in the kill zone. I couldn't believe how easily we had apparently killed everyone in the patrol. I felt that I had participated in an act of cold-blooded mass murder, and I was deeply bothered by it. I had volunteered for this war, and this wasn't the reaction I had expected toward killing the enemy.

When it started getting light, Sands made sure everyone was awake, and we waited through the dawn until it was light enough to see clearly. Then we saddled up, and Rat took the point to walk back to the kill zone. We approached very slowly and carefully, looking in all directions for other gooks. As we approached, I could begin to hear flies buzzing loudly. And I smelled an incredible stench, unlike anything I had ever smelled before. It was the stink of blood and emptied bowels and bladders, of intestines blown through with the steel shot from the Claymores, and of brains and eyeballs blown out, mixed in with what smelled like rotting fish.

Along with the other grunts, I made my way into the kill zone and forced myself to approach one of the NVA bodies. The dead soldier looked young, although it was difficult to make out his features well because there were holes throughout his face and body where the shot from the Claymores had punctured. Every hole was black with drying blood, and pieces of brain and gut oozed from the punctures. There were flies everywhere, and the buzzing was a dull roar. I looked at the body for only a moment before my stomach turned over, and I turned away and vomited.

None of the other grunts seemed disturbed by either the sight of the dead gooks, covered with buzzing flies, or the stink of them. But none seemed to think it strange that I had been sickened by the experience, either. "You'll get used to it, Cherry," said one of the 3-3 grunts.

There had been five NVA in the patrol, all dressed in khaki uniforms, wearing pith helmets and the famous Ho Chi Minh sandals that were made of truck tire treads and strips of inner tubes. They carried new-looking AK-47s and bandoliers of ammo. Their packs were light, and when Rat opened one he found only some brown rice, a couple of plastic packets we thought might be seasonings or sauces, and two 62mm mortar shells. Other packs contained similar stuff.

Only one AK and a couple of bandoliers of ammo had survived the Claymore blasts, and we policed them up along with the undestroyed mortar shells, and prepared to move out. I watched as one of the 3-3 grunts went from body to body putting 1st Cav patches on each chest. Another pulled a knife and began sawing on the ear of one of the bodies. Seeing him, Sands said, "Leave his fuckin' ears on his head. We ain't takin' none of that shit back with us. Those fuckers stink to high heaven before they dry out, and I ain't havin' 'em around." The grunt stopped sawing, shrugged, put his knife away, and stood up.

Then we all froze in place as we heard a quiet moan come from one of the North Vietnamese soldiers. The man wasn't dead, as he'd appeared to be. Three or four of the ambush team walked over to him, and I wondered what the procedure was to Medevac a wounded NVA. He looked too far gone to save, but maybe they could.

Instead, Sands put the muzzle of his rifle next to the man's head, turned his own face away, and fired a single round through the soldier's left eye. The bullet exploded the eyeball and the brain, and some of it splattered onto the low scrub growth around him, some of it onto Sands' rifle. Blood poured out the back of the man's head into the dead leaves and dirt below.

"He was gonna die anyway," Sands said to no one in particular as he wiped the muzzle of the rifle on the man's shirt. The rest of the grunts just shrugged and turned away. I tried to absorb what I'd seen; stood there looking bewildered. Jon saw the look on my face and just said, "You'll get used to that, too."

18

28 November 1969
Kansas City, Kansas

I woke with a start, the image of Sands killing the wounded NVA soldier fresh in my mind. For a few seconds I couldn't remember where I was, could only see the gook's eye exploding with Sands' bullet through it. I couldn't understand why I was naked and covered in sheets, and I sat up abruptly, thrashing wildly in our bed, feeling around for my weapon and gear.

Katie had fallen asleep next to me, and my thrashing elbow slammed into her ribs hard enough to knock the breath out of her. She let out a startled, "Ack!" and doubled up in pain. Awake then, I gathered her into my arms and whispered into her ear, "Oh, Katie, I'm so sorry. It was a nightmare. I'm so sorry." I began to weep with a deep sense of grief that I had brought that horrible war back home with me, and now I'd hurt my beloved Katie.

"It's OK, Mick," she gasped, once she had enough breath back to make a sound. And she held me close and smoothed my hair, crying with me.

We lay together for a long time, and gradually the weeping stopped. Finally, Katie rolled away from me, sat up on the bed, and said, "Why don't we get dressed and go out for some food, Mick? You probably haven't had a decent meal in a long time."

"Well, you're right about that. But I don't really feel like going out right now. Got any bacon and eggs? I'd love to have some if you do. I'll even cook."

"No, no, Mick. Lie still. I'll fix them. Your clothes are in the closet there, if you think anything still fits."

Katie stood, and I could see the beginning of a bruise under her left breast where I had hit her. "Oh, Katie. I'm so sorry." I hugged her again.

"It's OK, Mick. Don't worry. No ribs broken."

She smiled at me, got up, put on her robe, and went to the kitchen. Soon I could hear the beautiful domestic sounds of pots, pans, and dishes, and I could smell bacon and eggs frying and coffee brewing. It felt really good to be home.

I climbed out of bed and stepped back into the shower briefly, but the water was still only warm, so I washed off quickly, dried myself, and went back into the bedroom. I pulled a pair of jeans from a hanger and slipped them on, noticing that they were about two inches too big in the waist. The high school sweatshirt I found fit better, and I slipped on my old moccasins, and made my way into the kitchen. The coffee was ready, and I poured us each a cup and sat at the table, watching Katie finishing dinner/breakfast.

The food was wonderful, the first eggs, bacon, and toast I'd eaten since I'd left. We lingered over it, drank second cups of coffee, and then Katie slipped into my lap, and hugged me contentedly. We found ourselves back in bed again as the sun was setting outside, and this time we made love very slowly, very generously, and it was beautiful and satisfying for us both.

That night after Katie had fallen asleep I lay awake thinking of the events of the past few weeks, beginning with the firefight in which I was wounded. I remembered my surgery and treatment at the hospital in Chu Lai, and my eventual release back to my battalion rear head-quarters in Tay Ninh. There I was delighted to find that orders were waiting, for me to go home! When I'd left my Guard unit for Vietnam I'd been told that since I'd volunteered, I'd have to stay a full year even though the rest of the Guard would be coming home the end of November. So I was happy beyond belief that I'd be going home with them. "Probably because you got hurt, and they figure you're no good to them here anyway," the company executive officer said as he saw the smile on my face.

"OK by me, sir."

Technically even though I was home I was still under U.S. Army care, and I had to report to the military hospital at Ft. Leavenworth within a few days of my arrival in Kansas City. But, effectively, I was out of the Army and would be released to the National Guard and then discharged by mid-December.

I thought of my buddies still in Vietnam and fretted that I hadn't been able to exchange stateside addresses or phone numbers with them before I'd left. I had never returned to the field after being wounded that night and had simply lost contact with the closest friends of my life, men with whom I'd shared all sorts of misery and deprivation and loss, men with whom I'd endured the horrors of combat in that hellish place. I wondered how they were doing and where they all were at that very moment, who was still alive, who might be wounded, and who had been killed without me even knowing it. Did they have food and water? Were they, right then, in contact with the enemy? Perhaps surrounded by the NVA again, on the verge of being massacred?

I began to feel guilty about being home with Katie, knowing that my closest friends were still at risk, still there. I felt guilty about the hot shower and the clean sheets, the wonderful food she'd prepared for me. I felt guilty because I could go outside and smoke cigarettes at night without risking a sniper shot. I even felt guilty about being able to make love to my wife when my friends were still so far away from theirs. And I felt guilty that I was still alive, when Carl Engle, Tony Giles, Sugarbear, and so many others were dead.

I slipped quietly out of bed, pulled on my jeans and sweatshirt, and padded through the darkened house, absentmindedly checking the locks on the doors and windows to make sure the place was secure. I didn't remember having done that before Vietnam, but security seemed absolutely essential now.

Katie found me at 3:30 in the morning in the living room rocker, smoking cigarettes, a glass of bourbon in my hand, staring out the window at the streetlight outside, lost in my thoughts. She invited me back to bed by opening her robe and pressing her breasts into my face. But when we made love for the third time since I'd been home, I couldn't keep her from noticing that I felt a little ... distracted?

The nightmares continued night after night and became such a pattern that Katie took to sleeping as far away from me in bed as she could. Gradually, after the first couple of weeks I began to remember where I was more of the time, so the violent awakenings became less frequent. But I still talked in my sleep and made fearful noises, and thrashed around, although somewhat less violently. Katie had a hard time sleeping for more than an hour or two because of all that, and after a few days she was as exhausted as I was.

I made my mandatory trips to the hospital in Leavenworth and was discharged, pronounced healed, by the second week of December. I still walked with a limp from the shrapnel wounds in my leg, but that was gradually getting better. I was treated only for my physical wounds. The emotional stress I was undergoing wasn't discussed, and no one in the Army medical community asked how I was doing in that way. And I certainly wasn't going to bring it up if there was any chance it could delay my discharge. It was clear to me that, now that I'd served my purpose, the Army was as anxious to get rid of me as I was to be rid of it.

19

15 December 1969
Watertown, New Jersey
Angie Giles

Angie's grief continued to overwhelm her, and she lived on in total misery. Only the knowledge that she carried Tony's baby gave her the strength to carry on at all. Even with the pills the doctor had given her she tossed and turned for hours before falling asleep at night, and then slept only fitfully, dreaming every night of Tony. The dreams were very realistic, each a beautiful memory of Tony and the time they'd had together. But she woke each morning to the horrible realization that he was gone. Forever. And with each new morning also came the unrelenting uncertainty about the letter, fear that he might have died believing she was leaving him, that she didn't love him.

Though her belly continued to swell as the baby grew inside her, she actually lost more weight through the two remaining months of her pregnancy.

A month and a half after Tony's funeral Angie went into labor, and still gripped by the fear that she might well die in delivery, she rode to the hospital in the back seat of her dad's car, her mother holding her hand and encouraging her through each new wave of pain. But her labor was short and the delivery went more easily than Angie had expected. And only a few hours after the contractions began, the baby was born.

He was a perfect little boy, born with a full head of black hair and looking startlingly like Tony. Even in her misery at losing Tony and her ongoing sense of guilt about the letter, Angie couldn't help but smile into his beautiful little face. Without ever really considering any other choice, she named him Anthony Giles, Jr. But his grandparents quickly started calling him "Little Tony."

Little Tony immediately became the light of Angie's life and the delight of both sets of his grandparents, who adored him all the more because Tony was gone and he was Tony's son. Little Tony's presence in Angie's life helped her, very slowly, begin to heal. He was someone to live for, someone to get out of bed for, someone as yet untouched by the evil of the world and the sadness that had overwhelmed them all before his birth. And each day that passed, each day she cared for him, and saw more and more his father's eyes and his father's face, a tiny bit of the pain of Tony's loss went away. And a tiny bit of the agony of wondering about the letter went away. She would simply never know, and she eventually began, little by little, to accept that.

20

Christmas, 1969
Kansas City, Kansas
Mick Delaney

My National Guard unit reassembled in mid-December for a mustering out ceremony, and I once again, for the last time, wore the dress green uniform they'd given me in Oakland. As I'd carefully cleaned the spit stains from the lapels of my uniform jacket that morning, I'd thought about other wars and how proudly the veterans had returned home, marching in welcoming parades in their dress uniforms to the cheers and ovations of huge crowds that lined the streets.

But there would be no parades for us. Because so many people in Kansas City and all across America were demonstrating violently against the war, it was decided we would simply form up one last time as a battalion inside the armory's gymnasium, away from public view. There were a few words of thanks from our battalion commander, and then we were simply dismissed, to get into our cars and go home. I drove home with Katie, took off my uniform, hung it in the closet, and vowed never to wear green again in my life.

I reported back to my job at Langton Manufacturing the next day, and found that the company had moved its offices to a new location in downtown Kansas City, Missouri. I went there to find my old group and get back to work at my job as a draftsman. But things had changed a lot, and the people there seemed... distant? Even a bit apprehensive around me. The almost nationwide demonization of America's soldiers, who had fought the war America's government sent us to fight, seemed to have affected almost everyone.

My old boss Wayne Jensen welcomed me back warmly, then told me I'd earned my paid vacation for that year, and that I had just enough days left before year end to take it all. So, why not go back home and take it easy, and they'd see me after the first of the year?

Money was tight. I had sent almost all my pay home while I was in Vietnam, including my combat pay. But there had been some unexpected expenses while I'd been gone, so by the time we'd bought Christmas gifts for her sisters' kids, my sister's kids, and our parents, there was barely enough left for Katie and me to exchange modest gifts. I knew things would get better financially once I went back to work, but that wouldn't be until after the first of the year. I wanted to take my wife out to celebrate making it back alive and being home with her again. But there wasn't enough in the bank to do that and still pay the upcoming rent. So after I'd had long catch-up visits with my family while Katie was at work, I just stayed home and watched boring daytime TV until Christmas. Better than being shot at and sleeping in the mud, but not as exciting as I'd somehow imagined my return home would be.

Katie and I spent Christmas Eve with my mother, and Sarah and her family at Mom's home, eating a wonderful traditional Christmas dinner. Despite my happiness to be there in one piece with my family again, I found that gathering with all those people to be nerve wracking, especially the happy noise of the children. As the gifts were opened the laughing and screaming were like the screeching of fingernails on a blackboard to me. It struck me that I'd never felt that way before Vietnam.

On Christmas Day we went to Katie's' parents' home, where the scene was repeated, this time with a much larger, much more boisterous crowd. After a full day of it I found myself sitting alone at one end of the couch, watching the happiness and listening to the noise, and resenting it all, my nerves jangling. How could people be so happy in a world filled with so much horror, violence, deprivation, and death? Easy. They'd never experienced it. And I had. And I began to believe I'd never be able to erase the memories or stop worrying about my friends who were still there. I resented these innocent people, even the children, for their happiness, and their minds... minds not filled with the residue of war.

Finally, I got up slowly, went to Katie's side, and whispered to her that I had to get out of there, had to go home. She looked at me with concern first, but then a bit of anger showed through. Finally, she simply shrugged and said, "OK. You take the car. I'll get a ride home later." Then she turned back to her sister and continued talking.

As I walked away I heard her sister ask, "Is he OK?" I looked around to see Katie shaking her head, looking very sad.

I drove home through the darkened, icy winter streets, past all the Christmas lights and brightly-lit windows of joyous homes, alone. I went into our quiet, darkened house alone.

I was away from my buddies in Vietnam, with no way to communicate with them or know how they were. I felt different and separate from my own family. Clearly I had even made Katie angry and sad by leaving her family's Christmas.

I had never, ever, in my life, felt so alone.

21

1970 - 1974
Kansas City

I started back to work on January 2, 1970, in my old job in Product Development at Langton Manufacturing, where they made farm and grain storage equipment. I had been a good draftsman before I left in 1968, when my National Guard unit was activated for service in Vietnam. That first Friday and the following week were spent reviewing product manuals to "catch up" on updates that had been implemented since I'd left, and it was clear to me that there wasn't much for me to do. I felt lucky there were laws guaranteeing me my old job back.

Wayne Jensen began to give me actual drafting assignments during my second full week, and at first I was a bit challenged by the fineness of the work, my hands having become accustomed to much grosser tasks like chopping brush in the jungle and carrying a rifle. My right hand, my drawing hand, had suffered shrapnel wounds, and the fingers were still stiff from those. But the dexterity began to return after a few days, and I was quickly producing drawings I was proud of.

But the more senior technicians, including my boss, kept the most interesting parts of the work for themselves, including all the calculations of part dimensions and so forth. I was given sketches to produce finished drawings from, and the work didn't challenge me or occupy my mind. I had much too much time to think, to compare this boring, mundane work with the challenges, the excitement, and the fear, of leading, or helping to lead, an Army rifle platoon in combat.

My wages without the tax exemptions I'd been granted while serving in a combat zone, produced far less take-home pay than I'd made in the Army. And, of course, there were no clothing or quarters allowances, no meals provided, no free health care, none of those military benefits. With having to buy gas for our car and pay for rent, insurance, and other expenses, Katie and I found little extra money for anything.

Within a few weeks, a position came open for a supervisor in the order processing department. Since I'd done a little order processing work before I'd left and felt I had developed good leadership skills from my Army experience, I applied. I was quickly granted an interview and was excited that I might have a shot at something more interesting and more challenging, with better pay.

But that hope was quickly dashed during the interview. Alan Freeman, the vice president responsible for order processing, put me on the defensive right away. "As you know, our policy requires us to interview all internal job candidates who might be remotely qualified for a position. And especially since you're a recent veteran, I wanted to be sure to give you an interview. But I'm interested in understanding why you think you're qualified for this job, because from your job history, I don't see it."

"I did some order processing work for a time before my Guard unit was activated, and they said I was pretty good at it. But more importantly, I held a position as an infantry platoon sergeant, a staff sergeant, in Vietnam, with full-time administrative and part-time combat leadership responsibility for a platoon of about thirty men. That was leadership under very difficult conditions, and I was told I performed well."

"Well, it doesn't seem to me that leadership in the Army is much of a challenge. All you have to do is give orders, and the men follow them," said Alan, a bit sarcastically.

I looked at him for a moment before responding. "Well, Alan, that may be how it works in a peacetime Army. But it was very different in combat. There, if the men didn't respect you or didn't like your orders, they might decide to put a bullet in your head during the next firefight. You had to be good at what you did, and you had to have their respect, or you didn't last long. I believe I was good at what I did, and had their respect."

He gave a little smirk. "I'm sorry, Mick. I'm afraid I don't think your Army experience qualifies you for this position or any other supervisory position here. Maybe with a few more years' experience in your current job. And you might want to take some management courses at Junior College." Alan dismissed me.

Fuming, I went back to my drafting board, picked up my pencil, and resumed work on my latest drawing. That night, in a glum mood, I told Katie about the interview. "So I guess I get to go on connecting the dots on these product drawings for just enough money to live on for a while longer."

Within a few weeks of my return I became incredibly bored with my peaceful life at home. I didn't fully understand why, but I seemed to crave excitement. I started taking the Mustang to the drag strip on Fridays and Saturdays, but it wasn't enough car to be competitive, and I didn't have the money to build it up. I'd been a hunter and fisherman most of my life, loving the outdoors, the hunt, the excitement of catching fish or taking game. But after the death and suffering I'd seen in Vietnam, the notion of killing an animal or hooking and killing a fish for my own pleasure no longer had any appeal to me. I sold all my hunting rifles and shotguns, and gave away my fishing gear.

Life with Katie fell into a routine, as well. We worked five days a week and had little money to do anything interesting during the evenings and weekends. So we stayed home and watched television or visited with her family or mine. We made love less and less often. I still felt guilty about my clean, comfortable, sanitary life, when I knew most of my friends were still in Vietnam, maybe even wounded, or dead.

On April 30, 1970, Katie and I watched President Nixon's televised press conference, in which he announced that he had ordered the invasion of Cambodia, a sovereign, theoretically neutral nation, in order to allow American forces to attack the safe havens of the North Vietnamese, who had been taking refuge there since the beginning of the war. I was incredulous at the news and afraid for my friends, who I imagined would be spearheading the invasion. The Army had gone into Cambodia very near the area where my battalion had been patrolling when I left.

The press conference had a surreal quality to it, and Katie and I were among the many who at first believed that it might be the popular comedian, Rich Little, performing his famous "Tricky Dicky" imitation, as a joke. But it was not Rich Little. And it was not a joke.

Only four days later we were horrified to hear that a violent anti-war demonstration that had been fueled by the President's announcement of the Cambodian invasion had resulted in a shooting on the Kent State University campus. Thirteen demonstrators had been shot by members of the Ohio National Guard hours after the Ohio governor had made an inflammatory speech in which he described the anti-war demonstrators as "worse than the Nazi brown-shirts and the communist element and the night riders and the vigilantes. They are the worst type of people that we harbor in America."

Four of the demonstrators died. I couldn't believe this was happening in America.

Katie loved children and, despite all the political goings-on and our financial struggle, badly wanted to start a family. But I just couldn't make myself want that as well. I found that I had a bitter, cynical outlook on the world, and I struggled to see the wisdom of bringing children into such a place. I tried to explain that to Katie, but eventually realized that, try though she might, she would never understand. And I couldn't bring myself to describe in enough grisly detail what I'd been through, and seen, and done, that made me feel that way.

I saw the world through different eyes. When Katie and I took walks in the woods, I found myself searching the path for trip wires, scanning the forest for signs of an ambush. I often daydreamed, remembering firefights or sleepless nights on listening post. The days of Tony's and other friends' deaths were replayed in my mind a thousand times, always with a sense of guilt, and always with the question, *What if I'd done things differently that day?*

I was lost. I knew no one understood me. I was jittery, easily bored, and had a hard time keeping my attention on the things I'd found interesting before the war. I didn't realize that with day upon day of the terror of war I had eventually become addicted to my own adrenaline, a "thrill junkie."

I began to go out alone, took the Mustang onto winding back roads, and drove it hard. When that wasn't exciting enough, I took up sport parachuting. It seemed I was only able to produce the adrenaline that made me feel alive when there was some serious, immediate threat to my life.

Katie didn't understand me, the deadness I seemed to feel much of the time, the risks I took to feel alive. She had no idea why, after all the danger I'd been through, I'd want to put myself into more. She didn't understand why the life that had been so good for me before was no longer enough.

She went to watch me parachute jump only once, a day when my first jump ended in a bad, hard landing, and I had to lie on the ground for a couple of minutes before I could get up. She watched in horror from the side of the field while I lay there, barely moving. No one from the parachuting club came to help me since they assumed correctly what had happened, that I had merely taken a bad fall and wasn't really injured. And besides, it wasn't that kind of group.

Once I did get up, I gathered up the parachute and hobbled back to the packing area. Katie was again horrified when I had the chute re-packed and went back up to jump again. Later, on the drive home, she said simply, "People have to be out of their minds to want to do that." I only looked at her without comment. She was probably right.

Drinking became more and more a necessary part of my life. At first it was social, but soon I was drinking too often, and I often drank too much. I made new friends at work with two other Vietnam vets, both combat veterans, and the three of us frequently ended our work days in bars. Bars were noisy and anonymous, and no one expected anything from us there. And the drinking made the memories easier to tolerate, if only for a little while.

One Friday night after a few drinks, we somehow began talking about the Veterans of Foreign Wars, an organization all our fathers, World War II veterans, had been part of. We each remembered times when we were little kids when our dads had taken us to their VFW posts on a Friday or Saturday night for drinks, bingo, and dinner, and remembered how they'd seemed to enjoy that camaraderie so much. We decided we'd all go the next day to a VFW Post near our office and sign up.

But when we got there, perfectly sober and looking respectable, we were told in no uncertain terms, "We don't want you Vietnam sons of bitches in this organization. Fuckin' baby killers is what you are." I'll always remember those words, spoken so venomously by a man about our dads' age, wearing an Army Air Corps cap from World War II.

Maybe the saddest part was that we weren't really surprised.

We had all served honorably in Vietnam, none of us harming a child or indeed any civilian that we knew of, while we were there. But we knew there was no point trying to defend ourselves to the old man at the VFW post. And we didn't feel we should have to.

But Tom replied to the old man's hateful outburst. "You old bastard! You in the Army Air Corps in World War II? How many babies do you think you killed with all the bombs you fuckers dropped when you carpet-bombed Germany and Japan?" He glared at the man, who just glared back at him wordlessly. Then we simply turned around and left. And went to a favorite nearby bar, and drank. Again.

The months and years went by.

With my refusal to have children "yet" or buy a house "yet" Katie began to see the marriage, and me, as a dead end. We gradually drifted apart. My last months with her were lived mostly in silence, for I had simply quit talking to her and most everyone else outside work. I wasn't violent, wasn't even verbally abusive. I just stopped trying to communicate altogether. How could I communicate well with people who didn't understand me, and didn't seem to want to try?

Four years after my return from Vietnam I moved out of our house into a barren apartment. Katie, who had always been a loving, devoted wife, and who had endured the seven years of our marriage with never a complaint, was devastated. She never understood what happened. She only knew that the man who had come home to her from Vietnam was not the man who had left her a few months before.

We were divorced, the process finalized by some strange quirk of fate on my twenty-seventh birthday. I drank so much that night that I couldn't remember the next day how I'd made it home. I called in sick for work, then stayed in bed all day nursing my hangover. By late afternoon I felt good enough to get up, so I cleaned up and ate something. Then I became really depressed at my loneliness, my empty apartment, and what my life had become. If I'd still had any of my guns at that point I might well have ended that life. I certainly thought about it often in those days.

But I'd gotten rid of them all. So I went out to drink again, to forget the depression and loneliness. For the second night in a row, I couldn't remember how I got home.

The next night, after I'd had a quiet dinner at home and gone to bed early and almost sober, I had a dream that I've had many times since, and that I'll never forget.

22

LZ Sherman, Tay Ninh Province, Republic of Vietnam

Landing Zone Sherman was a bleak outpost in the vast rainforest of Tay Ninh Province, deliberately placed at the convergence of three major trails used by the North Vietnamese to funnel their men and supplies into South Vietnam from Cambodia. The LZ, as a base of our battalion's infantry operations, and with its artillery that could reach all the way to the Cambodian border and beyond, was therefore a major thorn in the side of the North Vietnamese Army.

There had already been three major ground attacks on the base earlier in 1969, before my battalion took over operations there in late May. With each attack, several Americans on the base had been killed, and many wounded. And with each attack scores of North Vietnamese and Viet Cong dead had been left where they had fallen.

The LZ itself was a football shaped encampment about a hundred and fifty yards long and a hundred yards wide, ringed by a dirt berm some four feet high. Along the berm, spaced about fifteen yards apart, were sandbag bunkers with gun slits facing outward, and overhead cover made of wood beams and more sandbags. An old dirt road from the French days ran through the center of the LZ from southeast to northwest, with a movable gate at each end of the football. The LZ took most of its resupply by helicopter, and the landing pad was on the dirt road just outside the southeast gate. Just northwest of the LZ, between the gate and a small river that flowed nearby, was a mass grave where the bodies of the scores of dead NVA and Viet Cong soldiers had been bulldozed to rot.

Outside the dirt berm, the LZ was ringed by rows of barbed wire and razor wire, and protected by hundreds of Claymore mines, trip flares, buried barrels of napalm "foo-gas," and other defensive munitions. Encircling the camp and extending outward for about fifty yards all around was the "kill zone," an area bulldozed clear of all vegetation that provided an open field of fire where the defenders could easily see, and kill, attacking enemy soldiers.

Beyond the kill zone, miles away on the horizon, sat Nui Ba Den, the Black Virgin Mountain. Nui Ba Den rose over 3,000 feet from the surrounding jungle, and was the only visible landmark in the otherwise dead flat terrain that surrounded the LZ. The mountain held deep spiritual meaning for Vietnamese Buddhists, being the source of many of their religion's historic legends. But to the GIs who occupied LZ Sherman it resembled a giant breast rising from the jungle, vaguely reminding them of the soft, warm bodies of the wives and sweethearts they'd left at home. It also provided them entertainment when they could sit on their bunkers or outside their hooches, and watch American B-52s drop their tons of high-explosive bombs on the North Vietnamese who often occupied its slopes.

Inside the perimeter of the base were gun pits where the 105mm artillery pieces were placed, and from which the cannons could support the infantry in the field and fire random interdicting missions onto the NVA infiltration trails. There were also a battalion headquarters bunker, a mess tent, an aid station, an ammo dump, and other facilities. LZ Sherman was a bleak place, bereft of any natural shade, where the air was constantly filled with gritty red dust during the dry season, and the ground was a morass of sucking red mud when it rained. It rained often.

This was the place the infantry, the grunts in the field, looked forward to coming home to after their four or five week patrols. Where there could be music in the daytime, where one could smoke at night behind the cover of a bunker. It was the place where the battalion even offered hot food of a sort, not by any means good food, but better than the constant menu of C-Rations that provided the only nourishment in the field. It was the place where a grunt could get a shower and a haircut and clean jungle fatigues. Where weapons could be thoroughly cleaned and maintained, and ammo and other equipment could be put back into shape before the grunts inevitably headed back to the bush.

Of course it was also the place where the grunts manned the bunkers along the perimeter and stood watch at night while the artillerymen and nearly everyone else on the LZ slept. Where the grunts would be the first line of defense against attacking enemy ground troops. Where the grunts still had to send out listening posts every night, outside the berm, outside the wire, and into the edge of the surrounding jungle, there to sit all night in groups of three, listening in the dark for approaching enemy.

The LZ was where the grunts were never allowed to actually rest in the daytime, but instead were placed on an endless string of work details, to refill sandbags and maintain bunkers, to check and re-wire the Claymore mines and concertina wire, and to burn the barrels of human waste from the latrines that dotted the LZ. Burning shit was an experience no low-ranking enlisted infantryman who survived Vietnam will ever forget. And the awful black smoke and sickening stench of the burning mixture of kerosene and human waste was a smell everyone who has ever been on an LZ will always remember.

In my nightmare, Delta Company had been on the LZ for three or four days, and Third Platoon, my platoon, had been assigned to man bunkers along the north side of the perimeter. The sun was dropping into the west, and the "Lifer Inspection," where the battalion commander and his staff marched around the bunker line and inspected each bunker for proper maintenance, and each soldier for proper dress and gear, was over.

Darkness was approaching, and with it the relative coolness of night. Our listening posts were out, gone to ground at the edge of the surrounding jungle. The first of the night's guards had taken their positions on top of the bunkers, fitted out with helmets, flak jackets, and weapons. And it was time for the rest of us to relax for a short while before sleep, later to be awakened for our turns at guard.

In my nightmare, LT Thorsen, Doc Benedetto, Firedog, and I were playing Hearts by the light of a red lensed flashlight, when we began to hear the "Thunk! Thunk! Thunk!" of mortar rounds being dropped into tubes somewhere out in the jungle. As we scrambled for cover, the rounds began detonating all around us, huge explosions, shrapnel whizzing through the air, peppering everything. Men in the nearby artillery pits were on the ground, screaming, groaning, rolling in agony.

I was unhurt.

The LT shouted, "Get down to 3-1, Mick! They'll need your help! I'll stay with 3-3!"

Quickly I pulled on my flak jacket, got my helmet on, and headed down toward the northeast gate, rifle in hand. Just then more "Thunk! Thunk! Thunk!" from the jungle, coming from all sides. *Where were the listening posts? Did they make it in?* In the nightmare, I never knew.

I never made it to the 3-1 bunker. As I was running, hunkered down, between bunkers a parachute flare popped right above me, and I looked out to see NVA soldiers just outside our wire, sliding Bangalore torpedoes under the entanglement. With a loud "Crack!" the first of the torpedoes exploded, blasting a hole through the barbed wire and sending dirt, rock, and shards of wire in every direction. I looked ahead and behind me, but couldn't see any of our men between me and the nearest bunkers.

I was all alone!

I dived to the berm, took a panicked breath, brought my rifle up and started shooting through the drifting smoke at the NVA sappers. Another Bangalore explosion, this one closer! Then I could see gooks running through the hole in the wire, at least a dozen of them, screaming, wide-eyed, firing their AKs from the hip as they ran. They were coming right at me! I kept firing and some of them fell, but more followed behind. They didn't care how many I killed. There were always more!

Terrified, I kept firing, emptying magazine after magazine into the enemy masses, fumbling full ones into the rifle with shaking hands to replace them. The gooks kept falling, but they were getting closer and closer! Where are the rest of our men? Why didn't someone come and help me?

Then from behind the rest came a big, tall enemy soldier, dressed the same as the others in a baggy khaki uniform, pith helmet, and Ho Chi Minh sandals, but almost a foot taller than them, with a strangely different face. Chinese? Mongolian? We'd heard rumors.

All the enemy were getting closer. Still there was no one to help me. I kept bringing them down with my fire, switching to full-automatic as they closed in, spraying rounds from left to right, right to left, hitting them in the chests, faces, everywhere. The bodies began to pile up.

Then there was only me and the one big gook left.

He was running right at me, firing his AK on full automatic from the hip, dirt spattering up around me. I put my rifle back on semi-auto fire, and with careful aim began pumping round after round right into the center of his chest. But he kept coming! I wasn't even slowing him down! I could see a smile spread across his big, ugly, terrifying face.

I reached down to grab another magazine as he was getting almost close enough to touch, and there were no more! I was out of ammo! I turned the rifle to use it as a club, but the red-hot barrel seared my hands, and I dropped it to the ground. I went for my belt knife, but it was gone! I looked up, and the big NVA soldier was coming over the berm at me, eyes wide and burning red in the light of the parachute flare, the shiny bayonet on the muzzle of his AK pointed at my chest, that hideous grin on his monstrous face!

***

I jolted awake, shaking, my heart pounding, sweat pouring from me, with a loud cry, "AAAAAAAAAAAAAAAAAAAAAAAAAAAAAA!"

I sat up, my heart still pounding. I was in my bedroom, alone in the bed, moonlight streaming through the open patio door blinds. From the apartment above me someone was pounding on my ceiling, shouting, "Quiet down there!"

"Sorry!" I yelled back.

Four hours later, and without another wink of sleep, with the image of that big ugly gook face still clear in my mind, I dragged myself from my bed. I soaked in a hot shower, got dressed, drank a cup of coffee, and headed for another boring day of my job at Langton Manufacturing.

It would be days before I felt comfortable going to sleep again.

23

1970s, Watertown, New Jersey
Angie Blake

When Little Tony was two years old, Angie began to leave him with her mother during the daytime to take a job at a local bank. But she came home and had lunch with him every day and rushed home right after work at night to be with him, to feed him, and play with him, and read him stories until he fell asleep. He was a very bright little boy, and he learned things quickly. And he reminded her in almost every way of Tony, almost as if he *was* Tony.

Many people in town knew the story of Tony's death and Angie's loss, and when she started work at the bank the others there were especially careful to treat her with kindness. She began as a bookkeeper, working in the back office. But a teller's job came open with higher pay, and she applied for that. At first it was difficult to force herself to greet each customer cheerfully. But gradually she found that the contact with so many people helped distract her from her constant memories of Tony and her constant sadness at his death. After a while some of the sadness truly left her, and from time to time Angie even smiled.

She developed close friendships with several of the other women who worked in the bank and with one of the vice-presidents, a man a few years older than her, named Loren Blake. Loren was recently divorced from a woman he had loved since childhood, and he suffered every day as he heard stories of her making the rounds of the local bars with her girlfriends and becoming involved in casual relationships with several different men. It was, after all, a small town.

After Angie had worked at the bank for more than a year, Loren asked her if he could meet her somewhere for coffee. So she met him on a Saturday morning, a day when Little Tony's grandparents had taken him to the park, and they sat and talked for almost three hours. He asked her straightforwardly to tell him about Tony, and she did, leaving out the part about her last letter, of course. Then she asked him to tell her about his ex-wife, and he did, speaking kindly as he described what he'd been hearing about her recent adventures around town. Angie decided that she liked Loren very much, and it was clear that he liked her, too.

On their next date, Angie took Little Tony along, and they went to a park across town that they hadn't visited before. Little Tony and Loren took to each other right away, and Loren had the boy giggling in delight as he chased him through the park, swung him high in the air, and pushed him on the little merry-go-round. They instantly became buddies, and after that Little Tony went along on most of Loren's and Angie's dates.

Three months later, Loren asked Angie for a date with just the two of them so he could take her to "a grown-up dinner not involving hot dogs, with maybe even some wine." She laughed at his invitation and accepted. They went to a French restaurant in a nearby town and spent two hours over wine, dinner, and dessert. Loren drove Angie home to her parents' house and in the car, parked outside at the curb, in almost the exact spot where Tony had first kissed her, Loren proposed.

"Angie, I know we haven't known each other all that long, but I feel like I've known you forever. I know we haven't had a lot of grown-up dates, and there really hasn't been much in the way of romance between us, at least up until tonight. But I love you, Angie, and I love Little Tony like he was my own son. Angie, will you marry me?"

From his silence on the way home Angie had guessed this was coming, and she'd spent the whole drive back thinking about her response. It had been more than three years since Tony's death, and while she still loved him and would always love him, she realized that she did love Loren, too. And she knew Little Tony needed a dad, and that he and Loren seemed like the best of friends.

"I had a feeling you might ask me this, Loren. And I've been thinking about it a lot on the drive back. As long as you understand how much I loved Tony, and that I'm not completely healed over his loss, and that maybe I never will be. If you can accept that, I do love you, and my answer is 'yes'." She smiled at him, and he kissed her fully and deeply for the first time, and after an initial hesitation, she responded in the same way.

"I am so HAPPY!" he declared. And he took out a small red box and opened it to reveal a beautiful engagement ring.

Angie had still been wearing Tony's wedding band on the ring finger of her left hand, feeling, and believing, that she'd always be married to him. Quietly, she slipped it off and put it on the third finger of her right hand. She held it up to Loren. "Is this OK?" she asked.

"Sure," he said. "I know you'll always love Tony. I have no need or intention to try to change that. In time, I hope you'll come to love me as much, but he was your first love. He was your true love. I know that."

Angie smiled. And then she held out her left hand so Loren could put the engagement ring on. And that time she kissed him.

Tony's parents accepted the news of Angie's engagement with genuine happiness for Angie and Little Tony, and they accepted Loren almost as their own son. Angie's parents were delighted that she would have such a good man for a husband, and that Little Tony would have such a good buddy for a step-dad.

Angie and Loren were married in a quiet ceremony a month after he proposed, with only Little Tony, Angie's parents, Tony's parents and brother, and Loren's parents attending. It was the week before Christmas, 1972, and Little Tony had just turned three.

They waited until their wedding night to make love for the first time. Angie was nervous about it beforehand, wondering whether she'd even be able to go through with it, this most personal of acts between man and woman that she had always thought she would only share with Tony. But Loren was very patient, very gentle, and very loving, believing he fully understood what she was feeling. He pretended not to see the tears in her eyes after he rubbed her back and caressed her for nearly an hour, when she turned to him and held him close and began to kiss him, gently at first, and then more passionately. He made love to her, very slowly and tenderly, showing concern only for her and what she was feeling, and seemingly none at all for himself. After what seemed like hours of his attention to her body and her face, he slipped gently inside her, and Angie came almost immediately, in a series of rolling waves. Loren came with her. She lay back, blissful, and they held each other through the rest of the night.

Early in January 1973, the new family went on a honeymoon trip to Jamaica where they had a full week on the beach. They came home tired, suntanned, and very happy. After two more days off to rest up, Loren and Angie went back to work at the bank, where a noisy celebration greeted the happy couple. A few weeks later they bought a house, conveniently near all three sets of Little Tony's grandparents, and moved into it together.

As time passed, Angie continued to heal. A little over a year after her marriage to Loren, when Little Tony was four, Angie became the mother of a second child, a beautiful little girl who they named Cynthia. Cindy was blonde, like Loren, and had his blue eyes.

One day not long after Cindy's birth, Angie found herself nursing her in the bedroom while listening to Loren and Little Tony laughing with each other while playing Legos in the next room. Angie was suddenly overcome with the feeling that this was a real family, *her* family, and more importantly, *Little Tony's* family. While she still loved Tony and missed him, she realized that this was her life now, and Little Tony's, and a good life. She wanted to do everything she could to make sure it worked as a family should.

That night, while she and Loren were snuggled up in bed, she told Loren that she'd like him to adopt Little Tony, and give him Loren's last name. There were tears in Loren's eyes as he told her that would make him very happy. They talked to Little Tony about it the next morning, in the simplest of terms. And with mock seriousness, but without much thought, he readily agreed. After they'd talked to all the grandparents about it and received their blessings, Angie and Loren started the legal work. Within three months, Little Tony was no longer Anthony Giles, Jr. He became simply Tony Blake.

Little Tony was six years old when he asked his mother for the first time why he had three sets of grandparents when most kids had only two. So she and Loren sat down with the boy, and Angie explained about Tony's birth father, and how he'd died in the war a long time ago, and that Loren was his daddy now. The boy took the news solemnly, but in stride, and remained as loving as ever to Loren. But he also asked about his birth father, and wanted to know more about him. So Angie opened a box she kept in her closet, and took out photos of her and Tony when they were in high school, of the homecoming parade and the prom, their wedding pictures, photos of Tony in his football uniform, and in his Army uniform, and some of him with his buddies in

Vietnam. She also brought out a frame with Tony's medals and patch-es, and the cigarette lighter she had given him.

It was very difficult for her, and she found herself crying through it. But Little Tony seemed to understand. He showed a particular interest in the Army photos, the medals, and the pictures from Vietnam, and he asked his mother if she would put them up in his room. Angie looked at Loren, who said only, "Of course." And the photos were framed and put up on the boy's wall.

By age seven, Little Tony was already a good athlete, playing soccer and Tee-ball, the teams usually coached by Loren. And he was a good student, always seeming to take his studies seriously, always doing his best. In fact, though he could play with his parents and grandparents and giggle and laugh when they tried to entertain him, Little Tony was for the most part a serious little boy, as though his spirit, his soul, was that of a much older, wiser person.

By then almost no one called him "Little Tony" anymore, even his Grandma and Grandpa Giles. But one day when he was playing on some swings at the park with them, and lying back in the swing so his head nearly touched the ground as he swung higher and higher, his grandmother shouted out "Little Tony!" to gain his attention and get him to stop being "dangerous." He calmly brought the swing to a stop, jumped out, walked over to his grandmother, and said, "Grandma, could you just call me 'Tony' instead of 'Little Tony'? It's embarrassing."

Of course his grandparents cracked up at the seriousness with which he delivered his request, using the big word "embarrassing." But when he stared at them, still serious, they stopped laughing and his grandmother said, "Of course. From now on you are 'Tony'!" And the Giles spread the word among his other family members, and no one called him "Little Tony" after that. That is, no one except his little sister, Cindy, when she was teasing him.

Angie lived on, for the most part very happy with Loren and her children and her new life. But sometimes, just sometimes, she found herself caught up by the pictures on her son's wall or some other reminder, and the empty place in her soul would re-open, and she would be consumed by sadness at Tony's death. When that happened she would often again open the letter she'd received from Lieutenant Thorsen after Tony had been killed, talking about what a good man he had been, what a good soldier and a good friend, and how much he had loved her. She would wonder again if Tony had received her last letter before he died, whether he'd died believing she no longer loved him. She would wonder about his friends, the men who had been with him when he was killed, where they were, whether she could somehow find them, so she could finally know, one way or the other, about the letter.

But then she would bury that thought, knowing that she could never bear to talk about that letter...with anyone.

24

1970s
Kansas City
Mick Delaney

By the time of my divorce from Katie, I had pretty much quit caring about anything. I showed up for work every day and did a respectable job out of some sense of personal pride, I suppose, and because I knew there was no one else in the world who could or would take care of me. But I ate just enough to stay alive, did my laundry when I ran out of things to wear, dated when I was horny, went to bed drunk nearly every night, and barely stayed alive.

I continued to think of taking my own life, just so I wouldn't have to endure those memories, those fears, those nightmares, that same haunted face in the mirror every morning, that sense of nothingness in my life. But something kept me from it. There was a little spark somewhere that kept me going.

About four years after Katie and I divorced I met another good woman, another soul as sad and tormented as I was with her own story of love and abuse and loss. Her name was Amanda, and she was a beautiful, slender, blonde girl. Somewhere in that relationship I found some remnant of myself that was still alive, and I began to settle down.

We were married in 1977, not only out of love, but out of hope of helping each other out of our sadness, I think. The next thing we knew, a child was born. He was a little boy who we named Hunter, the most beautiful child I had ever seen. Then two years later his little brother came along, and we named him Eric. They were the two most beautiful children, indeed the two most beautiful *anything,* I had ever seen. And they, and their mother, changed my life.

I had my own family to truly care about, people I loved dearly and who I felt responsible for, who were more important to me than my own issues and bad dreams. More important to me than my thirty-something, wrecked-up, "I-used-to-be-a-professional-killer-for-the-United-States-government" self. I became personally unimportant in the grander scheme of things compared to my new wife and my sons. So I quit thinking so much about the war, even quit thinking so much about my buddies, who had all long since come home, or died, anyway. I quit drinking. I quit smoking. And I turned my life around.

Holding down my regular job in the daytime and sitting up many nights rocking the babies while Amanda tried to catch some sleep between breast-feedings, I started a computer programming business of my own, on the side. I worked evenings after the boys were in bed and sometimes on weekends. Starting from nothing in my mid-thirties, with a pretty good head for the technology and a belief in treating people fairly, I grew the business quickly. Only a few years into it I quit my day job, so I could work at that business full time during the daytime and spend my evenings and weekends with my family.

I made it a point to be home for dinner every night, unless I had to travel or meet in the evening on business, which was seldom. I took most weekends off, and we took nice vacations every year. I made it a point to be at all the school activities, even acted as a "room mother" a few times. I was active in the boys' Cub Scout Troop, Pinewood Derby races, and pretty much every activity. I helped them with their homework. I coached their soccer and baseball teams, and was there for every game. When they were old enough, I bought them each a Mustang, and we had great fun together tinkering with the fast little cars, building them up for drag racing on the weekends.

I seemed to want desperately to learn from the poor example my own parents had set for my sister and me. I wanted to be the best father I could be.

At the same time, we had to eat, and I really enjoyed my work. Luckily, Delaney Enterprises, Inc., flourished. I turned out to be pretty good at following the technology trends, and by the time my sons were grown, the company had expanded to offices in four cities, and we had become…comfortable.

Sadly, though, the love between Amanda and me didn't survive the twenty-two years of our marriage. After our younger son, Eric, moved away to college, Amanda and I found ourselves alone in our big house, for the first time truly feeling the emptiness of our now-empty nest, and of our relationship.

We agreed to separate. Amanda wanted to keep our house, which we had built together, and I thought that was the right thing for both her and our sons. So I moved out into an apartment, and then later into a house of my own. A few months later we were amicably divorced, still friends, still a couple who shared parenthood of our sons.

Later, as years passed, I realized that sometimes people don't come together in marriage necessarily because they are to be the great loves of each other's lives. Sometimes they come together just to help each other past difficult times. And sometimes they come together simply to bring amazing children, like our two sons, into the world. And to raise them to be the wonderful adults they have become.

After the separation I spent more time at work, but I still had more free time, and I found my mind wandering more often back to the war. The nightmares that had been rare during the years of my second marriage began to re-emerge. I tried to bury myself even more deeply into my work, but even that began to lose interest for me. When I wasn't working, trying to spend time with my sons, or going on an occasional date, I would find myself again very, very, alone.

And thoughts of ending my life, which I'd kept well-buried for over twenty years, began to creep back into my mind.

During those dark days, when I became buried in memories of the war, I would sometimes take out the small box of artifacts I'd kept from back then; my Combat Infantryman's badge, the Purple Heart I'd received for my wounds, other medals and badges, a few photos of my buddies and me... and a separate envelope that held the photo of Tony Giles' wife Angie, and the last two letters she'd written him. I would again remember Tony's death, every moment of that morning still vivid in my mind. I would re-read those letters and look at Angie's picture, and wonder again how she could have done what she did. Even after all those years had gone by, my hatred for the bitch who I believed was largely responsible for my good friend's death would momentarily consume me, and I'd always wind up stuffing everything back into the box, and shoving it back into the closet where I kept it hidden from the world.

25

May 1988
Watertown, New Jersey
Tony Blake

Tony Blake grew up a serious boy and a bit of an anomaly, both a superb athlete and an excellent student. In high school he lettered in basketball, baseball, and football, where he was the starting quarterback, like his birth father. He seemed to have no difficulty with any of the studies and easily made National Honor Society with straight A grades. He had many friends among both the boys and the girls, but unlike most of his classmates, Tony didn't date much in high school, seeming not to notice when one of his girl buddies showed more interest than just friendship. He spent most of the time during his high school years working part time at a grocery store, studying, and playing sports.

At graduation in the spring of 1988, Tony delivered the valedictorian address. He wouldn't share its content with anyone before graduation day, when he delivered the address with great seriousness and unnatural polish and composure for a young man his age.

After acknowledging the faculty and staff of Watertown High and the family and friends of the graduates, he congratulated his classmates on their graduation and thanked them for their friendship and the support they'd given the school's athletic teams. He spoke of the many wonderful experiences they'd enjoyed together during the past four years, and of the bright future that lay before them in a prospering America and a world "largely at peace." And he wished them well in their future endeavors, in college or a trade, in their marriages, and in raising their families.

Then he paused, and his gaze swept over the audience, and he began to speak of other things.

"America's last war, the Vietnam war, ended officially for the United States in 1973, which is also the time that America ended the draft for military service. Since then, the world has changed enormously.

"In 1979, radical elements in Iran took over the American Embassy in Tehran and held fifty-two American citizens hostage for four hundred and forty-four days before releasing them in January, 1981. During that time America, as you know, launched a rescue mission that unfortunately turned out a disaster. So as a nation we seemed impotent, seemed to have no recourse except to sit and wait until the hostages were voluntarily freed.

"1979 was also the year the Chinese Communist Party announced a direction toward more liberalization of the government and a more western, capitalistic economic model. But we've seen the Chinese government struggle with that change and with the demands of its people for individual freedoms. And we've also seen China continue a very rapid expansion of its military in the years since, with continued aggression in Tibet, toward the Nationalist Chinese in Formosa, and toward some Philippine territories in the South China Sea.

"1979 was also the year the Soviet Union invaded Afghanistan, where they have been fighting ever since. In 1984, President Gorbachev announced a new direction for the U.S.S.R. toward Glasnost, or 'Openness,' in the Soviet government, and 'Perestroika,' restructuring toward more capitalistic and democratic ways. But the wall in Berlin is still standing, and much of Europe and Asia still lives under Soviet rule.

"In 1983, a radical militia element bombed the United States Marines' barracks in Beirut, Lebanon, and killed 241 American servicemen.

"Then coincidentally, just two days later, America invaded the island of Grenada. We went there to rescue American students and help the Coalition of Caribbean Nations restore the properly elected government of that island nation to power.

"There are many hot spots around the world this very minute, any of which could erupt into a serious, immediate threat to our futures and our freedoms, and the futures and freedoms of our children and their children. I speak of North Korea, Iran, Iraq, Afghanistan, India, Pakistan, Kashmir, Formosa, and many more."

He paused again and surveyed the crowd. People were looking at him with questioning expressions, wondering why he had decided to take his speech in this direction, to make it such a downer. Dr. Wilkins, the school principal, was beginning to consider the need to cut him short, and was trying to think of a way to do that graciously. Wilkins was wishing he'd made Tony show him that speech before he presented it, but Tony was such a good kid, Wilkins never suspected he'd take this direction.

Tony went on. "Many of you know that my dad, Loren Blake, who I love enormously, isn't my birth father. My birth father was a man named Anthony Giles. Anthony Giles...they called him 'Tony,' too, died in Vietnam in 1969, killed from ambush by the North Vietnamese while he was walking point through the jungle for an American rifle company.

"Tony Giles was drafted into the Army to serve his country, and he went and did his job, and he was killed. Whether anyone believes that was a 'proper' war or not, my birth father died protecting America's freedoms, my freedoms and yours, from what our government considered a very serious threat from the Communist nations in the world.

"One of my three grandfathers, Tony's dad Angelo Giles, fought for America's freedoms, too, in the Second World War. He served with General Patton in Europe, and helped defeat the Nazis after their murder of more than six million Jewish people and several million others, and their quest for world domination. He was fortunate to come home from that war with only minor physical wounds, and he thought war was behind him. But then only a few years later, he lost his son, my father, to the war in Vietnam."

Tony raised his voice slightly to regain everyone's focus. "I'm sorry to make this such a sober talk on such a happy and glorious day, but please bear with me, as I do have a point to make. Today there are hundreds of thousands, maybe millions, of students like us, graduating from their high schools all across America, and looking forward to college and wonderful, happy, prosperous lives in this land of the free.

"But in order for most of those graduates to go off to college and get into business or a profession, or go into a trade, and get married and have a family, and live the American dream... in order for most of us to do that, a few of us, just a small few, have to take a different course with our lives. A few of us must prepare to continue to defend America's freedoms from those in the world who would take them away. Those few must defend the rest of us from all those threats I mentioned, just as my father and my grandfather and a great many of you in this audience today have done."

He paused again. "It is my honor to announce to you, as I wish you all well in your long, wonderful lives of the American dream, that I have chosen to become one of those few. I am honored to announce that I have been accepted as an officer candidate at the United States Military Academy at West Point, as a member of the class of 1992."

Then there was silence. Tony stood tall and straight, smiling at the crowd, waiting for…something…applause maybe?… he wasn't sure what. It took the crowd a while, longer than he expected, to absorb what he had said about his birth father and his grandfather and his own decision to join the military. Many minds had wandered away from the content of his talk, put off by the discussion of all the uncertainty in the world, on this happy day. And it took them some time to reflect on his last words and realize that Tony's valedictorian address was over, and to absorb what he had announced.

Everyone knew Tony as an excellent athlete, an outstanding student, and a "nice kid." Few of the parents remembered his birth father or the circumstances of his death, and only his closest friends from among his classmates knew of him. And no one outside his immediate family knew of his decision to go to West Point and on to a career in the military. So at first, people were overwhelmed by Tony's message.

But then Dr. Wilkins, the master of ceremonies, stood up from his chair on the stage and began to clap his hands as loudly as he could, greatly relieved that Tony had managed to finish the talk in a rather uplifting way that put some sense to it. Dr. Wilkins was relieved that he wouldn't seem an idiot for not reading Tony's speech beforehand, and so his applause was very enthusiastic and genuine. And then the rest of the people on stage stood and began to applaud, and the next thing he knew Tony was looking out at the entire audience, on their feet, giving him a huge standing ovation. He smiled and shook Dr. Wilkins' hand and the hands of the others on the stage, and then he walked down the steps and over to join his parents and grandparents standing in the front row of the audience, applauding.

Angie stood between Loren and Angelo, and she applauded like everyone else, although perhaps not as energetically as some. But her heart was cold. She looked over at Angelo, and saw that he was applauding, but also wasn't smiling. He looked back at her, and the two of them exchanged wan smiles of mutual understanding, and some sadness.

When Angie had first heard of Tony's application for West Point, she had felt a heavy weight in her heart. She had thought she was through with the military, with war, and with waiting for someone she loved to come home. She had tried for a little while, as positively as she could, to convince the boy to take a different direction with his life. But she had stopped short of saying the words, "I don't think I could take it if you were ever to go to war." She loved Tony unconditionally and wanted him to do as he wished with his life. She wanted, more than anything, for him to be happy.

But as he spoke those words to the graduation audience that warm May afternoon, that cold chill once again ran up her spine. Angie was afraid for her son and realized that she now faced the uncertain future, maybe for the rest of her life, as the mother of a career Army officer.

26

Early 1990s

Tony excelled at West Point, with an exceptional academic record and strong athletic performance in both track and football. In football, he was backup quarterback for the varsity team and had the opportunity to play, always very successfully, in a number of important games. He graduated sixth in his class in 1992, and all his family made the trip up from New Jersey to attend. Angie, at forty-two, was still a very beautiful woman, though her face was beginning to show age from all the hardship in her life. Loren, as always, was by her side, a loving and devoted husband. Tony's sister Cindy also made the trip. She had graduated with honors from high school that same year, and was about to enter her freshman year at Rutgers with a full academic scholarship.

As Tony marched through with the other graduates in the cadet graduation parade, Angie felt pride in his accomplishments, but heaviness in her heart at what might lie ahead. It was May 1992, only months after the end of Operation Desert Storm, the war to liberate Kuwait from the Iraqis, and the Middle East remained in a state of unrest. Angie worried for her son's safety in a world that seemed full of threats, and now that Tony was graduating, she was constantly aware that he would soon be on active duty as an Army officer.

With Tony's excellent class standing at West Point he was given his choice of branches and specialties in the military. He chose the Army and the Infantry to follow in the footsteps of his father and his grandfather. He had already completed Army Jump School while still at West Point, and had proudly worn his silver Paratrooper wings on his cadet uniform. Along with the other cadets he had also completed the first segment of the Army's Basic Officer Leadership Course. So after graduation and a short leave at home, he left for Ft. Benning, Georgia, to attend the "B" segment of the Basic Officer Course, an Infantry Officer's school. Immediately after graduating from that course he passed the Ranger Selection process, and was admitted to Ranger School.

Ranger School began at Ft. Benning, then went on to the Mountain Training phase in the remote mountains of northern Georgia, and finally on to the third and final phase, in the swamps of Florida. It was grueling training all the way through, and Tony and the other candidates were required to function on short rations, with little or sometimes no sleep, all the while expected to demonstrate strong leadership skills and an ability to work well with other candidates in the harshest of environmental conditions. When he graduated, Tony had learned leadership, patrolling, and small unit tactical skills to a level he'd never imagined, had lost ten pounds from his already lean body, and felt like he was ready for anything. He was extremely proud of the Ranger tab he was authorized to wear at the top of the left sleeve of his uniforms.

As one of the top graduates of the school, Tony received orders to join Company B, 3rd Ranger Battalion, 75th Ranger Regiment, one of the Army's most elite units, as a platoon leader.

In August 1993, Tony landed in Mogadishu, Somalia, with Task Force Ranger, a special unit made up of Ranger, Delta Force, and other Army, Navy, and Air Force units. The task force was part of an international peacekeeping mission that included mechanized infantry units from Pakistan and Malaysia. Together they were assigned to provide security for the UN humanitarian mission that was attempting to deliver food, drinking water, and other supplies to the thousands of Somali refugees who had been displaced during the nation's civil war. Warlord and self-proclaimed Prime Minister Mohamed Farah Aidid and his Habr Gidr clan had been brutalizing, raping, and murdering the Somali refugees and interfering with distribution of the supplies, sometimes even stealing them at gunpoint from the UN vehicles for Aidid's own use.

Tony's first combat leadership experience came when he led his platoon on a mission to rescue a United Nations patrol that had been ambushed by Aidid's militia. He and his men were massively frustrated when they were only able to reach the scene of the ambush in time to find all twenty-three of the Pakistani UN troops dead and butchered. Tony thought he would never forget the sight of the mutilated bodies. Coming from his peaceful life as a kid growing up in civilized America, it was very hard for him to understand or accept this kind of savagery.

Only days later, Tony's platoon was deployed in Humvees to support other Rangers who had fast-roped from helicopters into the heart of Mogadishu, on a mission to capture two of Aidid's top lieutenants. The two clan leaders were successfully captured. But the operation turned into a fiasco when two Army Blackhawk helicopters were shot down, and masses of armed militia and Somali civilians began to surround and fire on the Rangers as they separated into smaller units to try to rescue the helicopter crews. Tony's platoon was able to fight its way out with the two captured clan leaders and some of the Rangers who had fast-roped in. But he and his men were unprotected from the barrage of enemy fire in the un-armored Humvees, and he lost two men killed and six wounded during the battle.

Some of the Rangers were unable to make it to safety, and spent the night cut off in small groups, fighting off continual attacks by Aidid's militia and other armed Somalis. Two Delta Force snipers who had volunteered to be dropped into one of the helicopter crash sites to protect the air crew were killed when they ran out of ammunition, and the surviving pilot they were defending was captured by the Aidid militia.

Early the following morning the Task Force commander assembled a rescue convoy, made up of Pakistani tanks and Malaysian armored personnel carriers, with soldiers from the Tenth Mountain Division as the primary American fighting force. With some recent knowledge of the Mogadishu streets and a sense of responsibility to help find the trapped Rangers, Tony volunteered to go along on the mission. But the rescue effort was another near debacle, since the Americans, Pakistanis, and Malaysians did not speak a common language, and there were no interpreters available. Nevertheless, they reached one helicopter crash site and rescued the air crew, and managed to bring almost all of the Rangers, even the dead, out of Mogadishu.

Arriving back at the American compound after the rescue mission, Tony watched in shock and anger on the little black and white television that had been set up in his company's ready tent, as German broadcasting repeatedly showed video footage of the body of a dead American Ranger being dragged through the streets of Mogadishu by Aidid's followers. As Tony watched the video in horror, he couldn't help but think of the man's parents, perhaps his wife and children, watching on TV as his shirtless body, tied to a rope, was pulled through the dirt streets of Mogadishu while thousands of the locals danced around it, fired their weapons into the air, and screamed their approval. It filled him with rage.

But there was to be no outlet for Tony's rage, and no revenge for the fallen Rangers. Tony was withdrawn from Somalia with other American forces in January 1994.

In all, sixteen Rangers and two helicopter pilots were killed in what became known as "The First Battle of Mogadishu." And several dozen more men were wounded in what was deemed the bloodiest battle fought by American forces since the Vietnam War. The only good news came a few days after the fight ended, when the captured American pilot was released to the International Red Cross and sent home.

Tony's perspective on his chosen career was never quite the same after Mogadishu. He always believed that President Clinton and Secretary of Defense Aspin had been wrong in committing soldiers to such a peacekeeping mission if they had no workable battle plan for the eventuality that the soldiers might have to fight, and they had no apparent stomach to finish the fight that did come. Tony particularly blamed Aspin for refusing his Task Force commander's repeated requests for tanks and other armored vehicles at the outset of the mission, leaving the Rangers and the other soldiers to fight either on foot or from un-armored Humvees against throngs of enemy militia armed with automatic weapons, RPGs, and other heavy weaponry.

Nevertheless, Tony was motivated more than ever to be "one of the few" who stood the line between America and those who would attack her. His performance in Mogadishu and his other assignments had been considered excellent, and late in 1995 he was promoted to Captain. With that rank, Tony became eligible to enter the selection process for the Army's Special Forces, the famous Green Berets. He successfully passed Selection, and began Special Forces training at Ft. Bragg, North Carolina, early in 1996.

From Ft. Bragg it wasn't too far up to Tony's home in New Jersey. And during breaks in his training Tony visited his parents and his grandparents as often as he could, knowing he would spend long stretches of time deployed overseas after his initial training was completed. On one of these trips in 1996, Angie introduced Tony to the daughter of a neighbor who had recently moved to Watertown, a beautiful young woman named Melissa Fenn, who was home for the summer from her teaching job at Rutgers. Melissa was an associate professor of American history, a happy, straightforward beauty with dark hair and eyes, just like Tony's mother. He fell for her almost instantly, and she for him, and, after a whirlwind courtship over that summer, they were married early in the fall.

Somehow, he never knew exactly how, he had convinced Melissa that she ought to become the wife of an Army officer, with the attendant long periods of his absence on one potentially hazardous mission after another. But the mid-nineties were a time of relative peace, and she seemed willing to make those sacrifices in exchange for a life with him when he was stateside. Besides, she had her teaching career, which she loved, and she imagined that he would retire from the Army after twenty years, a time only sixteen years away.

Melissa was pregnant with their first child before Tony left for his first permanent duty assignment in January 1997. He would be an Operational Detachment—Alpha (ODA) or "A Team" Leader with the 1st Battalion, 10th Special Forces Group, based in Stuttgart, Germany. He and Melissa had decided that she would continue living at home in New Jersey where she could keep her job at Rutgers and be near both their families, and that he would apply for leave when the baby was due to be born. But they were both prepared for long periods of separation.

The child was born in July, a little boy who they named Angelo after Tony's grandfather. He was a beautiful, perfect baby with dark hair and eyes like his mom and dad. Tony cherished every moment of the three weeks he was able to be home with Melissa and Angelo. But then his leave was over, and he had to return to Stuttgart alone.

27

Late 1990s

Tony served with distinction as a member of the NATO force during the second Kosovo war in April and May 1999, when he and a small team night-parachuted into Yugoslavia to pinpoint military targets for laser-guided bomb drops by American and other NATO aircraft. President Clinton regained some of Tony's respect for his conduct of that war and his leadership in saving hundreds of thousands of Muslim minority lives from "ethnic cleansing."

Tony and Melissa's second child, a beautiful little girl they named Lisa, was born while Tony was completely cut off from communications with his home, operating out of a safe house in Yugoslavia. By the time he was able to get home for a two-week leave, Lisa was almost three months old. The time with Melissa, Angelo, and Lisa was precious to him, and when he left again for Stuttgart, he did so with a growing sense that he was missing out on a critical part of his live.

Still, he soldiered on.

Later in 1999 Tony's excellent record as a Ranger and Special Forces A Team leader earned him a promotion to the rank of Major. He was reassigned from the 10th Special Forces Group, first to Ft. Leavenworth, Kansas, where he completed the Army's Intermediate Level

Officer Education program, and simultaneously earned his Master's Degree from Kansas State University. Then he went on to his next permanent duty assignment, as a company commander with the 1st Battalion, 5th Special Forces Group, headquartered in Ft. Campbell, Kentucky. The 5th Group was responsible for operations in the Middle East and Central Asia, some of the world's hottest hot spots. And Tony, as a company commander, held leadership responsibility for six A Teams.

Tony was delighted with the promotion and his next assignments for many reasons, not the least of which was his relocation to the U.S. mainland, much, much closer to home. Even though there were frequent overseas assignments with the 5th Special Forces Group, Tony was still able to spend more time at home with Melissa and his growing toddlers.

After the Al-Qaeda attacks on the World Trade Center and the Pentagon on September 11, 2001, Tony, together with every man in his company, volunteered for immediate deployment to anywhere in the world they might be needed, to hunt down Osama bin Laden and the rest of his killers. His company became part of Task Force Dagger, with responsibility for attacking and driving the Taliban, who had given Bin Ladin refuge, from northern Afghanistan. After a very short period of planning, Tony and his teams, along with other Special Forces and a massive military support organization, moved their headquarters to Karshi-Khandabad Air Base (known as K2) in Uzbekistan, near the northern border of Afghanistan. From there the A-Teams were deployed by helicopter over dangerous mountain passes to northern Afghanistan, to work with CIA operatives and the fighters of the Afghan Northern Alliance, in attacking Osama Bin Ladin's Al-Quaeda and the massive Taliban war machine that gave it refuge.

The performance of the Special Forces teams at the beginning of Operation Enduring Freedom was spectacular, far exceeding the highest hopes of President Bush and even the military high command. Small teams, often riding horseback with their Northern Alliance allies, were able to identify and laser-mark hundreds of Taliban targets for destruction by American and coalition air power, which was massive. The teams simultaneously trained, equipped, and led the Northern Alliance fighters in ground attacks on vastly larger Taliban forces, and again supported by overwhelming coalition air power, drove the Taliban out of Mazar-e Sharif, Bagram, and ultimately Kabul, the nation's capital. They accomplished this just 49 days after the Al Quaeda attack on the World Trade Center, and only 25 days after the first "boots on the ground" in Afghanistan. Seldom in history had such a small ground force achieved such an incredible victory over such a numerically superior adversary.

But due to the need for secrecy about the particulars of special operations capabilities, few people in America heard about these great successes at the time. Instead they heard later that after months of coalition operations in Afghanistan, Osama Bin Ladin and much of the Al-Quaeda organization had somehow escaped the country.

Tony and his company were ordered home nearly eight months later, back to Ft. Campbell to rest, re-equip, and prepare for their next missions. It so happened that they were there during the summer of 2002, and Melissa was able to bring Angelo, now five, and Lisa, now three, to Kentucky for almost three months that they spent together as a family. Tony was enormously happy.

Tony's company was relocated to Kuwait later in 2002, and from there the A-Teams deployed on a series of joint missions with CIA operatives, moving into locations all over Iraq to search for nuclear and chemical components, or other evidence of Weapons of Mass Destruction. They ran many similar missions over the following months, none of them producing any evidence of WMDs.

Still, Tony watched as more American forces arrived in Kuwait and

Saudi Arabia, gearing up for the invasion of Iraq. "Why," he wondered aloud to some of his buddies as they drank watered-down beer in a Kuwaiti bar, "are we starting this war when neither we nor anyone else has found any hard evidence of these Weapons of Mass Destruction we keep hearing about?"

No one there had an answer. In March 2003, President Bush ordered the invasion of Iraq, and Tony, being a soldier, followed orders. He and his men organized missions, and his teams were inserted into areas all over western Iraq, specifically to find any ballistic missile sites from which Iraq could attack America's allies, especially Israel. These missions were again very successful, and not a single Scud missile was fired from Iraq toward any other country during the invasion. After American forces took Baghdad but were unable to capture Saddam Hussein, Tony's unit was tasked to help hunt him down. Several months passed with no success by his men or anyone else in finding Saddam.

Angie and Melissa waited at home for Tony to return from his long deployment. Angie often wondered how Melissa endured these long absences, especially during Tony's active participation in the Iraq war. She herself worried about her son as much as she had worried about his father. The worry caused her to remember often the letter she'd written to Tony's father only days before his death. And with that memory came the guilt. The guilt that never really went away.

Tony came home on leave for nearly three weeks at the end of 2003, and he cherished every minute of his time there. Angelo and Lisa adored their father and followed him around everywhere he went. And Tony deeply loved them. At the same time, his love for Melissa continued to grow and deepen. He recognized that he was an entirely different man when he was home with his family, a kinder, gentler man who had enormous love to give, and who loved being adored by his wife and kids. He had enjoyed his career for the first few years, but ten-plus years of war in six different countries had darkened his perspective, and he began to genuinely look forward to his "twenty" when he could retire with a decent pension and look for work close to home.

28

I felt out of place. Not just a little out of place, completely out of place. Like a Martian at a movie premiere out of place. And I couldn't quite shake it.

I was dressed nicely enough. Nice light gray summer weight suit that had been custom made for my still "lanky" 6'2" frame. White Brooks Brothers shirt, reasonably subdued Jerry Garcia tie. Shoes were shined. Hair was short, combed. No facial hair, sideburns trimmed. I kept myself in good shape, stood up straight, nothing to be embarrassed about there. I even wore a tiny replica of a Combat Infantryman's Badge on my left lapel to let these lifers know that I had also served. I'd thought about wearing the ribbon from my Purple Heart and maybe the one from my Vietnam Campaign Medal, just to make sure they knew I was for real, and what war I was in. But I'd decided that would be overkill.

And as I arrived and began to look around, I realized that even with all that, it would still have been pretty *under*whelming compared to all the well-decorated uniforms in that room.

I was standing in the officers' dining room in the I-didn't-know-which-corner of the crazy labyrinthine second floor of the Pentagon building in Arlington, Virginia. I was jammed up against a sidewall by a couple hundred Army officers and a scattering of enlisted men and women, who had come together to honor my old platoon leader and now close friend, Ed Thorsen, now Colonel Ed Thorsen, on the occasion of his retirement from the United States Army.

And as far as I could tell, aside from Ed's father who was retired military and wore a business suit, and Ed's wife and mother and some other women in the family, absolutely everyone else in the room was wearing a uniform. Ed's son Dave was there, a West Point cadet, and he was wearing a Cadet Captain's uniform. Hell, even Dave's *girlfriend* was there, and *she* was a West Point cadet, and even *she* was wearing a uniform.

For a guy who'd done his four years in the Army way back in the sixties and had sworn when he got out that he would never again even own any green clothing, my strong sense of feeling out of place was almost enough to bring on a bout of paranoia. Except that with a little more age, two wonderful grown sons, a lot of success with Delaney Enterprises, and the attendant prosperity that had brought, I didn't get paranoid about much of anything by then.

But I had to admit, this room full of lifers came closer to intimidating me than anything else I'd experienced recently. And how in the world did I wind up standing next to a four-star general who was built like a fire plug and had the voice of Winston Churchill? *This guy,* I thought to myself, *has got four stars on each shoulder, three sets of braid, a ton of ribbons, including a Distinguished Service Cross and three Silver Stars, master Jump wings, a Combat Infantryman's Badge with two stars on it, a Ranger tab, a Parachute Rigger patch, and some junk I never even saw before. I was going to impress him with the little miniature Combat Infantryman's Badge on my lapel?*

Just then, the general looked over at me sharply, and I thought, *I didn't say that out loud, did I?*

But that had not been the reason. My mind snapped back to the podium, and I saw Ed pointing directly at me across the room and heard the words, "…and it means a great deal to me that my old platoon sergeant from Vietnam, Staff Sergeant Mick Delaney, has come all the way from Kansas City to be here at my retirement today!"

"Who you callin' old, Lieutenant?!" I shouted back.

Everyone laughed, including Ed. But then he went on. "Mick and I were very close in Vietnam, worked for months together on long range reconnaissance-in-force, slept in the mud, shared C-rats and cigarettes, even shared the shrapnel from a North Vietnamese 82 mm mortar round for dinner one night. He kept me out of a lot of trouble in Vietnam, and I really appreciate that he came today!"

The Army people, every single one of them, turned to look across the room directly at me, and began to applaud. "Wait! Wait!" shouted Thorsen over the crowd. "Just don't believe any of the stories he tells you. I was a much better officer than that!" and the crowd roared.

Winston Churchill, standing next to me, turned and grabbed my hand, started pumping it like a car jack, and simultaneously pounded me on the back hard enough that I thought there might be ribs splintering. "It was very kind of you to come all the way here today for this, Sergeant!" shouted the four-star. "We think the world of Ed Thorsen."

"So do I, General," I shouted back over the noise. "He was the finest officer I ever knew. He's the reason a lot of us from our rifle company in Vietnam are alive today. He's a hell of a good man."

"You got that right, Sergeant," said the general. "We sure hate to lose him."

"Well," I said, "after thirty-three years, West Point, Jump School, Ranger School, four overseas tours, two Silver Stars, two Purple Hearts, and a lot of other trinkets, I would think you could spare him. He's getting to be an old fart, sir. I mean, I'd hate to think what would happen if you pushed his old bones out of an airplane these days." I cracked a big smile, trying to lay on the charm. The general roared with laughter, and pounded me on the back even harder.

"How'd we let you go, Sergeant?" asked the general. "Seems like you're a pretty sharp guy. Why didn't you stay in?"

"Well sir, no offense, but I didn't see any future in the Army for me. I didn't have any college back then. I was just an enlisted infantry grunt. They offered me a chance to go to OCS and earn a commission when I got out, but if I'd taken it, they would've just kept sending me back to that fucked-up war until I didn't make it home again. Or at least until all my parts didn't make it home again. I couldn't see that. Did my bit, sir. Had plenty of the Army."

"Well, you're probably right, Sergeant. I do see your CIB there. I hope you've had a great life."

"Yessir. Gettin' better all the time, thank you." I pulled a business card from my wallet, and handed it to the general.

Delaney Enterprises, Inc.
Kansas City
Software and Internet Development Worldwide
Mick Delaney — President

"If you ever need any software or Internet development, hosting... whatever, sir, I'm your man. Give me a call."

"Thanks, Sergeant," said the general, glancing briefly at the card and tucking it into his shirt pocket. It was obvious he didn't expect to need my services. "It's good you've been so successful. The best of luck to you."

"Thank you, sir," I said, then grimaced to myself. No matter how badly I wanted to, I couldn't NOT call the general "Sir." Too much of the military still in me, I guessed.

The ceremony was over, and I wandered away from the general to find Ed, his wife Lois, and their family, to say goodbye. Though Delaney Enterprises owned a private jet, I hadn't used it for this trip because it had been tied up flying people on real business. So I had to catch a commercial flight out of Washington Reagan in a little over two hours. Not much time, considering I had to turn in my rental car.

"What war stories, you old geezer?" I began as I approached Ed, a big smile on my face. "You're the one always tellin' the war stories!"

Thorsen smiled, knew I was leaving, grabbed my hand and pulled me in. "Sure you can't stay longer, Mick? We have a big party starting up in a little while back at the house."

"Yeah, I know, LT. I'm sorry. When I scheduled my return flight I should have expected they'd delay this by four hours. It is the fuckin' Army, after all." I grinned. "I'm sorry to have to leave. But I'll be back up here in a couple of months for a software show, and I'll come and stay at your house, sleep in your bed, eat your food, drink your liquor…How's that?"

"Works for me," said Thorsen. "And I don't imagine Lois will mind too much having you around. While you and I are off telling war stories, she can get some peace."

Lois, standing easily within earshot, turned with a big smile, approached the pair of us, reached out with both hands and grabbed our respective cheeks between thumbs and forefingers. She was a beautiful woman in her mid-fifties, with red hair and a sparkle in her smile.

"What are you little boys discussing?" she demanded, lightly pinching each cheek.

Thorsen laughed. "Mick's invited himself back in a couple of months for a visit. Says he's coming back to sleep in our bed, eat our food, drink our liquor, and tell more of his famous war stories. So you'd better start laying in supplies now."

"You know you're always welcome, Mick," she said. "Hopefully, you two will have more time to visit next trip."

"I hope so, Lois. We didn't get much time to talk today. But it was really fun being here. Thank you both for inviting me."

"Wouldn't have been right without you here, Mick." Thorsen looked at his watch. "You'd better get out of here, my friend. You're going to hit rush hour leaving the Pentagon, and that can get ugly.

"Yeah, thanks, LT. I just want to say goodbye to your mom and dad and Dave."

I hugged Lois and Ed. "Congratulations, LT," I said. "I really hope you enjoy retirement." Then I put what I hoped was a quizzical look on my face. "Does this mean you're not a fuckin' lifer anymore?"

Thorsen smiled, punched me lightly in the ribs. "I'll always be a fuckin' lifer, and don't you forget it." But there was a little sadness in his eyes that I imagined was because he was leaving the Army that had been his home through all his adult life.

I found my way to Thorsen's parents who were standing with Dave, Ed's son. I hugged all three of them in turn. "I'm so glad for the opportunity to meet you all," I said. "Ed and I have known each other almost thirty years, and I've known Lois for a while. But I'm really happy to meet the rest of his family. Next time I see you, sir," I said to Ed's father, "I'd like to hear all about your experiences in World War II and Korea."

"Be glad to share with you, son. After all the times Ed told us you saved his butt in Vietnam, I owe you all the stories you want."

"Oh, you know how he is, sir. Always exaggerating. It was pretty much a cake walk for us compared to what you went through."

He shook his head. "Not the way I heard it, Mick."

I turned to Dave, wearing his West Point cadet's uniform. "You look just like your dad did when he and I were in Vietnam. You take good care of yourself, Dave. And try to stay out of trouble."

"But, Mick," said Dave, "I'm hoping to get into the Rangers. I'm supposed to get into trouble."

And with that I was gone. I threaded my way out of the Pentagon, across three parking lots to my rental car, which almost evaded me it was so anonymous there among the thousands of other cars. The day was warm, so I took off my jacket and tossed it into the back seat, started the engine, turned the air conditioner on full blast, and headed out of the lot. Reagan National was only a few miles south along the Potomac, and I checked the car in and made it to the terminal with a few minutes to spare before flight time. Then I had the opportunity to sit around for an extra hour because of a weather delay.

I had a briefcase full of work with me, as always, and plenty that needed doing. But I was much too distracted to work. Every time I saw Thorsen it took me back to the war and all those vivid memories. And I went back there then, sitting in a seat near my gate, staring out the window with what they'd once called the "thousand-yard stare."

29

It had been forty-two days since we'd left LZ Sherman, forty-two days living rougher than most people back in the world could ever imagine. Forty-two days without a bath, with only one change of clothes, bodies covered with pus-oozing sores that came from brush-snags, leech bites, and even the smallest scratch, and that stunk like death. With hair uncut, beards unshaven for a week or more at a time, and uniforms long gone to rags, we looked more like a band of guerrillas than a company of United States Army infantrymen.

We had left Sherman with a little more than a hundred men, but in six weeks we'd lost four killed; more than fifteen wounded; five to malaria, trench foot, and dysentery; three to R & R; and two lucky bastards who had gone home alive after finishing their twelve-month tours. One of the two grunts who had gone home had actually made it through his whole tour without being wounded even once. It was the first time anyone could remember a grunt from that company going home without at least one Purple Heart. Most went home with two or three, if they were lucky enough to make it home alive at all.

I was still a point man then. I was on day 78 of my 365-day tour, still fairly new in country, but I'd learned a lot in the time I'd been there. Danny Nakamura, the muscular little Hawaiian with the uncanny sixth-sense for danger, and I, and sometimes Tony Giles, who was still alive then, were the point team for our squad, and more often than we should have been, it seemed, the point team for the company.

Carl Engle was the squad leader. He was an Alabama boy with a thick southern accent. After his first tour in Vietnam with the 101st Airborne Division in '67-'68, he'd gone home and married his high school sweetheart and had managed to be stationed at Ft. Rucker, Alabama, near his hometown. But only a few weeks after his marriage, Carl had lost his wife to a car accident. With very little thought given to it, except perhaps the thought that he really didn't want to continue living without her, he had re-enlisted and volunteered to come back to Vietnam. He'd taken over the squad when Estevez went home a couple of weeks after I arrived in the company, and was a good squad leader and a good friend to us all.

We had lost one of our squad to a firefight the night before. Sugarbear, the poor guy who'd received so many letters from friends at home telling him how his wife was constantly cheating on him, had been shot through the chest by the North Vietnamese in a gunfight that erupted after our point squad had walked into some NVA anti-personnel mines. Captain Larkin, who was then our new company commander, had made the blundering mistake of calling the Medevac in to extract the wounded in the exact spot where the ambush had occurred. During its descent, the chopper had been shot to hell by a swarm of NVA, barely making it out. Two of their crew had been killed, all the rest wounded.

The ambush that fucked-up Sugarbear could have been easily avoided if Captain Larkin hadn't been such a "stupid motherfucker" as I so succinctly put it. OK, I was a tad judgmental sometimes. I admit it.

After that firefight was over and we had Medevaced Sugarbear and the other wounded, and without even running a patrol to check out the area, Larkin made another poor decision and ordered us to set up our night position in the exact spot where the battle had happened. So we spread out to the left and right of the bomb crater, and, as it turned out, only a few yards from where the gooks themselves were dug in, in a big bunker complex.

Engle then sent Danny Nakamura, Tony, and me out as a listening post on the side of the perimeter closest to the gooks. We only went out about twenty meters from the perimeter, since we could almost feel the NVA nearby. And it didn't take long after dark had fallen for the enemy to start moving around, even talking and laughing inside their well dug-in and reinforced positions, while we lay above ground behind a log we'd found. We'd called in artillery as close as we could get it with little effect, even thrown grenades out a couple of times. But each time, within only a few minutes, the gooks started talking and laughing again. "Terrifying" wasn't a strong enough word to describe what it felt like being out there in the dark all night with them so close, and none of us got a wink of sleep.

We came back to the perimeter shortly after first light, exhausted. We were nearly out of food and water, and almost out of cigarettes. I was pissed off that I'd been sent out on listening post the last three nights in a row, while Carl, as squad leader, had stayed inside the relative security of the company perimeter. This practice made sense when we were at full strength or near full strength, with nine or ten men in the squad, since most of the men would be inside the perimeter, and the squad leader needed to be with most of the men. But it didn't make sense to me when there were only six men left in the squad, and half of them were out on listening post on any given night.

So coming in after another interminably long night of fear, not knowing all night if I might die in the next few minutes, I picked that time to challenge Carl about not taking his turn on listening post. Being inside the perimeter had been no picnic, either, and Carl was just as hungry, thirsty, and tired as anyone. So he had reacted as I might have expected, if I'd thought about it at all before confronting him.

"Fuck you, Mick," he said quietly, but venomously. "I don't need you to tell me how to run this fuckin' squad. I been at this a hell of a lot longer than you have, and I know my job. I need to be in the perimeter at night with the company and the majority of the squad in case there's an attack."

Then I was really pissed. "Carl, now that Sugarbear's gone, when there's a listening post out, half the fuckin' squad's *outside* the perimeter. What difference does it make whether you're with the half on the inside or the half on the outside? And we all know the company rule. It's up to each squad leader to decide whether he goes on listening post or not! I've been outside the perimeter three fuckin' nights in a ROW, man! I'm TIRED!"

Carl stepped in closer to me, his face only inches from mine, looking up at me. "Like I said before, Mick. Fuck you! Don't try to tell me how to run this fuckin' squad! Now get back to your gear."

Thinking of nothing else, I heard myself say, quietly, "You are one sorry motherfucker, Carl." Then I turned and made my way back to Danny and Tony.

When I got back to them I was still angry at Carl's reaction to my request, or demand, or however I'd done it. I sat down for a minute, lit one of my last cigarettes, stared into the jungle, and felt my anger roll over me. I thought about how I'd volunteered for the war, how naive I'd been then, how long ago that now seemed. I thought about Katie, how I missed her, and how it was becoming difficult to remember what it was like to be with her. By then I could hardly remember what she looked like unless I was looking at her photo.

This was my world now, the gooks, the heat, the deprivation, and being at the mercy of the asshole company commander and the battalion commander, the little prick. I thought about Carl and his reaction to my demand. Carl wasn't a bad guy, and in fact he was a damn good squad leader and a good friend. He was just acting as he thought he should in this incredibly shitty situation. I realized I'd picked a lousy time to bring it up, and after thinking about it, also realized that I'd gone about it in the wrong way. Besides, what the fuck difference did it really make whether Carl went out on listening post or not? Nobody was getting much sleep those nights, no matter where they were.

After a while, the anger subsided, replaced by regret. I decided I'd try to make things right with Carl the next chance I got.

"Gotta be a resupply today," Danny said. "We're out of everything. This is the fifth day."

"Yeah," said Tony. "Maybe. Or maybe they'll pull us back to that clearing we crossed a-ways back, and airlift us out of here while they call in an Arclight and blow this place away. There must be a million gooks in there."

"That's the only thing that makes sense," I said. "This has to be a big bunker complex or the gooks wouldn't have stayed to fight yesterday like they did, and they sure wouldn't have stuck around all night. As fucked up as we are, half strength, out of everything and no sleep for days, there's no way they're gonna send us in there. Even if they were gonna do that, they'd pull us back for resupply first and work this place over with some serious artillery."

"That's what I thought, too," said the platoon sergeant, "3-5," walking up behind us. "But I heard 6 talking to Battalion, and there's bad news. We're going in there in just a little while. No resupply first. Lancelot said he wants us to get after these gooks before they have the chance to get away, and 6 is agreeing with him on every call. Trying to make up for his fuck-ups yesterday, I guess. You should have heard that fucker on the radio. Didn't even argue with him. Didn't even ask for resupply first. Just kept sayin' 'Yessir, yessir'."

"Oh, fuck," I said. And then, "OH, FUCK! We have the point to-day."

"Oh, fuck, is right," said 3-5. "I was just coming over to find Engle. You guys tell him I want to see him with the other squad leaders in five minutes, and to get the squad saddled up."

Danny, Tony, and I could only look at each other in despair.

I grabbed my rifle and helmet and made my way back to Engle. "3-5 wants you at his position in five minutes, Carl. We're going in there."

"Oh, mama!" said Carl. "We didn't even do a mad minute, and we've been so close to them all night we know the artillery didn't do any good."

He grabbed his rifle and made his way back to 3-5's fighting hole.

We heard a Huey land in a clearing not far behind us, then pull away. After a couple of minutes, we heard a commotion and looked back to see our favorite scout dog handler, Bill, and his big German Shepherd, Hassle.

Bill spotted us, brought Hassle over to where Danny, Tony, and I were getting our gear together, and sat down.

"Hey, guys," he said. "This as fucked up as I heard?"

I rubbed Hassle's ears, and Hassle stood next to me and pushed his body into my leg while I did. Hassle and I had become good friends over the past weeks, on the occasions when he and Bill had come out to walk point with us and smell for gooks. I really loved the dog. But I could feel the big Shepherd's tension against my leg.

"It's pretty fucked up. We were out there about twenty meters on listening post all night, and you could hear gooks talkin' and laughin' and shit, like they didn't even know, or care, that we're here. We fig-ure there's about a million of those motherfuckers right over there." I pointed into the jungle.

"From the way Hassle's acting, I'd say you're right," said Bill. "So I wonder what they need a scout dog for?"

"Who knows, man?" said Danny. "This 6 is one fucked up dude. Only thing he knows for sure is how to kiss Lancelot's ass. He's really good at that."

Carl came back from the squad leader meeting and pulled the rest of us and Bill together.

"OK, here's the deal. Third platoon has the point. We're heading straight in from here, but we're not just going with one squad on point, single file, like we usually do. 3-2 will be walking point for the company. We'll be on their left about ten meters out, walking flank security. And 3-3 will be on the right, doing the same thing. The Weapons Squad will walk behind 3-2, and the rest of the company will follow them. Bill, you and Hassle will be with the company point, with 3-2 in the center file.

"One more thing," he paused. "We got the word that Sugarbear died on his way into Tay Ninh last night. Two of the others from yesterday are dead, too."

"Oh, man. That sucks," said Danny. "Sugarbear was a good guy. All that trouble with his wife. I can't imagine how miserable he was. And now he's dead."

"I know, man," said Carl. "And that bitch'll get his Army life insurance."

There was silence for a while, and then Carl said, "Let's get saddled up." He looked straight at me. "I'm taking the point today."

I faced him squarely. "You don't have to do that, Carl. It's my turn to walk point. Besides, Danny and I are a team."

"Danny can back me up. You walk behind him and back us both up. I'm going to walk point." He glared at me. "We clear?"

"Look, Carl," I said. "I'm sorry I brought that up earlier. And I'm sorry for saying what I did. You don't have to do this."

"Fuckin' shut up about it, Mick," said Carl, his voice coming up, obviously getting pissed off again. He shrugged and shook his head in frustration. "Get ready to move out!"

I realized that I wasn't going to get anywhere arguing it further. I turned away and went back to get my gear. Before Carl came up I had been scratching Hassle's ears, and I reached down to give the dog a last pat as Bill put on his helmet and got ready to go, Hassle's leash in his left hand and his rifle in his right. "You guys be careful," said Bill. "We'll see you in a bit."

"Take care, Bill."

We finished pulling on our gear. At least with no re-supply, no food, and no water, the rucksacks were much lighter. I lit one of the three cigarettes I had left, noticed that Danny and Tony had none, and passed mine over to Danny. Danny took a couple of puffs, passed it to Tony. It went around a couple of times.

I noticed that my hands were shaking as I buckled my pistol belt and picked up my M-16. I took off my helmet and looked at the picture of Katie I had tucked into the webbing. I smiled at the picture, put the helmet back on, and stood, ready to move out. Carl had taken the point spot with Danny behind him. I followed Danny, then came Tony and Jon. Fragman brought up the rear.

A couple of minutes later the word came up that the main column was moving out. Carl stepped around the fighting hole and headed out into the trampled vegetation in front of it. We all moved slowly, taking turns crossing the downed log where Danny, Tony, and I had spent the night on listening post. "Hold up," came the word from behind. We all stopped. The Army way, moving in fits and starts.

To my right I could hear Hal, the 3-2 squad leader, talking on the radio. "6, the dog's got gooks to the front. He's bristled up real big. Bill says there must be a bunch of 'em."

I couldn't hear the reply. "Roger that. Can we send Bill back off the point? The dog's done its job."

Again I could hear no reply.

"But 6, there's no sense him bein' up here now. We know there are gooks."

This time I heard 6's voice from considerably behind me, raised loud enough that he didn't need the radio. "Move out, trooper! And the dog stays with the point. You got that?"

Well, I thought, hearing the conversation from ten meters away, and 6's voice from considerably farther behind, *if the gooks didn't know we were coming before, they sure as fuck do now.*

Carl and Danny began moving again. The rest of the squad followed, moving slowly into the vegetation in front of the fallen log. I could distinctly smell the gooks now, the smell of that awful fish sauce strong in the air.

30

Tay Ninh Province, Vietnam

Suddenly…Boom! Boom! Boom! From our immediate right, explosions, shrapnel tearing through the trees! Screams!

I hit the ground. I could see Danny dive to the ground ahead of me and Carl already down, half hidden by some heavy brush, but crawling forward. He had turned off to my right. I clicked the safety off my rifle.

Gook AK-47s opened up to our left, bullets tearing through the trees overhead, shredding limbs and leaves, tracers leaving green trails, the terrifying Pop! Pop! Pop! Pop! Pop! of automatic fire.

I looked left, looked right, could see nothing through the thick brush. I looked forward and saw Carl rise up on his knees, then lunge forward. A second passed, then… Boom!

Another deafening explosion! Another mine had been detonated, right where Carl was!

The AK 47 fire stopped. I saw Danny get to his knees, crawl forward. "Carl's hit bad!" he shouted back.

I dropped my rucksack, crawled toward them screaming, "Doc! Doc! Doc! Carl's hit!"

There was another burst of AK fire, this time straight from our front. I saw Danny dive to the ground, almost on top of Carl. I dived forward myself, still behind him, and took cover behind a clump of small trees. Bullets popped overhead from our left.

Carl was lying half on his left side, half on his back, clawing at the mess that had been his face. The top half of it was blackened by the blast, but still there. But the tip of his nose, most of his front teeth, and his lower jaw were gone, now only bloody pulp. He was awake, clawing at the place where his lower jaw had been, frantically trying to breathe through the remains of his upper neck, but producing only a wet sucking sound when he tried to inhale, and blood bubbles when he tried to breathe out. His bowels and bladder had released, and he lay in his own blood and shit, and struggled to hold onto life. Hearing Danny near him he reached out for help, his hands and arms covered with blood.

Danny was in shock, looking into the blackened, bloody gore that had been Carl's face, and terrified of the gunfire and mine detonations around him. But he was thinking clearly enough to know that he couldn't stay where he was, and he wouldn't leave Carl there. So he started crawling backward, grabbed Carl's feet, and began pulling him across the jungle floor.

I crawled out to meet him, and Danny dropped one foot for me to grab hold of. Together we crawled backwards, pulling Carl back toward the log. We stayed as low to the ground as we could, expecting more AK fire any second. For some reason, none came. I shouted, "Doc! Doc!"

Doc Benedetto crawled over the log to us, pushed Danny aside, and tore off Carl's pistol belt and bandoliers. He ripped open Carl's shredded, bloody T-shirt and pulled a surgeon's scalpel from his medical bag. He was trying to find a place for a tracheotomy to get air into Carl's lungs. He had to fight Carl's hands, as they kept trying to tear open the blasted throat. Danny and I each grabbed a bloody arm, and held Carl's hands away from his face.

After probing the mess at the base of Carl's face, Doc realized that there wasn't enough of Carl's throat left to allow him to open an airway. Knowing he was going to lose him, Doc dug into his pack for a morphine syringe to at least ease his pain. He jammed the syringe into Carl's thigh, and Carl seemed to relax a little almost immediately. Danny and I released his hands.

Over the next minute or so Carl's struggle weakened. With blood still pouring from his wounds and his fingers still pulling weakly at the ruins of his face, his chest stopped heaving, and his heart stopped pumping. He died there in front of the fallen log, tears still streaming from his eyes and sliding onto the bloody jungle floor.

The medic's head dropped. He sat back against the log, defeated.

"Did you see that?" said Danny, incredulous. "He dived on that fuckin' mine on purpose, man! He saw it, and was trying to smother the blast, so it wouldn't hit us! Jesus Christ! I never saw anything like that before! Carl gave his life to save ours!"

I kneeled over Carl's body and put my arms around him and just held him and rocked back and forth, tears streaming down my face, not making a sound. Deep in my heart I felt the intense guilt and sorrow of knowing that had it not been for the ugly words exchanged between us only a little while before, my good friend, who lay shattered in my arms, would probably be alive, and I would probably be lying there, the victim of that horrible death.

But…a part of me was also glad that it wasn't me there, dead on the ground. A part of me was glad that I had not suffered that horrible death, that at least for now Katie wouldn't be getting a visit from some anonymous Army officer, letting her know that I was dead.

The platoon sergeant, 3-5, was wounded during that same firefight. And among the other casualties in the platoon were the dog handler, Bill, and Hassle. All three had been peppered badly with shrapnel. 3-5's wounds were not life threatening, but he was pulled to the company rear for Medevac. Bill was hurt badly. Hassle, torn by shrapnel that had struck throughout his body, nevertheless tried to crawl nearer to Bill, to protect his beloved friend from any more harm. Out of his head with pain, he'd even snarled and snapped at the second platoon medic when he tried to help Bill.

Sadly, Hassle had to be shot so Bill could be saved. Even more sadly, the first shot fired to end Hassle's life had missed the vital spots, putting the poor animal through even more excruciating pain before another round was put through his brain. My last memory of Hassle alive was the series of unbearable shrieks the big, heroic dog made during the seconds between the first shot and the second.

Danny and I carried Carl's body to the small clearing where the other dead and the wounded were being gathered, and helped Doc Benedetto get him into one of the thick rubber body bags that were piled there on the ground. A few minutes later, a lone Huey came clattering in, and we helped load the wounded and the dead onto the chopper. I put my hand on the place where Carl's face would be, inside the hot olive drab rubber bag, and said goodbye to my friend one last time. Then we loaded Hassle's shattered body onto the chopper floor alongside the human dead, and the pilot pulled pitch on the main rotor and lifted the bird away. My last sight of my friends on the bloody floor of that chopper was of Carl's feet in the body bag, sticking out over the edge of the floor, and of Hassle's tail, hanging out the door, his beautiful black and tan fir blowing in the wind.

As Danny and I walked back through the company perimeter to pick up the rest of our equipment, Captain Larkin shouted at me, "Sergeant Delaney! I need a word with you!"

This surprised me. I didn't think Larkin even knew my name. Danny headed back to our position on the perimeter, and, shirtless and carrying my M-16, I approached Larkin. In my rage at the unnecessary loss of my friends' lives, and fully believing that Larkin was responsible, I didn't speak at first. I simply walked up to the captain and stood facing him with my rifle in the crook of my arm, the most insolent look I could muster on my face.

"You're taking Third Platoon," said Larkin. "Sergeant Miller was wounded this morning, and you're the senior NCO in the platoon now."

"I don't want the platoon," I spat back, the word "sir" noticeably absent from my sentence. "There are other sergeants here with more combat time than I have. Give it to them."

"It's an order, not a request, Sergeant! No one else wants the platoon, either, and you have more time in the Army than anyone else in Third Platoon. So you're the platoon leader until we can get an officer out here to replace you. And then you're going to be the platoon sergeant. Now get your platoon saddled up, Sergeant!"

I just stood and stared at Larkin for a few seconds, absentmindedly clicking the selector switch on my rifle from "safe" to "fire" and back again…"click, click, click." I'd never felt rage like that before, and I was having real trouble controlling it. I was seriously thinking about simply putting a burst into Larkin's chest, and walking away. I wasn't even remotely considering the consequences.

"Is there something else, Sergeant?" asked Larkin, a threatening tone in his voice.

A few more seconds went by while I stared into his face. "Engle didn't have to die, 6! All you had to do was pull back and call in the big stuff. He'd still be alive. And Sugarbear didn't have to die last night either!" I was shaking with rage now.

Sensing a real threat, Larkin's voice softened a bit. "Take it easy, Sergeant. I was just following orders. And that's what you have to do now." He paused, his eyes shifting away and then back to mine again. "Now get back to your platoon and get your men ready to move out."

I didn't answer. I stared at Larkin for a couple more seconds, the rifle pointed upward, my thumb still on the selector switch, my finger lightly on the trigger.

Larkin was scared now. He could sense what I was thinking. "Move out, Sergeant!" he commanded. But his voice cracked when he said it.

Somehow that little crack in his voice, that little sign of fear, settled it for me, broke me out of whatever trance I was in. I turned on my heel and headed back to the platoon, without another word.

I walked directly back to Danny and the rest of the squad and picked up my pack and other gear. My hands were still shaking with anger, and I was full of the other emotions of losing Carl. I was tired beyond limits, hungry, thirsty, wasted. But I knew that someone had to take the leadership of Third Platoon. So I worked to get it under control.

And so, on that horrible day I had lost one good friend in Sugarbear; was at least partially responsible for the death of my good friend Carl; had seen my buddy Hassle killed in a most horrible, painful way; and Hassle's handler, Bill, also a good friend, badly wounded. And several other men in the platoon, including the platoon sergeant, had been wounded, as well.

I had had the horrible selfish emotion of being glad it wasn't me who had been killed or wounded. And somehow, I had wound up as the acting platoon leader and future platoon sergeant of Third Platoon.

I knew I would never in this lifetime sort all that out. I could only remember that some of my last words to my friend Carl Engle had been to call him a "sorry motherfucker." And I could never take that back or make him know how very, very sorry I was that I'd said it.

Years later, I would learn that my friend Carl Engle, who had given his life so selflessly on that bloody day, had been awarded the Medal of Honor, America's highest award for heroism in combat.

***

I was grateful when the airline paged me by name, pulling me back from the past. "Kansas City passenger Michael Delaney, please report immediately to gate 34. Your flight is about to depart." And I snapped out of the daydream and back to the great life of Mick Delaney, successful basket case.

31

June 2005
Near Ramadi, Iraq
Tony Blake

The Iraqi village of Kubaisah, located northwest of Baghdad, a few kilometers west of the Euphrates River and Iraqi Highway 12, was not considered by the American command to be of major strategic importance. Unlike nearby Fallujah and Ramadi, larger cities that had been the scenes of major battles since the American invasion of Iraq in 2003, there had been very little insurgent activity in and around Kubaisah. So, no Coalition units were permanently deployed there.

Nevertheless, satellite and drone surveillance of the village could only tell the commanders so much about the activities of the residents, who were nearly all Sunnis, the sect of Saddam Hussein and his regime. In fact, a couple of the village's leading residents were known to have been active members of Saddam's Baathist Party. So periodically the Special Operations Command was given orders to conduct eyes-on surveillance of the village, just to make sure no major insurgent activity was being mounted there. This time, in early June 2005, the job fell to Major Tony Blake and his Special Forces company, then headquartered in an old aircraft hangar at Al Taji Air Base, north of Baghdad.

After receiving the order, Tony pushed his chair back from the rickety metal desk he used in his makeshift office, put on his field cap, and headed out to see if he could catch Warrant Officer Bob Wilkins, acting team leader for Alpha detachment 592. He was in luck. Wilkins and half of his team were cleaning weapons and loading rifle magazines, pulling MREs from their packaging and stowing them in their rucksacks, generally preparing for their next mission, whatever that might be.

"Morning, Skipper," said Wilkins as Tony approached. "Got something for us?" The team had been back from its last operation for five days, long enough to rest up, get some decent food and some exercise, and start getting bored and ready to move out again. Wilkins was acting as team leader for 592 because the regular team leader, Captain Everett Myers, had received minor wounds during their last op.

"Morning, Bob. Morning guys," said Tony as he approached.

"Morning, Sir," came the response from the team. No one came to attention or saluted, or even stopped doing what they were doing. There was very little formality in the unit as long as they were in a combat zone. Tony's men all wore long beards and long hair and sported skin well-darkened by the desert sun, the better to fit in with the locals.

"Everyone had their morning coffee? No one's all grumpy this morning, are they?" asked Tony. That brought a chuckle.

"Any word on Captain Myers, Skipper?" This from Wilkins.

"He's doing fine. They sent him up to Landstuhl because he caught some of that shrapnel in his lower groin, and they wanted to let the surgeons up there do the tricky work removing it. But that's all done now and he's recuperating well. His wife flew over from home and is with him, so I told him to take a few extra days and hang out with her. He should be back in about ten days."

"Won't be much fun with her if he's got shrapnel in his dick," someone said. Everyone laughed.

"I don't think there's any in his actual dick," replied Tony. "I'm sure he'll manage." He chuckled, and everyone laughed again.

"What's the word, Sir? We finally getting something to do? Pretty boring around here." It was Master Sergeant Andy Hanks, the team's Operations Sergeant. Hanks was a burly former high-school wrestler from Michigan. This was his third deployment, one to Afghanistan and two to Iraq.

"Yeah, Skipper. Pretty boring here. When do we get to go kill some people and blow some shit up?" That was Sergeant Barry Drake, a Las Vegas native who loved to crack jokes. *Kill people and blow up shit* was the well-used enlisted man's summary of what the infantry, and by extension the Special Forces, were paid to do.

Tony couldn't help but laugh. "Don't know about that, exactly, but this mission might get you a little closer to some action. Ought to get your adrenaline up a little anyway."

That got everyone's attention. "Interesting!" said Raj Maraki, an Indian-born American citizen, another sergeant, and a team medic. "What's up, sir?"

The team gathered around. Formally Tony's orders were going to Wilkins, but there was no reason for him to have to repeat the scenario to the other team members, so it made sense that they should all hear what Wilkins heard.

Tony spread a map out on a well-worn work table, directly under an overhead light. "We've been ordered to gather intelligence on any potential insurgent activity in and around the town of Kubaisah, about eighty clicks northwest of Ramadi and a few clicks west of Route 12, in Anbar Province. It's a Sunni town, home of a couple of Saddam's old ministers. Language like everywhere around here is Arabic with a bit of local accent because of their fairly isolated location. Agriculture drives the local economy. There are five major mosques and two major marketplaces within the town itself. Also, the usual collection of shops, garages, even a car wash. Intelligence has identified the mullah who leads each mosque and the location of their madrasahs where they teach the boys their evil ways. These and the marketplaces will be our points of focus. If you overhear a lot of radical talk coming out of a madrasah, you'll need to focus on that mullah, see where he goes and who he talks to, and see what you can learn. Tricky thing about this town is there's little through traffic. The main road into the city from Route 12 pretty much dead ends a few clicks west of the town, so they don't get a lot of people just passing through. Any questions so far?"

"Are we the only ones going on this op, Skipper? What about the rest of the team?" asked Drake.

Wilkins spoke up. "Sorry, I should have mentioned that. Williams, Rivers, Hernandez, and Milich are over with one of the SEAL teams, getting ready to go on a joint op with them. Sergeant First Class Williams will be the team leader on that one, reporting to the SEAL team leader. So there's just the four of us for this op. That should work, eh, Skipper?"

Splitting the team up to handle multiple operations wasn't unusual.

"Yeah, I think so, if you guys think you can handle it with four men. Any other questions?"

There were none.

"Then spend the rest of the day putting your operation plan together, take tomorrow to prepare, and then be ready to head out very early Tuesday. I have satellite photos and all the other intel here on the table."

Tony turned the operation planning over to Wilkins, and sat back to become one of the group, participating when he was asked questions but not commanding, letting the team put together a plan they could all buy into. They were all seasoned pros, expert at what they were doing.

There was some rowdy initial discussion. Sergeant Drake suggested they make a high-altitude night parachute jump into the valley south of the town and deploy from there, disguised as locals. Everyone liked the local disguise part of that plan and thought it was essential. They all spoke fluent Arabic and were extremely familiar with the local dress and customs. But nobody except Drake thought a HALO, high altitude low opening, insertion was appropriate for this mission, since by nature a night HALO jump carried a high risk of injury, and created other logistical issues. So that left a drop-off by Blackhawk helicopter (inherently noisy, certain to alert the locals that something was up), or just a drive over in Humvees. Eventually, after checking with Aviation and some other units, they decided to get a chopper ride over to a sparsely populated area west of Ramadi, where they would be picked up by Humvee and driven up Route 12 to a spot south of the village of Khauza. From there they would hump the last few clicks across the desert on foot.

They would make camp in a dry riverbed south of Kubaisah, change out of uniform into their disguises as locals, and recon the town in two-man teams. They would just casually walk in there from the edge of town, pretending to be locals. They would focus on the marketplaces and Mosques as places to learn what was going on or being planned. They would stay in the area for a week, carrying water and rations with them for that time, picking up extra water where they could. At the end of the mission, they would be extracted by Blackhawk helicopter from a spot near their camp. Didn't matter how much noise they made when they were leaving. The Blackhawk would be standing by during the whole operation, with one escort Apache gunship, to come get them out on a few minutes' notice if things came off the rails.

Piece of cake.

Satisfied that it was a good plan, Tony left the team to the detailed planning under Wilkins' leadership, and went back to his office to prepare a briefing for his boss. The team would brief Tony again on

Tuesday morning before they moved out, and he'd be given the actual team schedule for two man recon walks into the village.

The life of a Special Forces company commander could get pretty boring, with Tony spending most of his time at the Battalion headquarters as part of the "B Team," in and around the hanger at Al Taji. So after clearing it with the battalion commander, Tony decided he would ride along on the mission, as far as the drop-off point where the team would leave the Hummers and finish the trip on foot. It was Wilkins' first mission as a team leader, and Tony wanted to make sure the logistics of the drop-off went well for him. And... he just wanted to gear up and get out of the "office" for a while, if only for a day or so. He walked back down to where the team was still making preparations for the mission and let Warrant Officer Wilkins know about the ride along.

"Sure, Skipper. Glad to have you. There should be plenty of room in the chopper and the Hummers."

After finishing up for the day, Tony called Melissa from one of the satellite phones set up around the base. It was seven p.m. in Al Taji, noon in Watertown, New Jersey. Melissa would be having lunch when he called.

"Hello? Tony?!"

"Hey, Love, what's up?"

"It's so good to hear from you. It's been almost a week!"

"Yeah. Thank God for these SAT phones. Can't imagine what it was like for my mom and dad when he was in Vietnam. They never got to make calls."

"That would have been really hard. How are you? And what's with the 'Hey, Love'?"

"I'm fine. Been hangin' around with the SAS guys too much, I guess. Bunch of bloomin' Brits. Starting to sound like them. Wanted to let you know I'll be off the base for a couple of days, so I won't be able to email or call. Nothin' dangerous. Just going along on a drop-off, to make sure things go OK for a new team leader." He knew he was probably saying more than he should, but the calls were scrambled to the satellite, then unscrambled before being passed on to the U.S. So nobody worried about it.

"How are you? How are the kids?"

"I'm fine. Missing you a lot. The kids are good. Angelo's loving baseball, and his coach says he shows some real talent for pitching when he gets a little older. And he's swimming every chance he gets. Lisa's swimming, too, and I just signed her up for tumbling classes. I wish they were here to say hello to you, but they're out having lunch with your mom."

"Please give them my love. How are Mom and Dad?"

"Angie is good. We see her a lot, and she seems fine. She worries about you, of course, but I think she's doing pretty well overall. Loren's good, I think. Haven't seen much of him lately. Still at the bank.

"When do you think you'll be coming home, Tony?"

"Should be about another month. We're due to rotate at six months, and we came over late in January. So it should be the end of July. I don't have the orders yet, but that's not unusual. Nothing too big going on here now, so I don't expect a delay."

"I can't wait to see you, Tony."

"I know just how you feel, Baby. I can't wait to be back."

"I love you, Tony."

"I love you too, Baby. Been having some great dreams about you, all naked and stuff." He laughed.

"Me, too. Me, too. Wait'll you get home."

"I can't wait." There was a pause as they both thought about the upcoming reunion.

Finally Tony said, "Better go, Baby. Have to finish up some stuff. Talk to you in, uh, let's say, five days. I love you."

"I love you. Goodbye, Tony. Thanks for calling!"

Tony sat for a while and thought about his beautiful wife and his beautiful kids. Angelo was almost eight, already becoming a good athlete. But his grades in school weren't so hot. Tony would have to help Melissa with that when he got home. Little Lisa showed signs of growing up to be her mother; beautiful, poised, intelligent, and sweet. He was a lucky, lucky man.

Then he put those thoughts away and got back to work. In his line of work, it was best not to think about family too often or too much. It could be distracting. Tony of course had no idea how much he thought and acted like his birth father, Specialist Tony Giles.

32

June 2005
Near Ramadi, Iraq

At 04:30 Tuesday morning, Tony, Warrant Officer Wilkins, and the team boarded an Army Blackhawk that was already warming up its engines outside the operations hangar. They wore desert BDUs, body armor, Kevlar helmets, and each of the team members carried over a hundred pounds of equipment, rations, local clothing, ammo, and water. The Blackhawk took off in a great cloud of dust and was soon at 3,500 feet, headed toward the rendezvous with a small convoy of Humvees being provided by an Arkansas National Guard unit operating out of a base west of Ramadi.

The three Hummers sat in a column in a large clearing west of Ramadi, the engines and all the lights off. The driver of the second vehicle and commander of the convoy, a Sergeant Susan Helms, had placed a small signal light, visible only from above, on the roof of her vehicle as a homing point for the helicopter. The Blackhawk copilot spotted the light, right where it should be according to the GPS, and the pilot brought the helicopter to a soft, dusty landing a few yards away. Tony and the men quickly stepped out of the chopper, Wilkins waved thanks to the crew chief, and the men carried and dragged their equipment to the Humvees. Warrant Office Wilkins, as the team leader, dumped his gear in the back of the lead vehicle, and took the passenger seat. Sergeant Drake climbed into the back. Tony took the passenger's seat of the second vehicle, and Hanks and Maraki took seats in the back, their M-4 rifles pointed out the side windows. There was a .50 caliber machine gun mounted on the roof, and the gunner stood between Hanks and Maraki, his head and shoulders out of sight above the roof.

While the Blackhawk took off, Tony shook hands with Sergeant Helms. From what he could see of her in the near darkness she was a very pretty young woman, Tony guessed about thirty, with a lock of blonde hair hanging out from under her Kevlar helmet. "Any questions, Sergeant?"

"No sir. I don't think so. Just let me get the light off the roof here and tell the guys we're ready to go, and I'll run through my orders with you." She opened her door, reached to the roof, toggled the light off, and pulled it inside. She handed it to Maraki, who put it on the floor behind her. Then she radioed the other drivers, put on blackout lights, and the convoy took off straight ahead. They reached the two-lane concrete highway only a few minutes later, and with no visible traffic at that early hour, carefully made their way up onto the pavement. Once all three of the vehicles were on the road the lead Hummer accelerated, and the little convoy was soon making a respectable sixty kilometers per hour.

When they were under way, Sergeant Helms repeated her orders to Tony from memory. "As you can see, sir, there are three vehicles in the convoy. From here we're just going to take Highway 12 northwest until we reach the GPS coordinates for a spot about a click south of Khauza. We should reach there just at dawn. We'll pull into a clearing there by the river, drop your team off, and then immediately head back for our base. I have no idea where you're going from there and, in case of my capture by the enemy, I'm not to be told. That about got it, sir?"

"Perfect, Sergeant. Thank you. I'll be riding out with you, but I won't deploy with the team. Once we drop them off I'll ride back with you to your base, and catch a ride back to my outfit from there."

"Very good, sir."

"You have a bit of southern accent. Where you from?"

"Little Rock, sir."

"You're National Guard?"

"Yessir."

"You're the commander of this convoy?"

"Yessir."

"How many times have you been deployed?"

"This is my second trip, sir. Once in Afghanistan, now here."

"What do you do in your civilian life?"

"I'm a high school teacher, sir, although I may not be able to keep that job if we keep getting deployment orders."

Tony nodded. He understood. He was very familiar with the law protecting deployed Guardsmen's civilian jobs, but employers had ways around them.

"Well, I'm from Jersey." He deliberately pronounced it 'Joisy.' "Thanks for the lift."

"Any time, sir."

"You have family, Sergeant?"

"Yessir. My husband is in the Guard, too. He's driving that Hummer up ahead of us. He's a Spec 4, so I get to boss him around sometimes." She looked over at Tony and flashed a devilish grin. "We have two kids, a boy and a girl. They're with their grandparents until we get back. Really tough on them with us gone so much. I guess we didn't think that through when we joined the Guard. Really did it because we wanted to serve, but also for the extra money. No idea we'd be deployed so much."

"Tough deal, Sergeant."

"You have a family, sir?"

"Yeah. Wife and two kids, also a boy and a girl. Just got to talk to Melissa night before last on the SAT phone. They're hanging in there. Unfortunately, we're deployed much more than we're not these days, with Iraq and Afghanistan going on, and some other stuff over in Africa. Hope these wars are over soon."

An hour later, just at dawn, Susan's husband, the lead vehicle driver, radioed to let them know they were approaching an apparent accident ahead. The convoy slowed and in the growing dawn light Tony could see what looked like a small pickup lying on its side, partially off the road surface on the right shoulder, smoke wafting up out of the engine compartment. On the shoulder alongside the truck a small group of Iraqis stood talking, among them a man holding his left arm, and a woman, fully veiled, working to bandage it.

"Tell him not to stop, Sergeant. I don't like the look of this, so early in the day," said Tony sharply. But as he said it, he realized it was too late. An RPG rocket streaked toward the lead Hummer and hit its right side. The missile exploded into the un-armored Humvee and, through its back window Tony could see the men inside being slammed by the blast. Then a second explosion, an IED, detonated from the left side of the lead Hummer, lifting the vehicle up into the air and throwing it onto its side.

Sergeant Helms was accelerating, trying to get around the ambush even though she could see that her husband had just been hit. But then a blast erupted from the roadside to their left. Tony felt their vehicle lifted into the air, seeming to come apart in the process. Despite the lessons of Mogadishu and Afghanistan, America's forces had been sent to fight the Iraq war ill-equipped for the mission, and the un-armored Humvees offered little defense against massive roadside bombs.

The Hummer crashed back down onto the road surface, its tires flattened, fuel tank ruptured, the entire vehicle riddled with shrapnel. Tony looked to his left and saw Sergeant Susan Helms, the high school teacher from Little Rock, Arkansas, wife and mother of two, slumped over the mangled steering wheel, blood pouring from wounds all around her body armor, her arms and legs covered in blood.

"Hey, guys, you OK?" he called weakly to Hanks and Maraki. But there was no answer. Turning to look back at them produced enormous pain all through his body. He was greeted with the grisly sight of both his men and the vehicle's gunner literally shredded by the bomb's shrapnel. All that remained of the gunner was his legless torso, hanging from the rim of the roof turret. The entire lower half of his body was gone. There was blood everywhere, and pieces of flesh and bone and brain and gut were strewn about the inside of the vehicle.

Tony's door was literally blown off its hinges, so he dragged himself and his weapon out onto the ground. He was screaming mad and starting to hurt like hell, and he wanted to kill the raghead bastards who had done this to his team and to him. But the group that had been standing by the truck was long gone, and there were no visible enemies to engage.

His mind clouded by the blast, Tony looked down at himself there on the ground and saw blood streaming from many places on his body where the IED had sent shards of metal and rock into him. One place on his right thigh was bleeding heavily, maybe an artery cut. His right foot was twisted unnaturally, lying flat on the ground while his left stuck straight upward. His helmet had been torn off, and his squad radio was nowhere in sight. He couldn't call for help. And he couldn't seem to think clearly enough to know what to do next.

The Humvee smoked and smoldered beside him, no human sound coming from it. Tony believed everyone inside his vehicle was dead, but he wished he could raise himself up enough to check again. He just didn't seem to have the strength. He looked toward the lead Hummer, but it was just a smoking wreck, torn to shreds. And the one behind, which was at least sitting on its tires, looked only a little better.

Through the fog of his pain and the concussion, Tony saw a young Sunni boy emerge from the trees down near the river, about twenty yards away. The boy was small and skinny, dressed in baggy gray trousers and an old tan shirt, his turban a nondescript desert tan. He had an AK-47 in his hands, and a bandolier of banana clips strapped across his chest. He walked toward Tony, the AK at the ready, his face a mask of either fear or hostility, Tony couldn't tell. Somewhere there came the noise of a helicopter in the distance, maybe an American Blackhawk? He could only hope, because his vision was dimming, and he didn't have the strength to turn his head to see. He tried to raise his M-4 to take out the Sunni kid, but again, there was no strength.

The last thing Tony saw before he blacked out was the boy standing over him, the AK pointed at his chest. Were there tears in the boy's eyes?

33

12 June 2005
Georgetown, D.C.
Mick Delaney

I stepped out of an elevator in the lobby of the Latham Hotel in Georgetown and headed for the main doors. I had become friends with the hotel's evening-shift bell captain during my three days there, having stumbled onto the fact that we had both served as grunts in Vietnam, me in the Army and my new friend Wally in the Marines. Wally had seen the miniature Army Combat Infantryman's Badge that I always wore those days on my lapel, and that had started our first conversation.

"Good evening, Mr. Delaney," said Wally with mock formality. Wally was a black man, over six feet, with broad shoulders and a thin waist, except for the slight paunch that had settled in with middle age.

"Mr. Delaney, my ass," I replied, glancing to make sure no one else was within earshot. "It's Mick to you, Wally. You know I work for a living." I grinned back.

"Yes, suh, Mr. Mick." Wally shifted to a mock southern drawl. "Anythings you say, suh," he grinned.

"Fuck you, Wally. Fuckin' Marines, anyway. Never could teach 'em anything. Hadn't been for the 1st Cav, your ass would still be stuck in Khe Sanh."

"Uh-huh," replied Wally. "Hadn't been for the 3rd Marines up north of you there on the DMZ, the NVA woulda had you Cav pussies for lunch up in the A Shau."

We both laughed. "Where you headed tonight, Mick?"

"Up to see my buddy Ed Thorsen, my last platoon leader from Vietnam. Damn good man, except he stayed in, became a fuckin' lifer."

"You guys still buddies after all this time? That's great."

"Well, we weren't in touch for a long time; then one night I got a long-distance call out of the blue. It was him, calling to tell me our twenty-fifth anniversary was coming that year. We've been staying in touch ever since."

"That's great, Mick. He was a good officer, then?"

"The best. Absolutely the best."

"Well, that's great, Mick. You have a great time. If my shift is over when you get back tonight and I don't see you before you leave tomorrow, you have a safe trip home. And take good care of yourself." Wally shook my hand, wrapped me up in a big bear hug.

People around us looked over at us, a black man and a white man, obviously from two different walks of life, both in our mid-fifties, as we hugged unashamedly in the hotel lobby. Brothers in blood. It didn't take long to become fast friends.

After a second the hug broke up. "I will, Wally. You do the same. And don't work too hard." Then one last time. "Fuckin' Marines, anyway." And I smiled and walked away.

I stepped out into the beautiful summer evening in Georgetown. As I headed out of the portico, I had to sidestep a bellman unloading baggage from a Town Car. Then I smiled and said, "Good evening!" to an attractive woman who was stepping up on the curb from the back of the car. I jaywalked across the street and headed up the block toward

Wisconsin Avenue and dinner. The sun was almost directly in my eyes as I headed northwest up the busy street, waiting at the lights like all the other civilians.

I turned north on Wisconsin and made my way up a couple of blocks to Billy Martin's Tavern at Wisconsin and N. Stepping in through the little entryway, I noticed there was no one up front to seat anyone yet. But I spotted Ed sitting at a table outside on the deck, so I threaded my way through the light crowd and stepped out to join him. As I did, Ed glanced over and smiled.

I called, "Hey, LT!" as I approached him, and his smile broadened. It had been nearly a year since we had seen each other, and our re-unions were always great. He started to stand to shake hands but I waved him down, seeing the cane next to his chair. I shook his hand warmly, sat down next to him facing away from the setting sun. "How you been, LT? What's with the cane?"

"Just some arthritis in that knee, pretty bad. That's the one where I took the shrapnel in Cambodia, acts up now and then."

"Ever think about having it taken out? The shrapnel, I mean."

"And let those lifers saw on me more than they already have? Not much chance of that."

"Well, there are civilian doctors, although I don't think they're any better. And besides, you're a fuckin' lifer, so what do you care if the lifers saw on you. Be like old home week." I grinned.

"Fuck you, Mick. How's the software business?" Thorsen main-tained a mock-serious look.

"Gangbusters, LT. Gangbusters. If I was makin' any more money, I wouldn't know where to put it."

"Sorry to hear about the divorce," Thorsen said, no longer smiling. "How long were you married?"

"Twenty-two years." I paused, the smile leaving my face. "It's OK, LT. It had been a long time coming I guess. I think we were both just waiting until the boys were grown. Didn't seem right to take away part of their childhood. But it was time."

"She doing OK?"

"Yeah, I think so. We still talk often. Nobody's pissed off at anybody. We just weren't a good couple. Not like you and Lois."

"Oh, but we have our moments."

"Sure you do, LT. Everyone does. But there's real love there. Anyone can see it. It wasn't that way with us. Not for a long time, anyway."

There was another silence.

"Want a drink?" I asked finally.

"Nah. You know I can't drink, since the shrapnel in the brain. It's all those drugs they give me to keep me rational."

"Yeah. Sorry. I forgot. Drugs aren't working very well, are they?" I punched Thorsen lightly on the shoulder. "Mind if I have one?"

"Nope. Go right ahead."

We ordered a bourbon for me, a Coke for Thorsen.

"So how's life since you quit consulting, and really retired?" I hoped I wasn't being too obvious, but I worried about Ed and the frequent bouts with depression that Lois had told me about, that seemed to come on more strongly now that he had truly retired.

"Aw, you know. I think about the war a lot more now that I'm not so busy. Think about all those kids I lost in that shithole. I guess it's worse, with more time to think about it, about how we just picked up and left, turned it over to the fucking NVA after we'd lost 58,000 killed and God knows how many others fucked-up for the rest of our lives. What a goddamned waste of good men." The bitterness was clear, undisguised.

"I know, LT. And I know I wasn't with you the whole time you were there, but while I was, I never, ever saw you lose anyone because you fucked up. You were…are…the best leader I ever knew, LT. You shouldn't blame yourself for the kids who died. Lyndon Fucking Johnson and Richard Fucking Nixon should take the blame for them. You should think about all the ones you saved. There have to be hundreds of guys like me walking around in one piece right now because of your excellent leadership. You need to think about that more."

"Problem is, Mick, I don't know who those guys are. But I do know the names and faces of the ones who died. They are etched permanently into my mind, kind of like the shrapnel."

Another silence.

"Let's order some dinner." And we did.

As we were eating, Thorsen said, "Remember that kid who got killed on point with the Dear John letter in his pocket?"

"Sure. Tony Giles. Great guy. A very close friend of mine. I took his wife's picture out of his helmet liner and the Dear John letter out of his pocket after the gooks put five or six rounds into him, including the last ones right through the chest. The fuckin' bitch."

"You still talk like a soldier, Mick."

"Only when I think about it, LT. Most of the time my language is sweet as a baby's breath."

"Better that way. Anyway, I think about Tony a lot, as one example of my mistakes. If only I'd realized how distracted he was that day, I'd have taken him off point. I might have kept him alive."

"Yeah, and some other poor kid might be dead. Tony was the best point man we had, LT. If we'd pulled him off the point, someone else, not as good, would've probably died instead.

"Look, LT," I continued, "you gotta quit this. You're the one with the PhD in Psychology, not me, but anyone can see there's no point dwelling on things like that from the past. You were a hell of a good officer. The best. People died, sure, but it was a fuckin' war, run by a bunch of dumb fuckin' lifers who were trying to make rank or satisfy their fuckin' political constituencies, just like all fuckin' wars. You did your best, and your best was very damn good. Goddamn, I hate to see someone as good as you feeling guilty because people died under your command. You were nothing like Larkin, the incompetent asshole."

"You knew he was killed back then, didn't you?"

"Yeah. Helicopter crash. Originally I heard it was shot down by the gooks, but later heard it was a mechanical failure. I was saddened by the loss of the air crew and Joe the FO, who was riding with them on their recon, but honestly it didn't bother me at all that Larkin was killed. Sorry asshole."

There was another silence.

"Anyway," I went on, "I remember Tony well. He was a really good guy. Came in country just a little before I did. We were in the same squad for a while, walked point together. Broke my heart when he was killed."

"Yeah, I know. Broke mine, too. Just giving you an example of one of my mistakes that drive me crazy."

"I think about Tony's death all the time, LT. And I often remember that I had noticed he seemed distracted when I was giving him the azimuth for the march that day, just before we took off. I should have been sharper, made sure he was OK. But as you well know there was so much shit coming down from Larkin, and we were in such a rush to move out, I didn't take the time. I think about that a lot. And I can't get over being pissed at his wife for sending him that fuckin' Dear John letter. Never did figure that out. They were crazy about each other."

"I know, I know. Well," Thorsen raised his glass, "here's to Tony. Hope he's sittin' on a cloud somewhere, surrounded by beautiful angels, happier than a clam."

"I'll drink to that, LT."

"Gave Fragman and Danny Nakamura the Bronze Star with V for going out and pulling Tony back in."

"And they certainly deserved that and more. It was an incredible act of heroism. Two more really good guys."

"But you know, the gooks counted on us doing just such stuff as that, crawling out under fire to help a wounded man. Gave them an opportunity to maybe pick off a couple more of our guys. You wouldn't see a gook crawl out under fire after their wounded. Their doctrine would never allow it. No sentiment from those motherfuckers."

"That's why they'll never beat us," I said with a small grin.

"They did beat us, Mick."

"Oh, yeah." I laughed at my little joke. "Oh well, fuck 'em. As I often say, they may have beat 'Us,'" I held up my fingers in quotes, "but they didn't beat you and me. I don't remember losing any battles. You remember losing any battles, LT?"

"Oh, I guess you'd have to say we lost a few firefights. Some of those where the gooks killed one of our guys and then *dee-dee-mowed* the fuck out of there before we could get back at 'em. But any time they stayed and fought, we kicked their asses. Destroyed the motherfuckers."

I laughed. "By the way, now whose fuckin' language is startin' to sound like the fuckin' Army, LT?" We caught a glare from the well-dressed, white-haired man who had sat down with his wife at the next table, unnoticed by us.

"Sorry," said Thorsen, flashing a smile their way.

"Don't mind him, sir, ma'am," I added. "He's just out of the home for the evening. I'll be taking him back to his rubber room in a little while. Deranged Vietnam vet, you know? Caught him the other day on top of a building, shooting at some passers-by with an invisible rifle. Sad." I hoped there was an impish twinkle in my eye.

The man gave another glare. His wife, seeing my grin, laughed out loud. Thorsen shook his head sadly, but there was a smile on his face.

"More like it, LT. You used to laugh all the time, sometimes even in firefights."

"Yeah, well, I was young and carefree then."

"Yeah, carefree. Right. You were responsible for forty guys in a very dangerous combat zone, and you took it very seriously. I don't call that 'carefree'."

"Hey, you remember Nick Avery, got the Medal of Honor for that action in the spring of '70?"

"Maybe a little. That was after I came home. But I think he was in First Platoon when I was there. Nice kid, as I remember. That was the second Medal of Honor for our company in just a few months, wasn't it? After Carl Engle?"

"Yeah, it was. Very unusual. Anyway...Avery's coming to West Virginia this weekend. He and his buddy Ray Davenport were a machine gun team. Well, Davenport's son is getting married, and Nick's coming all the way from South Dakota to be there."

"And you know all this how?" I asked.

"Davenport invited me to the wedding."

"No kiddin.' That's great, LT. You guys stay in touch?"

"Not really. I got a call from Davenport a couple of weeks ago, asking me to come. Hadn't seen either of them since they were Medevac'd the night they got hurt, almost thirty-five years ago.

"You going?"

"I'd like to. You want to go? I'd feel better with someone else along. From there, you know?"

"Well, I'm supposed to fly out tomorrow, but I can change that easily enough, and go back Sunday instead. What time's the wedding?"

"It's at 4:00, out in the country on a farm. I hear the bride's riding in on a white horse."

"Have to say I never saw that before. Should be fun."

"And you can stay over at my place tomorrow night, and I'll invite some of the neighbors. Some of the newer ones have never met you, and they're curious."

"You been tellin' war stories again, LT?"

"Just about the time you took my grenades away because I bounced one off a tree."

"That's bullshit, LT. I never took your grenades away."

"Right after I got there."

"Nope. Not me. I taught you how to smoke, but I never took any grenades away."

The server brought us both coconut cream pie.

"So you're coming?"

"Sure. I'll change the flight when I get back to the hotel. How did Avery get the Medal of Honor?"

Thorsen told me.

"Jesus Christ," I said.

"Yeah. Good coconut cream pie, eh?"

"Yeah, LT. Great coconut cream pie."

34

12 June 2005
Georgetown, D.C.

It was after 11:00 when I left the restaurant. Thorsen and I had made plans for the next day for Ed to pick me up outside the Georgetown office of Delaney Enterprises at 4:30. I headed back down Wisconsin Avenue toward M, then decided to take a narrow side street, Congress Court, over to 31st and then down to M, to avoid having to jostle my way through so much of the crowd that always seemed to be out that late in Georgetown. My mind was back in the war to the day Tony was killed, just walking along, my hands in my pockets, lost in my thoughts. As I walked past an alley, I noticed a street sign declaring it "Corcoran Alley" and thought to myself *They even name the alleys here?*

Just as I was passing it I heard someone cry out from the semi-darkness, then a crash of something heavy falling or being thrown into cardboard boxes and trash cans, then footsteps running away.

I stopped, looked ahead and behind myself to see if there was anyone else on the street, but seeing no one, I took a step into the alley and called out, "Who's there?" There was only a muffled moan in reply. I looked up and down the street again, hoping for a police car, or at least another pedestrian, but there was no one. I didn't want to go into the alley, but I couldn't just walk away, either.

"Who's there?" I called again, louder. No answer at all this time. I looked around for a weapon, a board, a stone, anything. Nothing.

Cautiously, I stepped into the alley. I heard another groan, sounding like it came from behind some garbage cans and a stack of boxes and other trash. The hair on my neck bristled up. This was really stupid, I knew. But I couldn't just walk away and leave someone there hurt. I waited a few seconds until my eyes got used to the semi-darkness, then made my way a few feet farther, saw a man's leg protruding from behind the trash. I stepped forward then, rounded the trash can, and came face-to-face with a gun, pointed right at my belly. The man holding it was sitting propped comfortably against the wall of one of the old buildings, his left leg extended past the trash, his right drawn up so his gun arm could rest on his knee.

"Dammit!" I said, disgusted with my own stupidity.

The man pulled his other leg back and pushed his way up off the ground, the gun pointed steadily at my belly. He was a white man, almost my height but heavier, wearing work clothes that were only a couple of days dirty, not the filthy rags of a true resident of the streets. A snarl of a grin exposed crooked front teeth in an unshaven face.

"Well, stranger, that was a little stupid, don't you think? Just walking in here like that? But you know what? It works almost every time. I'm getting pretty good at faking that running away sound."

He looked at my left wrist. "That's a nice watch you got there. Why don't you hand it over?"

I lifted my left hand, looked at the watch, let it fall back to my side. Then I looked directly into his eyes. I didn't say anything, didn't blink. But I made no move to hand over the watch.

"I said hand it over, motherfucker! And your wallet, too. I bet it's nice and fat. Hand 'em over, or I put one in your gut."

I stuck out my lower lip, smiled a little. Then I shook my head slowly, still looking the man in the eyes.

"You fuckin' nuts? Hand 'em over or I kill you and take 'em."

I kept looking into his eyes. The surly confidence was leaving them, replaced by uncertainty, maybe the beginnings of fear.

Finally, I spoke. "Go ahead and shoot. You'd be doing me a favor. I've been looking for an honorable way out of this life, and I guess being shot by some low-life motherfucker like you will do just fine."

I paused, smiled at the guy. "Only I have to warn you. I've been shot before, and I guarantee if you don't kill me with the first one, you'll regret it. I'll take that gun away from you and shove it up your ass." And as an afterthought, "And then I'll pull the fuckin' trigger." I smiled broadly at my own little joke. His smile was gone now. "If I were you, I'd make it a head shot. Here, I'll stand real still." I stood up nice and straight. "Wouldn't want you to miss."

The smile again. I did have my charm.

His eyes widened in disbelief. I could see he knew I was serious, that I was not only unafraid but would welcome death. He'd picked on a real crazy one this time. Then I saw realization in his eyes, that *I* had *him* cornered. He started looking from side to side, for a way out.

I thought about stepping forward to force him to shoot, but figured he was so scared he'd probably miss, maybe hit me in some non-lethal spot and fuck me up more than I already was. I decided this was not my chance at a clean, honorable end to my life.

So I took a step backward instead.

With that opening, the man bolted to his right and sprinted down the alley into the darkness.

"You're fuckin' crazy!" he shouted back over his shoulder.

"That's what your wife said!" I shouted in return. Again, not a great retort. But the best I could come up with at the time.

I waited until the running figure disappeared around a corner, then picked my way back to Congress Court and headed for 31st Street. Around another corner, down a block, and I emerged into the late night crowd on M Street, starting to clear out a bit. I crossed over and made my way back to the Latham, finding myself whistling happily as I walked.

One of the things the war had cost me, I'd realized long ago, was my fear of death. I just wasn't afraid of it. I'd already faced it more times than I could count in Vietnam, and had found it to be like anything else.

You get used to it.

And with death, I believed, would have come peace at last. After the years of nightmares, the memories of friends lost and mistakes made, the bouts with depression, the anger that came over me sometimes that was so hard to control, and the eventual bad end to every relationship I'd tried to have with a woman, I would certainly have welcomed peace.

My volunteering for that fucked-up war had cost me both my wives, had put my mother through another year of hell, waiting for someone else she loved to come back from some foreign place where his life was constantly in danger. It had given me heart disease that I worked constantly to control. It had cost me most of my hearing and put permanent ringing in my ears. And was likely, I knew, through the Agent Orange I carried in my body, to end my life early through some miserable, drag-you-down-and-eat-your-guts-out disease.

Since the second divorce, I'd sometimes actually thought about how easy it would be to have a few drinks, put the muzzle of a handgun in my mouth, and pull the trigger. I figured I wouldn't know anything after that until I got my chance to sit down with God in the afterlife and discuss how I'd fucked this one up. I'd been looking forward to that conversation for a long time.

But there was one critical reason I could never commit suicide: I'd never want my sons, my sister Sarah, or anyone else I cared for to feel the guilt that all loving suicide survivors had, the feeling that they somehow could have done more to prevent it. They would never understand that there was really nothing they could do. The damage had been done all those years ago in the war, and I wasn't having much luck, even with a lot of help, getting it undone.

I found myself happy with my foolish little detour into the alley. That encounter with the mugger and my reaction to it had somehow clarified things in my mind. I had often thought that if I had the opportunity to leave this lifetime honorably, I would take it. But I'd never really known how I'd react to an actual opportunity until one came along. One had come, or almost come, and I'd reacted just as I'd imagined I would. Plus, I had to admit, I kind of enjoyed that little buzz I got from it.

"Mick," I muttered to myself as I entered the Latham, "you are one fucked-up dude."

35

12 June 2005
Georgetown, D.C.

Wally was still on duty in the lobby, standing tall and proud, his hands clasped behind him, a perfect Marine Corps parade rest. He turned as I entered the lobby and saw my smile, and a big grin took over his massive brown face. "How was your evening, Mick?" he called, his deep voice booming across the room.

"It was great, Wally, thanks. Colonel Thorsen is doing well. He seemed to be in better spirits than last time I was here. I'm going to stay over a couple more days with him and his wife. I guess a couple of the guys from Vietnam are going to be over in West Virginia this weekend together for a wedding. We're going over, have a little re-union. Bride's riding in on a white horse! Should be fun."

Wally threw back his head and laughed, a deep belly laugh. "It's so good to hear you guys are doing well, Mick. I'm really happy for you."

I said good night to Wally and headed into the hotel bar for a nightcap.

The attractive woman I'd seen stepping out of the limo as I'd left the hotel earlier that evening was sitting in one of the booths, a drink in front of her. She was well dressed, had a pretty oval face with very little makeup, maybe a couple of years younger than me. She wore a gray business suit with the jacket open, a conservative white blouse underneath. One strand of pearls and no other jewelry. No wedding ring. A very pretty lady. And attractive, well beyond pretty.

Across from her in the booth was a tall, thin man, a few years younger than her, chattering away, reaching over to pat her hand as he talked. "You're sure a pretty little thing," he said to her, a bit too loudly. "What's a pretty lady like you doing alone on a fine night like this?"

He paused to check his watch, and as he did the woman looked toward me, rolled her eyes up, then opened them wide. "Help!" she seemed to say wordlessly.

As smoothly as I could, I altered course away from the bar and toward the booth. "Oh, there you are!" I called to her with a big smile. "Almost didn't see you! Who's your friend?"

The man looked up at me and the smile vanished from his face. Foiled again.

"Just keeping the lady company," he said to me. Then he turned to the woman. "Well, g'night, Miss." He slid out of the booth, head down, not looking at me, made his way back to the bar.

I sat down across from her.

"Thank you!" she whispered. "He was being a pest. Had a bit too much to drink." Without extending her hand she said, "I'm Julie."

"Nice to meet you, Julie. I'm Mick. And it was my pleasure. You have very good facial communication skills."

"Thanks. You could see the desperation. I hope you're not planning to get drunk and become obnoxious, too," she smiled.

"Well, that was my plan. However, in consideration to your company, if only for a little while, I'll change that. Now I'll only get half drunk and become semi-obnoxious. How's that?"

We both laughed. "Sounds fair enough," she said.

"Seriously, if you like I'll sit here a few minutes, give you a chance to make an exit before the vultures start circling again. You know, if a pretty woman like you sits alone in a hotel bar, she's going to draw a crowd."

"I guess. I was just going to have a couple of drinks to take the edge off the day before I head upstairs."

"You travel much?"

"All the time. Since my husband died a few years ago, and with my daughters grown, I don't have much reason to be home. And the money's good. I sell prosthetics to doctors and hospitals. Up here for a couple of days to get a technology update at Georgetown."

"I'm sorry about your husband. He passed away pretty young."

"Yeah. Heart attack at age fifty-one. He'd been diagnosed with heart disease a couple of years before, and it just got steadily worse. He believed it was because of the Agent Orange he was exposed to during the war. He was an Air Force pilot in Vietnam."

"Ah. I'm so sorry." The fucking war, again. "We seem to be losing a lot of Vietnam veterans to Agent Orange. I've lost several friends to it."

"Were you there?"

"Oh, yeah. In '69."

"What did you do?"

"I was infantry. 1st Cavalry Division."

"Were you an officer?"

"Nope. Just a grunt. I was a platoon sergeant for a while before I came home."

"What do you do now?"

I pulled one of my business cards, handed it to her. "I've got this company going, out of Kansas City. We have an office here in Georgetown. Just up for a couple of days. Where are you from?"

"Chicago. North side."

"Ah. Got those chilly winters."

"Yes, indeed we do. You're not wearing a ring," she said. "Are you married?"

"No. Divorced a couple of years ago. Two-time loser. Got a couple of great sons out of this one, though. Really good young men."

"Are they married?"

"No, neither of them. Your girls?"

"The older one is. The younger one is still in college."

"Grand-kids?"

"Not yet. But I've got my fingers crossed."

I laughed. "Me, too. But I guess somebody ought to get married first."

"You seem like a bright, educated person, Mick. Obviously successful in business. How'd you wind up as a 'grunt' as you call it, in Vietnam? I thought most of the boys who went there as infantry were drafted, mostly poor, uneducated kids."

"Lot of people think that. It's not really true, at least from my experience. I'm in touch with a few of the guys I was there with and, as it happens, I know the current circumstances of the four guys who were in my platoon's 'CP,' the platoon command group. There was the platoon leader, a first lieutenant; the medic, who was a Conscientious Objector; the radio operator; and the platoon sergeant. That was me. Of the four, two now hold PhDs, one in psychology, the other in education. One holds a Master's in education, and I'm the fourth, with an MBA. One was a career Army officer and went pretty high up and is now a big-dollar consultant to the Pentagon and Congress. The medic is now superintendent of schools in Massachusetts, the RTO runs a non-profit education program for Navajo Indians in New Mexico, and I'm president of my own company. I got curious about it and did some research. Turns out that over 60% of those of us who served in Vietnam volunteered, and almost 65% of those killed were volunteers. Lot of bad data out there about Vietnam."

"So, how'd you wind up there?"

"Destiny, I think. Members of my family have been citizen soldiers since the Civil War. Had two great-great-grandfathers in that
one, on opposite sides. My grandfather fought in World War I. My dad
and most of my uncles fought in World War II. Then my mom's little
brother was killed in Korea. Changed her life, and not for the better.
Lot of stories there, but anyway, I wound up volunteering."

"Good lord, why?"

"My buddies were all going, and for some reason I didn't get called.
I think I just felt like I should serve because my family always had. Or
maybe in some perverse way I was doing it to get my mother's attention after she'd been so distracted all those years by my uncle's death.
Probably take a shrink to help me figure that one out."

"My husband was a volunteer, of course. Sure changed him."

"I think it changed all of us, more than many of us want to admit."

We sat and talked awhile. I found Julie to be interesting, intelligent, and very attractive. But a bit sad. I could tell she still missed her
husband.

After a few more minutes I said, "Just tell me when you're ready
to call it a night, and I'll make sure you get to the elevator without
another buzzard attack."

"Thanks," she said. "I'll have another drink if you don't mind sitting
a few more minutes."

"Sure." I turned and held up two fingers to the bartender.

"Prosthetics, eh? I've heard they're now able to attach prosthetic
hands to nerve endings in amputees' arms so they can actually move
the fingers."

"Oh, yes. That's one of the areas with the most advancement. With
the wars in Afghanistan and Iraq and so many IEDs and other explosives, a lot of soldiers are suffering multiple amputations. Really tough
going through life with no hands. That's what we're talking about at

Georgetown tomorrow morning. Then I guess we're going to Walter Reed in the afternoon to visit some of the patients who have volunteered to try some of the new prosthetic hands."

We finished our drinks, and I paid the tab.

"Ready?" I said.

"I am. Thanks for the drinks. I didn't mean for you to buy."

"My pleasure."

We stood and headed for the elevator. Wally was still at his post. "Night, Wally," I called over.

"Night, Mick." Wally's eyebrows raised a fraction. I shook my head.

"Friend of yours?" asked Julie.

"Yeah. Just since I've been here the last couple of days. Ex-Marine from Vietnam. Good guy."

"You guys stick together, don't you?"

"Well, there's this sort of bond thing that happens. Hard to explain. We feel so poorly understood by most regular people that when we bump into a brother from the war it often makes us instant friends."

We got on the elevator. "What floor?" I asked.

"Well… May I ask a favor?"

"Sure."

"You're so nice, and I feel like I can trust you. I don't sleep at all well when I'm alone on the road. Would it be too weird if I asked to come and sleep with you… just sleep?"

"You have to be the world's most trusting soul to ask a thing like that." I checked my own feelings about her, decided I could take a chance and trust her. "But… sure. Rather sleep in my room than yours?"

"Doesn't matter to me."

"All right. You want to pick up something to sleep in? I'm in 318."

"OK. I'm on 4. I'll go get my things and be at your door in a few minutes."

"Gotta warn you," I said. "I sleep in my boxers."

"That's OK."

"And there's only one bed."

"I assumed that."

I got off on 3, walked down the hall to my room, shaking my head. "Totally weird day," I said to no one in particular.

I let myself into the room, took off my jacket and tie, brushed my teeth, then sat down in the armchair and switched on the TV. Late night news. I was watching it, getting drowsy from the alcohol, when I heard Julie knock on the door. I opened it, and she slipped inside, her night gown and a robe over her arm.

"Welcome to my humble room."

"Thanks. I'll go get ready for bed."

"I'm ready, so I'll meet you there. Any side you prefer?"

"Farthest from the door."

"You got it."

Julie went into the bathroom and closed the door, and I undressed, hung my clothes in the closet, and climbed into bed. The TV was on, but for the sake of Julie's modesty I turned off the lamp, so the room was pretty dark. She came out a few minutes later wearing the robe, went around to the window side of the bed. I kept my eyes on the TV as she took off the robe and slipped under the covers.

"Want to watch TV?" I asked.

"No. Kind of sleepy. Want to take advantage of it." To my surprise, she snuggled up to me, her breasts pressing against my arm, kissed me on the cheek.

"You're sweet, Mick. Thank you."

It had been well over two years since I had made love to a woman, my ex-wife. I was instantly aroused. I turned on my side, facing away from her, embarrassed. "Good night, Julie."

But there was no response. Already asleep.

I lay quietly, wide awake at first, thinking about the day, the evening, the woman in bed with me, my life, my near-death, the future. Where did it lie? I didn't know. At the moment, I was too tired to care. Finally, I fell asleep.

A little later, even with enough drinks under my belt to numb things a bit, or maybe because of them, I had the dream.

36

It was again July 18, 1969. Danny and Tony and I came in off the listening post again, just as we had all those years before, and I was as angry as I had actually been at Carl's decision not to go out, and that I had to go out all the more often because of that. But in this version, I thought better of it before going to talk to Carl, and I took the point that morning myself, as I was convinced I should have in real life. It was me stepping out into the jungle at the lead instead of Carl, me seeing the gook mine to my front and diving for it, my hand on my knife to cut the wires. There was a bright flash of light and incredible heat in my face, and then I was blind and in horrible, unimaginable pain and only barely able to breathe through the blood that sucked into my lungs with each labored breath.

It was me who Danny and Doc Benedetto labored over, me who clawed at my face to get more air! More precious air! It was me they gave up on after I felt myself go still.

Only in this nightmare I wasn't really dead. And once I went still, I could see again, but as though from above. I could see them carrying me back to the helicopter pad, could see them lowering me into the infernal heat and awful hot-rubber smell of an Army body bag. I tried to talk, to move, to raise my hand, anything to let them know I was alive. But I couldn't move! Couldn't make a sound.

Then I felt myself being lifted and laid on the floor of a helicopter, and I felt hands on me and heard Danny and Carl saying goodbye, and then I felt myself flying and flying. In the body bag it was terrifyingly hot, and there was no air, and yet I lived on. I was repeatedly lifted and moved and set down and then lifted again.

Finally, the body bag was eventually unzipped, and there above me was the face of my wife, Katie, and she was looking down at me, crying, her tears splashing on my terrified face!

***

I bolted upright in bed, my hands on my head, trembling. "Uhhhhhh!" I cried out.

Julie, startled awake by my sudden movement and muffled scream, sat up, reached over, and turned on the lamp.

"Mick! What is it?"

I remembered then where I was and came back to reality. "Oh …I'm sorry, Julie. Nightmare. I should have warned you that I have those sometimes. Too much talk about the war today. Sorry. Turn out the light. I'll try not to wake you again."

She sat and looked at me for a second. "You sure you're OK?"

"Yeah. I'm fine. Sorry."

Julie's nightgown was cut somewhat low in the front, and my eyes fell momentarily to her breasts. I looked away quickly, but she had seen me look.

"Hey, Mick," she said softly. "I think I know how we can get back to sleep." She reached over her head and pulled her nightgown up and off. Her breasts were perfectly shaped, the nipples erect. She slid down to lie flat, turned on her side, reached over and took my hand and put it on her breast.

"Boy," I said, a little grin on my face, "that nightmare bit works every time."

She laughed, reached around, slapped me on the butt. But then she trailed her hand across my hip around to the front, and it found other things to do.

A while later she collapsed under me, her eyes closed, both of us exhausted.

After a few minutes, she turned her head and faced me, looked into my eyes in the near-darkness, and said with a smile, "I'm guessing you've done this before."

I smiled back. "Well... not lately, that's for sure."

"You didn't finish, did you?" she asked.

"Gee, that's kinda personal, don't you think?"

"Yeah. But I'm asking. Did you?"

"Well, no. But you seemed to enjoy yourself."

"Oh, I did, I did. But... there is one more thing I'd enjoy."

She pushed me onto my back, climbed on top, eased herself onto me. "This OK?" she asked.

"Oh .... yeah." I wondered if she could see my huge smile.

Despite Julie's prediction about getting back to sleep, we never did.

37

14 June 2005
Georgetown, D.C. and Springfield, VA

We got up at seven, exhausted but both very happy. I was amazed at what Julie had drawn from me.

"Want to meet for breakfast?" I asked.

"Oh, I'd love to, Mick, but I have to be at Georgetown by 8:00, and they always have a light breakfast there. I'll be rushing to make that."

She sat down, though, before leaving my room, took one of her business cards from her purse, and wrote her home phone number and address on the back. She handed it to me.

"You will call me, won't you?"

"Julie. Sweet Julie," I said, my face hopefully a mask.

Her smile turned into a look of concern. "What, Mick?"

I grinned. "You can absolutely count on it. Kansas City to Chicago is not even a real flight. When will you be back home?"

She punched me in the ribs, lightly, but enough to make me groan. "You're gonna pay for that, Mick!" With that she pulled open her robe, pulled down the front of her nightgown to expose her breasts, and just as I reached out to touch, pulled the nightgown up, closed the robe, stuck her tongue out at me, laughed, kissed me on the lips, and turned and walked out the door.

Where have you been all my life? I asked myself.

I had breakfast in the hotel coffee shop, one eye open, then made it to the Georgetown office of Delaney Enterprises, only a couple of blocks down the street, by a few minutes after 9:00. Just this once I wouldn't be there when the doors opened.

The branch manager, a sharp young man named George Randall, was waiting for me. I did my absolute best to stay awake and alert through the review we'd scheduled of several major projects, but George and the others could see I wasn't in top form.

"You feeling OK, Mick?"

"Yeah. Just tired, I guess. Didn't sleep well last night."

"Sorry to hear that. Too noisy in Georgetown?"

"Not really. Just...couldn't sleep." I smiled to myself.

Ed Thorsen picked me up outside the office right on the dot at 4:30. He was driving a gray, ten-year-old Mercedes convertible, his "second car." It was in immaculate condition. Ed loved his cars.

By this time, I was starting to revive a bit. "This is gonna be fun, LT. I'm looking forward to seeing your neighbors again, every single one of them. Even the crazy ones."

"Yeah, I told Don Rensler last night to let everyone know. Party's on my front porch. Better warm up your vocal chords, buddy. Going to be a long night. I laid in a good supply of Coronas for you and the gang, and you know how they like to talk."

"What time are we leaving for the wedding tomorrow? I have to get my beauty rest, you know."

"I thought we'd leave around nine, should get over there by around one o'clock. Wedding's at five, so that'll give us some time for a little reunion. I hope these guys are doing OK. They both really got messed up bad in that firefight when Nick earned the Medal of Honor. I can still remember their wounds. Worst mess I ever saw, thought they were both gone for sure. Nick with his guts all over the ground, Davenport with his legs in shreds, barely attached. And they were both still awake, in shock but awake. Medics threw tourniquets on Davenport, wasn't anything they could do for Avery except try to keep all his insides in one place and attached."

"Jesus, LT. How many of those memories you have in your head?"

"Way more than I can handle sometimes, Mick. Way more than that."

We made our way down George Washington Parkway to the 395, a little ahead of rush hour but still slow going. By the time we reached Thorsen's home in Springfield, it was almost 6:00. I pulled my bag out of the back seat, followed Ed through the front door. Lois was there, and I gave her a big hug and a kiss on the cheek. "Lois! It's sooooooooo good to see you! I have missed you guys! Thanks for putting me up for the night, or two nights, I guess, eh? How have you been?"

"Great! Good to see you, too, Mick. How's the world treating you?"

"Got no complaints, Lois. Got no complaints."

"I thought we'd start the party at 6:30, and, instead of dinner I have a bunch of snacks. If we're still hungry when you guys finish telling your war stories we'll order a pizza or something."

"Sounds terrific, Lois. Am I in the same room?"

"Yep. I changed the sheets, and the towels in the guest bath are clean. You should be all set."

"Thank you, Lois. I really appreciate it."

Ed had left the room, was back on the porch smoking a cigar, and petting the dog, Stonewall.

"I'm so glad you could stay, Mick," Lois said. "Ed's really looking forward to this wedding trip, to seeing these guys. But he's also a little nervous about it, too. And you're so good for him. He's always in a better state of mind when you're around."

"Well, I'm glad I could stay, Lois. And being around the two of you helps me, too. I have my down times, and it helps me to feel useful to Ed. So it works for everyone. And, of course, it's always an absolute delight to see you."

She kissed my cheek. "You're sweet, Mick. Now get out of here so I can get these snacks going. When you come back from putting your bag in your room, would you take the cooler outside?"

"Sure thing, Lois."

Ten minutes later I was on the porch, sitting back in one of the comfortable patio chairs, a beer in hand, watching Ed light his cigar. Stonewall was sitting at Ed's feet, a contented dog. The late evening sun was breaking through the trees to Ed's back, and there was the slightest of breezes. It was a perfect evening.

I caught movement out of the corner of my eye and turned to see a full-grown male Boxer running full speed straight across the yard toward me. I grinned, yelled, "Hey, Satan!" and the boxer ran to me, skidded across the concrete floor and wound up sprawled with his front feet in my lap. Stonewall barely moved. "Hey, buddy! How you been?" I scratched the big dog's ears and petted his shoulders. "Where's Don? Huh? Where's your old man?"

Don Rensler, Ed's next door neighbor, strolled across the yard toward us. "Jesus, Satan! Don't crush the man! How are you, Mick?"

"Doing fine, Don. Just fine. And Satan's not a problem. It's good to see you both." I stood, shook Don's hand, sat back down.

"Have a beer, Don." Ed opened the cooler, pulled one out of the ice, popped the cap.

"Thanks, Ed. So, what's up with you guys?"

"We're going over to West Virginia tomorrow. Couple guys from Vietnam, one's son is getting married. They invited me, and I figured Mick would enjoy it, so he's staying over to go, too. Bride's riding in on a white horse, never saw that before."

"Yeah," I added. "I wasn't there when it happened, but I guess they were in a terrible firefight, and one of these guys, Avery, rolled on a frag. Would have killed both of them and some others, too, except for that. He thought to put his helmet over the frag before he rolled on it or it would have blown him into a fine pink mist. As it was, I guess it blew most of his guts out, fucked up Davenport's legs pretty bad. The LT put Avery in for the Medal of Honor, and he eventually got it. That was in, what, April of '70, LT?

"Yeah. They used to call our company 'Deathwing Delta' but sometimes it should have been 'Dying Delta.' We were in a lot of shit there for a while," said Ed.

Don grumbled, "Wish I'd been there. Too young."

"No disrespect, Don," I said, "but are you out of your mind? Never feel bad about missing that fiasco. Wish I'd missed it. Then maybe I could sleep nights."

"You still have trouble sleeping?" Don asked.

"Yeah. Well, it's only been thirty-six years, so maybe I'll get over it."

"Same here," said Ed. "Really fucks you up."

Another neighbor, a tall, fit, blonde man of about forty, came up on the porch. "Hi, guys."

"Hey, Allen," answered Ed. "Want you to meet my platoon sergeant from Vietnam, Mick Delaney."

I stood again. "Nice to meet you."

"Allen's a light colonel in the Marine Corps, Mick. Just got back from Iraq."

"Yeah, and just got my orders for my next tour. Leaving again in five more months. Hardly going to get to know my kids again before it's time to go."

"Jeez, I'll bet Lana's pissed about that," said Ed.

"You ain't kiddin.' If I'd known I was going to spend this much of the time deployed, I'd have either chosen another line of work, or stayed single. It's hell on us, but major hell on a woman alone with four kids. This'll be my third trip."

"That sucks, Allen," I said. "I bitch about my one tour, and it was a short one."

"Yeah, but you guys were in the bush all the time. Don't know how you took that. At least we get to come into a compound most nights. Even have air conditioned Conex containers to sleep in sometimes. Different war."

"I guess so," I said. "But you're still in harm's way most of the time. Has to get on your nerves. I bet the PTSD is running rampant with you guys and the other veterans now."

"Yeah, a lot of it. Other thing they don't talk much about is all the suicides. My last deployment we had four in my battalion alone. And these were Marines. They're very well-conditioned to hardship. I hear it's worse for the Army units."

"Big difference. I don't remember any suicides in our unit in Vietnam. You, LT?"

"Nope. Lots of self-inflicted wounds, bullets through the feet, stuff like that. But I don't remember any suicides."

A young Hispanic man approached and, while Ed was still talking to Allen, introduced himself to me as Sal Duello. Sal sat down on a foot stool, listened to the talk for a while. When Allen got up to leave and things quieted down, Sal politely asked me, "What was it like in Vietnam, sir? Ed won't talk too much about it, but I'm very interested. You were a platoon sergeant, eh?"

"Yeah, Sal. What do you want to know?"

"Terrain, living conditions, how often you were in contact, stuff like that."

I did my best to describe it. Got into it pretty easily with someone who seemed so interested. Talked about how much of the time we spent off the firebase in the jungle, how often we made contact, every day sometimes, even more often sometimes, sometimes not for a week or more. Every time I would pause, Sal would ask another question. He looked so young I figured he was just out of high school, thinking about enlisting, wanted to know what war was like. So I told him the best I could. I was as honest as I could remember in the telling, not exaggerating it one way or the other. I didn't much like war stories, especially in situations like these.

"Is it true you took Colonel Thorsen's grenades away from him?"

"No, that's bullshit. I never did that. I taught him how to smoke and gave him his first cigarette, but I never took his frags away. That must have been someone else. He was this goody-goody little West Point grad," I teased. "Someone had to corrupt him."

"Yes, you did, Mick," said Thorsen. "You did take my frags. I remember it."

"Bullshit, LT. Never did that."

Sal got up to leave, shook my hand. "It was nice meeting you, sir. Thanks for the information. Take care."

"You too, Sal. Nice meeting you. Good luck to you."

"Know who that was?" asked Thorsen when Sal was out of earshot.

"Kid thinking about going into the military, I assumed. He was very curious, seemed very thoughtful."

"Not quite. That's Staff Sergeant Sal Duello. Ex-Army. Enlisted when he got out of high school, went Special Forces, was a medic. He did two tours in Iraq, one in Afghanistan. Wounded three times. Has two Silver Stars, three or four Bronze, three Purple Hearts. Tough little sonofabitch."

"Wow. He's got way more combat experience than I do. Could have fooled me. He seemed so curious, I didn't figure."

"Yeah. He's a good kid. After his third tour, he went over again for six months with Blackwater, earned enough on that one tour to buy his mother that house down the street."

"Bet he hasn't slept a wink in years," I said.

"Bet you're right."

We called it a night around 11:00. I turned in but couldn't sleep. Thinking about the evening, and the war again. I finally fell asleep about 1:00.

Sometimes I dreamed about the day Tony died. Sometimes I dreamed about my last night in the field, the night I'd been wounded twice in one firefight, the night we'd almost been overrun by the North Vietnamese. Sometimes I dreamed about ambushes I'd been on, or been in. Any number of small firefights I'd been through. But often when I dreamed about the war, I dreamed about July 18, 1969, the day I'd had something to do with Carl Engle's death.

Years after the war, the military and Veterans Administration doctors had come up with a term to describe what thousands of us would endure for the rest of our lives. They called it Post Traumatic Stress at first, and later, perhaps because PTS didn't roll off the tongue well as an acronym (too close to PMS?) they extended it to Post Traumatic Stress Disorder, or PTSD. I had finally gone to be tested for it, and they'd found my levels on both the scales they used to be very high. The doctors had been amazed by that, probably because I had managed to become successful in business and outwardly successful in life, and hadn't fallen out of society to live on the streets, a hopeless drunk or drug addict.

I had gone to the group therapy sessions, and they had helped some, I supposed. And I remained in private therapy and probably would for life. But I never got over it, and I doubted I ever would. And I still had the dreams.

It was a little after 5 am when I woke up from another nightmare, terrified, and sat up in the near-darkness, shaking. Then I remembered where I was and lay back down. I'd only slept four hours and had hardly slept at all the night before. In a little while my heart stopped racing, my blood stopped pounding in my ears, and my breathing slowed to normal.

But I didn't sleep again that night.

38

14 June 2005
Springfield, VA and near Kingwood,
West Virginia

We were up and away early in the Mercedes convertible, the top still down. It was chilly at highway speeds that early in the day, but the LT seemed to enjoy the cold, so I kept my mouth shut and shivered. We stopped for breakfast and coffee at a Burger King along the way, made it to Ray Davenport's bed and breakfast in the West Virginia countryside about noon. The place was a refurbished farmhouse about a hundred yards back from the road, most of the surrounding land in pasture and orchards with a few acres of forest, rolling hills in the background. It was a beautiful scene, a place like I would have liked to own, so peaceful there in the countryside.

Davenport came out to meet us as we pulled up to the farmhouse. He recognized Thorsen, cordially greeting him with, "Good morning, Captain. Thanks for coming! Looks like it'll be a beautiful day for a wedding."

Ed introduced me. "You remember Mick Delaney? He was my platoon sergeant in Third Platoon in '69, until we were both wounded in that big firefight the end of October. He went home not long after that."

I shook Davenport's hand. "How are you, Ray? You look good. Beautiful place you have here."

"Thanks, Mick. And thanks for coming. Should be an interesting day."

"Where's Nick?" Thorsen asked.

"He's up at the cabin. It's about five miles from here, up in the hills. My family doesn't live here. We operate this place as a bed and breakfast, leave all the bedrooms for guests. We live in some cabins I built back up in the hills. Wait'll I tell my wife where we're going, and you can follow me up there."

He turned and walked back into the house. Avery was wearing a pair of baggy khaki shorts with cargo pockets on the side, worn track shoes with no socks, and a faded gold and black West Virginia Mountaineers t-shirt. As he walked back into the house I noticed his lower thighs and calves were covered with ugly deep scars, severe indentations where chunks of muscle were missing.

He came back alone, and I saw that the front of his legs were just as badly scarred. I tried not to stare, but Davenport saw me looking. It didn't seem to bother him. "She's elbow deep in some cooking right now, guys. Wanted to clean up a little before she meets you. We'll catch up with her before the wedding. Want to follow me up to the cabin? I'll take that red pickup."

"Sure, Ray," said Thorsen.

We climbed back into the Mercedes, turned around in the driveway and followed Ray's truck out onto the road. It was a two-lane blacktop, but a mile or so north we followed him off onto a dry, dusty gravel road. Thorsen dropped back far enough to let the slight breeze carry most of Davenport's dust to one side before we passed through it.

"You gave me the short version of how Avery earned his Medal of

Honor the other night, LT. And I remember you said that Davenport was with him and had his legs torn up. But, Jesus! I'm surprised he can walk."

"Yeah. I haven't seen him since he and Avery were Medevaced. I'm kind of surprised he still has his legs, as badly mangled as they were. But he seems to get around pretty well. Glad for that."

"Tell me that story again, LT. The long version. We've got a few more miles here."

Thorsen nodded, paused for a moment to gather his thoughts, and started the story.

"This happened in April of '70, a few months after you'd gone home," he began. "By that time, I'd been promoted to captain and taken over as company commander. We were still operating off LZ Sherman, and we'd been there for about four days, doing lifer shit as usual, rebuilding bunkers, checking Claymores and concertina wire outside the perimeter, and burning shit in those big cut-down 55-gallon drums." He looked over at me and grinned. "One of the few benefits I ever saw of being an officer in that war was that I never had to personally burn shit. But the stink of it was bad enough, even twenty yards away.

"We got the word one afternoon that we were going back out the next day to try to intercept some NVA that had been spotted getting ready to cross the border from Cambodia. We'd barely had time for showers, haircuts, and clean fatigues, and the diarrhea, jungle rot, and ringworm were just starting to heal up, so there was the usual amount of pissing and moaning at the platoon leaders' and platoon sergeants' meeting I held that night. Of course I couldn't say anything to them, but I was just as pissed off as everyone else.

"I remember talking with Avery and Davenport on the lifer inspection that night, making sure everyone knew we were going back out. Those guys hated the lifer crap we had to put up with on the LZ about as bad as anyone, so they seemed pretty happy we were headed back to the bush the next day."

39

The Delta company grunts were spread out alongside the dirt road that led into LZ Sherman from the southeast, clustered in small, three-man groups, half of a six-man load on each side of the road so they could board quickly when the helicopters landed. The aviation people were busy that day so there were only four birds to move the company of about a hundred men. Avery and Davenport sat together as usual, the M-60 machine gunner and his assistant, clearly the best of friends. The mission was relatively routine, so no one was especially tense except for a couple of replacements who had recently joined the company. Avery and Davenport played Hearts with a worn deck of cards there in the sweltering heat, sitting as they were in the direct sun of a hundred-degree day. They were so used to the heat that they didn't seem to notice, and they were laughing and teasing each other as the game went on.

They rode out on the third lift, sitting on the floor in the door of the Huey, feet hanging out, catching as much of the cool breeze as they could on the way. Helicopter rides and rain storms were about the only time the grunts ever got cooled off in that part of Vietnam, and they made the best of every opportunity. Besides, grunts knew that if they sat up in the helicopter's seats instead of right at the edge of the floor, it would take another two or three seconds to get off the bird when it landed, and sometimes that two or three seconds was the difference between life and death if the LZ was "hot."

They were dropped off in a small clearing about eight hundred meters from the road they were supposed to ambush that night. It had been unsecured before the first two lifts landed, but by the time Avery and Davenport were on the ground the first and third platoons had a good perimeter set up, so that part of the mission was a cake walk. No one had taken any enemy fire so far that day, and as the two men stepped off the chopper and the Hueys pulled out, it was a nice, quiet, although blistering hot, day in the jungle.

The mission for that afternoon and that night was for the company to hump about six hundred meters to a night position that was about two hundred meters from a known infiltration trail coming southeast out of Cambodia, then send two heavy ambush patrols to set up right along the trail a hundred or so meters apart, to wait for the North Vietnamese to come down the trail from the north, or up the trail from the south.

The six-hundred meter march to the company night position went uneventfully, and they set up in a small circular perimeter. The men who weren't going on the ambush patrols dug fighting holes about twenty-five feet apart in a big circle there in the jungle. The grunts were as quiet as possible digging in and cutting fields of fire in the thick brush but, inevitably, still made considerable noise. The ambush teams gathered inside the perimeter, piling their rucksacks together in one spot, stripping down to fighting gear, rolling down their shirt sleeves, darkening their faces and hands with camouflage stick, and checking each other for anything that would make noise.

Each ambush team would carry several Claymore antipersonnel mines, which were the primary kill weapon, plus their rifles, one machine gun, and plenty of ammo. They carried their nylon poncho liners to wrap up in, but there were no waterproof ponchos on ambush since they tended to shine in the dark if it rained, and could give away their position.

Avery and Davenport were another M-60 team. Avery carried the gun and a couple of hundred-round belts of ammo, and Davenport humped most of the rest of the ammo, and provided security for the team with an M-16. By luck of the draw, they were assigned to the company perimeter as part of Thorsen's reaction force.

The two ambush teams, each consisting of eight men, left the company perimeter a little before dusk. They patrolled together for the first hundred yards, then separated, with one team going northwest, the other going southeast. The plan was for them to reach the trail about a hundred meters apart a little before dark, take a few minutes to set up the Claymores and position the men in the brush about twenty feet back from the trail, then settle in and wait. Ambush teams didn't dig fighting holes because it made too much noise and might warn away the NVA. Instead the men would find the best cover they could behind trees or fallen logs.

Things started going wrong when the northwest ambush team, the one closer to Cambodia, approached their position on the trail and ran into some NVA soldiers who were already moving down it. The NVA had apparently heard the Americans coming, because as the first men reached the trail they were fired on, a barrage of full-automatic AK-47 and light machine-gun fire. The man walking point was killed in the first burst of fire, his backup severely wounded. The grunts opened up on the NVA and in a matter of a few seconds the quiet jungle night was turned into a horrendous, deafening firefight, with red and green tracers flashing everywhere, the gun-smoke and fragments of trees and brush making it almost impossible to breathe.

Back in the perimeter, two hundred meters away, Thorsen was

quickly on the radio trying to assess the situation up on the trail. He ordered the second ambush patrol to pull back off the trail about twenty meters and then move toward the firefight, but to be especially careful not to fire on their own men. He called to Battalion with a report of the contact, and ordered in artillery onto the trail northwest of the fight. While he was doing that, the reaction force got ready to move. They consisted of the Second Platoon and an extra machine gun team from Third Platoon, Avery and Davenport.

"I've thought about this firefight a million times," Thorsen told me in the Mercedes that day. "Never could identify a specific mistake I'd made, but things got really fucked up."

As the second ambush patrol began making its way the hundred yards to the site of the firefight they were also fired on from the trail, with three men wounded in the opening bursts. Thorsen, by then making his way toward the first firefight with the reaction force, heard the outburst of fire, identified from the distinctive sound that most of the noise was coming from NVA weapons, and realized suddenly that he had two separate battles going on, and had to split his reaction force to help both teams. The NVA fire was heavy and concentrated at the site of both fights, so it was urgent that he relieve both teams as quickly as possible.

He grabbed the Second Platoon leader, told him to take two squads of the platoon and go help the team on the right. Thorsen would take the rest of the platoon and the extra machine gun team with him to support the team engaged in the first firefight, on the left. Then he called the Third Platoon leader back in the perimeter and told him to get started chopping and blowing down a helicopter pad inside the perimeter and get everyone saddled up and ready to move forward to engage the NVA if they were needed.

He did all that while on the move toward the first firefight, which was still going on intensely ten minutes after it had begun.

As Thorsen's group approached the site of the first firefight, he spread one squad out along a twenty yard front to maximize forward firepower. He and his two radio operators were just behind the forward element, centered on the twenty-yard front, with reserve squads following them. Artillery was screaming in from overhead, impacting up the trail and into the jungle on the far side of the trail. Green North Vietnamese tracers were buzzing through the jungle at all angles, and red American tracers were zipping out the other direction. In all the smoke and noise, it was impossible to tell where anyone was except by muzzle flashes and tracer streaks.

Within ten yards of where he thought the American ambush patrol was, Thorsen ordered his relief force to stop and go to ground, and called in an illumination round to be dropped overhead but slightly behind where he believed the NVA were. Thirty seconds later the round burst right on target, and the big parachute flare turned the darkness into daylight. The American relief force began advancing toward the fight, firing over the heads of the ambushed patrol, who were holding tight on the ground.

Avery and Davenport somehow wound up on the far-left end of the sweep, and moved forward with the rest of the Americans. Avery fired the machine gun from the hip, Davenport feeding him the belts of ammo. Thorsen ordered the relief team to hold up when his first men reached the devastated American ambush team, and to find cover and continue firing on the NVA.

Things began to quiet down, and the NVA fire began dropping off, indicating to the Americans that they were either pulling out or being killed by the American fire. Avery stopped firing his M-60, and the rest of the American fire began to slow as well. Thorsen and the medics he'd brought from the company position moved up to find the dead and wounded grunts and begin getting them back to the company perimeter to be Medevaced. Thorsen ordered the artillery to stop the illumination. The other firefight had quieted down as well, and he called the Second Platoon leader to see how things were there. The return call was grim. Three of the grunts in the other patrol were dead, everyone else was wounded. And the relief team had three wounded as well, two of them critical.

As the GIs were finding and accounting for the dead and wounded at the first ambush site and getting them ready to move, Avery and Davenport, who were out on the left end of the sweep, began to hear movement in the jungle. They could hear the men whispering, and the voices were clearly Vietnamese. The NVA soldiers were trying to flank their position, get in behind the Americans to cut them off.

Avery quietly shifted his gun around to his left and then opened up on the gooks, firing in eight-round bursts close to the ground. After a few bursts he held off on the trigger, and he could hear more than one of the North Vietnamese screaming in pain, wounded by the machine gun fire. Undoubtedly, he had killed some as well.

Just as he was about to begin firing again, Avery felt a heavy object hit the ground beside him, between him and Davenport. He knew instantly that it was a hand grenade, thrown with incredible accuracy right at the machine gun muzzle flashes. He reacted in a split second; took his steel helmet from his head, put it over the grenade, and then threw himself on top of it.

The grenade exploded, blowing Avery off his helmet and into the air, opening him up across the stomach and chest, pushing part of his stomach and intestines from his body. Davenport, right next to him, was blasted in the legs, his left leg nearly torn off below the knee. They lay there unconscious but alive, in a giant spreading pool of their own blood.

40

14 June 2005
Near Kingwood, West Virginia

Thorsen was finishing the story as we rolled into the dirt driveway leading to Ray Davenport's cabin.

"Those two guys out on the end of that line saved us from the NVA that night. The gooks were trying to sneak around us to attack from behind, and we were spread so thin they would have kicked our ass. Avery and Davenport killed so many of them with that M-60 that they broke it up. The gooks pulled back and the firefight ended. One of the medics and I got to them a couple of minutes after they were hurt, but they were so fucked up and losing so much blood I didn't think either of them would live. We carried them back to the company perimeter with everyone else, and the Medevac choppers were already rolling in. But we had so many other wounded and so few choppers available that I had to do what no commander ever wants to do. I Medevaced the guys who were badly hurt, but who our medics and I thought would make it, first. Avery and Davenport didn't qualify, so I let them wait.

He looked over at me, his face grim, tears in his eyes. "Having to do that really fucked with my head back then. Still does."

After a couple of seconds, he went on. "We propped them up

against the same tree, bandaged them as well as we could, got most of the bleeding stopped in Davenport's legs. Couldn't do much for Avery except try to keep all his guts in his lap, and up off the ground. It was forty-five minutes later when we'd Medevaced the worst of the other wounded, and I got back over to them, thinking they'd both be dead. The doc had set them up with IV bottles to keep fluids in them, and he'd given them both a little morphine to cut the pain, but couldn't give them full doses because of the shock. Avery was passed out, but the doc checked his pulse and said he was still alive. Davenport was awake on and off, out of his head some of the time, but alert enough to say, "He rolled on that frag, Captain! He rolled on that fuckin' frag, or we'd both be dead!"

"We loaded them onto the Huey and off they went. I expected to hear they were both KIA, but a couple of days later I heard they were both probably going to make it and had been sent to Japan for more surgery.

"Davenport wrote me a letter about a month later telling me what Avery had done in more detail, taking his helmet off and putting it on the frag, then rolling onto it, just like he'd been rehearsing it all his life. Saved both their lives, and probably the lives of some of the other guys around them, plus breaking up the NVA sneak attack. I put Davenport in for the Silver Star, and Avery for the Medal of Honor. Davenport got the Silver Star right away, of course. But it took over a year for the Army, and I guess ultimately Congress, to make a decision on Avery's Medal of Honor. They can declare a war in an hour, but it takes those motherfuckers over a year to decide what to do about a Medal of Honor. Thorsen looked over at me with a wry little smile, acknowledging that now it was he who was calling on his soldier's vocabulary.

"I haven't seen either of them since the night they were hurt, although I get a letter or a call from Avery from time to time. He hasn't worked a regular job since the war. He lives very modestly on his VA disability pension and I guess some money his mother left him. Uses his time to take care of some of the older veterans from World War II and Korea."

Thorsen said it again, obviously a little nervous about the meeting. "This will be the first time I've seen either of them face-to-face since we loaded them onto the Medevac that night."

The cabin was a small home-built affair, nestled into beautiful surroundings but looking a bit unkempt. The yard was full of stuff, kid's wagons and bicycles, a home-made trailer, other odds and ends. Another cabin, about the same size, sat on the opposite side of the dirt driveway.

Davenport pulled his pickup off the driveway onto the grass, got out, and motioned Thorsen to park on the grass on the other side. Ed and I got out of the Mercedes, and Davenport led us to the back of the cabin where there was a little stoop of a porch. Nick Avery was sitting on the stoop in his shorts with no shirt on, snapping green beans and throwing them into a big pot. He looked up as we approached and rose to his feet, a huge smile on his face.

"Hey, Captain Thorsen, how are you, 6?" He made the two steps down off the stoop, and threw his arms around Thorsen, who returned the hug warmly.

"I'm really good, Nick. Damn, it's good to see you. You look good! How have you been?"

"I been good, 6. Gettin' by, you know?"

Thorsen and I were both trying not to stare at Avery's chest and abdomen, which had the texture of used bubble gum, crisscrossed by long, linear scars, each bearing stitch marks.

"It's OK, 6. I'm used to it. Quite a mess, isn't it? I never thought I'd live through that. Thought I was dead for sure. But I woke up one day a couple of weeks later, and someone had put all my guts back inside, and given me this great stitch job." He laughed. "I guess they took off six or eight feet of intestine, but everything still works. How lucky can a man be?"

"You were very lucky," Thorsen said. "Or you were livin' right. Hey, do you remember Mick Delaney? My platoon sergeant from Third Platoon, went home a few months before you were hurt."

I shook Avery's outstretched hand. "Good to see you, Nick. Afraid I don't remember you well. You know how it was... we kind of stayed in our own platoons most of the time."

"Sure, Mick. Good to see you. You were wounded too, weren't you?"

"Yeah, the LT and I were both hit by the same mortar round one night about dinner time. We were arguing over who was going to eat which C-Rat, not paying close enough attention, and the suckers got us. Then I got hit again later that same night. Luckily, we walked away from that one. You guys were there, weren't you?"

"Yeah, we were there, in First Platoon then. Hairy night. I guess we're all lucky to be alive."

"Guess so. What are you doing?" I asked.

"Snapping green beans for the reception tonight."

Davenport said, "Let me get you guys a beer. Bud OK?"

"Sure," I said.

"Not for me," replied Thorsen. "I can't drink alcohol. Got a Coke around?"

"Sure." Davenport came back with beers for him and me, and a Coke for Thorsen.

We all sat down on the stoop, which was shaded from the afternoon sun. It was a perfect day, about 75 degrees with a clear sky and a slight breeze. I couldn't help taking in the beautiful hillside behind the cabins. Avery went inside, came back out with a second big grocery sack full of green beans.

"Mind helping me snap beans while we talk?" he asked. "Ray's wife is coming to pick these up in an hour or so for the reception dinner, and I'm running behind schedule."

"Sure thing," I said. We made ourselves comfortable on the stoop, snapping beans together in the pleasant afternoon shade.

Ray was the next to speak. "You guys been back?"

"You mean back to Vietnam?" Thorsen asked.

"Yeah. Nick and I went back about... what was that, Nick? Six years ago?"

"Yeah, '98. Kind of a thirty-year trip. We flew into Hanoi, which was weird. Toured the city, drove down through the old DMZ, visited Khe Sanh, Hue, then went back up and spent a week helping the people in some village build a community center. Then we flew down to Ho Chi Minh City, Saigon to you guys, drove up to Cu Chi, went through the tunnels the NVA had dug there, which were amazing. Then we drove up to Tay Ninh, and out to where LZ Sherman was. There was an excavation crew there from the Hanoi government, digging for the remains of NVA and VC soldiers in that big mass grave we had made outside the wire on the northwest side of the LZ.

"If you remember, the NVA hit Sherman really hard three or four times early in '69, took a lot of KIAs. Killed and wounded a lot of our guys, too. Got where the bulldozers were just shoving the NVA bodies into that big pit and covering them up."

"I remember that grave," I said. "You guys remember Fragman? That tall skinny black guy in Third Platoon? He took a skull out of that grave one day, cleaned it off, and wired it to the back of his rucksack. When we were on the LZ he would put a boonie hat on it and a cigarette in its teeth. Called it 'Luke the gook.' Kind of a mascot."

"Well, you should have seen how carefully and reverently the excavation people were sifting through the dirt for remains, cleaning off what they found, trying to piece the bodies back together, find any kind of identification they could. During the war I always thought the NVA didn't give a shit about their soldiers, making them live in the jungle for years at a time, not enough to eat, poor medical care, all that. You get an entirely different perspective if you go back," said Davenport. "They have a strong respect, almost reverence, toward their families and their ancestors." He paused. "Best trip I ever made."

"What's crazy," began Nick, "is that the Vietnamese people welcomed us with open arms. We didn't go out of our way to tell them we'd been there fighting during the war, but one day one of the tour guides saw me with my shirt off, and asked me about it. So I told him. Turned out he had fought for the NVA, and was in South Vietnam himself for almost nine years without ever getting to go home. A grunt just like us. We were there at the same time. When he found out I was a soldier there he shook my hand really hard, wound up hugging me. Felt like my brother."

We sat without speaking for a few minutes, snapping beans, throwing them into the pot, and sipping our drinks, lost in thought.

Then Nick said, "You're right, Ray. Best trip I ever made, too. Those people where we helped with the community center, they were just really nice, straightforward people, happy for our help. They kept thanking us for coming, and the night before we left they threw us a big party. Great food, some local wine. Even though I got the impression they didn't even have enough to eat themselves all the time.

"The Vietnamese consider the American people their friends because it was the American people who got the war stopped. They still don't like the American government, but they have nothing against our people. Kinda weird that they can differentiate like that, but they do. Even when the people we met in North Vietnam found out we'd been soldiers there fighting against them, they still treated us as friends."

I said, "You know, not long after I came in country, my first Delta Company commander, Captain James, was leaving the field, transferring the company to another captain, and he got all the platoon leaders and NCOs together and made this little speech. Basically said that we were there fighting a war America was no longer trying to win, and that our priority should be to keep ourselves and our men alive and get them home in one piece. He recalled for us that in 1945 America considered the Germans and Italians and Japanese to be, and I still remember his exact words, 'the most heinous motherfuckers on the planet.' But then he said that here we were only twenty-four years later, and the Germans and Italians and Japanese were our best friends, and now the North Vietnamese were the 'most heinous motherfuckers on the planet.' He said that twenty-five years from then, the North Vietnamese would be our new best friends, and somebody else would be 'the most heinous motherfuckers on the planet.' But we'd still be just as dead if we got killed there.

"His last words were 'Don't let yourself or one of your men be the last poor sonofabitch to die in this fucked-up war.' Sounds like he was exactly right."

Thorsen: "He really said that?"

"Yeah. Pretty much those words."

"Well, we all thought it, but I'm surprised he put it into words. He could've been court-martialed for that."

Nick said, "Now, that's fucked up, 6. Court-martialed for telling the truth?"

To lighten the mood, Thorsen said, "We ought to come up with an agreement for what you guys are gonna call me. Mick calls me 'LT' most of the time because I was a First Lieutenant when we worked together closest. But then sometimes he calls me 'Colonel' because we got back together when I was still in, and I was a full colonel then. You guys called me 'Captain' earlier because I was a captain most of the time we worked together, but Nick, you just called me '6' because, as we all know, my call sign was 'Patriot 6.' So, how about a compromise?

That war's well over, thank God, and none of us is in the Army now. How about 'Ed'? That work?"

All three of us started shaking our heads, everyone having some sort of problem with it. "Gee, I don't know," said Ray. "Doesn't seem to show the proper respect. Don't know if I can call you 'Ed.' Guess I can try."

"Yeah, I guess we can try it, Ed," I said. "Doesn't exactly roll off the tongue, though." We all laughed.

It got quiet again.

I stood up to stretch my legs, stepped off the stoop into the shade of the cabin's back yard. Avery followed me. I turned, and he walked right up to me. Put his hand on my neck, just where the right shoulder connected. I was a little uncomfortable with the familiarity of it but didn't pull away or, hopefully, didn't flinch.

"Where were you wounded, Mick?'

"Oh, man. I wasn't hurt anywhere near as badly as you were, Nick. Mine were scratches compared to what got you."

"That doesn't matter. You were wounded, it had to hurt. You still carry the pain, don't you?"

"Sometimes."

"So, where were you hit?"

"Took a bunch of shrapnel up the right side of my body. From my hip to my head."

"Where was the worst of it?"

"Two places. One right where your hand is. The other just above my right temple. Both places felt like I'd been hit with a baseball bat, but the chunks of shrapnel weren't that big. The one where your hand is went in about three inches deep, almost to the top of my lung, but not quite. It's still floating around in there somewhere. Freaks the doctors out every time they see it on a chest X-Ray. The one in my head eventually came out on its own, several years after I was home. I still have little pieces working their way out, even this many years later."

I thought about it. "How'd you know to put your hand right there? You can't see the scar with my shirt on."

"I could sense that you'd been hurt there. And it felt like that was the worst of it."

"Oh," was all I could say.

"You can see into people's hearts, can't you, Mick?"

"Huh? What do you mean?"

"I mean, you can tell almost immediately when you meet someone whether they're good, sincere people out to help others and try to do right in this lifetime, or they're self-serving, perhaps deceitful people who can't be trusted."

"Well, yeah, I can, Nick. But I thought that was just me. It's been my great gift. I've been very successful in business, not because I'm smarter than anyone else, but because I can read people like nobody else. Takes me about two minutes to get what I need from a job interview, and bores me to tears when others want to drag one out for an hour or more. Same way with people I meet socially. Takes me about thirty seconds to size them up, and if they're the self-serving, self-promoting, insincere types, I never have much use for them. But if I meet someone who's good, out to make the world a better place, help others, and so on, I can make friends really fast. You and Ray are both that way. I can already tell. The LT certainly is." I'd already forgotten our agreement to call Thorsen "Ed."

Davenport and Thorsen had overheard. Davenport spoke. "We all have that gift, Mick. We can all see into people's hearts. Nick and I got together for the first time about a year after we were wounded, and we've been close ever since. It became apparent to both of us that the war had changed us, and we talked about it a lot. One of the things we both realized was that we could size people up really fast, see into their hearts. I've read as much about it as I can find. Some people claim it's because we learned to trust our instincts more than most people ever do when we were in combat and facing death every day. So we somehow have a heightened instinctive ability to assess people from their speech and actions. Some people claim it's some sort of supernatural gift we've been given because we lived on the verge of death for so long. Maybe it's both. But we all have it. I can tell by how you and Ed behaved toward us when you first saw us that you have it. You already trust us. You believe every word we say because it's the truth. And we feel the same about you."

41

14 June 2005
Near Kingwood, West Virginia

Thorsen said, "You know, I studied everything that was known about Post Traumatic Stress Disorder back when I got my PhD, and one of the symptoms of it is that you feel 'different' from ordinary people who haven't been in a war. That makes you feel isolated and alone, with the obvious negative effects of that. Maybe one of the reasons we all feel different is that we have this gift that most people don't develop very well. I know I've been in a lot of situations where I was in a group, and everyone else in the group seemed to be going in some direction because they believed what, or who, was being presented to them, based on some intellectual analysis, I suppose, and I knew in my heart that they were making a mistake. I'd argue against it as best I could, but often I couldn't present a good argument based on the facts, because I didn't have the tangible evidence. I just knew what I knew. Usually I was right, but most of the time the mistake was made anyway. I've even had other people come to me later and say, 'You were right? How'd you know?' I'd say, 'I just knew.'"

All this time Avery and Davenport were nodding, agreeing, because they'd had similar experiences.

"And you're saying this is because of the war?" I asked.

"Well, did you have this ability before the war?" asked Nick.

"Now that you mention it, no, not much. I can't remember exactly when I began to trust it, but it wasn't long after the war that I did. Somewhere in my mid-twenties, is what I recall. I do remember that when I was in Vietnam, later in my tour, I became very confident in my ability to function well there, to make good decisions. I was pretty comfortable being the platoon sergeant."

Avery had long since taken his hand off my neck and turned to participate in the bigger conversation, but he turned back and spoke just to me.

"That grenade," he said, "the one that got me?"

"Yeah...?"

"Well, I never really saw it that well, it was so dark by then."

"Yeah...?"

"I'm ALMOST sure it was an NVA stick grenade, but I've had lingering doubts that it might have been one of ours. You know, maybe one they found or took off a dead GI, something like that. For some reason, it bothers me that it might have been one of ours."

"I don't see what difference ...?"

"Well, the gook grenades, they weren't as powerful as ours. I thought it was one of theirs, and when I heard it hit the ground between Ray and me, I didn't know what to do, you know? And not a lot of time to think about it. At first I thought I'd pick it up and throw it back, but I was afraid it would go off up in the air in my hand before I could throw it, and maybe hurt a lot more of our guys. So I decided to do what I did. I pulled my helmet off, put it over the grenade, and then laid on top of it, to smother it. I guess I figured the helmet might contain all the blast, or almost all the blast, of a gook grenade."

"Important thing is, you lived through it, Nick. One of the bravest things I ever heard about."

"Well, didn't seem very brave at the time. I was scared shitless all through that firefight, but we heard those gooks coming around us and had to start firing on them. Then came that frag.

"Besides..." he went on. "What else was I going to do? No time to get Ray out of the way and run. Afraid to throw it back. I just put the helmet over it to protect us as much as possible. Guess my head was workin' a little at least."

"Probably that refined intuitive ability we were just talking about. Whatever it was, it was working great. You're here to talk about it thirty-plus years later."

"You know, after I put the helmet down and rolled onto it, it seemed like it took forever for the frag to go off. I remember having all these second thoughts. You know, *Maybe I should have thrown it back after all,* that kind of shit. It seemed like it took so long that I thought maybe it was a dud, or that some gook had thrown it without pulling the fuse, or the pin... something like that. I remember thinking that I ought to get off the helmet and pick it up and get rid of it after all. And then it went off.

"I remember this enormous 'bang' and a bright flash, and I sort of went out of it, and next thing I knew I was laying on my back on the ground, and I looked down... It was bright as day... the captain must have called in more illumination... and I saw my guts sticking up out of this huge hole in my stomach...I was bleeding a lot but my guts weren't covered with blood. At first... you'll laugh at this... I remember thinking that my intestine, stickin' up, looked like a fuckin' tuna... all blue and shiny.

"And then I just had this great sense of peace. It was like God had taken me in His arms and was holding me, and I felt safe and warm and comfortable...and at peace. It was the best feeling I ever had in my life... still is. Pure, absolute, safe, peace."

Ray and Ed had been in a conversation of their own but had overheard Nick's words and had fallen silent to listen. I was speechless... coming up with only, "Jesus, Nick."

"I was in and out of it a couple of times, but I remember the captain waking me up...I was sitting under a tree by then...and telling me we were up for the next Medevac. And then I don't remember much for a while. I do remember that the feeling of peace and safety had gone by then, and I was scared and in a lot of pain... more than I'd ever imagined possible.

"Next thing I remember clearly was in the hospital in Japan. My mother had heard about my wounds and had flown over to be with me. She spent all day every day there looking after me and helping the other guys. There were so many of us, and so few doctors and nurses, that guys would call out for hours just for a drink of water, and unless my mom had been there, there would have been no one there to give it to them. Guys laying for hours in their own shit, critical wounds seeping blood. Guys strangling on their own vomit and spit. It was worse than the fuckin' war.

"The worst part, though...the absolutely worst part..." His voice began to crack, and his face started to break up, tears began rolling down his cheeks, "...were the guys who died alone there in the dark at night without anyone to help them." He sobbed. "They'd call out into the darkness, sometimes saying things like 'I'm not going to make morning, guys. Somebody give my love to my family.' We were all in such bad shape none of us could get up and go over to them, but we'd yell back things like 'Hang in there, man. You're gonna make it!' But after a while the guy would quit talking back to us, and we'd know he was gone. And then later when a nurse finally did come around and find him dead, we'd hear them cover him up with his sheet, and then in the morning they'd come and take the body away." He sobbed again. "Those poor guys, all they went through, and the fucking government spending all those billions bombing the Vietnamese and putting all of us there, and the motherfuckers couldn't scrape up enough money to hire enough nurses to hold a guy's hand while he was dying."

He sobbed again, raised his arm to his face and wiped away the tears, took a drink of his beer. We all sat quiet for a moment, out of respect for his experience and those memories.

Then he said, "I thought for sure I was going to die. There in the firefight, and after the grenade had gone off, with that feeling of safety and peace, I thought for sure. Even when I'd made it to Japan and woke up and found out where I was, with all those guys around me in pain, suffering, crying out, calling out... I thought I would die like so many of them did. There were a lot of times I hoped for it, prayed for it, there was so much pain. I'd wake up and see my mom there holding my hand, trying to put on a brave face, but I could see in her eyes that she didn't think I was going to make it, either. Still don't know why I did.

"And when I finally did get back home and knew I was going to live, by then I was addicted to the morphine, so while I was still healing and still had a lot of pain, I had to go through withdrawal, and that was almost as bad as the rest of it.

"I often wished for death, never knew why I lived. Still don't.

"Then one day well over a year later, I got a letter saying I'd been awarded the Medal of Honor. I was discharged from the Army by then, but they invited me and my mom to Washington, and there was this big ceremony with all these colonels and generals and people from Congress, and President Nixon put it on me himself. That whole experience was just... surreal."

He seemed to lapse into his memories. I looked over at Thorsen, then at Ray Davenport, who seemed to remain absorbed in Avery's story.

"What about you, Ray? What was it like for you that night, and afterward."

"Oh... I don't like to remember it much. It was just like Nick said in the firefight. We opened up with the machine gun, and kept firing. And then they threw that frag. I guess it was one of theirs. In the flashes of light from the other explosions and gunfire I remember Nick taking his helmet off and rolling on it. I was about five feet away, could only put my head down before the blast. I was never unconscious but couldn't feel the pain in my legs at first. Just remember looking down and seeing all that blood. Thought I was going to die for sure.

"The captain came over with a medic a little later, they put tourniquets on my legs and gave me a shot. I kind of drifted off after that. I do remember waking up, and Nick and I were sitting propped up against a tree next to each other. I looked over and saw his guts hanging out, thought we were both dead. When the captain came to tell us we were on the next Medevac, I wanted to ask him to just leave us there, let us bleed out and have it over with, but couldn't get the words out. Shock, and the morphine, I imagine."

"They worked on me a lot in Chu Lai, and a couple of times the docs would come by and say they were trying hard to save my legs but didn't know whether or not they'd be able to. I might lose one or both of them. They sent me to Japan, too, but I didn't see Nick there. I thought he was dead for sure. Eventually, they sent me back to the States. I was in Walter Reed for quite a while, which was good because I wasn't too far from where my folks were. When I got better I started checking around and found out that Nick was still alive. So I tracked him down, and we got together, and we've stayed best friends ever since.

"It's nice having you guys here. There aren't many other people we're comfortable talking to about all this, who maybe understand some of it, you know? You'll meet my wife and my kids later this afternoon. They're terrific. But I have trouble relating to them. As much as I love them, I just can't seem to really connect with them. You guys know what I mean?"

"Yeah, I do," I said. "Been through two marriages and a couple of other relationships since the war, and after a while I just can't seem to relate. Things my wives and women I've dated think are important seem like trivial nonsense to me. After a while they get tired of it. I think about the war too much, talk about it too much. They get tired of me waking up with the nightmares, sitting and staring off into space. I've worked hard to have good relationships with my boys, make sure they stayed out of the military. And I know they love me as much as I do them. But I still think they look at me as a stranger sometimes."

Thorsen nodded his head. He'd been through his own broken marriage and faced some challenges with Lois and his kids that he didn't talk about much to others.

We finished snapping the beans in silence, each of us lost in our own thoughts. Then Nick and Ray went inside to shower and change clothes for the wedding, and Ed and I sat on the back stoop and waited for them. In a little while a red Pontiac convertible pulled up the drive and a pretty young woman of about eighteen got out, walked up to the stoop.

"Hi," she said. "I'm Amy Davenport, Ray's daughter. You must be his friends from Vietnam."

"Yeah. I'm Mick Delaney, and this is Colonel Thorsen."

"Call me Ed." Thorsen shook her hand. "Your dad and Nick are inside."

"Nice to meet you." She climbed the steps, opened the screen door, stuck her head inside. "Daddy!" She shouted, seeming suddenly cross. "Mom says we need the beans down at the farm house. Sent me to get them! And you need to be there in half an hour. I think she's kind of mad that you're not there already."

"OK! OK! Take the beans and tell her we'll be there in a few minutes. The wedding doesn't start for another hour and a half!" he shouted back at her.

Ed looked at me, said nothing. Amy went inside, came back out with the large pot of snapped beans. She smiled wanly at the two of us, got back in her car, turned it around, and headed back down the drive.

There was hostility there in both directions that neither Ed nor I understood. Obviously, just the latest episode in a longer story. After a few more minutes, Ray and Nick came back out dressed in khakis and sport shirts, ready to go.

"Follow us back down, guys. Road's kind of tricky. Watch for that sudden ninety-degree turn about a mile down. For some reason, it's worse in this direction. We get about one dead farm kid a year on that turn, taking it too fast."

42

14 June 2005
Near Kingwood, West Virginia

The drive back was uneventful. Both Ed and I were lost in our own thoughts. We pulled back into the driveway of the bed and breakfast. Both sides of the drive were now lined with cars, and people were walking along the grass toward the farm house. The men all seemed to be dressed as Ed and I were, in khakis and golf shirts or sports shirts. The women wore sun dresses or shorts and tops. A very casual wedding.

Ray led us into the house and introduced us to his wife, a pretty woman named Karen who seemed a few years younger than Ray. Then he went back outside, leaving us there. Karen dried her hands on a towel, shook hands with Ed, then with me. "Ray's talked a lot about you, Captain Thorsen. But I don't remember him mentioning you, Mick."

"I was just in town visiting Ed, and he invited me along. I hope you don't mind. We were all in the same company in Vietnam, but I was in a different platoon than Ray and Nick so we didn't know each other well."

"Were you there when they were hurt?"

"No, I'd gone home by then. But Ed was there. He was the company commander then."

"Ah." She turned back to Ed. "Well, thanks for taking care of him back then. Although some days he doesn't seem very happy about the outcome. He's had a really tough life since the war. Can't seem to get over it."

"I know, Karen. Doesn't seem like any of us really can."

Ray came back into the kitchen, said abruptly, his words harsh, "Where's Devon? He's supposed to be here by now."

Karen's words were equally harsh. "I don't know, Ray. Try calling him on his cell phone."

"Kid's going to miss his own wedding, for Christ's sake!"

Karen turned away from him, went back to something she was doing in the sink. Ray stormed back out, slammed the screen door behind him. Ed and I went back outside and sat down at a table that had been set up under a canopy, the obvious location of the wedding's reception.

"Wonder what that's all about?" asked Ed.

"Don't know. Everyone sure seems to have a chip on their shoulder."

In a little while we followed the crowd to an area in an open field behind the farm's barn, where straw bales were set up in rows, like the pews in a church. A woman who looked to be in her fifties stood at a microphone at the front. She wore a white summer dress and had a Bible in one hand.

Ed leaned to me. "That's Ray's sister. She's an ordained minister." I nodded.

After a few minutes, the rest of the guests were seated and things quieted down. It was warm there in the afternoon sun, and I could see people fanning themselves with their hands or the little programs that had been handed out. A young man came in from one side and stood near the microphone. He was wearing khaki slacks and a white short-sleeved shirt. The groom.

"I guess Devon turned up after all," Ed said with a smile.

Soon, a man stepped in from the right wearing black jeans, a black western shirt, a black western hat, and a close-trimmed black beard. He carried an electrified acoustic guitar and leaned down to plug it into the amplifier that stood at his feet. After a couple of seconds of tuning, he began a processional, playing softly but with great feeling. From behind, with a cute little flower girl ahead of them, the bridesmaids began walking forward in a long, slow, single file. The groomsmen appeared beside the groom. With everyone in place, the guitarist finished the processional, then began the Wedding March. I heard a horse neigh softly behind me and turned to see the bride sitting side-saddle atop a bare-backed white mare coming up the aisle. An older man who I assumed was her father walked alongside, one hand holding the horse's bridle, the other steadying the bride.

"Never saw that before," whispered Ed. "I like her spunk. Takes guts to ride bareback side-saddle, especially at your own wedding."

I looked around, saw Ray standing with his wife on the front row. Couldn't spot Avery.

When the bride and her mount reached the front, her father helped her to the ground, then gave the horse's reins to another man who led the mare away.

The wedding ceremony was about the right length, I thought, for an outdoor session in the warm spring sun. It was beautiful, the minister's voice clear and strong, the bride and groom each reading their vows. After the "You may kiss the bride" part, the bride and groom led the party back down the aisle on foot.

"Awww... I'm disappointed," I said. "I thought maybe they were going to ride out together on the horse."

Ed looked at me and smirked.

We followed the rest of the well-wishers out of the "church" and back up the hill to the reception tent. We were served beverages by plainclothes waiters and waitresses carrying trays of champagne through the crowd. The guitarist from the wedding had set up a few feet outside the edge of the tent and began playing country love songs, still solo. We were standing off to one side, Ed with a Coke and me with champagne, when another man about our age approached.

"Are you the fellas who were in Vietnam with Ray back during the war?"

"We're two of them," replied Ed. "There's another of us around here somewhere."

"Understand you all have Purple Hearts."

"Yeah," I said. "Ray and his buddy Nick Avery were wounded very badly...nearly died. Colonel Thorsen and I were hurt in a completely different action, not quite so badly, but bad enough."

"I was there in 1970 with the Air Force, flying F-4s out of Bien Hoa Air Base."

"You might have flown some close air support for Ed here and his boys. I left in November of '69," I said.

"It's good to see you fellas. Did you come far?"

Ed joined in. "I live just south of D.C. Mick's from Kansas City."

"Well, I know Ray's really happy you're both here for this. He was telling me about it before the wedding. I imagine the four of you will be treated like rock stars at this little shindig. It's good to meet you."

"You, too," said Ed. "Come back later and we'll tell each other some war stories." He laughed.

"I'll do that." The man wandered off.

Ed and I took a seat at one of the tables, and soon the wedding party came back from taking photographs, formed a reception line at the edge of the canopy, and people made their way through, congratulating the bride and groom. Ray was there with Karen, next to the groom, not looking much happier than when they'd had sharp words with each other earlier.

Ed and I stood in line with the others and made our way to the wedding party. We were near the end of the line, and the bride and groom were looking a little weary by the time we made it to the front. But they greeted the two of us warmly nevertheless. "I'm Devon," said Ray's son, "and this is Mary." He introduced his new wife. "You're my dad's friends from Vietnam, aren't you? I'm glad you came. I'd like to talk to you later if you're going to be around."

"Sure," said Ed. "We'll be right here. Wouldn't miss a great party like this. We'll look for you."

Devon nodded. Mary gave each of us a warm hug. "Thank you for coming," she said. "I'd like to listen in when you talk to Devon, if that's OK."

"Sure it is," said Ed. We wandered into the crowd. Ed got into a conversation with someone sitting at one of the tables and sat down with them. I moved on alone, stopping by the buffet table for some crackers and cheese, finding a cooler with more beer. I was standing alone at the edge of the tent, lost in thought, when a young man approached.

"Hi." said the kid, holding out his hand. "You're one of Ray's friends from Vietnam, aren't you?"

"Yeah. Mick Delaney." I shook his hand.

"Nice to meet you, sir. I'm Doug. Just got out of the Army myself, about a year ago. Right before they invaded Iraq."

"Oh, yeah? What did you do in the Army?"

"Military Police. With the 101st Airborne."

"Yeah? Thank you for your service. And great you got out before Iraq."

"Well... maybe. I'm kind of struggling with that. Most of my buddies are still in, and they're in Iraq now, and I guess it's pretty bad. I feel bad for getting out and leaving them just before they went. Guilty, you might say. We did a tour in Afghanistan together, and that was bad. But I hear things in Iraq are worse."

"Went through a lot of that myself after I got home from Vietnam, so I know that feeling. It's pretty normal when your buddies are at war and you're home safe. What do you do now?"

"I'm in school at Penn State. Studying architecture. Going to be a city planner someday, I hope."

"You married?"

"Yeah. My wife's not here today. She's pregnant with our first kid. Due in a couple of weeks."

"How long were you in?"

"Four years. Went in right out of high school. Tell you what, though, I've thought about going back in since this second war started. Really feel bad I'm not out there with my buddies."

"Looking for some advice?" I asked.

"Sure."

"Your place now is right where you are. Imagine how you'd feel if you were in Iraq right now and your wife was at home alone having this baby. Or what it would be like after the child is born if you weren't here to be around during the first part of its life. Even worse, imagine how it would be for your wife if you were badly wounded or killed, and she had to go through life like that. You did your part. You served for four years in a tough job, defending America. That's a lot more than 99% of Americans ever do. So don't be so hard on yourself. You know what?"

"No, what?"

"If your buddies knew how you were feeling right now, they would appreciate it. But they would also tell you to take it easy on yourself. They'd tell you you'd be stupid to go back in when you have this great life ahead of you here. And they'd be right."

"Yeah, you're right. I've been writing to some of them, and I told one of my best buddies how I felt. He wrote back essentially what you said. 'Don't be an idiot. Stay home and take care of your wife and baby.' Then he wrote, 'If you re-enlist and come over here, I'm personally going to kick your ass.'"

I laughed. "The friendships we have in the military are some of the great benefits. A lot of people never get that close to anyone else in their lives. But your life is here now."

"Yeah, I know you're right. Thanks for talking to me. I feel better. Have a great visit. I'm going to go talk to the bride and groom."

"You take care."

43

The day turned into evening and the evening into night. I wandered around by myself mostly, checking in every so often to make sure Ed, Nick, and Ray were doing OK. They were all generally lost in conversation with someone, and I was content to let them talk. A couple of hours into the party I bumped into the bride and groom, and we sat down together at a table.

"Tell me about what happened to my dad in Vietnam," said Devon.

"Don't you know?"

"Not really. I know he was hurt pretty badly. You can see these horrible scars on his legs. But he never talks about it. What happened?"

I told the story as best I could, not having been there, and having only heard it in detail myself that day.

"My God!" said Devon. "You mean he almost died?"

"Yeah. If it hadn't been for Nick rolling on the grenade, I imagine both of them would have died."

"So that's why he's so close to Nick. I always wondered about it. My dad's never really been that close to me, even though sometimes I could see he wanted to be."

"Well, I'm sort of a student of Post Traumatic Stress Disorder," I said. "Got some of it myself, it turns out. But in my opinion, your dad has it pretty bad. One of the effects is a difficulty in being as close to people you love as you want to be. Some say that's because we've lost so many people we cared about that we're afraid of becoming close to others and then losing them. Some say it's just because the things we experience make us 'different', so we're never really comfortable with the closeness. Still others say it's because we can never find the words to accurately describe what we've experienced, so our attempts to help other people understand us just leave us frustrated. I think it's all of those, and maybe more. I have two sons myself, and I love them more than my life. I know they love me, too. But I do think it's been hard for them to understand me and for us to really relate as well as I'd like. I just keep doing the best I can.

"When you go to war, especially when it involves that kind of violent, close combat, you come back changed. And it's a lifelong thing. You can get better. But I personally don't think I'll ever get over it."

"Do you think my mom knows any of this? She and my dad always seem to be at each other about little things that don't mean much."

"I don't know if she does. If you didn't know, I doubt she knows much of it. Maybe you should tell her."

"Yeah, maybe so." He seemed to lose himself in thought.

"Well," I said, rising, "it was a beautiful wedding. Mary, I'll always remember you riding in on that white horse. Beautiful. I hope you'll be very happy."

Devin stood, shook my hand. "Thank you, sir. And thank you for sharing about my dad."

Mary stood up and hugged me, said goodbye. The couple sat back down and began what seemed to be a rather intense conversation. I walked away.

It was completely dark by then, the soft glow of the lights in the tent barely penetrating the blackness surrounding it. I couldn't see Ed, Nick, or Ray. I went to the cooler and grabbed another beer, sat back down at a table by myself. The crowd was beginning to clear out a bit, but the cowboy musician continued to play. In a little while a woman of about forty approached me, a beer in her hand. She seemed unsteady on her feet.

"You're one of Ray's friends from Vietnam."

"Yes, I am."

"Nice of you to come to the wedding. Where are you from?"

"Kansas City. How about you?"

"I live down the road a little ways. One of the neighbors." The longer she talked, the more I realized she was very drunk.

"So you drove over?"

"Yes. But don't worry about me. I'll just crash on the couch and go home in the morning."

I saw a wedding ring on her finger. "Didn't your husband come with you?"

"No. He's somewhere between here and Iraq. He's been over there for about six months with his National Guard unit. He was hurt in some kind of bomb blast four days ago, and he's supposed to be on his way back to the States. But I don't know where he is right now, and I don't know how badly he's hurt." She sat down and started to sob. "They won't tell me anything. They gave me a phone number to call for updates, and the people that answer are very nice, but they keep saying they don't have any more information. It's driving me crazy."

"I'm sorry," I said. "I know they fly most of the wounded from Iraq to Germany and then keep them there until they're stable and can make the longer flight home. I bet he's there now. Could be my friend Ed Thorsen can help you find out how he is. He's still got connections at the Pentagon. When I find him, I'll have him come and talk to you, get the information so he can see what he can find out."

Karen approached from the kitchen door, sat down next to the woman, and put her arm around her. "Come on inside, Raelene, and we'll get you some coffee. You want to stay here tonight, honey? I don't think you should drive, and the guest rooms are empty." She stood and helped Raelene up and walked her toward the house.

I sat alone for a while longer, my mood turning decidedly gloomy. Some of it was the beer, I knew. But most of it was from all this talk of war; my war, and now these current wars in Iraq and Afghanistan, and of all the suffering that came from them. Suffering for the service people and their families that went on for a lifetime after the war itself was over. And what few people who hadn't been there thought about; the unimaginable suffering of the millions of civilians who lived in Vietnam and Laos and Cambodia and Iraq and Afghanistan.

I hoped Raelene's husband would be OK, but my optimism about such things wasn't strong. More often than not, the wounds from one of those blasts were very severe.

The evening passed. The cowboy singer eventually finished his gig, said good night, packed his gear, and left. It was starting to get late, and I hadn't seen my buddies for a while. I walked to the reception tent again, didn't see them there. I widened my search out to the barn, the edge of the garden, then down the drive toward Ed's car. I heard them there before I saw them in the darkness, strong harsh voices coming at me through the night.

"No, you don't understand, Captain. We're not pissed off because you Medevaced the others before you Medevaced us. We understand that! You had to save the ones you thought you could save, and I know we looked like we weren't gonna make it." It was Nick's voice.

"Why didn't you just let us die there, Captain?" Ray almost shouted. Then he realized others might hear, and lowered his voice to a loud whisper. "Look at us! Nick's never married, still having nightmares most every night after more than thirty years! And me! I've got this great family I can't even relate to. My wife's probably going to wind up leaving me. My kids avoid me. And I don't blame them! I drink too much. I'm depressed a lot of the time. I can't sleep. Why didn't you just let us die? It would've saved us and a lot of other people a lot of grief."

"Jesus, guys, I ..."

"Hey, you guys." I walked up, pretended I hadn't heard. "Been looking for you. Party's almost over. Really nice wedding, Ray."

In the near darkness, I saw Ray wipe tears from his face. "Thanks, Mick. Guess we were giving the Captain a hard time here, and he doesn't deserve it. You were a great officer, Captain. It's just that ..." his voice trailed off.

"I know, guys. I understand you aren't angry at me. It's that fucked up war and what it's done to all of us."

"Can I make a suggestion?" I said. "I don't know how long Nick is going to be here, but we're not that far from D.C. Why don't you three guys sit down together in the light of day, without the influence of the beer, and talk it out? Ed has a PhD in psychology that he got specifically because he wanted to help other veterans. I bet the three of you could really help each other."

"That's a good idea, guys," said Ed. "Why don't you come down to my place for a couple of days, and let's talk this through. Maybe I can help."

Yeah, I thought to myself, *and maybe they can help you, too.*

They agreed to the trip and shook hands all around.

"Thank you both for coming," said Ray. "It's been great to see you, Captain. And great to see you again, Mick."

"It was a beautiful wedding, Ray. Glad we could come. Nick, really good to see you, too. I won't forget today. Not ever," I said.

"Nor will I," said Ed.

The four of us made our way back to the house, and Ed and I said goodbye to Karen. I told Ed about Raelene's husband, and Ed gave Karen a card to give to her, so she could contact him the next day, and he could try to get more information. We said our goodbyes to Nick and Ray and crunched our way back down the gravel drive to Ed's car.

As we pulled out of the drive into the darkness of the country road, Ed turned to me and said just one long word, from the old days.

"Un-fucking-believable."

44

28 June 2005
Tony Blake

Special Forces Major Tony Blake awoke slowly, the space around him seeming surreal, mostly white, with light that seemed like sunlight coming from his left. He was on a soft surface and covered in some kind of cloth. His arms and legs felt constrained, but he couldn't detect handcuffs or ropes or bonds of any kind. The air was cool, cooler than he'd felt for a while. After a minute he heard voices nearby, and he braced himself for what might come next. The Hajis coming for him? Was he a prisoner somewhere? Would he be tortured, or perhaps decapitated on camera for the world, including his wife and children, to see over and over again? If only he could move. If only he could open his eyes. But his arms and legs wouldn't seem to move, and his eyelids wouldn't respond to the instructions from his brain. He was a brave man and had fought many fights and faced death many times. But he was afraid. Very, very afraid. Gradually he drifted off to the blackness again.

Hours, or perhaps days later, he awoke again, a little more quickly this time. He felt like his eyes were coming open, but there was only a dim light as though he was looking through water from way down deep. He strained to move his arms, but got only sharp pain in both of them for his efforts. He struggled to move his legs, but again there was only searing pain. He tried to speak, to call out, but the sound that came from his throat was only a muffled cry. The fear came back, started in his stomach, seemed to move through his whole body. He wanted to cry out, but again nothing came. He wept silently, felt the tears run down his cheeks. He had to get a handle on this fear!

The third time he woke up the space around him was light, the air still cool. He managed to open his eyes, and this time he could see a bit more. There were people around him, moving around in light green clothing. Someone was holding his left hand. Taking his pulse? Someone else was holding his right hand. He still couldn't move his legs. It was like there were heavy weights on them. He turned his head to the right a bit, blinked, blinked again... and saw Melissa's face there next to his. She was holding his hand, smoothing his hair with her other hand. She was smiling at him! Was he dreaming? This must be a dream. Last he remembered, the Haji's had him. Didn't they? How'd Melissa come to be with the Hajis? Where the fuck was he? He tried to sit up, but he couldn't. Didn't have the strength. He drifted off again.

Then he heard Melissa's voice in his ear. "It's OK now, Tony. You're safe! It's OK. These are doctors and nurses, and they're here to help you. It's OK!"

Weakly, he forced his eyes open, turned his head toward Melissa's voice, and tried to smile. He hoped it looked like a smile. He wasn't sure. Then he fell back asleep.

There was a recurring dream. He was in a convoy in Iraq, riding in the shotgun seat in an un-armored Humvee, next to the driver, who was a woman. There was an overturned truck in the highway ahead of them. And then there was deafening noise and blinding light, and the Humvee lifted off the ground and came crashing back down, and people seemed to come apart next to him, and there was blood everywhere, and pieces of bone and flesh. And he looked around and saw everyone dead, only the gunner's shredded torso hanging from the gun turret, his lower half a pulverized mess all over the inside of the Hummer. Hanks' and Maraki's bodies were an unrecognizable, bloody mess. Tony was covered in blood, but the door was open and he crawled outside. He managed to drag his rifle out with him, and he flipped the selector to "Auto" and made ready to shoot it out with whoever had blown them up. But there was nobody to shoot at.

And he looked down and there was all that blood on him, and he felt weak. And then this Haji kid came over carrying an AK. And then...what?

It was another full day before Tony came fully awake. This time his eyes opened all the way, and he could see pretty clearly. Melissa was sitting there holding his hand, smiling at him again! His head throbbed unmercifully at the light, and his neck ached, and his whole body hurt. But he was alive, and the Hajis didn't have him. He was safe. And he was somehow with Melissa. *How did I get here?* he thought. He tried to smile back at her, tried to open his mouth to speak, but it felt like someone had glued his jaws together, and he only got out a muffled word that sounded to him like "lurb." That made Melissa smile even more, and she brushed his hair with her free hand, and kissed him on the cheek. He could feel his stubble against her lips.

"I'm so glad you're awake, Tony. Thank God you're awake. Thank God you're alive!"

He could finally smile. Slowly, he raised his head from the pillow and took stock of himself. His right hand and arm were bandaged, but didn't hurt too badly. Melissa was holding his hand. His left arm was in a cast, but he could see his fingers sticking out of the end of it, and the fingers moved when he willed them to. They all seemed to be there. He looked down for his legs, saw they were both in casts, but both still there. He could see all his toes. Thank God!

Melissa fed him a couple of ice chips, and the cold and moisture wet his mouth enough that he could try some more words. "Glad you're here," he squeaked out. "Where are we?"

"Landstuhl Medical Center in Germany. You've been here for over a week, completely out of it. In a coma."

A woman in hospital clothing with a captain's bars on her collar came in, smiled at him, walked over to the bed. "Welcome back, Major Blake. So good to see you awake."

"Thanks," he replied weakly. "Where are my men? What happened to them?"

She glanced over at Melissa. Then back to Tony. "The men in your vehicle were all killed, Major. I'm sorry. And everyone in the lead vehicle was killed, too. Your driver, a Sergeant Susan..." she looked at her clipboard... "Helms is alive, just down the hall. But she's very badly wounded. We're trying hard to stabilize her so we can get her back to Walter Reed.

"I'm sorry about the men you lost, Major. You're lucky you're still with us."

Melissa saw Tony's face go dark. "Thanks." He went silent, thinking. Then he shook his head as though to move on. "Are you my doctor?"

"Yes. I'm the primary. There are several others working with you."

"How am I?"

"Well, you have a bad concussion... traumatic brain injury, but I think we're past the worst of that. You took a lot of shrapnel in your legs and arms, and both your legs and your left arm were broken in multiple places. Your right leg is pretty bad, but we're working hard to save it."

Save it! His mind reeled. Out loud he said, "You mean I might lose it?"

"I'm sorry, that was too abrupt. There's a lot of infection, and the bones in your ankle are pretty badly broken. We're giving you all the antibiotics we can, and we'll get you fully stabilized before we send you back stateside. We're doing everything we can but, yes, there's a chance you'll lose the leg. And if you do keep it, it's difficult to know how badly your mobility will be affected. We'll just have to wait and see. But... you're very lucky to be alive, Major. You get some rest, and I'll be back to see you again soon." She glanced over at Melissa, then turned to leave the room.

"What about ...?" Tony croaked after her.

She turned back. "Your genitals are still there and intact, Major, no apparent injury. And no severe internal injuries. Sorry, of course I should have mentioned that." She paused a moment to give him a chance to ask more, but when no more questions came, asked, "Anything else I can do for you right now?"

"Not right now. Thanks, Doc."

Tony turned back to Melissa. "Sorry for the scare, Baby. But I'm going to be OK. I can feel it."

Melissa closed her eyes, as if in prayer, and held and kissed Tony's hand. Then she said, "Tony, I'm so glad you're alive. I was so scared. The kids are with your mom, and you can imagine how petrified she is. In a little while I'm going to give her a call and tell her the good news."

***

Angie sat in an old wooden rocking chair in her living room, rocking gently back and forth in the darkness. Angelo and Lisa were asleep, as yet unaware of their father's injuries, and Angie was alone. She sat, thinking back over her life, the time she'd spent waiting for someone she loved to come home from a war, the agony and anguish she'd somehow made her way through. But now she was dealing with the news that Tony had been badly wounded in Iraq, with his exact condition unknown. Melissa had called her after arriving at the military hospital in Germany with the news that Tony was in a coma with brain injuries, and bad shrapnel and blast wounds to his arms and legs. Melissa had done her best to sound calm, but Angie could tell she was covering up her own terrible fear.

As she sat and rocked, Angie thought back to 1969 and Tony's father's death and the horrible thing she'd done by sending him that letter. She was sure, somehow, that God was punishing her now for what she'd done then. And she was certain that she deserved it. Tears streamed from her eyes there in the darkness, and she whispered over and over again, "Please, God, let him be OK. Please don't punish Tony for something I did."

The phone rang beside her. She picked it up, answering urgently, "Hello?"

"Mom, it's Melissa. There's someone here who wants to talk to you."

Then there was Tony's voice, and over the long distance line, with all that had happened to him evident in every syllable, he said, "Hello, Mom? I'm so sorry I scared you like that. I'm going to be OK. Should be back Stateside in a few days, and hopefully you can come and see me." His voice sounded just like his father's, so many years ago.

"Ahhhh, Tony." She wept. "I love you so much. I'm so glad you're going to be OK. Please come home!"

"I will, Mom. I'll be home soon."

***

The next day Tony was more alert, coming farther out of the shock and concussion. Melissa was there with him, and they talked about the kids and the rest of his family. He asked Melissa to check on Sergeant Helms. The doctor's summary of her condition the day before hadn't been altogether hopeful, and Tony had grown to like the young woman in the few minutes they'd shared as she'd driven him along Iraqi Highway 12.

Melissa came back looking grim. "She's not in good shape, Tony. She's already lost both her legs, and her doctor told me they'll probably take her right arm. It's shattered badly, and there's a lot of infection. When she comes to they said she's very depressed, cries all the time. Her husband was driving the lead vehicle in your convoy, and she saw him killed right in front of her. What an incredible tragedy."

Tony just shook his head but kept his thoughts to himself. He had never believed the Iraq war to be necessary, and after the invasion in 2003 when no Weapons of Mass Destruction had been found, he was sure of it. *How many Americans and other coalition forces would die or be maimed by this tragic mistake? How many Iraqi civilians would die or suffer unbearable hardship because of it?*

***

Tony was sent back to the United States aboard an Air Force hospital transport with many other wounded from Iraq and Afghanistan. Melissa had taken a civilian flight to Germany to be with him there and had been required by the military to do the same coming home. There was no room for her on the hospital transport, and it was "against regulations" for her to accompany Tony on the flight. She met up with him again three days later at Walter Reed Hospital, just north of Washington, D.C. And this time Tony's mother was with her.

Angie was shocked when she saw Tony there in the hospital bed. He had casts on both legs and his left arm, and there were IVs and other tubes protruding from many places. His skin was dark from the sun, but beneath that there was a grayness, the pallor of someone incredibly ill. Melissa had told her of the damage to Tony's right leg, but she hadn't imagined the horrible look of his foot protruding from the cast, and the smell of infected flesh. She was terrified all over again but tried her best to conceal it. Tony, a master at reading faces, could see his mother's fear.

"It's going to be OK, Mom. Don't worry. The doctor's saying my leg is more than holding its own. It'll just take some time."

"Oh, Tony." She leaned over the bed clumsily and hugged him. "I've been so scared."

"I know, Mom. I know. I'm sorry. Guess I never realized how awful this career of mine has been for you and Melissa and the kids. And after what happened to my birth father... well, you've had more of this than one person should ever have to deal with. I'm so sorry."

He looked into his mother's eyes. She was fifty-four years old, but her hair was streaked with gray, and her cheeks were sunken and without color. The worry and grief, and the guilt he never knew about had aged her well beyond her years.

"Is Dad with you?"

"No, Tony. He couldn't come. Tony, your Dad has been very sick himself. He was diagnosed two months ago with pancreatic cancer, and he's been taking chemotherapy and radiation treatments ever since. So he can't travel at all, and I'll need to be getting back to him pretty soon. He's pretty weak."

"Is he ... ?"

"I'm afraid the prognosis isn't very good, Tony. The cancer is pretty advanced, and ... they don't think he has too much time left. They're just trying to slow things down with the treatments, but they don't give much chance at all of a cure, or even long-term remission." Angie was crying as she told Tony about Loren's illness, the awful cancer that was taking yet another loved one from her.

"I'm so sorry, Mom." He looked over at Melissa, then back at his mother. "You need to be telling me these things," he said softly.

"You have so much on your mind with your job, Tony. Loren asked us not to worry you with it. And we knew you were due to come home in another month anyway, and that would have still given you plenty of time with him. He has some time left."

Tony only nodded. He understood them wanting to protect him, but it was terrible news.

45

Tony was treated at Walter Reed for nearly a month before the antibiotics won the battle against the infections in his body and the surgeons
could put his ankle back together. He came out of that surgery with a
plate and several screws in his lower leg, but the prognosis that with a
lot of physical therapy he might well walk normally again.

A few days after the surgery, Tony was taken off all IVs and his
catheter, and was able to move around for the first time since the roadside bombing. Once in his wheelchair he asked Melissa to push him
to the nurse's station where he inquired about the location of Sergeant
Susan Helms.

"She's in 4118," was all the nurse said.

Tony and Melissa took the elevator to the fourth floor, and she
pushed him to 4118.

"You may want to wait out here." Melissa nodded, and Tony clumsily wheeled himself in.

Susan Helms was asleep, her head partially elevated in the bed.
There was a noticeable absence of both legs under the sheet that covered her torso, and her right arm was only a bandaged stump from just
above the elbow. There were IVs and other tubes attached to her body,
and machines beeped softly in the background. He watched her for a

while, and when she still didn't wake up he wheeled himself closer to the bed, and touched her arm.

"Susan."

Her eyelids fluttered open. She looked at him through eyes blurred by trauma and drugs. He smiled at her. At first she didn't recognize him, but then she blinked, made a sad face. A tear rolled down her cheek. She couldn't speak around the respirator tube and the feeding tube. He wisely didn't ask how she was doing.

"I'm Tony Blake. I was with you in the Hummer when we hit the ambush."

She nodded, just a bit.

"I'm so sorry for your wounds," he said. Then he paused. He saw her eyes going over his body, to the cast on his arm, and the casts on both legs. She began to cry more.

"You're going to make it," he said. "These doctors work miracles."

She nodded. He thought of her husband, killed in the lead Humvee, of her kids back home, staying with their grandparents. He wondered how much they knew about what had happened. But he couldn't ask her questions. And he didn't want to make her think of anything sadder than her own injuries.

"I just wanted you to know I'm right down the hall, thinking about you. My wife is here, too. If there's anything we can do …."

She nodded again.

"You hang in there, OK? You'll get better. This is the worst of it. It gets better from here."

She nodded. Still plenty of tears.

"I need to let you get some rest now. But I'll be back to see you again."

She nodded, reached over with her left hand, the only one left. He took it in his right, squeezed her fingers gently. She squeezed back as best she could. He smiled at her and gently placed her hand back on the bed. Then he turned the wheelchair and left. Melissa saw tears streaming down Tony's face as he wheeled himself out of Susan Helms' room.

After two more weeks, he was pronounced fit enough to be moved to the regional military hospital at Ft. Dix, New Jersey, less than an hour from his home in Watertown. He visited Susan Helms every day while he was still at Walter Reed. On his last visit, he met her son and daughter and Susan's parents, who were looking after them. The whole family seemed incredibly sad, and he couldn't blame them. After talking to Susan for a moment he turned to her family.

Looking directly at the kids, he said softly. "Your mother is an incredibly brave woman. She has given nearly everything so that you can grow up in a country that is free, where you can do anything you want, be anyone you want. She also fought so that the people of Iraq could have the same kind of freedom we have here." This last part he had trouble believing himself, but he said it nevertheless.

"Times are hard for you right now," he said, "but it will get better."

"What happened to our dad?" asked the boy, about twelve. "We know he's dead, but Mom can't talk right now, so we don't know what happened." Tony looked at the grandparents, and they both nodded. It was OK to tell them.

"He was with us when we were ambushed, driving the vehicle ahead of us. Your dad was also a very brave man. Sadly, he was killed instantly by the first blast. I saw it, and it was very quick. You can believe me when I tell you he didn't suffer."

He paused, then, "You're very lucky your mom is alive. And she will get better."

They just nodded. The grandfather said, "Thank you."

Tony thought often about how lucky he had been to come through that ambush no worse injured than he was.

Melissa had stayed with Tony much of the time while he had been at Walter Reed, and Angie had brought Angelo and Lisa, now seven and five, for two visits. Even Tony's half-sister Cindy, who was married and living in California, made the trip to Washington to see him. But once Tony was at Ft. Dix the visits by his immediate family became even more frequent, and he was able to see Angelo and Lisa every weekend.

A month after he reached Ft. Dix, Tony was released to go home on rehabilitation leave with the stipulation that he return to the hospital three times a week for physical therapy. Because of his prognosis of nearly full recovery and his critical skills and experience, Tony was told that he would not be medically discharged from the Army. Instead he would be allowed to convalesce at home until he was pronounced fit for service again.

Living at home again after so many years of overseas combat deployments and Army posts was a bit strange at first, but Tony settled in quickly. Melissa was able to take a sabbatical from her teaching job at Rutgers, and they became reacquainted to the extent of falling in love all over again. Melissa fantasized that somehow Tony would never have to be deployed overseas again, and soon she convinced herself that her fantasy was real. Tony, knowing the Army, knew better, but he kept that to himself and enjoyed the time he had with her as best he could.

After nearly six months at home Tony was pronounced fit for service, and ordered back to duty, this time at Ft. Bragg, North Carolina A couple of weeks after he arrived there he took part in a ceremony honoring the dead and wounded Special Forces soldiers from the last several months in the Iraq war and in Afghanistan. Among those honored were Warrant Officer Robert Wilkins, Master Sergeant Andy Hanks, Sergeant Barry Drake, and Sergeant Raj Maraki.

After the ceremony, Tony was called to the office of his new boss, Colonel Abe Goodrich.

Tony entered the Colonel's office and saluted.

Goodrich returned the salute and said, "At ease, Tony. Please sit down."

"Thank you, sir."

"How are you feeling? How are your wounds?"

"Still a few twinges now and then, sir, but nothing serious. I'm good to go."

"That's good to hear. As you know, as a routine matter we ran an inquiry into the ambush that cost us four of our best men, plus five Arkansas National Guard troopers dead and three wounded. Not to mention your very serious wounds and those of Sergeant Helms. You were interviewed extensively about the incident while you were still in Walter Reed, since you were the company commander and with the team when you were ambushed."

"Yes, sir."

"I thought you would want to know the outcome of that inquiry."

"Yes, sir."

"Well, we were looking for leaks in our communications systems, even looked at locals who were employed at Al Taji who might have somehow got hold of some info about the mission and got word to the insurgents who ambushed you. It seemed a little too weird that you were driving up Highway 12 just at dawn and ran into a random ambush."

"Always seemed that way to me, too, sir. I've thought about it a million times and can't come up with a single idea about how they knew."

"And that is our conclusion too, Tony. We couldn't find a single leak. The insurgents who ambushed you couldn't have known about your mission or even who you were. They might have had people down the road, somewhere after you got onto the highway, who saw your three Hummers in convoy and called it up the line so the crazies could set up the ambush. But their information didn't come from your team or anyone else involved in the planning."

"So my men and all the others who were killed and wounded were just the victims of a random act of violence against Americans?"

"I'm afraid so, Tony. It's a dirty war."

"Sure is, sir. But, thank you for the information."

"Sure, Tony. But... please stand up."

Tony did.

The colonel came around his desk and shook Tony's hand.

"I'm glad to see you back on your feet and fully recovered, Tony. You didn't have to come back active, you know. Those were very serious wounds."

"I know sir, but I want to keep helping out the best I can. At least until the fight in Iraq is over."

"Thank you, Tony. And by the way ..." the Colonel took a small box from his desk, and opened it to reveal a pair of silver oak leaves. "Congratulations on your promotion, Colonel."

Tony had been promoted to Lieutenant Colonel, a little earlier than most.

"Thank you, sir. I'm very pleased."

Throughout his recovery and during his time back at Ft. Bragg, Tony stayed in touch with Sgt. Susan Helms' parents, hoping for ... he wasn't sure what. Some sort of miraculous recovery, he supposed. He learned that she had stayed at Walter Reed for nearly two years, eventually recovering from the Traumatic Brain Injury and healing enough that the doctors could begin work to fit prostheses to the stumps of her legs, both of which had been amputated above the knee. But he knew from these conversations that Susan remained in a constant state of depression, despite anti-depressants and psychological counseling. She had lost her husband, her legs, one of her arms, and seemingly, her will to live. The only time she brightened at all, the parents said, was when she first saw her children on one of their necessarily-infrequent visits.

They were young and having a very difficult time themselves with the loss of their father and their mother's grievous wounds.

Susan would smile when they entered her room. But then when the kids were shy around her because of all the damage to her body, her mood would begin to darken again. The conversation would go flat, and Susan's parents would take the kids away, for a tour of Washington's many historic sites, or just some fun outside the hospital. Susan's depression would deepen after each of their visits, and she would often go for days afterwards without speaking to anyone.

Sgt. Susan Helms was ultimately released from Walter Reed Hospital with prostheses for both legs and her right arm, and transferred to the VA Hospital in Little Rock. She was medically discharged from the Army and the Arkansas National Guard at that point, several years short of eligibility for any military pension. Later, after only a short delay for "processing," she was awarded full VA disability benefits; a tax-free monthly pension of about $3,000 with which to live and raise her children, and fully-paid VA health care for life.

Since she was certain that no man would ever want a romantic relationship with a woman who had no legs and only one arm, Susan was convinced that her life was essentially over. Her only reason for not actually taking her own life was her two children. But sometimes, sitting alone in the darkness late at night, unable to sleep because of the frequent nightmares about the day her husband was killed and she was maimed, not to mention the continuing pain from her injuries, she would come very, very close.

46

30 October 2005
Santa Barbara, California
Mick Delaney

"What were you dreaming about last night, Mick?" Julie was brushing her hair at the dressing table in our hotel room on the beach at Santa Barbara. She was wearing only a towel, and the towel was wrapped around her waist. She sat unembarrassed, her breasts fully exposed, reflecting well in the mirror. She seemed unaware of her nudity.

"Why?"

"You were talking in your sleep again, thrashing around, even yelled a couple of times. Hard to sleep when you're doing that.'

"Butterflies."

"Butterflies? You have nightmares about butterflies?"

"Yeah, well, not exactly. By the time I got to Vietnam just about all the wildlife was gone. Don't remember ever seeing a bird. Certainly no tigers or elephants anymore. A monkey once in a while, but not often. A few snakes. All the bombs, artillery, and Agent Orange either killed them or drove them away. But there were butterflies. Saw them almost every day we were in the bush."

"And that was somehow scary?"

"No. It always made me feel good. Gave me a little hope to see them floating around, like maybe there was still something normal about the world, like maybe I'd actually make it home."

"You didn't think you'd make it home?"

"Not after a few weeks. So much contact, so many of our guys getting killed or hurt. So many gooks around where we were. After a while, one day I can remember quite clearly, I had this epiphany. And the epiphany was that I wasn't going home alive. Just didn't seem possible. I think a lot of guys felt that way, especially early in their tours when there seemed to be so much time left to do. Seemed like the odds were against you."

"So the butterflies?"

"Well, this one day we were humpin' through the jungle as usual. I was about halfway back in the column, and it was slow going, also as usual. The point man had to take it slow, even when the way was fairly clear, to try to make sure he wasn't walking into something... an ambush, booby-trap, mine... whatever. Hard to believe, but it got really boring sometimes when you were just walking along, big heavy rucksack on your back, nothing much to do except walk a few feet, stop, look around, and so on. Waiting for the point man to make our way. Smoking cigarettes from time to time; maybe drinking some of the hot, putrid water from a canteen; wiping the sweat out of your eyes with a towel that stunk like death.

"So this one day there were a lot of butterflies around, and it gave a kind of peaceful feeling. Big yellow ones. Beautiful. Delicate. Everything that the war, and the rest of my life then, wasn't. I was enjoying them, and they kept coming closer and closer, and finally one landed on my shoulder. I could see it there, out of the corner of my eye. It just sat there, very slowly flapping its wings, not moving otherwise.

"I was kind of afraid to move because I didn't want to scare it. But then the man in front of me moved on, and I had to. So I took a few steps, watching it, careful not to move around too much. And it stayed. It went on for like an hour like that. I couldn't believe it. I started thinking maybe it had died or something, from the Agent Orange or whatever, but every so often it would move its wings.

"Then a while later, just before we were going to take a break to eat lunch, we heard someone up front, maybe the point man, yell 'gooks!' and immediately fire his weapon on full automatic. Well, normally I would have hit the ground, looked for cover, in case they came at us from the sides, but there was this butterfly, and I didn't want to move too fast. I remember that. I was having such a time with that butterfly on my shoulder that I slowly dropped to my knees, still watching it out of the corner of my eye. It stayed with me.

"Then of course we got the word to move forward, to fan out and start putting down fire to cover the point squad. I was the platoon sergeant, so I had to start moving fast, help to direct the squad leaders. There was more gunfire in both directions. Kind of a standard firefight for us. Hell of a lot of noise. When I checked for it later, the butterfly was gone, of course. I always wondered what happened to it. Hoped it just decided to fly away, didn't get crushed as I was moving around, or whatever. And I thought about how far it came with me, away from wherever it had been living. I even remember hoping it found other butterflies to live with. All this time a firefight going on, all that noise and fear and craziness."

"So why the nightmare. Sounds like a pretty good memory."

"Oh, yeah. Well, when we got up to the front, I took cover next to one of the guys from Second Platoon, a Canadian kid who had volunteered to be there. This kid, whose name was Mitch something, had come in country the same time as me, we'd gone through Cherry School together, were both assigned to this infantry company, but put into separate platoons. We got to be pretty good friends during those first few days, had some interesting talks. Intelligent, good-natured kid.

I liked him. But after we'd been assigned to different platoons, I hardly ever saw him."

"And?" she asked, impatient now.

"Well, we were talking, things were quieting down, most of the firing off to our left. I looked away or something, maybe to see if that butterfly had come back, and when I looked back, Mitch was dead. Clean bullet hole through the forehead, just under his helmet. I remember it really made a mess coming out the back of his head. He was just lying there, blood running down his nose, eyes sort of staring at me. That's what I was dreaming about. Sorry I disturbed your sleep."

"Jesus, Mick."

"Yeah, sorry."

"When are you going to get some help?"

"I've tried that. Group therapy, private shrink. Helps some, but... sometimes I still have these... dreams. Guess I'm just stuck with it."

She turned and faced me, clearly angry. "You keep saying the war is behind you. But you're pretty fucked up." Her language, after I'd gotten to know her awhile, had surprised me. And I couldn't quite understand her anger. Now I was getting angry myself. Couldn't she be more understanding?

"Yeah, well. What I heard was, life's a bitch and then you die," I snapped. I went back into the bathroom to finish getting ready for our day trip, north of Santa Barbara along the coast.

"Pain in the ass," she said under her breath.

I pretended not to hear.

A half hour later we were in the rented car going over the map. I'd been in Santa Barbara on business, had brought Julie along on a mini-vacation. By way of thanks, she'd been irritable and bitchy the whole way. And that mood seemed to be more the rule than the exception lately. *Another fucked-up relationship*, I found myself thinking.

When am I going to get a good one? When am I going to quit fucking up the good ones I do get? When am I going to get myself out of this one?

Later, we were having lunch at a Mexican restaurant in Solvang, a Danish-American community not far from Vandenberg Air Force Base. It was the Saturday of the annual Danish Festival, and we'd come to see what a Danish Festival could possibly be about. Still crabbing at each other, the day and the trip were not going well. I was eating my tacos in silence, absorbed as usual in my thoughts. Julie shoved a festival brochure under my nose, pushing my paper plate out of the way.

"Maybe you want to see this guy while we're here."

Her finger was pointing to a line in the musician's bio where it said "...decorated Vietnam combat veteran." I looked at the line, then at the name under the photograph, and then the photo itself.

"I know this guy!" I said, excited.

"Really?"

"Yeah. Jon West. We were good buddies in Vietnam."

"No way."

"Yeah. I remember he lived somewhere in southern California. We were gonna' come home, buy a boat, take our wives with us, and sail around the world together. But when we both got wounded and came out of the field, I lost track of him. Tried to find him over the years. Drove a lot of 411 operators nuts looking for him. But this is the guy. I'd recognize him anywhere. He was a pretty good musician back then. Got hold of a guitar somewhere every time we came out of the field, and played and sang for us. Looks like he's still doing it. Let's find out where he is."

"No way."

"I'll show you."

We went off in search of whoever was managing the festival and, after a bit of a walk, found the office on a side street in Solvang. I approached the older man at the counter, held out the brochure, and asked, "Do you know this musician?"

"Sure. Everybody knows Jonathan West. He opened the festival last night. He's playing again tomorrow afternoon as we close it down. Lives over in Lompoc."

"He and I were together in Vietnam. Haven't seen him in thir-ty-five years!"

"No kidding. I think I have his phone number here somewhere. Let me see...Yeah. Here it is."

"Thanks!" We walked back outside, and I dialed the number on my cell phone. A woman's voice answered.

"Is this the home of Jonathan West?"

"Yes, it is."

"Do you know if he was in Vietnam in 1969?"

"Yes, he was."

"Well, my name's Mick Delaney. I've been looking for him all these years. We were great friends there. I'm over in Solvang at the festival, and I saw the brochure. Wow, this is great!"

"He's mentioned you," she said. "I've heard him say more than once that he'd like to find you, but he couldn't remember where you lived."

"Wow. Great! Is he home?"

"No, he's playing a private party right now. And he won't be home until late tonight. He's playing again at the festival tomorrow. Will you be able to see him then?"

"I'm afraid not," I lamented. "Have to go home tomorrow morning. But... tell him I'll call him. And I'll come back out in a week or two, whenever he's free. I'd love to see him." Then I paused, thought back. Jon's wife's name had been Linda. "Is this Linda?"

"No, I'm Rachel, his second wife. He and Linda were divorced not too long after he got back from Vietnam. After they broke up, he took his band on the road. He and I met in Salina, Kansas, in 1975."

"Oh, I'm sorry, Rachel. That was thoughtless of me."

"No problem, Mick. Kinda neat you remembered his wife's name after all these years. You and he must have been very close."

"Yeah. We really were. I'm sure disappointed I won't see him this trip. But I'll be back."

"I know he'll look forward to seeing you, too, Mick. And I'll look forward to meeting you."

"Give him my phone number, will you? It's … …."

Back at the hotel that night I had a hard time sleeping again, as usual, and wound up in a nightmare that woke both Julie and me.

After breakfast, we loaded luggage into our rental car and drove north to the Santa Barbara airport in Goleta. We were picked up there a little while later by the Delaney Enterprises corporate plane, a Learjet 60. Both Julie and I were in poor moods, having argued again over breakfast about my frequent nightmares and lapses in attention when I thought about Vietnam. I, of course, had brought up Julie's apparent disinterest in any sort of affection anymore.

I had been excited to find Jonathan after all these years and couldn't wait to get back to California to see him. But I knew that seeing him again would bring back a lot for both of us, and I was preparing myself to face that and to try to deal with it.

Julie had continued to live in Chicago near her children during our relationship, and I had continued to live in Kansas City, near mine. But her travel schedule allowed her frequent visits to Kansas City, and my work allowed me to get to Chicago on many weekends and sometimes during the week. So we'd seen each other often. The subject of marriage had come up, and we'd planned it, without announcing an engagement, for a year out.

But I could see that it wasn't working out. And I could sense that Julie felt the same way.

When we landed in Chicago to drop her off, the pilots told me that they'd need at least two hours to get the plane refueled, since there was a queue for refueling at the busy Midway airport.

"I'll take you home," I said to Julie as we were exiting the business terminal looking for a cab.

"Oh, you don't need to do that, Mick. I'll be fine." She kissed me on the cheek, kind of like a sister.

"Julie, I ...."

"No need to say it, Mick. I know. It's not working out between us. I'm sorry for my part in that. I really thought it would."

"I'm sorry too, Julie. I thought it would, too. I do love you, you know?"

"I know, Mick. I love you, too. You're a wonderful man. But sometimes love isn't enough. We seem to have a lot of differences, and I think we're both just getting tired of it. Honestly, that fucking war you were in has caused me a lot of grief in my life. It took my husband from me. And now, every few nights it causes you these nightmares that absolutely terrify me. I can't take it anymore."

I looked down sadly.

"I hope you get to meet up with Jon West soon, Mick. He seems like someone you were very close to."

"Yes, he was. I'm excited to have found him ...."

"And I hope you get some more help. You need it."

I didn't respond to that.

"Well, here's my cab, Mick. Take good care of yourself." She gave me another peck on the cheek.

"Goodbye, Julie. You take good care of yourself, too. If you ever need anything ...."

"Thanks, Mick. But I'll be OK. I have my kids and the material things I need. I'll be fine." With that, she was in the cab and gone. I stood there, looking after her, feeling that very familiar sense of loss I'd felt so many times in my life when someone I'd loved had died or left or somehow been taken from me. Or perhaps driven away by me. By me!

I turned and went back into the business terminal, sat staring dumbly at the television for a few minutes in a sort of shock that our relationship had ended so abruptly. Then I shook my head as if to shake off that feeling of loss, took out my cell phone, and dialed Ed Thorsen.

"Hello?"

"Hey, LT! Guess who I found!"

47

1 November 2005
Kansas City

My office was on the northwest corner of the 19th floor of the BMA Building, in midtown Kansas City, Mo. I believed that this particular office, on this particular floor, of this particular building, offered the best view in the city. From it I could look down to the north and see the famous Scout statue, a lifelike bronze sculpture of an Indian scout sitting his pony, one hand up shielding his eyes as he surveys the horizon. Beyond the Scout was Union Station, and farther north, beautiful downtown Kansas City. I could look west past the railyards to the Kansas River, the Kaw they called it, and follow its path northward to its confluence with the Missouri. Or I could look southwest past the University of Kansas Medical Center toward Johnson County, Kansas, the affluent suburb where I lived. I especially enjoyed that view during the spring and summer when frequent storms approached from the southwest, and I could watch their progress toward me from certainly the best vantage point in this part of Kansas City. And sitting in that office during a violent rainstorm, as I had done many times, was almost exciting enough to get my adrenaline going.

Delaney Enterprises occupied the top five floors of the building, and the space cost the company a great deal of money. But we were very profitable and could easily afford it. Delaney Enterprises was a national contender in many forms of technology, from software and website development to hosting, network management, and consulting services. We were doing very well for ourselves, and I was very proud that all the company's employees, who benefited from partial owner-ship in stock, a rich profit sharing program, and many other perks, were doing very well individually, too.

But more and more often those days I found myself with a sense of general discontent, not unlike my first few months home from the war more than thirty-five years before. When my boys had been young and I'd been working hard every day just to keep the company going, I'd been so busy that I'd had little time to think back to the war days. But now the boys were grown and on their own, and the business pretty much ran itself, having benefited from my war-given talent at picking the best people for key leadership positions. And I was bored. Bored and disturbed.

And now I'd lost Julie. The last in a long string of failed relation-ships. The really tragic part, I thought, was that, try as I would, I couldn't feel much of a sense of loss about it.

I unlocked and opened the bottom right hand drawer of my desk, where I kept the mementos of the war that I'd moved to my office when Amanda and I had separated. There was an album with the few photographs I had of some of my buddies and me, including one photo of some of us with a big python we'd killed one day and eaten half raw because we were out of food. In the album was also a great picture of Jon West. It was taken one afternoon on a rare respite from the bush, in Phuoc Vinh, the division base camp, where we'd had a few hours of stand down. Jon was sitting on a pile of sandbags, his shirt off, a guitar in his hands, playing and singing for us. Off to the left in the picture was Carl Engle, a beer in his hand. And Hal Wilson…. Tony was there, and the Fragman.... Termite and Sugarbear, Doc Benedetto, and a few others. As always, my heart came alive seeing all those guys in the photograph.

I was excited I'd found Jon and couldn't wait to get back to California to see him again and meet his family.

I put the album back in the drawer and took out a heavy black plastic bag with a zip closure. I held it in both hands for a while, then unzipped it and took out the contents. It was the picture of Angie, Tony's wife, that I'd taken from his helmet the day he'd been killed. And the letters. The Dear John letter was in its envelope, the corner stained by Tony's blood that had long ago dried and turned black. I took it from the envelope for the hundredth time and read it again.

Tony,

I'm sorry to have to tell you this, but it has to be over between us. I want a divorce. I can't stand this waiting anymore. Not knowing every night while I lie awake in our bed whether you're alive, or dead, or hurt somewhere in the jungle. I know I'm a coward, but I have to stop caring about you. I just can't live like this anymore.

Angela

I put the letter back in its envelope, looked once more at the picture of the beautiful young woman who had written it, then put both letters and the photo back into the black plastic bag, zipped it closed, and dropped it back into the drawer.

I turned my chair away from the desk to face the window, looking west toward the train yards and Kansas City, Kansas, where I'd grown up.

Still can't fuckin' believe you did that, I thought. *Still can't fuckin' be-*

lieve I didn't read Tony better that morning when we started the march. If I had, I bet he'd be alive today.

48

Stan McDermott, the company CFO, walked in. "You wanted to see me, Mick?"

I spun around in the chair. "Hey, Stan. Yeah. Thanks for stopping by. You all ready for the employee meeting?"

"Sure. Not hard to get ready when the news is good."

I smiled. "Very true. Hey, you know I took the company plane to Santa Barbara last week, for the meeting with Capstone. We flew to Chicago first to pick up my girlfriend Julie, and then back there to drop her off on the way back. Would you get hold of the flight logs and calculate my share of the cost of that trip, and deduct it from my next quarterly bonus? Want to make sure we're all square. And... I'm going to take the plane back to California this week, on a trip that's strictly personal. I'm going to announce that at the employee meeting so everyone will know what I'm doing. It's really important to me that everyone understands that I don't fold personal expense into the company expense. I've already cleared this week's flights with the scheduler... they didn't have the plane scheduled for anything else, so no conflict there."

"Sure, Mick. Happy to do it. And thanks for keeping it all square. Last company I worked for the owners were always loading what I considered personal expense into the company, then wanting the operating units to absorb it into our operating costs. So it affected our profits, by which our performance was judged. It made me pretty uncomfortable, being the financial guy, and it made a lot of the employees pretty angry. I know a lot of people do that, but it's just not right."

"I couldn't agree more, Stan. Thanks for your help on this. What people like that don't realize is that the folks who work for them always see it, and then they don't trust their leadership anymore. That's a recipe for disaster. I truly believe there's no substitute for operating in a totally ethical manner, and as transparently as possible. It's about *trust*.

"You learn all that at Rockhurst when you got your MBA, Mick?'

"Well, we sure talked about it there. We had a course on Corporate Social Responsibility that had a heavy ethics component to it. Excellent professor named Gerry Miller taught it. I'm actually teaching that course now, as an adjunct. But that's not really where I learned it."

"Really? Tell me. I'm very curious."

"OK. We have a few minutes before the meeting. You knew I was in Vietnam?"

"Yeah. Heard something about it. Not many details though. You've never talked about it much, with me at least."

"I try not to bring it up around here. But...I was an infantryman there. An enlisted man. A grunt, we called it. Wound up as a platoon sergeant the last few months before I left. But my highest rank was as a staff sergeant. Not too high up. I saw a lot of unethical behavior there, at pretty much all levels of the Army. But most of it from the higher ranking officers. The ones at the battalion level and above, who weren't in the field with us. It seemed like the higher up they got, the more all they wanted to do was make more rank, and the less they cared about the lives of the men like us who were actually doing the fighting. They'd order us to do things that were just absolutely stupid, to unnecessarily risk our lives, so they could be credited with more body count.

"On the American side at least, that war was all about body count.

Supposedly, we could tell whether or not we were winning by whether we killed more of the enemy than they killed of us. The higher level infantry officers were rated based on the body count they turned in each week, month, and so on. So then the company level officers were rated by the battalion commander based on body count. But much of the time, there was no way to actually confirm the body counts that got turned in.

"So to keep the battalion and higher up officers happy and off their backs, the people in the field would lie all the time, turning in a higher body count than we actually had, to make the 'lifers' as we called them, happy. I think the formula our company commander used after a firefight was, if we saw one blood trail, it equaled two or three bodies for the body count. If we had an actual 'step-on,' that was worth five or six bodies for the body count, and some 'probables.'"

"I've heard about that," Stan said.

"Yeah. Most everyone who was around back then has.

"But then to get more body count, so he would look better, our battalion commander would order us to do things that absolutely made no sense. Keep in mind, now, that this was a war we weren't even trying to win. We were just marking time until we could be withdrawn.

"I remember one night he ordered our company to walk into a bunker complex where another company had been in a firefight earlier in the day, so we could count bodies for him. It was after dark when we got there, and raining, so dark you literally couldn't see the man in front of you. Our CO, the first one I had, he was a good officer. He called the battalion commander and told him we needed to wait until morning. I could hear the battalion commander screaming at him over the radio, from back at the firebase, that we had to go in immediately. So he had no choice. We did it. Went in as quietly and carefully as we could. But a couple of our guys on the point got killed, and a couple more hideously wounded, maimed for life, when we were ambushed going in there. And of course there were no gook bodies to be found."

"Jesus."

"Yeah. Another time my squad leader, a really good guy from Alabama, got killed because we were ordered to walk directly into a known bunker complex, where we could actually hear the NVA talking right in front of us. If anyone at battalion had been even a little concerned for our welfare we would have been pulled back away from there first, so the artillery could shell the hell out of it, or maybe we could call in a bomber strike, like they did on all the invasions in World War II. And then we would have gone in. Would have given us a much greater chance of survival. Instead we walked right into it, my buddy was killed right in front of me, and we lost several other guys wounded that day, and a really good scout dog killed, because that asshole didn't want to risk us not getting a body count for him."

"Good God!"

"Yeah. That same battalion commander had the skids on his personal Huey helicopter chromed somehow, so you could always pick him out when he was flying overhead, safely out of 'small arms range' at 3,500 feet, when we were in a firefight. Supposedly he was locating the enemy for us, but we already knew where they were... they were shooting at us. You know? This one firefight, I remember, I saw red tracers from a machine gun being fired at his helicopter. It wasn't the gooks. They had green tracers. It was one of our gunners shooting at the battalion commander, honest to God.

"We were in another little skirmish a couple of days later, right after we'd made a helicopter landing in another area, got a couple of rounds fired at us, nothing significant. We were then ordered to 'secure the area' and wait in place. That puzzled us, since we would normally have started humping through the jungle right away. About an hour later, we're sitting around, eating C-Rations and smoking, joking around, enjoying the break. In flies the battalion commander's helicopter, and he jumps off like he's in a hot LZ, and comes running over like he's under fire, and hits the dirt right next to us. We looked at him like, 'What the fuck?' And he gets up and says 'Hello, men,' runs back to the bird, and they take off. Later that night I hear him on the radio to our company commander, telling him that he wants him to write him up for the Silver Star, for making a 'hot combat assault'. Silver Stars weren't given out easily in that war, to the grunts at least. You had to do something really heroic, really risk your life, to be recommended for one. But he wanted to be written up because he'd faked a hot LZ landing. The more medals he got, the better chance he had of making more rank.

"Of course, we hated the guy. Didn't trust him. Knew he didn't care a damn what happened to us. Result was, we weren't nearly as aggressive in the field as we could have been, didn't kill nearly as many gooks as we could have, if he'd been a good leader and we'd really wanted to fight for him. As it was, all we wanted to do was keep our heads down, try to make it home alive and in one piece.

"I could go on for hours with stories like that, but I'll spare you. And don't misunderstand me. I know there were excellent officers at all levels in Vietnam. My first company commander and my last platoon leader were two of them. But my personal experiences with my battalion level leadership taught me a lot about how NOT to be a leader. All the lessons I learned from them translate directly to this business, and all businesses, as far as I'm concerned.

"If you want an organization to perform well, you absolutely must lead it ethically, and transparently, with respect and high regard for the people at all levels, and sincere concern for their welfare. Share the rewards. I've tried very hard to do that here at Delaney, and it seems to be working. Look what a great company we have."

I looked at my watch. "We'd better go. And... sorry for the language. When I get to talking about the war, I'm afraid I slip back into the old me a bit."

"No worries, Mick. And thank you for the talk. Fascinating. I'd like to hear more some time. I get it. And I couldn't agree more." We shook hands.

I stood and put on my suit jacket, and we walked to the elevator together and took it down to the basement cafeteria where all the home office employees were assembling. We walked in together and made our way to the front of the room, stopping to say hello to several people who had spoken to us along the way. The podium and a large projection screen were set up. One of the IT guys had set up a computer and projector, and the first slide of a PowerPoint presentation was already up. I took the podium first.

"Welcome, everyone, to the Delaney Enterprises monthly employee meeting. It's good to see you all. This will be the usual agenda. I'll make a few introductory comments, and then we'll ask each of the Regional General Managers to update us on activities in their regions. And then Stan McDermott will come up to update you on monthly, quarterly, and year-to-date financials and the payout on the profit sharing plan. As always, if you have any questions along the way, please hold them until the end of that presenter's talk, and we'll take whatever time we need to make sure you get answers. OK?"

Someone shouted, "OK, Mick!" and everyone laughed. These meetings were always boisterous affairs, the employees really appreciating the openness of the communications, the sharing of the financials, and the employee participation in the company's profits.

"So, sort of a personal item first for me, but it has business implications, so I want to share it with you. When we were in Santa Barbara last week meeting with Capstone Software I had my girlfriend Julie with me. We took the company plane and flew up to Chicago on the way out to pick her up and then back there on the return trip to drop her off."

It was quiet, people wondering why I was bringing it up.

"As is the case every time I or anyone in this company has used the plane for personal travel, I've just asked Stan here to calculate the cost of the portion of the flight that was personal for me, going out of our way to fly to Chicago to pick up my girlfriend, and then out of the way back to drop her off... fuel cost, pilot time, aircraft depreciation and overhead cost, and so on, and deduct that from my next quarterly bonus. I just want to make sure it's clear to everyone how this is handled, and that a part of our company's profits don't go toward my personal use of company equipment, or anyone else's."

Someone in the middle of the crowd of employees started a slow clap, and then everyone joined in the applause.

"Thanks," I said. "But I'm not looking for applause. It's really important to me, and I think to everyone in the company, that you understand that we're all in this together, and that the other company officers and I are always going to be honest with you and as open as we can be. There are some things we can't discuss openly with you, like individual employee salaries or planned acquisitions of other businesses, and I know you understand why those have to remain confidential. But where we can, we'll always be completely transparent with you.

"Now I have another little announcement before I turn it over to our general managers. While I was in Santa Barbara I ran across an old friend of mine from the Vietnam war, a fellow named Jonathan West, who I was really close to during a very difficult time in our lives. Jon is a regional entertainer out there, has a band, and plays in some pretty big venues, makes his living that way. So I'm going to take a few days off the end of this week and fly out there and visit him and his family. It'll be the first time we've seen each other in thirty-five years ... we couldn't get together in person when I was there last weekend. Anyway, since the only airport near his home in Lompoc is a small regional airport without good commercial connections, I've checked the flight schedule for our plane and find that it won't interfere with other company business if I take it out. So I'll be doing that, and of course, paying for this trip out of my next bonus as well."

My openness, what I hoped was my open friendliness to the other employees of the company, and what I hoped was my honest, sincere, and inclusive leadership style, seemed to make everyone feel comfortable speaking their minds and talking to me about anything. One of the programmers near the back of the room, a young man known to have a great sense of humor, stood and shouted, "Hey, Mick, is there any danger you're going to grow your hair long and become lead singer in your friend's band? We'd hate to lose you!"

There was enormous laughter, including mine.

"Well, you've obviously never heard me sing. I'd say there's absolutely no danger of that at all."

More laughter.

"Any questions on any of that?"

"Glad you found your friend, Mick," someone else shouted. "Bring us some pictures!"

I smiled. "I'll do that. Next meeting. Maybe we'll even get Jonny and his band back here to play for you." I paused. "OK then, my overview of the business last month. First slide, please. Revenues for the month were up 3.3% over the previous month and almost 9% from the same month last year. Thanks to our company-wide cost reduction program, costs were only up 2.1% over the previous month and 5.9% over last year. So operating profit was up, meaning this will be your thirty-third consecutive month of payout for the profit sharing plan. Each of the regions brought in considerable new business last month, and our repeat business remains strong. Quotes for future new business are up as well, meaning that if we continue to improve our closure rate and continue to manage our costs well, we'll see this profit sharing payout trend continue, and the payout percentages increase.

"Any questions on that?" There were none.

"OK, then. Now let me introduce Ellen Spangler, Senior Vice President and General Manager of the Northeast Region, who will be with us today via video conference."

There was a momentary pause, then Ellen's smiling face appeared on the giant projection screen at the front of the room. Ellen was a beautiful black woman of about thirty-five, who had an incredible innate warmth in her face, and her smile, and her demeanor. "Good morning!" she exclaimed.

49

The Lear Jet landed at the Lompoc Airport and taxied to the executive terminal, a small metal building along the south side of the field. I stepped out, set my bag on the ground, and stretched. The little Lear was economical to operate and very fast, but it was a bit small inside for a tall guy like me, and I always felt a little claustrophobic, even in the luxurious leather seats with all those windows. Eric Wang, the pilot, followed me out of the plane, walked with me to the terminal. "If it's OK with you, Mick, Lilly and I are going to rent a car and go down to Santa Barbara until you're ready to leave." Lilly was his wife and the co-pilot. They made a great team.

It was a Friday, and I planned to stay the weekend.

"Sure. Let's plan to leave Monday morning. What time can you be back up here without having to rush?"

"8:30?"

"OK. I'll meet you here at 8:30 Monday morning." Lilly had joined us. "You two have a nice weekend in Santa Barbara."

"Thanks, Mick," replied Lilly. "Where's your friend?"

"Probably waiting inside there."

298

They walked into the building and sure enough an older version of my close friend from Vietnam was standing near the front door. He was wearing jeans, a tan shirt, and black leather vest, and a big, black, broad-brimmed ten-gallon cowboy hat. He had long hair down to his neck and a goatee and mustache, and he looked just like the photo I had seen in the Solvang festival magazine.

"Mick!" he shouted, rushing over. "Boy, it's good to see you!"

We came together for a big hug, then stood apart and looked at each other.

"You haven't put on a pound since '69, Jon. You look great!"

"So do you, Mick. I'm so glad you ran across that brochure over at Solvang. Sorry I missed you, though."

"No harm done. I'm here for a couple of days, so we can catch up. Let me introduce Eric and Lilly Wang, our company pilots."

Jon shook hands with them. "Welcome to Lompoc. Will you be joining us for dinner tonight?"

"No, thanks, Jon," said Eric. "Lilly and I are going down to Santa Barbara for the weekend. When we flew Mick out here last week we weren't able to stay because of other flights. So we're going to go enjoy the town."

"Well, have a great time."

With that the Wangs went to the service counter to make arrangements for the refueling and tie-down of the plane, and Jon and I left through the front door. He was driving a beautiful red 1994 Pontiac Trans Am, and I threw my bag into the back and slipped into the low-slung passenger seat.

"Nice car."

"Thanks. It's fun to tinker with. How you been, Mick?"

"Doing fine, Jon. My boys are doing well. Hunter's in construction, Eric is a mortgage banker. I really enjoy the company I started a few years ago, working with some great people, traveling some."

"No woman in your life?"

"Not at the moment. Just broke up with a really nice lady from Chicago. She lost her husband to Agent Orange a few years ago, and had trouble with my PTSD. Can't blame her."

"Sorry to hear that. You were married, what, twice? You were married when we were in Vietnam. We were going to come home and buy a boat and sail around the world together."

"That's right. I looked for you many times after the war but couldn't remember where you were. I do remember calling the Santa Barbara area code 411 operator, but she couldn't find you."

"We've been in Lompoc a long time. We were in Florida for a while."

"So I talked to Rachel on the phone the other day from Solvang. She told me you have three kids?"

"Two girls and a boy. Actually, two women and a man. My oldest is my daughter Shelly. She just had her first child, a little girl, about two weeks ago. There's also my son Jason and my younger daughter Cathy. My sister and brother-in-law live here, too. You'll meet everyone at dinner tonight. We're going to Shelly's house up on the mountain for dinner. Great view of Vandenberg Air Force Base."

"And you're an entertainer! That's neat."

"Yeah. It's what I always wanted to do. When I came home, I grew my hair out long, grew a beard, and started a band. We got a contract right away with the old Decca label, and they put us on the road to tour for a couple of years to make a name for ourselves. My wife, Linda, couldn't handle the travel and couldn't handle me being away that much, and she left during one of my road trips. We were divorced in '74."

"My first divorce was in '74."

"I remember how much you talked about Katie. I'm sorry for that."

"Well, the war really messed me up. I was very lost for a while and started drinking and hanging out with some other combat vets. That breakup was really my fault. I've always felt bad that I couldn't handle the PTSD better. So how'd you meet Rachel?"

"She's from central Kansas. I met her in Salina while my band was touring, a year or so after Linda and I were divorced. She was eighteen, I was twenty-five. But I knew it was meant to be from the first moment I saw her. She says I chased her until she caught me."

I was greeted warmly at the house, first by Rachel, a beautiful woman in her late forties, then by the son and daughters and their partners. Jon's sister and her husband were also there. Everyone treated me like family from the first moment, and I couldn't remember feeling more at home. They weren't wealthy, but lived a comfortable life, happy with their family relationships and the work they'd chosen to do. Jon's son-in-law, Will, played in Jon's band and helped with the production of his several CDs and a patriotic music video he'd made. They were about the happiest, most contented people I had ever met, and they immediately adopted me as honorary "uncle." I also became honorary grandpa to Shelly's and Tom's beautiful baby girl Lana.

I stayed at a small local motel, but Jon and I spent every possible moment together for the days I was there. Jon and Will were playing a gig on Saturday night at a local dude ranch, so I went along. Remembering the comment at my employee meeting, I resisted the urge to add my voice to the beautiful singing that came from the pair, and smiled to myself when I thought about it.

During the moments when Jon and I were alone we talked about the war. Do you remember this day or that day? Sad day that Sugarbear and Carl died. Sad day that Tony died. Sad days that the others had died or been badly wounded.

"You know," I said during one of those conversations, "I'm in touch with LT Thorsen, and I see him a lot. I've spoken by phone with Doc Benedetto up in Boston, and I'm planning a visit with him one day soon. And now you and I have re-connected, and that makes me really happy. Tony, Carl, and Sugarbear are gone. I'd sure like to find Danny Nakamura and Fragman and Termite. I honestly don't remember Fragman's real name or Termite's, do you?"

"No. Always called them by their nicknames."

"Going to be hard to find them that way. They probably don't go by 'Fragman' and 'Termite' now," I laughed. "But I ought to be able to find Danny. He was from Hawaii, right? Do you remember which island?'

"Kauai, I think. Have you looked for him lately?"

"Honestly, no. Last time I was over there I was on Oahu and Maui. But I've never been to Kauai. Several years ago, I called the 411 operator in Honolulu and asked her to look. She didn't see a Danny or Daniel Nakamura, but there were tons of Nakamuras on Oahu, and she said there were a lot more on the other islands."

"Might find him on the Internet."

We went to Jon's computer and searched for "Danny Nakamura Kauai."

The search engine turned up several references to Nakamuras in Kauai, but no Danny or Daniel. One reference was to a woman, Ishio Nakamura, as the owner of a restaurant.

"His mother owned a restaurant! I bet that's her," I declared. "Is there a phone number?"

There was. I dialed it on my cell phone. It was Sunday afternoon in California, mid-Sunday morning in Kauai. I got an answering machine but hung up, deciding not to leave a message about a soldier in Vietnam on a restaurant answering machine.

"I'll call them later tonight or tomorrow. See if I can get hold of someone who might know Danny."

The reunion ended early Monday morning when Jon met me for breakfast at 7:00. I felt like we were just getting re-acquainted and I had to leave. It wasn't enough time.

"I feel like part of your family, Jon. You have an incredible family, and they made me feel really welcome. Just the warmest, friendliest people I've met in a long time. Please tell everyone 'thanks' for the wonderful hospitality, baby rocking opportunity, home cooking... all things I don't get very often these days. I had a terrific visit."

"Well, they are your family, Mick. They all just instantly fell in love with you. Knowing we were in the war together and that the friendship has lasted all these years without us seeing each other... that means a lot to them.

"Hey, I brought you a gift," he said. Jon handed me a small gift bag. Inside were copies of all Jon's music CDs and the patriotic DVD he'd made. "Hope you enjoy these. We sure enjoyed making them."

Eric and Lilly Wang arrived around 8:00 and prepped the plane for the return flight. So right at 8:30 I hugged my good friend good-bye, took my bag and the gift CDs, and boarded. I turned to wave to Jon, who was inside the building at the window. Then I stepped inside, pulled up the steps, and closed the door. As the plane taxied away from the terminal I put one of the CDs into the built-in player and treated Eric and Lilly to Jon's wonderful tenor voice all the way home. He was a truly gifted musician and a dear friend. In ways, it was as if the thirty-five years had been only a few weeks.

50

7 November 2005
Kansas City

I was back in my office in Kansas City by 3:00 that afternoon, and with no one to go home to I stuck around to clean up paperwork through the early evening. At about 8:00, well after dark, with Kansas City spread out before me, I again dialed the phone number Jon and I had picked up from the internet for the restaurant in Kauai where Ishio Nakamura was listed as owner.

"Land and Sea Restaurant, may I help you?" A woman's voice.

"May I speak to Ishio Nakamura, please?"

"May I ask who's calling?"

"It's a personal call. I'm trying to locate a man named Danny Nakamura. He was a very close friend of mine in Vietnam back in '69. I thought Ishio might be his mother because his mom owned a restaurant in Kauai and used to send him all kinds of treats that he'd share with the other guys in our squad."

"Ishio is his mother. I'm his sister, Anna. Perhaps I'd better do the talking for us. My mom isn't well. Can you hold until I can get back to my office?"

"Sure."

There was a click, and some Hawaiian elevator music, and then another click.

"I'm sorry, sir. I didn't get your name."

"Mick Delaney. I'm in Kansas City. Danny and I were in the same rifle platoon, even the same squad for a while, in Vietnam. He's a very good friend, and I'm so happy to have found him. Do you have a number where I can reach him?"

"I'm afraid not, Mick." She paused. "Danny passed away last year."

"Oh, no." I went quiet for a moment. "May I ask the cause?"

"Well, it was a heart attack. But Danny hadn't been well since he came home from the war. When he came back in December of '69 he moved back into our mom's house with her and me. Kind of kept to himself, didn't say much to us about the war, and we didn't pry. He enrolled in college for the spring semester and started taking classes, but it seemed like he wasn't at all the same person who had left just a year before. He was withdrawn, didn't talk much, spent a lot of time alone in his room playing his guitar, watching TV. Sometimes he went for walks on the beach.

"Then one day in mid-February he came home from school, sat down on the couch, and put his head in his hands and started to cry. I happened to be there and I went over and put my arm around him, and asked if he wanted to talk. He started pouring out these stories, about his friends who had been killed in the war right in front of him, and how afraid he'd been, and how he felt partly responsible because he was supposed to be helping them watch for the 'gooks,' I think he called them. He was particularly upset about a boy named Carl... and another boy named Tony. I'll always remember those names. Carl, he said, had lost his face from a mine blast and died right in front of him. Tony had been killed just as he was being pulled to safety. It was horrible, the way he described those deaths.

"I didn't know what to say," she went on, "so I just hugged him and told him it would get better. But after a while he quit talking and just sat there, became unresponsive. We couldn't get him to talk any more or do anything except by kind of leading him around. We took him to the VA and they said it was delayed combat stress and admitted him to the hospital. But after several months there he was no better, so we took him out of there and put him into a private hospital. He eventually got to where he would talk to people and started playing his guitar again, but when they talked to him about leaving the hospital, he just said he didn't want to. Danny lived in a special shelter for mentally challenged adult men until he died last year. They found him dead one morning of a heart attack. He was kneeling in prayer, his head resting on his folded hands beside his bed. He was fifty-six years old."

"Oh, my God," I said. "I'm so sorry. I wish I'd found him years ago. But that explains why I could never find him in a phone book or with directory assistance. He didn't have a phone. We were such close friends. I can't begin to describe how close we were. I hate that the war affected him so severely for the rest of his life. I hate that he's gone and I never got the chance to talk to him. I'm so very sorry."

"We don't know much about what he did in Vietnam except that he was in the infantry. He had been in the Hawaii National Guard and was activated in 1968. He went to Vietnam in March of '69, and came home in December."

"Would you like to know more?"

"We certainly would."

"Well, generally what we did was walk around in the jungle in what they called 'Reconnaissance in Force' patrols, company sized units, maybe seventy-five or eighty soldiers. We patrolled through the really dense jungle until we found the North Vietnamese, or they found us, and then usually a firefight would break out. Danny often walked point, first man in the line of march, and chopped a path through the jungle for the soldiers following him. It was the most dangerous job in the company because the point man was usually the first to make contact. We lost several point men killed and wounded. He was so good at it that he survived. The incidents he talked about with Carl Engle and Tony Giles, on those days he was the backup man and they were walking point. In both cases, Danny was right there when they were hit, and in both cases he heroically pulled them back to where we could tend to them. I'm sure he was given at least two Bronze Stars for heroism for those incidents.

"We lived really rough, in the jungle for four or five weeks at a time without a shower, maybe one change of clothes, mosquitoes and leeches and every other hostile critter you can think of, sleeping in the rain without any kind of cover, often running out of food and water. Just incredible filth and deprivation. And then there were the North Vietnamese, who were trying to kill us.

"Danny was an incredibly good soldier. He toughed his way through all that, and almost always had a smile for you, a kind word. He had a great sense of humor, kind of dry but incredibly funny. He'd share anything he had with you, even his last cigarette or his last sip of water. And he had this uncanny sixth sense about the enemy and could often tell when they were near even when there was nothing in sight. I'm absolutely certain that he saved my life more than once. I can't tell you how sad I am that he's gone and that I never got to tell him how much he meant to me. He was a really good friend."

"I don't know if he would have seen you even if you had found him, Mick. One of his other buddies from the war was also from Hawaii and did manage to find him. Danny talked to him on the phone once but told him he didn't want to see him and didn't want him to call again. He just didn't want to be reminded of it."

"That's so sad," I said. "A fine young life like his, ruined by that damned war. His name should go up on the Memorial in Washington,

D.C. He's a casualty of the war as much as anyone who was killed there."

"But we're not certain the war caused his death. He died of a heart attack."

"Is there other heart disease in your family, Anna?

"Well, no."

"And do people in your family usually die in their fifties?"

"No. My mother is now in her late eighties and still doing pretty well. Our dad lived to be ninety. And all our grandparents lived at least into their eighties."

"Well, maybe there were other factors, but I'm betting it was the Agent Orange we all worked in while we were there that caused the heart disease. I have heart disease myself, had stents put in last year, and no one in my family ever had heart disease before. The VA is looking at heart disease now as what they call a 'presumptive' disease brought on by Agent Orange. I expect one day soon they'll classify it that way, basically saying that if you were exposed to Agent Orange and have heart disease, there is such a high probability that the Agent Orange caused it that they'll just presume it is the cause and give health benefits and some disability pay."

"Guess that won't do Danny any good."

"No, I'm afraid not."

The conversation began to slow, and I could tell that Anna was being absorbed by her thoughts of Danny.

"I have some photos of Danny and some of the rest of us taken during the war that you may not have. Would you like me to send you copies?" I asked.

"That would be great, Mick. And I'll send you copies of the ones he brought back, in case you don't have them." She paused. "I really miss him. We were very close. But you know, I felt like we really lost him back in 1969. When he came back from the war, he wasn't the same man anymore. They don't warn you about that before it happens."

"No, they don't. I don't imagine it's any sort of consolation, but every one of us I know from the war is still struggling with it."

I got the e-mail address where I could send the photos, and we said goodbye, promising to stay in touch. I hung up, then sat for a while staring out the window at the beautiful night sky above Kansas City. Then I picked up the handset again and dialed Jon West in California.

"Hey, Jon. I found Danny Nakamura. It's bad news I'm afraid...."

After that sad call, I called Ed Thorsen with the same bad news. Like Jon, Ed seemed to take the news with stoic sadness, but we spent a few minutes remembering Danny as he'd been in Vietnam, a tough, resilient man of short physical stature but great spiritual strength who always seemed to take difficulty in stride. Ed reminded me that Danny's favorite expression when things went wrong, as they often did, was "Fuck it man, it don't mean nothin'."

When the calls were over, I once again sat staring out the window, into the dark night sky, tears welling up in my eyes. *When*, I thought, *will that fucking war ever be over?*

But then I answered my own question. *When we're all dead!*

And then I said out loud, just to myself, "Fuck it, man, it don't mean nothin'!"

51

2006 - 2007
Tony Blake

Major Tony Blake spent over a year at Ft. Bragg as executive officer with the Special Forces Training Command. He was given responsibility for developing updates to the counter-insurgency training manuals for new Special Forces officers, incorporating what he'd learned in all those years in Afghanistan, Iraq, Somalia, and Eastern Europe. The job turned out to be a lot more difficult than he would have thought since every change had to be reviewed by a panel of junior officers, a panel of field-grade officers, and a series of senior officers, including the Chief of Staff of the Army, all of whom had their own strong opinions on what the manual should say. He often wished he had the ability to read minds, as that seemed the only quality that would ensure a smooth acceptance of his work. Soon he began to feel as though he was running in quicksand, and he was pleased when he was able to hand off the assignment, only partially completed, to another recent veteran of Afghanistan.

A few months into the assignment at Ft. Bragg, after a routine check-up, he decided to have the screws and plate removed from his broken ankle, in hopes that the joint would fully heal and his leg would be back to full strength. The surgery went well, with an excellent prognosis for full recovery, and six months later, after another check, he made his first parachute jump in almost two years, using one of the newer square parachute rigs that could be flown in and "stalled out" for a soft landing. He found the new ankle sound. He decided he was in pretty good shape for an old guy of thirty-six, and although his body was amply populated with scars, he returned to his daily runs, weight training, and endurance exercises.

In the Spring of 2006, Tony took special leave from his assignment at Ft. Bragg to be home with Loren, the man he considered his dad, and his mom, during Loren's last days. He hated seeing his dad as weakened and emaciated as he became during those final days of his life, and he hated to see his mother suffering with the tragedy of another loss in her life. He spent many hours sitting with Loren in the hospital, reading to him, watching sports, and simply sitting and holding his hand while he slept. Loren and Angie were both Catholic and had raised Tony and his sister Cindy in the church. Despite all he'd seen and done, Tony remained devoutly religious, and when it became apparent that Loren's last hours were near, Tony asked him if he'd like Tony to pray with him.

Loren agreed, and Tony led a prayer spoken directly to God, speaking frankly about the short time Loren had left on the earth, and asking God to look after him as he crossed over to Heaven and provide him a special place there. Loren seemed more at peace after that frank discussion of his upcoming transition, and only a few hours later he lapsed into a coma. Tony, Angie, and Cindy were all there with him when the priest came later to give the last rites, and Angie was holding Loren's hand early the next morning when he took his last breath.

The funeral was held a few days later in Watertown. All six of Tony's grandparents, including Loren's mom and dad, Angie's parents, and the Giles, though all in their eighties, were doing pretty well. The entire extended family attended Loren's funeral and mourned the loss of a very good man.

Tony took a thirty-day leave late that summer and took Melissa, Angelo, Lisa, and his mother on an extended vacation, first to the beach at the Isle of Palms, South Carolina, for two weeks, then up into the Catskills, to a cabin on a lake for nearly all the rest of the time. They swam and surfed, hiked and fished, played golf, played catch, played cards and board games, walked on the beach, and just sat on the porches of their cabins and relaxed. There was plenty of time to talk about things, catch up more on the kids' school, sports, and friends. Angelo and Lisa asked serious questions about the wars going on in Afghanistan and Iraq, and the kind of work their dad did. He told them as much as he could, citing the government line on America's reasons for being there, though deep inside he doubted the validity of most of what he was saying. And describing the kind of operations his Special Forces teams took on, without getting into any of the grizzly details. Angie generally sat quietly during these discussions, rarely commenting or asking questions. Tony could see the pain and concern on her face when he talked about what they did. But he could also see an occasional smile that he interpreted as an expression of her love for him and the man he'd become.

During a conversation one night at dinner toward the end of his leave, Angelo asked his dad how much longer he would be in the Army and when he might be able to stay home with them more.

"Well, Angelo, that's a good question. Nothing would please me more than to be able to be home with you all the time, and frankly, I'm getting a little weary of these wars and the operations we're on much of the time. Your mom and I have opted to have the three of you live in Watertown, even when I'm stationed at Ft. Bragg, since I never know how long I'll be in one place and wouldn't want you to have to change schools all the time.

"But the answer is, I need to stay in until I get my twenty years in so I can draw retirement when I leave the Army. And I need to make as much rank as I can before I retire, so my retirement pay will be as high as it can be. Then I can get a good civilian job, maybe teaching like your mom, and we can live comfortably and have enough money to put you and Lisa through college.

"So…. Bottom line is, I need to stay in for a little less than six more years, until May of 2012. You're ten now, you'll be fifteen then, and Lisa will be thirteen. So I'll be home for your high school years. And I promise to be at home as much as I can between now and then. With the injuries I had a couple of years ago in Iraq, I imagine I'll be drawing more stateside assignments between now and then. I'll be with you all as much as I can until I retire."

Tony could see the serious looks on everyone's faces, including Melissa's and his mother's. *Six more years? Six more years of war?*

52

2006 – 2011
Mick Delaney

Over the next two years I made several trips to California to visit Jon West and his family, and we met a couple of times in a small town near Wichita, Kansas, when they all came back to visit Rachel's parents. We found over time that we had a lot more in common than our wartime friendship, and the relationship flourished. Jon and his son Jason were tinkerers, as my boys and I had been, and were always fixing up some old car or making some elaborate Halloween contraption, an animated skeleton or Grim Reaper with fiery eyes and a swinging scythe. I helped with whatever gizmo they were working on when I was in town, and we spent many hours together chatting like schoolkids as we hammered and sawed and drilled and soldered together.

I went along on several of Jon's band gigs, even tried helping out on vocals a time or two. Jon taught me a few chords on the guitar, and sometimes I'd play a little from the back, just for the fun of it. But, as I'd told my fellow employees back at Delaney Enterprises, there was never any danger that I'd become a real musician. Just didn't have the talent.

Shelly's daughter Lana grew in spurts between my visits, and we became very close. I would always bring her some little gift at every visit and delight in the joy she seemed to get from even the smallest things. Almost exactly two years after Lana was born, Shelly gave birth to another beautiful little girl, Morgan, and the two of them were as sweet as any two little girls could be.

Meanwhile, Jason was married to a beautiful young woman named Danielle, and they settled in to a peaceful life, living just a block from Jon and Rachel.

Jon's kids all seemed to have only one real goal in life: to follow the excellent example their parents had set, and become parents themselves. It was about as close a family as I'd ever seen, and I took great joy from being a small part of it.

My own sons had grown to be wonderful young men. We saw each other often and did a bit of tinkering of our own, fixing one of our cars or making improvements to one of our homes together. Or we'd go to Kansas City Chiefs football or Royals baseball games together. I had spoken to them often about joining me at Delaney Enterprises, but they were both doing work they loved elsewhere, and I didn't push it. I couldn't blame them for wanting to follow their own paths and their own passions. In fact, I had a lot of respect for them because they did.

My own father, who I'd seen very seldom since he'd left Kansas City when I was thirteen, moved, along with his wife of thirty years, to Springfield, Missouri, and bought into a progressive-care retirement community. My sister and I began visiting them there, only a three-hour drive from Kansas City, or a one-hour flight if the Delaney jet wasn't busy. But it wasn't easy to make a relationship out of the fact that we were blood relatives, when he hadn't been around for much of our lives and hardly knew my sons or my sister's kids.

I dated some during that time, and sometimes a relationship would go on for weeks, or even months. But I didn't seem to connect seriously with anyone. Friends were constantly trying to fix me up with someone they thought "perfect" for me, but on the occasions when I'd go on a blind date, nothing clicked.

I traveled often to Virginia to visit Ed and Lois Thorsen, and we had many great weekends together seeing the sights, eating in great restaurants, even kayaking some on the local rivers and bays. And, of course, Ed and I would always find a few minutes, or sometimes hours, to remember the old days, the friends we'd lost, and those we'd found who were still with us.

Mid-September, 2007, I made a call to Jon West. "Hey, Jon. How are you?"

"Pretty good." But he didn't sound like his usual cheery self.

"Called to let you know I'm coming to Santa Barbara the first week in October for the Capstone Software conference. My company bought Capstone late last year, so I'm giving an opening address at the conference and will then be in and out for the following two days. But there should be plenty of time for us to visit. I can come up to Lompoc, or maybe you and Rachel want to come down to Santa Barbara and stay at the Fess Parker, the conference hotel. I'm sure we can find you a room."

"Aw, Mick, I'm sorry, but I don't think we're going to be able to visit much this trip. I've had some bad news. I've been diagnosed with throat cancer. Trying to get the VA to look at the case, since my civilian doctor says it's fairly common after Agent Orange exposure, but you know how they are."

"Oh, God, buddy. I'm so sorry to hear that. That's terrible news. I don't know what to say. How are you and the family holding up?"

"Well, it's scary as hell, and it's pretty advanced. But the doctor says with radiation and chemo treatment, there's a good chance I'll get past it."

"Well, if anyone is strong enough to do that, it's you. After all you've been through, can't let something like this get you."

"That's my plan. But... pray for me Mick, will you?"

"Of course. Is there anything else I can do?"

"Not now, but I'll let you know if that changes. I'm going to fight this as hard as I can, Mick. I've got this beautiful family... way too much to live for.

"So, call me when you get to Santa Barbara, Mick, and I'll let you know how it's going by then."

"OK, buddy. Take care."

I sat staring at the phone after we'd hung up. Cancer. Jesus!

We stayed in close touch over the coming weeks, and of course I let Ed Thorsen in on the news and kept him up to date as best I could.

One day months later, Rachel called me with tears in her voice to let me know the VA had still made no determination on whether Jon's cancer had been caused by Agent Orange. When she contacted the local office, she was told that the case was still under review with the administrator citing "months of backlog in the review procedure." Meanwhile, Jon and Rachel had exhausted their meager savings, and their health insurance was beginning to balk at more advanced treatments to try to bring the cancer into remission.

I had no connections with the VA myself, but I knew Ed Thorsen had been at West Point at the same time as the current Secretary of Veterans Affairs. So I gave Ed a call and asked if he had any strings he could pull to help out. Ed made some polite calls to the VA in Washington and asked for an inquiry into the case. A few weeks later Rachel called to let me know they had received a determination, and that the VA ruled in Jon's favor, claiming his cancer was likely caused by Agent Orange, awarding full disability, taking over Jon's health care and sending them a check for well over a year's disability back pay. She thanked me profusely for helping, but I told her all I did was make one call. I gave her Ed Thorsen's phone number so she could thank him personally, and of course she did. But he said the same thing. All he did was make a couple of calls. None of us was certain that Ed's calls had helped, of course. It was entirely possible the VA had resolved the case with no strings pulled. But we'll never know.

Jon fought on and regained some strength. But the damage to his mouth and throat from the radiation treatments was extensive, and he had to live on with a permanent feeding tube. He couldn't eat or drink normally, and it was very, very tough for him and Rachel and their kids. When I'd visit we'd usually go out to dinner, and Jon would always go along. But he'd never be able to eat.

In March of 2010, Rachel called to let me know that their youngest daughter, Cathy, was to be married in April.

"She was originally going to be married in September, Mick. But Jon's cancer has spread to his lungs now, and he's so weak that she moved it up so he can be there. It hasn't been that long since you were here, but I'll just say that if you want to see him alive again, you probably ought to come to the wedding."

"Oh, Rachel. I'm so sorry. Thank you for calling. I will be there."

And I was. It was a beautiful wedding, held in Shelly and Will's back yard. To my great surprise, Jon conducted the ceremony himself. He wore an English top hat and tails, and though he looked very frail, he stood up straight and proud through the whole thing.

"Is this legal?" I smiled at Rachel as the ceremony went on.

"Oh yes. Didn't you know? He was ordained as a minister when we lived in Florida. All perfectly legal." She seemed very happy with the wedding ceremony, and I had to admit it was beautiful. But then later I caught her looking at Jon when he wasn't looking her way, and the look of sadness that came over her face nearly broke my heart.

Jon pronounced his daughter and her new husband man and wife, the bride was kissed, and the happy couple glided down the aisle and into an alcove for pictures. Rachel went to Jon and helped him down the aisle to join in the photography, and he stayed for just a little while after that as the reception took off. He said goodbye to me before she took him home, and apologized for his weakness. "I wish we had more time together, Mick. I'm sorry I'm so weak."

"That's OK, Jon. You get some rest, and I'll be back soon for another visit."

But I wasn't. From my conversations with Rachel I knew that Jon was continuing to fight, going back into the hospital for course after course of chemo and radiation. He fought on longer than I ever would have, because he wanted to have as much time as possible with his lovely wife and their kids and their granddaughters. It never worked out that I could go back to see him again.

Rachel called me one day early in 2011 to let me know that Jon was leaving the hospital after yet another course of chemotherapy, and that he was very weak. She then called me two days later to let me know that he was gone. When he got home from the hospital that last time he told her, "I'm sorry honey, I can't do this anymore. I love you and the kids more than you can ever know, but I'm just so tired." And a few hours later he was dead.

Her phone call came as I was leaving the office, as I got into my car. When Rachel told me Jon was gone, I just sat in the car and sobbed, couldn't even speak to her for a couple of minutes until I got hold of myself. My own father had passed away late in 2004, my stepfather in 2006, and my mother in 2009. Those deaths all hurt, even my father's, though we'd been estranged from each other most of my life.

Jon West's death affected me more, made me sadder, made me feel a greater sense of loss, than even the deaths of my own parents.

Jon was cremated, and a few weeks after his death Rachel called to tell me there would be a memorial service a few days later in Lompoc at the VFW hall. The Delaney Enterprises jet was busy during those days so I flew commercial into Santa Barbara airport, rented a car, and drove up.

The memorial was beautiful. The hall, which had a capacity of about two hundred people, was jammed with twice that many, people lined up along every wall, some even outside standing at the door. Jon was well known around town as both as an entertainer and a man who would do anything for his neighbors. His son, his daughter, and her husband played and sang several of Jon's favorite songs, and there was a flag folding and a number of eulogies. I was able to give one, and talked about my first day in the field in Vietnam when Jon had greeted me so cordially, what close friends we'd been there, how we'd found each other many years later, and how his family had welcomed me so openly.

Jon had been wounded twice in Vietnam and had been awarded two Purple Hearts. The tradition while we were there was that a soldier with three Purple Hearts was allowed to go home. At the end of my talk at his funeral, I presented Rachel with a Purple Heart medal of my own, telling the crowd of friends about the tradition.

"Jon's death was caused by Agent Orange from his exposure in 1969 in Vietnam. Certainly that ought to qualify as a wound, since it ultimately took his life. Here was a good man who came home from the war believing he was safe, only to find so many years later that it was killing him at the young age of 60. Rachel, I'd like you to have this third Purple Heart for Jon, whose name should certainly be engraved on the Vietnam Memorial wall in Washington.

"Now he can go home," I said, my voice cracking as I forced out the words.

The memorial lasted for hours. I stuck around afterward to help clean up, but it was clear that everyone in the family was exhausted, and they decided to leave the cleanup until the next day. So while they headed for home and a night's sleep, I found a bar and drank.

And I was once again, very, very alone.

***

When I reached my office late the next day, after clearing away some pressing business, I called Ed Thorsen. "Hi, Ed. I just got back from California, went to Jon West's memorial service. It was beautiful. The family seems to be doing OK. I guess that's the natural result of watching someone you love fight cancer for four years, going through all that pain and weakness and just becoming very tired."

We talked a while about what a good man Jon West had been, how he'd entertained us all with his guitar and his beautiful voice in Vietnam, and all he had done with his life, and what a great father and husband and grandfather he had been. And what a waste it was that the Agent Orange had taken him so young.

53

2011

Ed Thorsen had been working for the last few years as a volunteer case manager with the severely wounded from Iraq and Afghanistan who were being treated at Walter Reed Hospital in Bethesda, Maryland. His work involved helping the families of the wounded find quarters near the hospital where they could live during the extended periods of treatment there; helping them financially with living expenses; working with the many doctors at Bethesda who might be involved in treatment; coordinating with the Army, Marine Corps, Air Force, or Navy on issues of medical retirement; and helping coordinate with the Veterans' Administration on disability benefits and treatment after discharge from the military.

It was tough, often emotional work, but Ed seemed to thrive on it, having found a way he could still be useful to his brothers and sisters in arms, helping the heroes of the present-day wars during his retirement. We talked often by phone of the individual cases, and Ed told me of a little group he'd formed at Bethesda who were all 1st Cavalry Division combat veterans. He sent me a photo of them, himself in the middle, all wearing 1st Cav T-shirts, some sporting broad brimmed cavalry hats. They were all smiling. Some were in wheelchairs, some missing arms or eyes or hands. But they were all together, and in that photo, at least, they were all smiling.

Ed himself had received traumatic brain injury the night we were wounded by mortar fire way back in 1969, and underwent drug therapy for it during his entire Army career and in all the years since. He was also severely affected by Post Traumatic Stress Disorder, a cause for his own periodic depression. So he was a perfect person to help these wounded warriors with their case issues because he understood them so well. They in turn responded better to him than to most others who tried to help them, simply because he understood them, and they him, as wounded combat veterans. He and I talked often about how difficult it would be for a Psychologist or Psychiatrist to treat a disorder they could not possibly understand, having never shared the grotesque war experiences that so often produced PTSD.

I began to accompany Ed to the Bethesda Hospital whenever I was in town visiting him, when he happened to have appointments there.

Once while I was staying with Ed and Lois, Ed got a call on Saturday night from the wife of a PTSD victim who was being treated as an outpatient at Bethesda and living in a nearby apartment that Ed had arranged for them. For no apparent reason, the man had suddenly begun carving on his arms with a razor blade, which terrified both the wife and their four-year-old daughter, which in turn drove the man to lock himself into their bedroom. His wife was very frightened that he might take his life and called Ed to ask for help.

Ed called 911, then we rushed to the apartment to see if we could help. The emergency response team was just arriving as we drove up, and after a short conversation they deferred to Ed to try to talk the man out. After a few minutes talking with Ed, the man unlocked the bedroom door and came out, his arms, shirt, and jeans covered in blood. The EMTs gave first aid, then took him to a nearby civilian hospital. Ed and I followed with his wife and child, and I looked after the little girl while her mom and Ed were talking with the patient. A few hours later, two Army nurses from Bethesda showed up to reclaim their patient, get him discharged from the civilian hospital, and re-admit him to Bethesda.

Ed told me later by phone that the possible reason for the incident had been that our patient was being given five different anti-depressant drugs, along with other medications, to treat his PTSD. After a review brought on by the near-suicide, the doctors at Bethesda decided they would cut him back to only two anti-depressants. No one seemed to understand why he was given five, except that so many doctors were involved in his treatment at different times.

After a few days on the revised treatment, the man returned to a much healthier state of mind, and was released again to out-patient status. He and his family have since relocated back to their home town in Texas, but Ed still gets letters and phone calls from him every few weeks, letting Ed know that his "patient" is doing well, and thanking Ed for his life-saving case management, and his friendship.

On another of my visits, Ed and I met with two Army Special Forces master sergeants and their wives and children in the Heroes Cafeteria at Bethesda to review their cases over lunch, and try to lay out the next steps for them. Both of these men were in their late thirties and were professional soldiers who had intended to make the Army their career. They were strong, intelligent men, one black and one white, who had dedicated their lives to the defense of America, and I was struck by how they truly seemed to be the best and brightest our country had to offer. So many civilians I talked to were caught up in what I called "first world" problems, like whether their children would be admitted to the best schools, or how they could get the latest iPhone, or that next party coming up, or the updated landscaping at their homes. These men had focused their lives and their careers on making sure Americans could sleep well at night, adequately defended from their enemies. And now they were suffering the consequences of their selfless, heroic actions.

They were both severely disabled. One had lost both his legs and his left arm to a roadside bomb blast in Iraq, had received traumatic brain injury and severe internal injuries from the shrapnel, and had Post Traumatic Stress Disorder. He sat at our table in a wheelchair, his beautiful wife nearby managing the kids, trying to show a face as brave as his.

The other sergeant had also been wounded by an Improvised Explosive Device, or IED, while he led a patrol in Taliban country in Afghanistan. He, too, was missing both legs above the knee, and had lost his right thumb and a good sized chunk out of his right forearm, to the blast. Again, there was traumatic brain injury and PTSD. He had received internal injuries and damage to his testicles. His beautiful wife was also there with their daughter, trying to be brave.

The men had both been treated at Bethesda for extended periods, the Iraq veteran for nearly two years. And, coincidentally, they were both only then recovering enough from their wounds so that the doctors could begin to discuss with them the fitting of prosthetic legs and arms, and the long course of therapy and training that would ultimately, hopefully, get them walking again. Thus the reason we could meet with them together, aside from the fact that they had become very close friends during their stay in Bethesda.

I sat in the fourth chair at the table, kept my mouth shut, and basically just made sure everyone had something to eat and drink while Ed worked them through the various issues under review. Ed had introduced me as another combat veteran, his platoon sergeant who had been wounded alongside him in Vietnam, and they immediately accepted me as one of their own. I was honored.

The primary issue under discussion that day was retirement. Neither of these men would be allowed to remain in the Army longer term, given the severity and permanence of their wounds. Both were near their "twenty" and would soon be eligible for regular Army longevity retirement. One man was only eight months away, the other about eleven months away, and both were inclined to try to stay "in" until their twenty, so they could receive their regular military retirement benefit, which would be 50% of their regular military pay, taxable as income, plus access to TRICARE retired military medical coverage for them and their families, for life.

Ed was an expert on the subject, and patiently explained to them and their wives the difference between regular longevity military retirement and military disability retirement, which could give them up to 75% of their regular military pay (NOT taxable as income). They were both also likely to be rated at 100% disability by the Department of Veterans Affairs (the VA), which would give them a second pension, plus health care for them, plus a death benefit for their wives if they died as a result of the factors that caused their disability. It was a long and complex discussion, but Ed was gifted (and well-practiced) at presenting the material, and he did that in such a way that it was easily understood. I was very impressed. But no matter how the men's retirement worked out, or their long-term health care, no one at that table, nor their wives, were kidding themselves into believing the men and their families would ever have a normal life again. Those young wives and children would watch their husbands and fathers struggle with severe disabilities, PTSD, and bouts of depression for the rest of their lives. And the stress from that on the rest of the family would be enormous.

As Ed and I drove back to his house after the meeting was over, we were both struck by the same thought. Ed put it into words first. "I'm an old man now, fucked up by this shrapnel in the brain, lots of other stuff going on with my health because of Agent Orange, and often very depressed by the PTSD. I'd gladly trade my life if I could just buy one of those men his arms and legs and health back, give those young families a good life back."

"And if you were able to do that for one of them, I'd damn sure trade my life to do the same for the other one," I said.

And we both damn sure meant it.

54

Late 2011

My life went on. Delaney Enterprises, staffed as it was with excellent people at all levels, was on a path of steady, profitable growth, and everyone who was a part of the company was benefiting from that. I was largely out of the day-to-day operation of the business, having turned most of it over to the division heads and a small core staff of corporate leaders, including our excellent Chief Operating Officer, Ellen Spangler, who we'd promoted from Regional VP, and Stan McDermott, still our Chief Financial Officer and Treasurer. But I still showed up early at the office every workday I was in town, and I still worked closely with the R & D team, the corporate officers, and the board of directors, as chairman. It was a very enjoyable business.

I hadn't dated anyone seriously since Julie but could usually call on one of a couple of lady friends to go to dinner, to a play or film, or sometimes to a baseball or soccer game. We nearly always had fun, sometimes even wound up sleeping together, but I just couldn't seem to want to take a relationship farther than that.

I found time to do some writing, which I'd always enjoyed. And I found that the subject I was most passionate about was the war. So I began a memoir, dictating my memories into a digital recorder on my way to the office every morning, then listening to what I'd dictated that morning on my way home that night. Just the process of remembering the war, incident by incident, dictating the stories into the recorder, then listening to what I'd said and how I'd said it, seemed to help me emotionally. One particular story made that clear to me, and serves as a good example.

It was from one of the worse firefights I'd been in, the night Sugarbear was wounded and later died. The night before Carl Engle was killed. The company had walked into an ambush, and my platoon had moved forward to reinforce the point platoon as we were getting ready to Medevac the wounded by helicopter. When the Medevac Huey arrived and began descending into a small clearing to winch up our guys, the NVA opened up with automatic rifles and machine guns from the nearby trees, and all hell broke loose as they tried to shoot the chopper down.

I found some cover behind a small clump of trees and began firing at the NVA, trying, along with everyone else, to suppress their fire and save the Huey and its crew. I looked up at one point to see the door gunner on the side nearest the gooks slumped over his gun, obviously either badly wounded or dead. The bird began to wobble in the air, the tail rotating around the main rotor, almost out of control. I started thinking it was going to crash on top of us.

But the pilot, who we later learned had been badly wounded himself, regained control, and somehow managed to pull the bird up out of the hole in the jungle trees, and get it headed back to Tay Ninh.

When that happened, the gooks shifted their fire toward the grunts on the ground. It was somewhere in there that Sugarbear was badly wounded.

I hadn't been in many firefights that were as intense or as sustained as this one. The NVA just wouldn't stop firing. So we kept pouring out all the fire we could. It was total chaos. Of course there was supporting artillery fire, but as usual we couldn't get it in close enough to do us any good.

In the chaos, I had seen smoke puffs coming from a spot up in a tree just across the bomb crater from me, and could see leaves and small branches being blown off the tree by the outgoing fire of the gook, who was up there with an AK, shooting on full automatic.

It became my personal mission to kill that motherfucker.

So I started firing at that one spot in the tree, round after round of well-aimed, semi-automatic fire. But there was seemingly little effect, as the fucking gook just kept shooting.

A few minutes into it the gooks, all of them, finally stopped shooting, and 6, our CO, started yelling, "Cease fire! Cease fire!" But I remained unconvinced that my personal gook was dead, so I ignored 6 and kept on shooting. Finally, he personally walked over to scream at me, "Cease Fire, trooper! I said cease fire, Goddamn it!" Still I kept shooting. He just stood there glaring at me in disbelief. I basically ignored him.

And then, a few seconds later, before 6 could haul off and kick me in the side of the head, or whatever he was thinking he'd do, I saw an AK fall from the tree where my personal gook was hidden, and drop, banging on limb after limb, to the ground. 6 and a couple of guys near me saw it, too.

"I got that motherfucker!" I screamed. I was elated. I didn't know at that point that Sugarbear had been hit, and I was happier than I'd been since arriving in the shithole that was Vietnam. It wasn't often during that particular war when you actually got to see an enemy go down from all the ammo you fired, and I was ecstatic.

6 didn't say anything. He just shook his head, turned around, and walked back to whatever company commander duties he had coming next. I turned around behind my little tree, pulled a pack of Marlboros out of my shirt pocket, and lit one up.

All those years later, as I listened to my own voice telling that story from the recorder that night as I drove my very comfortable, air-conditioned, leather-upholstered Lexus home from work, I was stricken by something. For more than thirty years I'd carried the memory of that incident, the killing of that NVA soldier, with great joy and happiness. I had smiled every time I'd thought about it. I had killed one of the enemy who had been trying to kill my pals and me, maybe the one who actually shot Sugarbear, and I was damned happy about it.

Only, listening to it from where I sat that day it didn't make me happy. It made me sad. I had taken the life of some poor North Vietnamese kid, maybe only fifteen or sixteen, who had probably been conscripted just like many of the GIs I was with, forced to walk hundreds of miles down the Ho Chi Minh trail, constantly afraid of American B-52 strikes, fighter-bomber attacks, artillery fire, and other devastating weaponry, only to die in a tree in this filthy, mosquito infested, mold-ridden section of the jungle. And his family probably never knew what happened to him, were never able to reclaim his body.

As that realization, and the sadness, came to me, I felt like I was growing up a little, maybe even getting past some of the pain of that miserable war a little. My emotional response to the incident was finally, after all those years, appropriate to the event.

I was beginning to see the light.

As some of my memoir reached paper, I shared it with Ed Thorsen and a couple of other veterans I'd met in Kansas City, and they encouraged me to finish and publish it. It took a while, but it finally made print. I got a good deal of feedback that it was helping other Vietnam combat veterans explain to their wives and families what the war was like. Many had never been able to talk about it directly because it was simply too painful.

With publication of the book came invitations to do book signings, and to speak about the book and its subject matter. I began doing talks at local gatherings of Rotary Clubs, Kiwanis, Lions, veterans' organizations, and school and church groups. I was invited to talk to some rather big audiences on Veterans Day and Memorial Day, and I always focused my comments on veterans and their families and the families of those who had died in one of America's many wars. My sole purpose was to raise awareness among civilians of the sacrifices being made by members of our military on their behalf, so they could live safe, secure, happy lives in The Land of the Free.

Often after a talk people would approach me with a request for some direction for themselves or their loved ones, usually about getting help for someone who was struggling physically, emotionally, or financially with the aftermath of my war or another war. So I became acquainted with some of the many veterans' organizations around Kansas City and a bit with the Veterans' Administration, and I could often send them in the right direction.

My trips to Washington to visit Ed and Lois Thorsen became a regular thing, and I'd often go up three or four times a year. They were always an enjoyable couple to spend time with, and I both relished and dreaded the visits to the hospital at Bethesda. I wanted to help, at least in some small way, and began donating money to Ed when he would call with some veteran's family's need that couldn't be covered by other donors or by the small fund his organization ran to support case managers like himself. But seeing these great American heroes, who had sacrificed so much of themselves to defend their families and other Americans against the terror in the world, often affected me very profoundly. I always came away very sad. And when I would leave the hospital and go back out into the city, I was always stricken by how little anyone seemed to know, or care, about the wars we were fighting or the brave Soldiers, Marines, Navy, and Air Force men and women who were fighting them.

One day in late October, 2011, I called Thorsen from my office.

"Hey, LT. I'm coming up on Thursday morning for a meeting at our office in Georgetown. Any chance you and Lois are free Thursday night? Don't want to wear out my welcome, but would love to take you out to dinner. Can you both make it up to Georgetown?"

"Probably could, Mick. But are you free on Friday? I'm going back to Bethesda Friday if you'd like to come along again. Seemed like you got a lot out of it last time."

"I can make that. Might have to catch a commercial flight home, but I can free up the day. I'm about half retired anyway, and I think the people here in the office prefer it when I'm not around."

"Then I'll pick you up at your office in Georgetown Thursday at about 5:00, bring you down here, and we'll eat here and you can stay over. Then Friday we'll go to Bethesda, and afterward I can drop you at the airport."

"If you're sure I'm not imposing."

"Well, you are, but what are friends for?" He laughed, seemed almost happy.

So Ellen Spangler, Stan McDermott, and I took the corporate jet up to Washington National, then hopped a cab to the Georgetown office. We were there by 9:00, got right into the meeting, held a working lunch, and were wrapped up by 2:00 that Thursday afternoon. I sent Ellen and Stan home on the jet, having already made a commercial flight reservation for myself for Saturday. Since we'd finished early and Ed wasn't coming to pick me up until 5:00, I decided to take a walk down to the Mall in downtown Washington where the Vietnam and Korean War memorials had been built.

It was probably my twentieth visit to the Vietnam Memorial since its construction in the early eighties. But I still tried to get by there as often as I could when I was in the area, even though it always affected me emotionally. It helped me to feel close to Tony and Carl Engle and Sugarbear, and several other friends who had died during the months

I was in Vietnam. And it was only a short walk from there over to the Korean War Memorial. There I somehow always felt closer to my uncle Tim, who had been killed in Korea when I was four. I would look up his name in one of the kiosks there, put my fingers on the little electronic certificate that would pop up, and somehow feel kind of close to him. Then I'd stroll solemnly past the statues of American soldiers on patrol, sculpted in so much lifelike detail in mock Korean rice paddies, and look into the faces of so many who had served in Korea from all branches of the service, etched into the panels of the wall there.

On this warm October day, I stopped at the Vietnam Memorial first.

When the Vietnam Veterans Memorial Fund Committee began to circulate concept drawings of the proposed monument back in the late seventies, I was initially appalled at the winning design, submitted by a young Asian-American woman, an architect from New York City. Whereas most war memorials I'd seen had included statues of some of those who served, this memorial was initially represented in design drawings as a long, black slash in the earth, like one might imagine the entrance to Hell. But the first time I'd been there, later in the eighties when the wall was completed, I'd been incredibly impressed by the perfect appropriateness of the huge, long, shining, marble wall, engraved with the names of the more than 58,000 dead and missing Americans from the more than fifteen years we had fought in Vietnam.

It has always been particularly humbling for me to walk slowly past the panels, reading some of the names as I go, seeing the things people have left in memory of the loved ones they lost during the war. Heartbreaking actually. There are baseball gloves, teddy bears, Boy Scout merit badges, packs of favorite cigarettes and chewing gum, cigarette lighters, combat boots, and many other mementos. And photographs...hundreds of photographs of the young Americans who died or went missing during that awful war, or of their wives, girlfriends, sons and daughters, or other family.

Once while Amanda and I were still married, the summer after Eric had graduated from high school, I'd managed to talk her and the boys into a short vacation trip to the Washington area. After we'd spent a few days at Virginia Beach I'd even managed to drag them into D.C. for a whirlwind tour of the monuments and museums. Nothing the boys had looked forward to, but after days of fun in the ocean, they'd grudgingly come along.

We had all walked along the Vietnam Wall together just an hour or so before sunset on a beautiful August evening, the boys silently taking in panel after panel after panel of the names of the dead and missing. Afterward we sat on the steps of the Lincoln Monument nearby, and as the bright reflection of the setting sun behind us had illuminated the reflecting pool, I'd said, "You know, guys, I have some friends whose names are up on that wall. And if it hadn't been for the grace of God, my name would be there and you wouldn't be here right now. Something to think about." I hadn't talked to them much during their lives about my service. And they were teenagers, interested in girls, cars, sports, video games, and the usual stuff. But for a brief moment, I felt like we connected really well around that thought, and they seemed to absorb it solemnly. I gave them both a hug, which I knew they hated, and then we went off to a wonderful late dinner in Georgetown.

55

On this particular warm October afternoon, I was there to visit the names of my three closest friends who had died in Vietnam, George Wendt, who we had called Sugarbear, Carl Engle, and Tony Giles. I knew the panel and line numbers by heart, having looked them up several times before.

Names on the memorial are listed in order of date of casualty, beginning with panel 1East at the center, one of the two tallest panels, and moving panel by panel down the slope toward the east end of the monument where panel 70East contains only one line of names. Then the sequence re-starts at panel 70West at the westernmost end of the wall, where there is again one line of names, and moves back toward the center of the monument, where it ends on panel 1West, where are listed the last casualties of the war. The last casualties are listed on the panel next to the panel with the first casualties, in some sort of interesting symmetry.

As I passed the west end of the wall, I was again reminded of something I'd discovered on an earlier visit: all the young men whose names are listed on the westernmost four panels, 70W thru 67W, were killed on a single day, May 25, 1968, during some of the heaviest fighting of the war. Passing those panels on the way to where my friends' names were located always reminded me of the incredible waste of the Vietnam war. *All those good young men,* I thought, *killed on a single day? For what?*

I reached panel 20W, where I knew I'd find Sugarbear's real name on Row 81, and Carl Engle's name on Row 82, about 16 rows up from the bottom of the panel. And there they were. It was a sacred place for me.

I touched the engraved letters of Sugarbear's name first, tracing each letter with my fingertips, remembering vividly how he had died unnecessarily because Captain Larkin wasn't smart enough to pull back from an ambush site before he Medevaced the wounded. I felt all the old emotions again, the sense of loss for my sad friend who'd spent his last days knowing that his wife, safe back at home, was cheating on him. The anger at his unnecessary death. My hand paused there for a while as I remembered how he'd soldiered on in silence under the emotional burden he'd carried, how he'd savagely attacked the ground each evening with our pick, digging the night's fighting hole and letting out some of the pain and anger that were consuming him.

Then I moved my hand to Carl Engle's name, and traced each of the letters there. I remembered our argument the morning of his death, and some of my last words to him, calling him a "sorry motherfucker." I recalled his insistence on walking point that morning, and how he'd willingly sacrificed his life to protect the rest of us in the squad from that mine blast. It had been July 18, 1969, the day after his twenty-first birthday. I could hear his Alabama drawl in my ears as clearly as if he'd really been there, saying his favorite exclamation, "Oh, mama!" I remembered his face with the horrendous damage from the mine blast, remembered him clawing at his ruined throat for air that never came. Tears came to my eyes as they always did, and I wept unashamedly.

As I was wiping my face I noticed a woman standing at the next panel over, 19 West, with her fingers also on a name on the wall, but looking over at me with a pitying look on her face. There were tears running down her cheeks, too. She was about my age, slender to the point of looking frail, with dark hair streaked with gray. It was easy to see she had once been a very pretty woman, and in many ways she still was. But she looked so ... worn.

"Sorry," I said. "Hope I didn't embarrass you. This fellow here was a good friend of mine. I was with him when he died. I've probably been here twenty times, and it happens every time." I smiled.

She smiled back, wanly. "I understand. Always happens to me, too."

I looked where her finger was touching the name on the wall, noticed that it was very close to where I knew Tony's name was engraved. Then I looked closer and saw that her finger was actually touching the name:

Anthony B. Giles

"You knew Tony? Tony Giles?" I was incredulous.

A look of shock, maybe fear, came over her face. She dropped her hand, turned, and started walking away to the east, away from me, at a very fast pace.

I followed after her. "Wait, please. Did you know Tony? Please, wait. Tony was my friend! I was with him when he died!"

She glanced back over her shoulder as I said that. But then she picked up the pace, walked away even faster.

I followed her to the east end of the Wall, and she looked back over her shoulder again, fear in her eyes. "Wait, please," I pleaded.

But she didn't.

Finally I gave up. What was I going to do, tackle her? Force her to talk to me? Grudgingly I went back to Tony's panel, stared at his name, touched it with my fingertips, remembered again his gruesome, sad death. Then, still baffled about the woman who had been touching Tony's name, I said goodbye to my friends again, and walked slowly over to the Korean Memorial, on the other side of the Reflecting Pool, and spent a little time there remembering and honoring my Uncle Tim. Then I headed back for Georgetown, still thinking about the woman at The Wall.

That night, when Thorsen picked me up, I told him about the strange encounter.

"Who do you think it was, Mick? You say she was about our age? Maybe his wife or his sister? Did he have a sister?"

"I don't know about a sister, LT. But he certainly had a wife. Remember? The bitch who wrote him that Dear John letter?"

"I remember. But if she wrote him a Dear John letter back in 1969, why would she be touching his name on the wall with tears in her eyes in 2012? Seems to me she'd have forgotten him long ago."

"You're right, LT. Probably his sister or maybe a cousin or someone else who remembers him from high school. Wonder why she took off like that, though?"

We drove back to Ed's house, chatting about his day and my day, the incident temporarily forgotten. Back at home, Ed insisted on making dinner while Lois and I caught up over a beer on the front porch.

"How's he doing, really?" I asked her, when I knew we were out of earshot.

"Oh, he has his good days and his bad days. Often when he comes home from Bethesda he's kind of down. The wounded there really affect him, but at the same time I think he benefits some from helping them."

"Yeah. I can relate to that. The last time I was here and went to the hospital with him, it affected me for days afterward. Just seeing those men and women in the terrible shape they're in, fighting as hard as they do for as much recovery as they can hope for, will break your heart. And then you look around out here where everyday Americans are living their lives, and it's like nobody notices. There's hardly ever anything on the news about the wars. Certainly not like Vietnam, where everybody watched it unfold at 6:00 every night."

"No, not at all like that."

"I have a theory. Want to hear it?"

"Is it a long theory or a short theory?" she grinned.

I swatted her gently on the arm.

"During Vietnam, which was ultimately seen by many Americans as an unjust war, there were college campuses on fire, hundreds of thousands of people marching on Washington, draft cards being burned, people shouting 'Hell NO! I won't go.' Most Americans supported the war in the beginning, but when it dragged on for years and years, American bodies started coming home by the hundreds every week, and we didn't win, it became an 'unjust war', and the government lost popular support.

"Fast forward to now. Are any of the wars we're in now any more 'just' than Vietnam? Was the second Iraq War, based on a premise that Saddam Hussein had weapons of mass destruction that he didn't actually have, and that resulted in the near-total destruction of the country's infrastructure, and chaos for the people, with tens of thousands of civilian casualties... was that war any more 'just' than Vietnam?"

"Well, I sure don't think so, Mick."

"Right. In Afghanistan, I agree we were well justified to go there initially to bring Osama Bin Laden and his gang to justice after the 9-11 attack. But that was ten years ago. Are we still justified in being there, in a war we evidently can't win, with all the civilian casualties and 'collateral damage' we're bringing about?"

"No, I don't think we are."

"So why aren't the college campuses on fire? Why aren't there hundreds of thousands of people marching on Washington to protest these 'unjust wars' and try to end them?"

"I don't know. Good question."

"My theory is it's because there is no draft now. Kids don't have to worry about being drafted to go fight in a war they don't understand and don't support, so there's no, or very little, protest from them. Parents aren't worried about their kids having to go fight, so they don't protest, or even object that I can tell. I bet you that if America still had a draft today, the country would be in the same chaos it was in toward the end of Vietnam. In other words, for most people at least, I don't think it was because of a high sense of morality and justice that they protested the Vietnam War. I think it was their sense of self preservation. They didn't want to get drafted."

"That makes sense to me, now that you put it that way." She looked thoughtful.

"The federal government, Congress and these recent presidents, have figured out a way to have wars without the people protesting. Just don't draft anyone. Make the military all-volunteer and then, when that doesn't provide enough fodder for the cannons or IEDs, go out and hire 'contractors' at very high pay to do the rest of the dirty work."

"And Congress hasn't passed any laws restricting how much can be spent on contractors. They only restrict how many people can be active in the military at one time," she observed.

"Right."

"What do we do about that, Mick?"

"I'm not that smart. I don't know. I'd say 'elect people to change those laws,' but that never seems to work. I do have a thought, though."

"I thought you might." Again, that grin.

"Maybe we should have mandatory military service for every American at age eighteen. One or two years. At least that way everyone could share the burden of national defense. Everyone would have some understanding of what being in the military is like. They would be trained in basic combat skills. They could be called upon, even years later, if we really needed a large military for a big war. Like Israel, or Switzerland, or other countries do."

"That sure would improve discipline among the young, maybe bring some of them to some focus in their lives," she said.

"Yeah. As much as I didn't like the Army, and as much as the war has messed me up, I did learn a lot there about enduring hardship and what it feels like to work for someone who really doesn't have to like you. How to lead and even how and when to follow. Stuff like that. And the other thing it would do would be to have Americans, the young and the old, actually care about what foreign wars we get involved in. Especially the ones that come across as 'optional' or that don't seem to have a path toward any kind of victory, or even resolution."

We sipped our beers and thought about it all, the beautiful fall evening slipping away, crickets and tree frogs chirping.

"Dinner's ready," hollered Ed through the open screen door. "Mick has to do the dishes. That's a job for enlisted personnel."

I stayed on the porch a minute after Lois had already gone in, caught up in my thoughts. As I sat there, staring into the evening sky, a beautiful Red-tailed Hawk came gliding in silently from the woods down the street to flare his majestic wings perfectly and land delicately on a phone line, right in front of the house. He sat completely still, facing me, seemingly staring right at me, not a feather moving on his graceful body.

"What a strange day," I thought. I watched him for a while. He was still there, apparently staring at me, when I got up and went in to dinner.

56

"Mick, Mick! Wake up, Mick! You're having a nightmare! Wake up!" It was Ed Thorsen shaking me, Lois looking over his shoulder from the door of my bedroom.

I pulled myself out of the deep well of sleep I'd been in, the dream vivid in my mind.

"Sorry, guys," I said groggily. "I guess going to the Wall yesterday brought back some bad memories. I'm OK now. You can go back to bed. Sorry I woke you." I rubbed my eyes.

"Sure you're OK?" Lois, from the door.

"Yeah, I'm fine. Unfortunately, those happen often enough that I'm pretty used to them. I usually don't make that kind of ruckus, though. Or I don't think I do. I'm fine."

But I wasn't. I had been back in August 1969, reliving the day Tony died. I'd dreamed about the first shots fired, the fear I'd felt, dropping my rucksack and crawling forward to that log, watching Danny and Fragman dragging Tony back to us. And finally, the bullets blasting through Tony's chest just as we were about to get him to safety. The blood splatter, the light going out in his eyes. How limp and wasted he looked in death. My rage. Kicking that dead gook soldier into the spider hole and spitting in his face.

And the letter. Finding the letter.

Seeing that woman touching Tony's name at the Wall had really done a number on me.

I mulled it all over for more than an hour and finally drifted back to sleep again. But this time in my dream I saw that Red-tailed Hawk from the evening before, sitting on the telephone wire in front of Ed and Lois's house. The hawk was staring at me, straight at me, unmoving. As I stared back I began to see the hawk's face morphing into Tony's face. It was startling at first because of the fierceness there. But then Tony's face softened, and he smiled at me.

And he said, "Remember Angie, Mick. Remember Angie. Remember how much I loved her."

I sat up in bed with a start, suddenly wide awake. *What the....? Where did that come from? Was the woman at the Wall Angie, his wife? The bitch who wrote that Dear John letter? Why would she be there?*

Next morning at breakfast Ed and Lois were both kind of quiet, looking at me a little like my arms and legs might fly off.

"What?" I said finally.

"You have those nightmares often?"

"Occasionally, LT. Happens more when I'm around something that reminds me of the war. Don't you have them anymore?"

"Sometimes. That was pretty violent last night. What were you dreaming about?"

"Shouldn't I lie down on the couch, Doc?"

"Quit being a smart-ass. What were you dreaming about?"

"The day Tony Giles was killed, August 17, 1969."

"Oh. You dream about that often?"

"Not so much anymore. Seeing that woman touching his name at the Wall yesterday obviously stirred things up. Then, after I went back to sleep, I had another dream. You'll want to lock me up for this one."

"Go ahead. I can't wait."

"Remember that Red-tailed Hawk I showed you both last night, sitting on the phone line out front?"

"Sure."

"Well, in the second dream, the hawk was sitting on the wire, staring at me. And as I stared back, its face morphed into Tony's face. And it was very fierce. But then he started to smile, and he said, "Remember Angie, Mick. Remember how much I loved her.""

"Hmmm. What do you think that means?"

"I don't know. That I'm insane?"

"Well, we know that. Be more specific."

"I don't know. That woman at the wall yesterday, you have to admit that her behavior was strange. I guess it brought everything back. C'mon, Doc! Give it up. You're the psychologist. What do you think?"

"Fuck if I know, Mick. I'd say you're crackers. Looney Tunes. Now eat your breakfast. We need to get to the hospital."

We were at the hospital by 9:30. We made our rounds, or rather Ed's rounds, at the hospital for more than two hours, moving from room to room. We were visiting with the patients themselves where they were awake and aware, but most often with a wife, or in one case the husband of a severely wounded woman, and sometimes the children who were there. Ed would always stop in the hall before we reached a given patient's room and, still out of earshot, brief me on the individual's background, including their branch of the service, rank, specialty, the nature of the injuries, and particulars about the family, where they were staying, and what Ed and his group were doing to help.

The patient in Room 4125 was an Army Special Forces lieutenant colonel, wounded during a rocket attack on an outlying Special Forces camp in northeastern Afghanistan while making a routine inspection of the post. It had been just a freak thing, really, since the colonel was only to have been on the post for a couple of hours.

He lay on his back in the bed, his torso elevated, bandages covering much of his body. What looked to have been a handsome face was pale and strained, and one eye was bandaged. A trachea had been inserted in his throat, and there was a breathing tube in the trachea through which a ventilator pumped air to his lungs. His left arm was shattered, riddled with shrapnel, the bones broken in several places. It was suspended at nearly shoulder level in a cast. He was missing his left leg from just below the hip, the amputation having occurred at a level so high up that, as Ed had explained, it was questionable whether he'd ever be able to use a prosthesis, assuming he recovered from his other injuries well enough to try. There had also been a head injury, the blast having torn a chunk from his skull, also on the left side. And there were some internal injuries from the shrapnel and the effects of the blast itself.

Lieutenant Colonel Anthony Blake's eyes were half open, glassy. He stirred when we entered the room and his eyes opened fully, and there was a warmth there when he saw Ed. He tried to speak and there was some vocalization, but no intelligible words came out. He squinted in frustration, apparently knowing what he wanted to say but unable to get the right messages to his mouth.

Ed smiled at him, said in a voice loud enough to reach past the noise of the ventilator, "Hello, Colonel! How are you doing today?"

Colonel Blake nodded slightly, but didn't, or couldn't, smile back.

At the foot of the bed was Colonel Blake's wife, who Ed introduced as Melissa, a beautiful woman in her forties with dark hair and eyes, a lot of stress showing on her face. Sitting beside the bed in a chair, working with an iPad, was their son, who Melissa introduced as Angelo. Angelo was fifteen, a handsome young man with coal black hair and dark brown eyes. He stood up as he was introduced, reached across the bed to shake my hand, smiled wanly. Near the foot of the bed was their daughter Lisa, a beautiful girl of thirteen. She was also very polite but spoke quite softly, obviously saddened by the situation. Ed introduced me as a veteran who had served as his platoon sergeant in Vietnam, told about our wounds back in our war.

He explained to me that Colonel Blake had been wounded nearly three months earlier, and that he'd been in Bethesda for about nine weeks. Ed had helped Melissa and the kids find a temporary house in the area since they lived in New Jersey, too far away to commute. Melissa wanted the family to be near her husband as much as possible, and they had made special arrangements with the schools in New Jersey so the kids could visit Bethesda often.

Ed chatted with Melissa, asked how the house was for them, how they were making out in the neighborhood. He told her in front of Colonel Blake that the doctors believed he would be in recovery for at least four more months before his brain function would be restored as fully as it could be, his arm would be healed, and they might be able to work with a prosthesis for his missing leg.

While all that was going on I stepped over to the Colonel's bedside and impulsively reached down and grasped his right hand, which lay at his side. He looked over at me, squeezed my fingers in response. I smiled down at him, took his hand into both of mine, and just stood there holding it.

A crackling sound began to develop in the ventilator from within the colonel's throat. He didn't seem to notice it, but I was a bit alarmed, looked around to see if someone wanted to call a nurse. But before anything else could happen, Angelo put his iPad down, stood, reached over and gently pulled the ventilator tube out of the fitting in the colonel's neck, and took a suction tube that was apparently kept nearby for the purpose, placed it into the fitting, and sucked the phlegm out of his father's throat. Then he replaced the suction tube into its receptacle, replaced the ventilator tube into its fitting, sat back down, picked up his iPad, and continued doing whatever he had been doing.

Apparently this was old hat to Angelo. But watching that simple act, done so routinely, and realizing that this man's son, at this tender age, had already become accustomed to his father's horrendous wounds and the needs that resulted from them, tore at my heart. I imagined what it would have been like for one of my own sons to have been sitting there in that same situation had I been somehow in Colonel Blake's place. I blinked back tears the best I could, but my eyes began to burn, and soon they were streaming down my face.

I turned my face toward the wall, hoping no one would notice that I was crying.

We stayed for a while, Ed talking to Melissa, giving encouragement, me standing next to Colonel Blake, still holding his hand and feeling him hanging onto mine.

I was watching Ed talk to Melissa when I saw movement in the door out of the corner of my eye. I looked over, and found myself looking directly at a somehow familiar face.

57

The woman I'd seen at the Wall the night before had been looking at Melissa as she walked through the door of Lieutenant Colonel Blake's room, a warm, sympathetic smile on her face. Then she saw Ed, and then she saw me, and she did a real-life double take.

"Who are you?" she asked, looking suspiciously at me.

Melissa spoke up. "Mom, this is Ed Thorsen, a retired Army Colonel. He's Tony's Wounded Warrior case manager. And... I'm sorry... Mick?"

"Delaney," I said. "The colonel and I served together in Vietnam. I'm here from Kansas City, visiting, and he allowed me to come along to visit with some of the patients here."

She looked down, saw me holding Colonel Blake's hand.

"This is Tony's mother, Angela Blake," said Melissa.

They tell me I'm a pretty smart guy. But I have to tell you, sometimes I'm a little slow on the uptake. I didn't know what to say. *Angie?*

"You were at The Wall yesterday," I finally managed to say.

"Yes," she said.

"Touching Tony Giles name. You're Angie. Tony's wife."

"Yes," she said again. The suspicion on her face had given way to a look of ... acquiescence? Perhaps defeat?

"But ... ?"

Ed looked at me, then at her. I just stood there.

"I was Tony's wife. This man, whose hand you're holding, is my son. And he's Tony's son."

"But..."

"Maybe..." she said. "Maybe we should go somewhere and talk."

"That would be good."

"Please let me visit with my son and his family first."

"Of course." I looked over at Ed.

"I think we're about done here, anyway," he said. He shook hands with Melissa, then stepped over to Colonel Blake's bedside.

I gave the colonel's hand a final squeeze, looked into his eyes, said, "Goodbye, Colonel. If it's OK with you, I'd like to come and visit you again."

He squeezed his eyes shut once, barely nodded his head. It was OK with him.

"Goodbye, Melissa. Goodbye, Angelo, and ... Lisa."

They all said goodbye. Melissa thanked me for coming. I stepped back from the bed.

"I'll be back next week with an update, Colonel," said Ed. "You just keep getting better."

Again, his eyes squeezed shut, he nodded almost imperceptibly. You could clearly see the pain in his face.

Angie said, "Why don't we meet in the cafeteria in half an hour? We can talk there."

"Can we make it an hour?" asked Ed. "We have two more patients to visit."

"Of course. An hour, then."

***

We were waiting in the cafeteria forty-five minutes later. Ed had moved quickly through the next two patient visits to make sure we were there on time.

"I've visited with Colonel Blake several times before and have met Melissa and the kids before. This was my first time to meet the Colonel's mother. Her name is Angie?"

"Yeah, LT. Tony Giles' widow. The more I looked at her... she must be what, early sixties by now? The more I looked at her, the more I began to recognize the face. She was a very beautiful young woman. Tony showed me her picture many times, and...I've kept her photo, the one I took from his helmet, and that fucking Dear John letter she wrote him, all these years."

"Jesus, Mick. Little obsessed, don't you think?"

"Yeah, no doubt. But Tony and I were so close. I loved the guy, you know? And that Dear John letter has to have been a factor, at least, in his death. Don't you remember, after the mail that morning, he'd asked us to talk... said he needed an R & R to see his wife?"

"I do remember, Mick. But that was over forty years ago. What do you intend to say to her?"

"I don't know. Seeing Colonel Blake there...can you believe he's Tony's son, and is going through this?"

"No. Too much to take in. Sometimes this job overwhelms me."

My attention was diverted as I saw Angie get off the elevator. She began looking around the cafeteria for us, so I stood and waved her over to our table. She started our way, unsmiling. We both stood as she approached, and I held out a chair for her.

"Thank you," she said, as she sat.

"Thanks for coming down," I said. "This is kind of overwhelming for us, bumping into you after all these years, and finding out Tony had a son, and then seeing him so badly wounded. We're both terribly sorry for what he's going through, for what you and the rest of the family are going through."

"Thank you." She started to cry, tears streaming silently from her eyes.

"Ed and I, that is, Colonel Thorsen and I, served with Tony in Vietnam. Ed was a first lieutenant then, Tony's platoon leader. I was the platoon sergeant. We were with him when ..." my face dropped.

"When he was killed?"

It took a moment before I could answer. "Yes," I finally said. "When he was killed."

Ed said, "We're very sorry for your loss, Mrs. Blake ..."

"Thank you. Sometimes I think I've gotten over it. But now, this, with my son."

"You must have remarried," said Ed.

"I did. A few years after Tony was killed. Little Tony, we used to call him that, he needed a father. And Loren Blake was a very good man."

"Was?" I asked.

"He died. About five years ago. From pancreatic cancer."

"Oh my, Mrs. Blake. We're so very sorry," said Ed.

"Yes ma'am. Very sorry," I said.

There was silence for a few moments, no one knowing quite what to say.

Finally, Angie spoke. "Sometimes ... I think God is punishing me."

"Punishing you? For what?" asked Ed.

"For something I did a long time ago."

Ed and I looked at each other. All kinds of thoughts were whirling through my mind.

"You mean ... the letter." There. I had it out there.

She looked me straight in the eyes, hers brimming with tears, then began to sob.

"You know." A statement, not a question.

"Yes, ma'am. We know."

She dropped her head and sobbed. Ed put his hand on her shoulder, but she seemed not to notice. I knew from the old days that she was a couple of years younger than me, but she seemed so frail, so worn, so...old.

Sadly, people in the Warrior Café at Bethesda Military Hospital are used to people at other tables crying. There is so much sad news that is communicated there, it is unfortunately not even noteworthy. This day only a couple of people looked over at us, sadness on their faces at someone else's tears.

"I've always wondered about that letter." Despite the pity I felt for her, the anger was still there too. "Tony talked about you all the time. Showed off your picture. He was so in love with you and believed you were just as much in love with him. But then there was that letter.... A Dear John letter? Why would you do that?"

"Oh, God!" she sobbed.

"I wrote that letter out of desperation. It was the biggest mistake of my life. I was only nineteen. I was six months pregnant with Tony's baby from the last few days before he went to Vietnam. I never told Tony because I didn't want him to worry about me and the baby. But I was desperate to get him home. I loved him so much! I didn't think I could live any longer without him.

"A girl friend told me that someone she had known had been sent home when his wife wrote him a letter breaking up their marriage, and with no other choices, I decided to try it. I regretted it from the moment I sent it. And I've never known, until today, whether or not he got it before he was killed.

"But I guess he did, because you know about it. Oh, my God! I feel so horrible. Tony died thinking I didn't love him anymore, that I wanted a divorce! Oh, my God!" She sobbed uncontrollably. People around us were staring over at us now, as though I... we... were doing something horrible to this beautiful, sad woman.

Maybe I was.

"Angie, I..." but I stopped what I was going to say. I'd carried this anger for her around for so long, over forty years. It had become almost a part of who I was, remembering that letter every one of the thousand times I'd remembered Tony's death with so much pain, so much sadness, so much grief.

"What?" She looked at me through bloodshot eyes, her tear-streaked face as pitiful as anything I'd ever seen.

Now, finally, had come the only chance I would ever have to let her know what she had done. To give her back some of the pain I'd felt all those years, losing my closest friend because she'd distracted him from his job, got him killed with that damned letter.

I looked over at Thorsen. He looked sharply back at me, his biggest frown on his face, and I could read his thoughts. *"What are you doing, you asshole?!"*

I looked away from them both.

"What?" she asked again, her face a mask of pain.

I was staring off into space, remembering that day again. Handing Tony that letter after the morning resupply, seeing the joy in his face as he saw it was from Angie.

Then again, as we were saddling up to move out and I was giving him the compass azimuth for the day's march. The distracted look on his face, his apparent agitation, my acceptance of his explanation of having dreamed about Angie the night before. I remembered my attempt to joke with him a bit to lighten things up and put him in a better frame of mind. And my sense of urgency to get the column moving so the LT wouldn't catch any unnecessary shit from 6. My failure to see that Tony shouldn't be walking point that day, or perhaps my recognition of that and my choice to ignore it just so we could get moving.

I remembered the ice that had spread through my veins when I heard the gooks open up on us, the fear that Tony might have been hit, then the stark horror of seeing him down out in front of that log, alone, his blood spreading around him.

I remembered how selflessly and heroically Danny and Fragman had crawled out, exposed themselves to the intense enemy fire, made their way to Tony, and dragged him back, all while hundreds of rounds of gunfire exploded around them.

I remembered us all struggling together to get Tony back over that log, the pleading in his eyes as he looked into mine, then those last bullets that tore through his chest just as we were about to get him to safety.

I remembered the light going out in my friend's eyes and what I felt when I knew he was gone. The absolute, horrible sense of loss of one of the best friends I'd ever had. A fine soldier and a good man who was like the brother I never had.

I remembered later that night opening Angie's letter, reading it and re-reading it in disbelief, handing it to the LT. Staring at her beautiful, loving face, unable to comprehend, or believe, that she'd done what she'd done.

I looked back at a now much older Angie, who only barely resembled the sweet young woman in the photograph from so long ago. A lifetime of sorrow had etched long, deep lines into her face. The sadness she had obviously carried every moment since she learned of Tony's death was palpable. It was excruciating to witness. I was sure it was the saddest thing I'd ever seen in my life, and I'd seen some really sad stuff.

I made up my mind.

58

"Tony never read that letter," I finally said.

"He didn't?" There was pure disbelief on her face now, her eyes wide, the tears suddenly stopped.

"No, he didn't."

Colonel Thorsen's face went from full angry to half-angry, half curious.

"As platoon sergeant, one of my jobs was to hand out the mail. We had just taken re-supply that morning, and I'd just given Tony the letter when we got the word to move out. He was walking point, so he had to be the first one to saddle up and head out. He didn't get the chance to open it.

"Later, when I was..." I paused.

"What?"

"I'm sorry to have to describe this. Later, after he was killed, when I was going...through his pockets... before we sent his body back..."

She started sobbing again.

"...I found the letter."

"But..."

"It was still in the envelope, Angie. Unopened. I know I shouldn't have. But we were such close friends, and I was so saddened by his death.... I put it in my own pocket, along with some of his other effects. And later that night, I opened it. I was very shocked when I read it. I showed it to Ed here, and we've always wondered why. Now I know."

"Are you sure he didn't read it?"

The lie was getting easier, especially after I'd seen the look of relief on her face. This agony had gone on long enough for all of us. "Yes, I'm sure. The envelope was still sealed. He never saw that letter. And... I'm sorry, but I read the other letter from you that he was carrying in one of his other pockets, from a few days earlier, and it was very loving and supportive, very hopeful. That was the last of your letters that he'd read. That's part of why we didn't understand. Tony talked about you a lot, Angie. He was so very happy in his marriage. All he ever wanted was to come home safe, to be with you again."

She sat back, put her hands over her face, and rocked back and forth, still crying, in pain, in relief, in disbelief. Just trying to get it all straight in her head, trying to be sure there was no mistake. *Tony never read that horrible letter!*

Ed and I sat there quietly with her. Ed looked over at me and gave me one of his rare full-face smiles. There were tears in his eyes, too.

I gave him a tiny smile in return, and a wink, with the eye Angie couldn't see.

She remembered something. She looked at Ed, said, "You're the one who wrote the nice letter, letting me know about how Tony died, saying all those nice things about him. But if you'd seen the letter...?"

"Like Mick said, Angie, Tony never saw that letter. Mick was sure of that. So I didn't see any point in mentioning it or saying anything other than what I said. You lost a very good man there, and we lost a very good friend and a very good soldier. I didn't see any reason to create even more sadness around Tony's death."

Now Ed was in on the lie, too. Co-liars. Might as well be. We'd done pretty much everything else together.

She nodded. Then she turned to me. "Thank you," she said finally. "You don't know what it means to me to know this after all these years of wondering. Thank you." Tears still trickled from her eyes.

"I'm glad we finally had the chance to clear this up. We're both so sorry for all the sadness you've known all these years. So sorry about your son and what he and his family are going through. So sorry for all the loss you've known. Ed comes here all the time to manage cases. I get up here from Kansas City once in a while and he lets me come along. But it is so painful, seeing these brave men and women with these terrible wounds."

"My son…Little Tony…Colonel Blake. His whole life, all he ever really wanted was to be a soldier like his dad. He was just a few months short of retirement when this happened. He was already hurt pretty badly a few years ago, but he recovered fully and stayed on active duty. Now this…."

She looked at Ed. "There are so many doctors who attend to him, so many people who come and go from the room, Melissa and I are having a hard time finding out how well he's likely to recover. Do you have any idea?"

"I'll ask for his hospital case manager to come by and talk to you," Ed said. "But the last I've heard they believe his arm will eventually be 80 to 90%. Their real concern, other than his leg, of course, is with the brain injury, and they won't know about that for sure for some time. They'll do surgery, maybe more than once, to repair his skull once they're sure the internal bleeding and swelling are gone. It won't be for several weeks after that until they know how fully he'll recover. His leg… they hope he'll eventually be able to handle a prosthesis so he can walk again."

She looked down at the table again. "Thank you. Thank you for this talk, and thank you for helping my son and his family. I really can't tell you how much we appreciate what you do, Colonel."

He smiled again.

"Mrs. Blake, you'd be surprised how much good it does for me, too. It is an honor and a privilege to help these brave, selfless warriors."

She smiled. A real smile. "I'd better get back up there now."

She rose from her chair. We rose from ours. She went to Ed, folded herself into his arms and hugged him. Then she came to me for a hug, one that seemed to go on for a very long time. I'll always remember the smell of her hair. It smelled like .... sunshine.

Then she was gone.

59

I stayed over with Ed and Lois again on Friday night. We had a quiet evening on the porch, Ed filling Lois in on what had happened, her looking back and forth at us, a bit incredulous at this story that had come to an end forty-two years after it began.

I turned in early to be up early Saturday for some kayaking with Lois before heading back home in the afternoon. I went to bed that night dreading the dreams I knew would come after the events of the day and so much talk about the war, and Tony's death, and his son.

But I was surprised. Somewhere during the deepest part of my sleep, Tony came back to me again. This time he didn't morph from the face of a hawk. Instead I began to see a star-filled sky and then began to move through it, not fast, but at a peaceful pace. And a little while later Tony was there in front of me, first very far away as just a bright point of light, then a little closer where I could barely recognize him. And then closer, until he seemed to be only a few feet away.

He was smiling.

"Mick," he said. "Thank you for what you did for Angie today. You've taken away some of her pain, maybe the oldest part of it. She'll be able to go through the rest of this lifetime without so much sorrow, without the guilt she has felt about that letter. I've learned from where I am now, here with God, that Angie came into this lifetime to have these experiences, to feel this sorrow once and for all. Some amount of that is necessary in order that she, in later lifetimes, can know it and feel it and fully sympathize with it in others. It's necessary in order that her spirit fully evolve."

"Ah ... that makes sense, Tony. It makes perfect sense."

"And you've learned a valuable lesson, too, Mick. The lesson of forgiveness. I know you feel good about it."

"Yes, I do, Tony."

We just looked at each other for a while.

"Then, Mick," he said finally, "why don't you try using that lesson to forgive your mother ..."

I nodded.

"... and your father ..."

Again, I nodded.

".... and yourself."

Maybe I would.

"And the last thing before I go, Mick. I want you to experience my death, my passing from that lifetime, the way I experienced it. I want you to know what it was like for me at the end. That's the only way I think you'll ever fully understand."

And suddenly I was back there. I was seeing things through Tony's eyes, and feeling things through his heart. I felt his pain when he read the Dear John letter that morning, the horrible shock of it. I saw and felt the daydream about Angie and him making love, the feeling of emptiness and loss when he was brought back to reality. I felt the bullets hit his legs, experienced the fear as he realized he would die if he couldn't get help quickly. I felt the gratitude, the love for his friends, as he watched Danny and Fragman crawl out to get him, felt them drag him back and push him up over the log. I felt the new fear when his shirt snagged and he was stuck there. I saw myself through his eyes, as he looked at me in fear from his exposed position on that log. And then I felt the bullets hit his back, and tear through his chest.

I felt the numbness overtake him, and the darkness. And then I saw and felt the light approaching him, and then overwhelming him. I felt his calmness, his total absence of fear, as he felt himself cradled in pure love. I saw his last earthly vision, Angie there on top of him, smiling, making love with him. And then I felt his perfect bliss as his spirit was carried away, to be with God.

It was overwhelming. I wept.

After a little while he said, "So Mick, you're a writer now. You wrote a book about the war and what it was like for you."

"Yes I did, Tony."

"Maybe you should write another one now. Maybe you should tell my story, and Angie's, and more of your own."

"Yes, Tony, I think I should."

Tony said goodbye then, and his spirit left my dream, and went to be with God again. I slept peacefully through the rest of the night, and awoke the next morning feeling at peace with myself for the first time in many, many years.

60

I returned to Washington, DC, several times over the coming months to accompany Ed on some of his visits to Bethesda, and we always stopped to see Colonel Tony Blake and his family. Melissa was always there, and the kids were there through the summer until they had to go back to school in New Jersey. On most occasions, Angie was there as well. She, Ed, and I would often visit outside the room, and Angie told us stories about what a great athlete and wonderful young man her husband Tony had been, the day of their meeting in high school, how they'd fallen in love and married so young, how happy they'd been.

She also told us about what it had been like for her to be at home, alone and pregnant, while Tony was in Vietnam in such a dangerous spot. The nights she couldn't sleep after watching the war news on TV. The horrible anguish of it. How she'd finally, in desperation, come to write that letter.

She told about the day only a couple of weeks after she'd sent the letter, when the two Army officers had come to her home to let her know that Tony had been killed. The waiting for his body to be returned home, the horrible experience of seeing him dead there in that coffin. The funeral. The words of Tony's father, Angelo, wondering how it came to be that his beloved son, Tony, had been killed in a war that so many Americans protested against; that the rest of Americans seemed not to care about.

How torturous it had been ever since, not knowing whether Tony had seen the letter she'd written, whether or not he had died thinking she no longer loved him and wanted a divorce.

Then she told about her second husband, Loren Blake, how she'd met him, how he'd fallen as much in love with "Little Tony" as he had with her. How they'd finally come to have a good life together, how he'd adopted Little Tony and they'd been such good buddies. And she told about Tony Jr. growing up, what a good student and athlete he was, what a good person he was, his high school valedictorian address, his announcement of acceptance to West Point. How she'd worried for him so in the Rangers and Special Forces through those many deployments. His earlier wounds from the roadside ambush. How he'd been so saddened by the plight of Susan Helms, the National Guard Sergeant who had lost her husband, her legs, and one of her arms, in the roadside bombing of their convoy. How he was almost to his Twenty when he was hurt this last time. She told about Loren's fight against pancreatic cancer, and how she'd lost him too.

But despite all the horror that had been a part of her life, Angie seemed to be more at peace. Each time I saw her she seemed a little more alive, a little...younger, perhaps?

It was really good to know that one small, extremely white lie had done so much good for her. And for me.

Colonel Blake, Tony Jr., is one very tough, very resilient man, with so much to live for. Less than six months after my first visit with him his arm was fully healed, the surgeons had patched the hole in his skull, he had regained most of his brain function, and he could talk again, although still with some struggle. At my last visit with him in the hospital, just before Christmas, 2012, he had been fitted with one of the new prosthetics for his missing leg and was beginning the rigorous physical therapy that would eventually see him walk again. Never like he had. Never again a six-mile-a-day runner. But he eventually walked again.

On that last visit in the hospital he asked me to tell him what I remembered of his birth father, and we spent a couple of hours together in the Heroes Cafeteria, drinking tea, me telling stories of one of my best friends in life, how he had lived and fought so well, how he had died. How much he had loved Angie. I had my notebook computer with me, and showed Tony pictures of his dad and the rest of our squad from Vietnam, ones he'd never seen before. I pointed out Danny Nakamura and Fragman, who had tried so bravely to save Tony's father on the day he died.

Of course, I never mentioned the Dear John letter. I had destroyed it, and Angie's old picture, as soon as I'd returned to Kansas City from the visit when I'd met Tony and Angie and their family for the first time.

We came to the end of the talk about Tony's dad with no more questions from Tony and no more thoughts from me. We sat silently for a while as we both took it all in. And then Tony's face brightened, and he said, "Hey, Mick, guess what?"

"What, Tony? Must be good. You have a huge smile going there."

"I was out taking exercise up and down the hall a few days ago when I ran into an old friend. Someone I hadn't seen since shortly after I got hurt back in '05, an Arkansas National Guard sergeant named Susan Helms, who was driving my vehicle when the Sunnis blew an ambush on us. All four of my men and several others in the convoy were killed, and I was hurt pretty badly."

He paused, and I could tell he was thinking about his men who had died that day. Then he went on.

"But poor Susan...she lost her husband, who was in the same Guard unit and was driving the vehicle ahead of us...he was killed right in front of her. And she lost both legs and her right arm. She and her husband had two kids… it was horrible for her.

"Well, she's been in here for several weeks, this many years later, and she's become one of the first veterans, man or woman, to receive a full arm transplant. I guess they take an arm from a compatible cadaver donor, and spend hours and hours attaching it, the bone, the muscle, even the nerves. I couldn't believe it, but when she saw me here, limping along with crutches on my new prosthesis, Susan got out of her wheelchair, stood up on two artificial legs of her own, and shook my hand. With her new right arm! She had a pretty good grip, too. And she said she had feeling in the fingers and everything!

"I hate these awful wars, Mick. And I especially hate seeing all these brave people coming back with so many traumatic amputations, so many brain injuries, so much PTSD. Poor Susan…she was one of the most depressed people I've ever known when we were here together after we were wounded. But at least the military and the VA are putting time and money into these new experimental procedures to fix as much of the damage as possible.

"Susan said that when you have no legs and only one arm, life is incredibly difficult. It's just about impossible to do anything, including putting on your leg prosthesis, without help. She mentioned something I'd never thought about…When you're a woman with only one arm, you even have to have someone else help you put on a bra." He paused to let the thought of that humiliation settle in.

"But when you have no legs and two arms, it's an incredible difference. You can do so much more for yourself!

"She actually smiled at me, Mick! I hadn't seen her smile since before they blew those IEDs on us, all those years ago."

61

Tony Blake will never again be the perfect male specimen he had been as a younger man, before all the wounds. But he went home to take up his life again, to be a very good husband to Melissa, an involved, at-home father to his children, and a wonderful, caring son to his mother, Angie Blake.

Melissa told me later about the depression Tony often experienced, because of what he'd seen, and done, and lost. But he was wise enough to go to the VA for help with his PTSD, and he was managing it. He was learning to live with it, to bring himself back from the depression, to work his way through the anger that sometimes came for no apparent reason, to survive the nightmares, to look on each day as a new opportunity, to be thankful for all he still had, that so many others who had gone to war with him had lost.

Tony went back to school, eventually earning his PhD in secondary education, and he is now very proudly the Principal of the Watertown, New Jersey, High School. He is the Post Commander of the Watertown VFW Chapter and an active member of the Military Order of the Purple Heart and the Disabled American Veterans. He often travels to Washington D.C. to appear before Congress, sponsored by the Iraq and Afghanistan Veterans of America, to testify on behalf of disadvantaged veterans, and appeal for better VA benefits.

Retired Army Special Forces Lieutenant Colonel Tony Blake is a true American hero.

Ed and Lois Thorsen still live in the same home in Springfield, Virginia. Though now in their mid-seventies, they both live happy, productive lives. Ed is still a very active case manager with the Wounded Warrior Mentoring Program at Walter Reed Hospital in Bethesda, Maryland. Lois, a retired Army nurse, volunteers at several military centers around Washington, mostly as a teacher to new parents among the military families, and a counselor for families dealing with PTSD and other afflictions brought about by one or both parents' time at war. And she is a serious recreational kayaker, among her many other interests.

Jon West's widow and their kids and grand-kids live on. After these several years have passed since Jon's death, they've come fully to terms with his loss. They go through life loving each other, happy as they can be, but always with a bit of sadness at the loss of such a good husband, father, grandfather...and man.

My sister, who looked after me so well when we were kids, is now seventy-six years old. She lives close by, near two of her three daughters. And she still looks after me a bit from time to time (and sometimes I look after her, just a bit). Together we look after our dad's widow, our step-mother, who is ninety-eight, almost blind, almost deaf, and almost unable to recognize us. Our step-mother has been an opportunity for both of us to show forgiveness to our father, who abandoned us when we were in our teens.

Then there's me. Eight months after I first encountered Angie and the Blake family at Bethesda, I walked into a retail store near my home in Kansas City and met the love of my life. She is a beautiful, vital, energetic red-head, with the most amazing spirit! She is intelligent, compassionate, loved by everyone who meets her, and above all.... happy. She is a wonderful friend, a passionate lover, a muse, a lover of animals and all forms of nature, music, and art. And she is someone I can talk to even in my darker moments, which I do still have, as I'm sure I always will. She has brought incredible brightness and joy into my life.

Exactly two years from the day we met we were married in a four-person ceremony on a mountaintop in Colorado, with deer and hummingbirds and chipmunks in attendance. We have a photo of a hummingbird floating inches above one of the flowers in her bouquet, just as we said our vows. And just as we were finishing the ceremony, hugging each other happily, a beautiful Red-tailed Hawk flew directly over us and gave a brilliant, clear cry. Moments later one of his tail feathers floated down, to land at our feet.

I have tried to be a good man all my life. I've tried to help others. Tried not to be too prideful. I have always, or at least nearly always, tried to do the right thing. Tried to face life with courage. Tried always to be honest. Thinking it over carefully, though, as I am wont to do, I have decided that the little white lie I told Angie that day in the Warrior Cafe in Bethesda somehow earned me enough credits with the powers above that they, or He, decided I should have my wonderful wife to enjoy my old age with. Or, if that isn't the case, I still like to think it is.

She, along with my amazing sons...and now my beautiful, sweet daughter-in-law, my grandsons, my sister, and a few really close friends, make life a true joy.

I am enormously grateful. And despite the hypertension and heart disease I earned through my Agent Orange exposure while in Vietnam, the hearing loss and constant ringing in my ears, my continuing symptoms of PTSD with the nightmares and bouts of depression, and the very high likelihood that I won't live the normal lifespan of someone who didn't go to that war, I am, at this old age, happy.

One last thing: These days as I walk the nature trails near our home, or as I drive around, wherever I go...I always notice the hawks, especially the Red-tails. I often see them flying above me, sometimes alone, and sometimes in pairs. Beautiful and graceful and free.

Or I see them perched in trees or on phone lines or sitting on top of utility poles or street signs. When I do, they always seem to be staring straight at me as I pass. And every time I see one, I think about my good friend Tony Giles, who I now know is in a very good place. And I see him smiling at me as though to say, "Thanks, Mick! You did the right thing!"

Epilogue

Angie…Angela Giles Blake, passed away on August 15, 2017, two days before the anniversary of Tony Giles' death in Vietnam in 1969. She was sixty-seven. Her grandson, Angelo Blake, then nineteen years old, found her apparently asleep in her front porch rocker one afternoon when he came by to mow her grass. She had a very peaceful expression on her face, Angelo later said, even the hint of a smile.

The medical examiner indicated on her death certificate that her passing had been due to "natural causes." Privately he told Tony that it had apparently been her heart.

At the funeral, which I was honored to attend, Angie's son Dr. Tony Blake, standing somewhat uncomfortably on his prosthetic leg, gave a beautiful eulogy. He spoke lovingly of his mother; the great love affair she'd had with his birth father, Tony Giles, who had died in Vietnam; the sacrifices she'd made to give him and his sister Cindy a good upbringing; the loving wife she'd been to his adopted father Loren Blake; the wonderful grandmother she'd been to Angelo and Lisa. He talked about how much he loved his mother and how much she'd loved him.

Then Tony opened a blue box that he'd taken to the podium and withdrew a Silver Star Medal that he'd received for his heroism during an action in Afghanistan, a Bronze Star Medal with V-Device for heroism in actions in Iraq, and a Purple Heart medal with two Oak Leaf

Clusters, that he'd received for his wounds on three different occasions while at war for America.

"These are medals I was given during my time in the United States Army, during my deployments to Iraq, Afghanistan, and many other combat areas. They are for heroism and for wounds received in three different actions.

"But I don't feel like any sort of hero," he continued, tears in his eyes, "and I never have. I was simply doing my job. The job I'd volunteered for. The job I wanted to do.

"No, the real hero in my family is my mother, Angela Giles Blake, who lies before you in that casket. She endured my birth father's deployment to Vietnam, the agonizing days and nights of worry for a man she loved so dearly. She endured his death in combat there, the horror of knowing she'd never see him again. She endured my birth and the struggle of raising me alone until she met and married my adopted father, Loren Blake. She endured Loren's later illness with cancer and his eventual death from that horrible disease. And perhaps most difficult of all, along with my beautiful wife Melissa, my sister Cindy, and my son and daughter, she endured year after year of my deployments to different combat areas around the world, and my twice being severely wounded.

"I can only imagine what it was like for my mother, sitting up alone during all those sleepless nights of worry, remembering my birth father's death, and again not knowing whether someone she loved was even still alive, or perhaps hurt with no chance of recovery. Just wondering and worrying.

"So my mother, Angela Giles Blake, is the real hero of our family. Because she endured all that and never, ever, once complained about it, or asked me to leave the Army early, or for any concession at all to what she was living through.

"I am giving my mother these medals as a token of my love and respect for her, to be buried with her. My mother, and the others who wait while people they love go to war, are the true American heroes."

With that, tears streaming from his eyes, Tony went to the casket and placed the medals next to his mother's folded hands. He leaned down, kissed her one last time on her cold cheek, and then took his seat in the front row of the audience between Melissa and Cindy. Those attending the funeral were silent, except for the sound of quiet weeping.

The minister went to the podium and led the audience in singing "Amazing Grace." And then the hundreds of people who attended Angie's funeral began the final review of her body, with Tony and Cindy and Melissa at the head of the line.

One short hour later Angie's graveside service was over, and everyone except Tony had left. He stood alone with his mother's casket as it sat ready to be lowered into her grave, remembering the wonderful lifetime she had given him. With tears in his eyes, he placed a single red rose on the closed casket lid. And then he turned and, using his cane, slowly walked away.

Tony's war would continue for the rest of his earthly lifetime.
But Angie's war was finally over.

Author's Notes

An anonymous American Marine seeing his buddies dying around him during a bloody battle in Iraq, wrote on a well-placed wall:

America is not at war.
The Marine Corps is at War.
America is at the mall.

Perhaps the greatest tragedy of the several wars America is engaged in today is that most Americans aren't even aware of them, certainly not of the sacrifices being made by Americans on the various battle-fields, ostensibly for the security of our nation. These warriors, these brave few, willingly go to desolate foreign lands to fight wars on behalf of people who don't even recognize that we are at war.

Our federal government, it seems to me, has done an excellent job of enabling Presidents and their cabinets to send our young men and women to war most anywhere they choose without ruffling many feathers among the citizenry. They abolished the draft back in 1973 after Vietnam was nearly over, quelling most of the backlash from that war when young people no longer feared having to go. They created an all-volunteer military, with kinder, gentler treatment of recruits, high enlistment incentives and higher pay, better active duty benefits, and more VA benefits than my generation of soldiers had. Then they augmented the military with seemingly endless supplies of "contractors," many of whom are no more than mercenaries. They keep war news out of the news, limiting battlefield coverage, and even restricting photography of the flag-draped caskets of the war dead. So the public knows little of what goes on, where we're fighting, or our casualties.

This all continues because most of us don't care enough to do anything about it.

Can anyone tell me why we're still fighting in Afghanistan seventeen years after we went there to track down Osama Bin Ladin? Apparently, the Secretaries of Defense and State are having a hard time explaining that to our President.

I wish that every American could visit Walter Reed Hospital in Bethesda, Maryland, as I have been privileged to do. During those visits, I was humbled at the great tragedy and sacrifice of the severely wounded Soldiers, Marines, Sailors and Airmen I met there. These men and women are veterans of the recent conflicts in Iraq, Afghanistan, Syria, and other unnamed foreign places, with wounds so severe that the visitor must steel himself in order to keep the victim from seeing his shock. Missing arms and legs, even multiple traumatic amputations are common. Severe traumatic brain injury is common. Horrible burns, grossly disfiguring facial wounds, and blindness are common. Post Traumatic Stress Disorder is rampant. A few of these poor, brave souls suffer from all of these.

American medical skill and technology have saved the lives of many who were so severely injured that they would surely have died in earlier wars. But it has sentenced these survivors to lives of hardship unimaginable to most of us. These brave Americans, and those I served with in Vietnam, and the families who have waited at home for them, or who try their best to support them after they've suffered these horrible wounds, have been a great inspiration for me to complete and publish *Angie's War*. If you were ever to go to that hospital and meet with some of these amazing men and women, it would change your life, I am certain, as it has mine.

I started *Angie's War* a few months after publication of my first novel, *One Young Soldier*, when the first few paragraphs of Chapter 1 just showed up in my head one day, out of the blue. After hurriedly jotting them down, I began to think about what to make of this new story. I would work on it diligently for a while, then run out of inspiration and ideas, and stop, sometimes for years. But then America would get into another war, and another, and another. And I would marvel at the incredible tragedy of those wars for those who fought them, and those who waited for them at home, and the civilians in the countries where they were being fought. And I'd be inspired to continue this story. Now that *Angie's War* is finished, I look back to see that the pauses I would take in writing it were appropriate and timely. I was merely waiting for the next real-life incident, such as my visits to Walter Reed, to occur, so they could inspire part of this story. I learned that if you allow life to progress at its own pace, it all happens as it is supposed to.

I owe a great debt to retired Army Colonel Jonathan B. Dodson, who as a young First Lieutenant was my last platoon leader in Vietnam. Jon's wise and caring leadership as an infantry officer there undoubtedly saved many young American lives, and I know several of us from our infantry company walk around in one piece today because he was an intelligent, thoughtful, courageous, caring leader. I also owe Jon my deepest thanks for allowing me to accompany him on visits to Walter Reed, where he now works as a Volunteer Case Manager for the Wounded Warrior Mentoring Program, and where I learned so much, so quickly, about the casualties of America's current wars. Jon's wonderful wife, AJ, has been hostess during my many visits with her and Jon at their home, and is also a great friend.

I am honored by the friendship of John Baca, a soldier from my infantry company in Vietnam who was awarded the Medal of Honor for his heroism in saving the lives of the men around him, and who received such fierce wounds in the process. Thankfully, he lived to tell about it. John is a very wise and caring soul, and has dedicated his life to helping others. His thoughts expressed during our private conversations have been incredibly educational for me, and his life example has been an inspiration.

My very close war buddy Jonathan Wild died in 2011 from throat and lung cancer caused by his exposure to Agent Orange back in 1969. He suffered bravely through that horrible illness for four years before finally succumbing to it. Jon was a caring friend and a wonderful husband and father, and his death saddened me more even than the deaths of my own parents. I still miss him. His widow, Jamie, and his kids and grandkids are people I love as my own family.

Mitchell Hamabata was a young Hawaiian National Guardsman who walked point with me in Vietnam, and whose uncanny sixth sense about the enemy undoubtedly saved both our lives more than once. Mitchell died in a mental institution in Kauai, Hawaii in 2004, of heart disease, another victim of PTSD and Agent Orange. I still miss Mitchell too, and he appears often in my dreams about the war.

I also literally owe my life to Sergeant Rodney Evans, who died one day in 1969 when he smothered the blast from an enemy mine with his own body, saving Mitchell's life and mine, and probably more. Rod was posthumously awarded the Medal of Honor for his sacrifice. In 2004 I had the great honor of connecting psychically (that's psychically, not physically) with Rod through a now-famous medium named Rebecca Rosen, and we had a wonderful conversation about friendship, and love, and forgiveness, and peace. It was another life-changing experience.

My good friend Basil (Baz) Clark served as a squad leader and platoon sergeant with my infantry company in Vietnam, and was awarded the Silver Star for his incredible heroism there. Baz is now a retired university professor, and is the author of several excellent books on war and a wide range of related subjects. Baz recently spent four years as a volunteer teacher and mentor with prisoners at Georgia's Walker State Prison. He's also a frequent speaker to military groups, assisted living facilities, and school groups, and stays in touch with many of our war friends. He is a man who has clearly made the most of life, despite the challenges he's faced as a combat veteran.

Greg Ciardi was our platoon medic in Vietnam, a Conscientious Objector who didn't carry a weapon of any kind as he repeatedly exposed himself to enemy fire in order to help our wounded. He survived the war to take up a career in education, and retired recently as a superintendent of schools in western Massachusetts. He and his beautiful wife Margaret are dear friends, living happy lives in retirement near their kids and grandkids. Greg seems to me to be the model of how a soldier should be able to survive a war and come home to live in peace. He was able to do that probably because he doesn't carry the guilt of having harmed another human being in battle, and indeed personally saved many lives. I admire him enormously.

Lieutenant Colonel Chris Morris, an Army Special Forces officer who served in both Iraq and Afghanistan, was a great help to me in finishing this book, kindly giving his time from an extremely busy schedule to proof-read the manuscript and give great advice on young officer rank and assignment possibilities. These helped enormously in finalizing the story of Tony Jr. and his Army career, and I am very grateful for his help. Chris is currently an active duty officer serving in Ft. Carson, Colorado, and I hope to have the opportunity to meet him face-to-face someday, and thank him in person.

First Lieutenant Steve Koeppenhoefer served as an infantry officer in Vietnam in a sister battalion to my own, at the same time I was there. We only met about a year ago when I spoke at his OCS class reunion, but we've become close friends, and we've shared a great deal about the war. Steve helped me greatly with this book, as a source of inspiration, an editor, and a technical advisor. I am very grateful for that assistance and support, and for his friendship.

Bob Babcock, the principal of Deeds Publishing, is a former Army officer who served as an Infantry platoon leader and executive officer in Vietnam with the 4th Infantry Division. Bob has himself written and published a number of books about the military and veterans, and I can't thank him enough for his encouragement and support as I finished *Angie's War* and we took it together through the publishing process. He has become a great friend.

Linda Hughes is an author, an editor, a teacher and a speaker, who survived the loss of her first husband to Agent Orange-induced cancer only a few years after his return from the war in Vietnam. She has surmounted the sadness of that loss and gone on to remarry and live a happy and exemplary life. I am extremely grateful for her very professional final edit of *Angie's War*, and am truly enjoying the friendship we've developed through the process.

My close friend and spiritual coach Ruth Walsh has helped me so much these last several years through her understanding, her astonishing insight, and her life-advice. Anyone who knows her loves Ruth, a truly beautiful soul who has overcome terrible hardship in her own life to become someone totally dedicated to helping others. My deepest thanks go to her for her friendship, her encouragement, and her spiritual guidance as I've written this story.

My psychologist, Dr. Mike Moffitt, began treating me for PTSD in 2011, and has been a huge help to me during these past eight years in understanding my disorder and navigating some of the rough spots I've encountered in my life since then. He is an excellent listener, and has responded to my ramblings with well-spoken tidbits of very sage advice, at just the right times. One of my favorites is an observation of his that I have written down and hung on the wall right behind the desk where I write: "Storytellers have the power to change the world."

I hope so.

My sister Shirley took care of me when we were young children, through our mother's struggle with grief and depression after the combat death of our uncle in Korea. Shirley raised three wonderful daughters of her own, then was primary caregiver to our mother and stepfather during their last years. More recently she and I have shared the care for our stepmother, our father's widow, who recently passed away at the age of ninety-eight. I am honored that Shirley and I are still so close, and can share most anything. She's been a wonderful supportive sister, daughter, mother, grandmother, and great-grandmother, and I'm so fortunate that she has been a part of my life.

My sons John and Jeff are a constant inspiration, wonderful young men who have survived their own hardships and conquered their own demons, and now live truly happy lives. I've never loved anyone more than I've loved them. Jeff is now married to a wonderful young woman, Christine, and they are the happy parents of beautiful twin boys, Graham and Wyatt. He is a model husband and father, an excellent athlete, and a very competent professional, a great young man whom I truly admire. John lives a happy life on his own terms as a single man, and when I look at him I see a very wise old soul who I suspect has spiritual insights I've yet to understand. His love for family and friends, his stoicism and toughness through great personal difficulty, and his calmness and strength as he works every day in a demanding and dangerous profession, have been an inspiration to me.

As you can tell, I am one proud father and grandpa.

My wife Kitty and I are relative newlyweds, having been married now for just over four years. Kitty is a sweet, beautiful woman who actually seems to love everyone and everything she encounters. She has been very encouraging, patient, and understanding as I've lived my life as a PTSD victim and finished writing this book, and I am sincerely grateful for that. She's also a heck of a lot of fun, and a pure joy to be around.

I know the secret to world peace. Simply give each person a partner as wonderful as Kitty.

Kitty's parents, Wayne and Lynne, have also been inspirational and encouraging to me as I've written *Angie's War*. They are in their mid-eighties, and both struggle with physical challenges. Yet they are two of the happiest people I know. They set an incredible example for living peaceful, grateful lives, *no matter what.*

There are many, many other people, far too many to name, who have given me great feedback on my first novel, *One Young Soldier,* and who have encouraged me greatly through the writing of *Angie's War.* I am so very grateful to all of them.

As you can see I am one very fortunate man. I've had a beautiful, experience-rich life, and live each day in gratitude for it. And that's all I believe any of us can ask.

Thank you for reading *Angie's War*. I hope it has been both entertaining and informative for you, and that you will remember its stories. Everything in this book is fiction, but real events like this go on all the time in the American society we live in. I hope you'll remember that.

God bless us, every one.

About the Author

Gary DeRigne is a frequent speaker to groups of all kinds, captivating listeners with his stories of the Vietnam War and its aftermath, and encouraging their support for America's veterans and their families. To schedule a talk or book signing, contact him at Gary@GaryDeRigne.com.

A portion of the proceeds from the sale of each copy of *Angie's War* are donated to non-profit veterans' organizations, such as: Veterans Community Project, at www.VeteransCommunityProject.org; St. Michael's Veterans Center, at www.smvets.org; Iraq and Afghanistan Veterans of America, at www.IAVA.org.

Gary served as an Army infantryman and platoon sergeant in the Vietnam War, an experience that indelibly altered his spirit, and his life. Since the war he has been a husband; a father and grandfather; a youth baseball and soccer coach; a business executive; an entrepreneur, a philanthropist; an adjunct professor of ethics and corporate social responsibility; and a Storyteller, a novelist and speaker. He lives near Kansas City with his wife, Kitty, close to his sons and their families. *Angie's War* is Gary's second novel, a sequel to *One Young Soldier*.